D0374846

DISCARDED

UNIVERSITY OF WINNIPEG
PORTAGE & BALMORAL
WINNIPEG, MAN.   R3B 2E9
CANADA

INFANTS
OF THE
SPRING

BOOKS BY
ANTHONY POWELL
NOVELS
Afternoon Men
Venusberg
From a View to a Death
Agents and Patients
What's Become of Waring
A DANCE TO THE MUSIC OF TIME
A Question of Upbringing
A Buyer's Market
The Acceptance World
At Lady Molly's
Casanova's Chinese Restaurant
The Kindly Ones
The Valley of Bones
The Soldier's Art
The Military Philosophers
Books Do Furnish a Room
Temporary Kings
Hearing Secret Harmonies
BIOGRAPHIES
John Aubrey and his Friends
PLAYS
The Garden God and *The Rest I'll Whistle*

PR
G031
.074Z52
v.1.

The Memoirs of
Anthony Powell

INFANTS

OF THE

SPRING

HOLT, RINEHART AND WINSTON
New York

Copyright © 1976 by Anthony Powell

All rights reserved, including the right to reproduce
this book or portions thereof in any form.

Library of Congress Cataloging in Publication Data
Powell, Anthony, 1905–
Infants of the spring.
(His To keep the ball rolling)
Includes index.
1. Powell, Anthony, 1905– —Biography.
2. Novelists, English—20th century—Biography.
I. Title   II. Series.
PR6031.074Z516   823'.9'12 [B]   77-71357
ISBN 0-03-020991-9

Infants of the Spring is the first volume of an
autobiographical series by Anthony Powell
entitled To Keep the Ball Rolling.

First published in the United States in 1977.

Printed in the United States of America

1 3 5 7 9 10 8 6 4 2

for
my grandchildren

To keep the ball rolling I asked Marlow if this Powell
was remarkable in any way.
'He was not exactly remarkable,' Marlow answered with
his usual nonchalance. 'In a general way it's very difficult
to become remarkable. People won't take sufficient notice of
one, don't you know.'

JOSEPH CONRAD: Chance

Acknowledgments

The photograph of Eric Blair (George Orwell) is reproduced by courtesy of University College London (Orwell Archive); that of Cyril Connolly kindly lent by Mr Noel Blakiston; and Maurice Bowra's by the Countess of Longford. Other portraits, prints and photographs that make up the illustrations are in possession of the author.

Contents

I.	From Whence Clear Memory	1
II.	Go, Bid the Soldiers Shoot	19
III.	The Wat'ry Glade	33
IV.	The Grove of the Evangelist	47
V.	The Game and the Candle	60
VI.	Arcades Ambo	81
VII.	The Close and the Quad	105
VIII.	Cymbals in Naxos	120
IX.	Skins: Thick, Thin, and Changing	141
	Appendix:	165
	Family Chart	166
	Origin of Species	167
	Family Phantoms	188
	Index	207

I

From Whence Clear Memory

I was born in London, 21 December, 1905, the winter solstice ('´'tis the year's midnight, and it is the day's'), feast of the sceptical St Thomas, cusp of The Centaur and The Goat; the hour, towards one o'clock of a Thursday afternoon; the place, 44 Ashley Gardens, Westminster, a furnished flat rented for the occasion in one of the several redbrick blocks ('towering though monotonous', says an ecclesiastical journal of 1856; yet more so since rebuilding), in that rather depressing area between Victoria Street and the Vauxhall Bridge Road. My father, Philip Lionel William Powell, lieutenant in a regiment of the Line, had been married to my mother for a year and a day. She was second of the three daughters of Edmund Lionel Wells-Dymoke, barrister at-law. Both her parents were dead.

Expected to survive at most two days, I seemed about to follow them, so christening took place without delay in the flat. Later, a more formal ceremony was held over the way at St Andrew's, a Gilbert Scott church destroyed in the blitz, its site now a car park. The names given were 'Anthony Dymoke'; the first, whim of my parents, no relation possessing it, nor special association invoked; the second, from my mother's surname. That was how things started. Why, one wonders, did it all come about? Like Gauguin's picture: *D'où venons-nous? Que sommes-nous? Où allons-nous?*; a journey in my own case tackled under the momentum of a slow pulse, lowish blood pressure, slightly subnormal temperature.

My father found family history uncongenial to a degree. Regarding his

1

own advent into the world as a phenomenon isolated from the main stream of human causation, he was not merely bored by genealogy, he was affronted. He possessed little or no sense of the past; still less curiosity about the circumstances of other people, alive or dead. I have heard him argue that Christopher Columbus was a figment of legend; and, watching a resurrected news-reel of troops embarking for the South African War, he became very angry, supposing the short jerky steps endemic to primitive moving-picture projection were a deliberate attempt to make fun of his own generation. Most potent of all, when it came to probing family origins, he suffered a gnawing apprehension that, once begun, skeletons would emerge too gruesome to stomach. Taking the shorter view, that disquiet—perhaps a kind of race memory—was not wholly without justification.

Unlike my father, I have always found pleasure in genealogical investigation. When properly conducted it teaches much about the vicissitudes of life; the vast extent of human oddness. To dismiss the subject with one of those arch (though not necessarily uncomplacent) generalizations would on my part be hypocritical, concealing the manner in which I have spent a good deal of spare time. Nevertheless, since there are those who share my father's view, the two chapters of these Memoirs that deal with family history have been placed at the end of this book.

2

My earliest recollection is of snow descending in small flakes outside the window of an hotel bedroom. Several old women in black were scurrying round. This was the winter of 1907, or early months of the following year. I was therefore just about two years old. The place was Chudleigh in Devonshire. The scene predates the arrival of my nurse, Clara Purser (I avoid the word 'nanny' as too professional), my care then undertaken by mother's much beloved former housekeeper, Pavey, whom I do not remember, as she died not long after.

Chudleigh was probably a short period of leave before my father took up duties as adjutant of The Kensingtons, a battalion of London Territorials. (Some literary connotation is here established by the regular army fathers of both Cyril Connolly and Christopher Isherwood doing tours of duty as Territorial adjutants.) The Honorary Colonel of The Kensingtons, General Turner, a distant relation, had no doubt suggested putting in for the vacancy. At that time a Rifle regiment, the unit was soon after my father's appointment reconstituted as Infantry of the Line; becoming the 13th (Princess Louise's Kensingtons) London Regiment, part of the Grey Brigade, so called because, instead of changing over to the scarlet tunics of the Line, they retained the grey uniforms of Rifle Volunteer days.

Seeking somewhere in London to live, my father inspected a flat in Albert Hall Mansions, several blocks running south from Kensington Gore, the area named from the former Gore House, where Lady Blessington had lived with d'Orsay, and entertained the London literary world. After her bankruptcy (at the famous Gore House sale of 1849, a French ormolu clock had been knocked down to my maternal grandfather), the Blessington residence was demolished; the Albert Hall built on its site. This flat, which was on three floors, faced Kensington Gardens. The rent asked being decidedly more than he could afford, my father looked over the flat chiefly from curiosity. It turned out that the owner (for some substantial reason I have forgotten) wanted a tenant for immediate occupation on almost any terms. He accepted an offer of about a quarter or third of the flat's market value. In consequence, 25 Albert Hall Mansions became our home for the next five years.

While moving in, we stayed at the Kensington Gore Hotel, where I remember the genial head-waiter's huge moustache. Clara's régime had begun by then. Starting life as parlourmaid, she derived from before the move to London, when for a short time my father had been stationed at Gravesend, a small garrison in the Thames Estuary. Clara said it was a favourite place of retirement for ships' pilots, who would fly the Red Ensign from a yard-arm in their gardens. Although they came from Gravesend, Clara's father, a bricklayer, lived at Croydon. Mr Purser, who had a large family, all a credit to him, held strong views on correct deportment, particularly at meals. Above all he objected to people who put their elbows on the table. I have never done so—even momentarily over the port—without thinking of him.

Fascinatingly, one of Clara's brothers was not only Purser by name, but by vocation purser on a vessel. One of her sisters was married to a petty-officer in the Royal Navy, whose photograph showed him wearing a cocked hat. Clara herself was a sensible kindly intelligent young woman,

3

to whom I became much attached. She had favourite phrases like 'wooden razors' for blunt table knives, and would describe a sense of malaise as 'small aches and pains from which few people die of'. In this last connexion, she used to suffer the curse with unusual severity; something that should have prepared one in the future for feminine disorders of health and temper at these regular intervals. In middle life Clara married a widower, she too surviving to ninety or just over.

I do not remember a great deal about early childhood, a season that has never consciously obsessed me. My nursery (night-and-day), the flat's former billiard-room, was not one of the rooms looking out over the park; nevertheless, the shining gilt serrations of the Albert Memorial's spire; the great groups of white statuary—Europe, Asia, Africa, America—the wide flights of marble steps leading to the frieze of figures representing the arts and sciences throughout history, the rich greenery of Kensington Gardens beyond, together formed the central landmark of my first continuously remembered existence. The Albert Memorial was at that epoch never mentioned by anyone with the smallest claims to aesthetic sensibility (and many without) except in terms of the heartiest contempt. I always nourished a secret affection, which I have retained, for its absurdity, ornateness, and verbosity, 'which neither spring nor winter's frown, can aught improve or aught impair'.

I enjoyed playing with other small boys in Kensington Gardens, but did not as a rule greatly like children's parties, of which I do not remember a great many taking place. The area of operation in the park was roughly bounded by the Flower Walk, the Broad Walk, the Round Pond; the last judged rather dangerously far north for safety, even if less remote from civilization than the paved precinct, usually known as the Water Garden, from which could be viewed the ominous roofs of Bayswater. There would also be occasional forays into Hyde Park: Rotten Row, the Serpentine, the Powder Magazine with its guardsman sentry.

Controversy took place from time to time about who was allowed to play with whom, not so much for reasons connected with the children concerned, as on account of the nannies' preference for sitting with other nannies who were personal friends. No doubt the possibility also loomed of charges disappearing for ever over the horizon with other bands of altogether unknown children. The park always seemed to me to be filled with mystery. I once noticed a little girl kneeling in front of an empty seat, her face buried in her hands. For a long time this terrible grief haunted me whenever I thought of it; grasping only years later that she was evidently playing hide-and-seek.

At home my main amusement was drawing—I cannot remember a time when I did not draw—combined with deployment on the nursery floor of a respectably large force of lead soldiers. These manoeuvres were apt to be restriced to only small detachments withdrawn from the cupboard at any one time; not unreasonably, as it was usually Clara who undertook their final return. There were frequent expeditions to Kensington High Street: Barkers', Derry & Toms, St Mary Abbots Church. The two big shops were overawing on account of their size, but enthralling in the manner that bills and receipts whizzed through the air with a loud buzz, from counter to cash-desk, by the agency of a Heath Robinson contraption of wires and pulleys. In one of the turnings off the High Street an excellent Punch-and-Judy show sometimes mounted a performance, though sufficient time was never allowed to appreciate the full development of the drama.

The Kensingtons' Regimental Headquarters, situated in an alley running south from the High Street called Adam and Eve Mews, always conjured up a vision of naked biblical figures, and on this corner, or a short way further west, stood one of London's few moving-picture houses. I was sometimes taken to this primitive cinema, though the first film I ever watched (without the smallest notion of what was happening) was shown at the Blue Hall in Edgware Road; now an office of the North Thames Gas Board, the exterior of which retains traces of its former exotic splendour.

At the Kensington High Street Picture Palace I remember a film about a sailor who had a wife in every port, and in retribution for his sins lost his life in a fire at sea. Shots of the fire were projected against a background of pink or mauve. One of the cinema's programmes was called *Dante's Inferno*. The posters outside made me desperately anxious to see this film, but it was considered 'too grown-up' for that to be allowed. Constant Lambert, within a month or two of my own age, then living somewhere off the top of Kensington Church Street (in those days just Church Street), told me he suffered the same cultural deprivation for the same reason.

The remote northern regions known as 'the other side of the park'

5

could be approached by a lane called Holland Walk, at the Kensington end of which an outdoor photographer had his pitch. From time to time I was taken there by Clara to be photographed. The photographer, a tall spare man, with a drooping moustache and straw boater, was an old soldier. He astonished me by saying that several of his contemporaries in the army, men younger than himself, were now Chelsea Pensioners. He always looked far too spry to be pottering about in a red frockcoat with a stick.

Clara and I were once walking through a tunnel beneath the road in the neighbourhood of South Kensington Underground Station (always a mild adventure), perhaps on the way to the Victoria and Albert Museum. Suddenly Clara announced to a man hanging about there that she would send for the police. Undersized, with a cap, and small moustache, he looked like a workman. He was apparently a 'flasher', who had just exposed himself. I saw only his embarrassed grin as he sidled off. I think no attempt was made at home to disguise what had happened, nor make heavy weather of the incident.

My mother (and Clara) used often to read to me; I wish I could remember more clearly which books, and at what age. The first literary work I myself read aloud unaided was *Little Black Sambo*, but I do not remember how old I was then. There were fairy stories (Andrew Lang), later the historical novels of Harrison Ainsworth (*The Tower of London, Old St Paul's,* and many more, as he became a passion); the latter now altogether unreadable. *The Children's Encyclopaedia* also played a major part, especially when I was equipped to dip into that extraordinary compilation myself. George Orwell has pointed out the large dose of American myth (Paul Revere, Barbara Frietchie, etc) on which children in this country were brought up. *Uncle Remus* is a rather different American example. I remember unending laughter about the Tar Baby. *Three Men in a Boat* (its unexpectedly Paterian undertones noticed only years later) made me laugh a lot too; notably Uncle Podger hanging a picture, and the story of the Cheese.

The Albert Hall Mansions flat had a small dark entrance hall, a place of coats and umbrellas, which opened into a somewhat larger inner hall. One afternoon (it must have been May, 1910), when I was nearly four and a half, the bell rang about teatime. My mother was expected, and I was told I could open the door for her. This was perhaps a customary routine. It is a reminder that latchkeys were not in general use; perhaps in this case ringing the bell a method indicating arrival home for tea. When I ran into the small hall a glow of red was visible through the frosted glass panels. Even so, I was unprepared for the sight of my father, in scarlet and spiked helmet, returning from the rehearsal of Edward VII's funeral procession. My father thus dressed was a rare spectacle. Officers of the period are sometimes shown today as wearing uniform among civilians, but, in fact, regulations were very strict as to being never seen in uniform except on duty. Permission was sometimes granted for full dress to be worn by a bridegroom and his brother-officers at a wedding; one such taking place at Albert Hall Mansions. Clara (who had a strong sense of such things) explained that, in spite of my enthusiasm, the 'nicer' regiments preferred top-hats and tailcoats.

When the day came for the King's funeral, I was taken by my mother and Clara to watch from the Mall. There was a lesser crowd than would assemble today for such a procession; even so I could see nothing but the bobbing plumes of the Household Cavalry. Behind the gun-carriage bearing the coffin were led King Edward's horse, saddled and bridled, and his terrier, Caesar. When this group passed the place we stood, I was held up (I think by a good-natured man in the crowd), but failed to discern Caesar—a great tear-jerker in the rôle of dog-mourner—though, as easiest way out, I pretended to have done so.

I must, however, have glimpsed for a moment the officer of 2nd Life Guards commanding the escort riding a short way behind the gun-carriage. This was the (5th) Earl of Longford, later killed at Gallipoli; father of my future wife. Accordingly, the photograph of the funeral procession reproduced in this book includes my father-in-law, as well as my father: Lieutenant-Colonel Lord Longford on his charger just behind Caesar's kilted attendant; Captain Powell among the group of regular army adjutants (recognizable from the darker tone of their uniforms), standing at attention with drawn swords, in front, and somewhat to the left, of the files of grey-uniformed Territorials.

I watched George V's coronation in rather more style from seats along the façade of St George's Hospital at Hyde Park Corner. My mother enjoyed processions, but brought to them all her passionate feelings about things. At one point some red-clad figures in slouch hats—whom I take to have been North-West Mounted Police—rode by. My mother said: 'I believe they're Boers—I shan't clap.' In rather the same critical spirit, watching what must have been one of the earliest colour films (at the Scala) of the Durbar, the royal visit to India of 1911, she exclaimed, of officers in military frockcoats and pith helmets having garlands of flowers hung round their necks: 'How silly they must feel.'

One afternoon—I was about five or six—we had returned from Kensington gardens, and were waiting outside the door of the flat to be let in. After the park and the street the interior of the building seemed very silent. A long beam of sunlight, in which small particles of dust swam about, all at once slanted through an upper window on the staircase, and struck the opaque glass panels of the door. On several occasions recently I had been conscious of approaching the brink of some discovery; an awareness that nearly became manifest, then suddenly withdrew. Now the truth came flooding in with the dust-infested sunlight. The revelation of self-identity was inescapable. There was no doubt about it. I was me.

> So rounds he to a separate mind
> From whence clear memory may begin,
> As through the frame that binds him in
> His isolation grows defined.

3

In contrast with what might be called my father's Sandhurst personality, he possessed, as a young man, certain *fin-de-siècle* leanings. In one form, these were expressed by delight in the drawings of Aubrey Beardsley, though this attraction for the *Décadence* was balanced by disapproval of much that it stood for. In South Africa, according to himself, he had caused eyebrows to be raised in the Mess by drinking absinthe, dripping water in the traditional manner over a lump of sugar balanced above the glass. In general drink of any kind played only an infinitesimal part in his later life, even if there had been sprees in younger days.

Family legend embodied one of these nights-out, spent in the company of a Grenadier friend called Hermon-Hodge (later Lord Wyfold), Sandhurst contemporary or comrade-in-arms of South Africa. 'Hermon' was staying with his extremely rich father-in-law at a house in Grosvenor

Square. On arrival back at this residence in the small hours, the front door was opened by an elderly man in black. Hermon-Hodge was fairly tight, and my father (representing himself in the story as far the more sober of the two) pressed a coin into what he supposed was the butler's hand; with the request that Mr (possibly Captain) Hermon-Hodge be conveyed to his room, and nothing said the following morning of this unsteady arrival home. The money was quietly accepted; the message evidently well understood. In due course my father found that he had tipped Hermon-Hodge's father-in-law, Robert Fleming (grandfather of the writers Peter and Ian Fleming), a banker as rich as any in the country. This P. G. Wodehouse episode, and its *dramatis personae*, would not have been at all typical.

As well as Nineties artists like Beardsley, Conder, Ricketts, my father liked the illustrators who followed them, such as Arthur Rackham, Edmund Dulac, and Hugh Thomson. Rackham was praised as an early Surrealist by André Breton himself, and I believe admired by Picasso. There was also a host of minor Art Nouveau derivatives. My mother did not at all share a taste for Beardsley (preferring the cosiness of Hugh Thomson), but she would seek out Nineties books as presents for my father. She had little or no critical interest in pictures, though she could do small drawings herself, and always encouraged my own drawing. Her disinclination for Beardsley was accompanied by laughter rather than moral disapproval, and, when I reached an age to hear art seriously discussed, I was amazed to find Beardsley's pictures—familiar as Tenniel's Alice or Beatrix Potter's Tom Kitten—spoken of with awe as evil incarnate.

My father also possessed a huge volume, the first reproductions in this country of Léon Bakst's Russian Ballet designs; the Chief Eunuch in *Schéherazade* seeming to me a picture of incredible beauty. That must have been after we moved to the country, as the date on the title-page is 1913. This comparatively sophisticated attitude towards the arts was something never carried through in a manner to bring my father much lasting satisfaction or inner support. Quite why—having progressed so far—all somehow melted away, I have never entirely understood. In certain respects my mother's way of looking at things—no doubt owing to the generation to which her father belonged—was almost pre-Victorian. She would use 'Early Victorian' as a pejorative epithet for anything she thought absurdly prim; though at the same time regarded as architecturally 'dull' a Georgian foursquare redbrick house with a pediment. Hating remarks that suggested unkindness, she was at the same time capable of sharp observations, such as that it was 'the greatest misfortune to be the best looking in a plain family'.

Byproduct of these vaguely intellectual interests was a sprinkling of perceptibly bohemian friends. Of these I wish I knew more. The level at which my parents would have made such contacts represents a side of Edwardian life about which comparatively little has been written; concentration usually on the larger fish of the era. Among the Territorial officers (tending to be stockbrokers) who used to visit the flat was one named Howard (perhaps killed in the war, as the battalion was early in action), who was a sculptor. He was shown a selection of my drawings, and later gave me some special modelling clay, which he pronounced superior to plasticine, my accustomed medium in that art. I remember laughter, and the words 'Post-Impressionism', which dates the incident to 1911, the year of the famous show, or soon after.

One drawing depicted Mephistopheles, a diabolical figure who (either on account of some illustrated *Faust* belonging to my father, or a poster of the *Inferno* film) played a great part in my imaginative life of that time. Mephistopheles had been portrayed by me in profile, wearing a kind of glengarry cap, surmounted with a long feather. The sculptor, Mr Howard, remarked that the spine of the feather ran in a direct straight line with the devil's slanting eyebrow. 'That continuation of line is something only children do naturally,' he said.

This comment made a deep impression on me (then probably about six) at the time, but seven years later, when Sidney Evans, the Eton drawing-master, pointed out the balanced pattern created in a picture, I had altogether forgotten about such conscious principles of design. The idea of a pattern in drawing returned as an entirely fresh revelation. What picture did Evans show? I seem to recall two separate groups of figures on one canvas in a book of reproductions, each group forming a kind of arch, one large, one small. Peter de Hooch? Watteau? Millet?

More adventurous social frontiers within my parents' purview are suggested by an encounter of my mother's when lunching with friends living on the outskirts of London. To reach the house entailed a journey by train. At the station my mother noticed getting into one of the compartments a man whose appearance made her feel a sudden sense of extreme repulsion. At her destination, this man reappeared on the platform. She found herself almost praying that he would not be her fellow-guest at luncheon. Needless to say he was. It was the magician, Aleister Crowley — to use his own preferred style—The Beast 666. Asked what he talked about at lunch, my mother simply replied: 'Horrors.' I don't think my father ever met Crowley (who gave me lunch at Simpson's in the Strand twenty years later), but he owned a set of *The Equinox*, and one or two of Crowley's other publications. The Beast's name would have been familiar, if in no other way, through an army friend, Captain (later Major-General) J. F. C. 'Boney' Fuller, a great Crowley adherent in those days. Fuller, regarded by his military superiors as able in professional matters, though too eccentric to be taken overseriously, was also an early partisan of the armoured vehicle in warfare.

On the occasion of the Crowley luncheon party, the hosts were perhaps Herbert and Olive Vivian, the latter a friend possibly dating from my mother's girlhood days. Herbert Vivian, journalist and writer of travel books, with some notoriety in his day, appears in a disagreeable light in Oscar Wilde's letters; first courting Wilde, then abusing him. The Vivian marriage did not last long, but was still going at this period. Olive Vivian, in consequence of a Russian trip they took, gave me a Russian picture-book illustrated by Bilibin (another Constant Lambert link, as he too knew Bilibin's pictures as a child), the flyleaf inscribed: 'For Antonio, from the Russian dwarf who came out of the egg.' I do not remember the Russian dwarf, but the Edwardian affectation of Italianizing words is recalled, and the then popular song, 'O! O! Antonio!'. Mrs Vivian lived to some considerable age, corresponding with my father up to the last; long chatty letters full of Edwardian daring, chronicling sinister barons and charming contessas met in the obscure Continental pensions where she ended her days.

The Vivian ménage could have provided an entrée into a world more exotic than that of fellow Territorial adjutants, though some of these (many killed in the war) seem to have been livelier figures than the routine regimental officer. My father usually took his 'leave' abroad. Family associations with Naples (see Appendix) were kept up to the extent of calling on Alberto Oates (son of the cavalryman and lady-in-waiting, who had been somewhat reduced by the advent of United Italy), a visit to become one of my mother's favourite stories: 'We were ushered into a room

11

where the fattest man I have ever seen was lying in bed under a tartan rug.' Why Alberto was indisposed was never revealed; perhaps just old age. Conversation in French had not been easy. It was the final rencontre between the two families. When in Naples in the middle 1950s, I was unable to trace any of the name of Oates, though I believe the stock survives in Sicily.

It was to Albert Hall Mansions that James Gomme came as cook. An impressive figure, fond of making sententious remarks, James was said to cook superbly. He was, indeed, wasted on my parents, who did no more than the minimum of entertaining required by good manners or duty; neither of them at all greedy, my father always complaining about his digestion. When my mother was ordering the meals for the day, James once remarked: 'I should not wish to cross the Captain in any of his appetites.'

There used to be great spreads in the kitchen, sometimes attended by the parlourmaid's Swiss fiancé, a waiter, who paid me a compliment (first and last) on my French accent. A conspicuous member of the household was Pekoe, my mother's pekinese, so huge in size that he was once mistaken for a St Bernard puppy. Albert Hall Mansions represents, I think, the happiest interlude of my parents' married life, a peace and coherence never quite achieved again. My father's military duties took a civilized form; my mother liked London, its largeness leaving her comparatively untroubled by social obligations, and giving opportunity for the unobtrusive 'good works' to which she liked mainly to devote herself. As stock subject for humour, or serials in boys' magazines, there was, of course, always talk of the impending German invasion.

4

In the early months of 1913, the tour of duty as Territorial adjutant terminated, my father rejoined his regiment; this time the 2nd Battalion of The Welch, then stationed at Bordon Camp about a dozen miles from Aldershot. We lived in a large bungalow of Indian type, let furnished, its situation on the top of a lonely hill, surrounded by heather, gorse, pines, sandy hollows skirted with bracken. The village was only a mile away, but the house seemed infinitely remote from all other human habitation. Here I must digress on a matter scarcely avoidable in the context.

The less novelists descant on their own works the better. Nevertheless, autobiographical material produced by a professional novelist is bound to raise speculation as to how much direct experience has found a place in his fiction. I will therefore, though unwillingly, make a few comments on a subject that can be tedious unless approached with businesslike severity. I choose this moment because a fairly close description of the bungalow (though not its domestic staff, except for certain aspects of James) appears in *The Kindly Ones*, sixth volume of my novel, *A Dance to the Music of Time*, in which the house is called Stonehurst; a name that will serve in these Memoirs too.

Most novelists draw their characters and scenes in some degree from 'real life'. If a character in a novel bears no resemblance whatever to any human being one has ever met—nor could ever meet whatever the circumstances—there is likely to be something wrong; a principle just as true of fantasy (say *Alice in Wonderland*) as of 'naturalistic' writing. On the other hand, the images that present themselves to the mind of any novelist of more than amateur talent take an entirely different form when the same writer attempts to describe 'real people' known to him; the former altogether more complex, free-wheeling, wide ranging.

There are no doubt exceptions to this rule, especially minor figures in the background of certain novels, drawn directly from life, but playing little or no part in the development of the narrative. The 'real person' who sets going the idea of a major 'character' in a novelist's mind always requires change, addition, modification, development, before he (or she) can acquire enough substance to exist as a convincing fictional figure. These alterations come not so much from thought on a novelist's part as from the uncontrolled subconscious instinct that gives a 'character' life; while the smallest deliberate change made by a novelist to suit the story's convenience means, in truth, that all genuine dependence on the original model ceases—in contrast with traits (possibly inconvenient from a fictional point of view) that must unavoidably be chronicled about a 'real person' in Memoirs or Autobiography.

'Real people' who merge successfully into fictional 'characters' are comparatively rare; and much bad novel-writing can be laid at the door of the misconception that, because someone has an outstanding personality, he (or she) can be easily assimilated into a novel. In fact, strongly 'realized' persons simply move through a novel as themselves, not on the fictional plane demanded by 'art'. In Dostoevsky's novel *The Devils* (sometimes called *The Possessed*) the Russian historian, Granowski, is adapted to create one of the great comic characters of the European novel, Mr Verkhovensky. In the same book, the writer Karmazinov is admittedly modelled on the writer Turgenev.

Karmazinov, in contrast with Mr Verkhovensky, never quite comes off. This is in some part because Dostoevsky allows personal spite—a fatal ingredient in any novel—to enter into his representation of Turgenev; but the flaw is even more from the interest attaching to Turgenev existing in his being Turgenev; not Turgenev watered down to Karmazinov. Once you turn Turgenev into a character in a novel—even in what is perhaps the greatest novel ever written—no true life is left in him. Proust clearly recognizes this principle in his projection of Anatole France as Bergotte, omitting all sorts of comic aspects of Anatole France's true character that might have been included in an unfriendly portrait (or caricature) by a lesser novelist, but would, in the context, have ruined the purpose for which Bergotte is intended.

This rule—that 'realized' personalities are likely to be unsuitable as characters in novels—does not apply only to individuals who have made a name for themselves. The obscure 'realize' themselves just as much as the celebrated; and can prove an equal trap for novelists lacking the right instinct. In any case the example of Granowski (unknown as an historian to most readers outside Russia, possibly to many within) shows what an insignificant matter 'identification' is, so far as appreciating a novel like *The Devils*. Often, of course, no model exists to 'identify'; invention is total; yet naturally even invention too must be undertaken in relation to the observed, or inwardly understood, manner in which human beings behave.

Notwithstanding these things, readers love to think of a 'real person' as always portrayed, and literary detectives have sometimes brought off discoveries in this line by no means without interest to those seriously concerned with writing. On the other hand, cocksure attributions infinitely wide of the mark can grate on any novelist's sensibility. May I demonstrate the pitfalls in jumping to facile conclusions by an illustration from my own works?

When I wrote in the Appendix of these Memoirs about Alfred Turner — a general, a distant relation, an eccentric—I saw at once that General Turner (among other things keen on psychical research) could be marked

14

down as model for General Conyers in my novel. So far as General Conyers had a model (he is in any case composite in his rôle of courtier), that was a cousin on my mother's side, Brigadier-General R. L. A. Pennington (grandson of the Peninsular veteran and in his regiment), a soldier of altogether different stamp from Major-General Sir Alfred Turner. The latter never crossed my mind when projecting General Conyers, but the principle is thereby illustrated of the novelist's attempt to create a 'character' based on someone known, who will be of more universal application than the mere sketching (as in Memoirs) of a familiar figure . To the novelist the characters in his novel are known as those in a dream are known; the texture too complicated to be explained.

I have paused—perhaps too long—on this subject, because Stonehurst was, indeed, much as suggested in *The Kindly Ones*, even if not in every character and incident. Among the factual elements was the strange cult, with odd costumes and bearded leader, going for runs past our gate. James was our cook (until he left to get married), and some of his remarks as Albert are authentic. My father's soldier-servant was Thorne (later wounded at La Bassée, and visited in hospital), who used to accompany rides on my donkey, Jock, and disparage the military policemen jogging through the heather. Thorne also took me to see an inter-regimental rugger match at Bordon; but he did not in the least otherwise resemble Bracey, the batman in the novel.

These small items would be scarcely worth mentioning, were it not for the Stonehurst 'ghosts'. The bungalow, built towards the turn of the century, looked the last place on earth likely to be 'haunted', but certainly various individuals (who could not have been in contact to discuss the matter) found reason to say there was something 'spooky' about the place. The appearances, such as they were, took two main forms; the more commonplace—if least easy to accept as genuine—a whitish shape, misty, of no great density but some height, that materialized at the bedside of successive maids when they woke up in the morning. This apparition—most traditional of spectres, except in manifesting itself at morning instead of night—was laughed off as 'imagination'; never reaching a pitch where a member of the domestic staff even suggested giving notice on that account. The matter was treated as a joke, if a joke with a basis in possibility. This benefit of the doubt was allowed to some extent in the light of quite other unusual experiences undergone by my mother.

The Stonehurst household, as customary with my parents, included several animals; the redoubtable Pekoe, a white cat called Binks, the latter possibly understudied by one or more cats of lower status, and at one moment a rather unsatisfactory labrador, for which another home was found. That is to say the minimum animal establishment was two, and I suspect usually somewhat in excess of that. I make this point because, in order to convenience any domestic pet wanting to take a nocturnal prowl—then re-enter the house in the small hours—my mother was accustomed to leave the lower half of her bedroom window open to facilitate an easy return. When the domestic animals used this form of access, they were accustomed to sleep the rest of the night on her bed. I emphasize this arrangement, because in certain respects the story, as a ghost story, would be more convincing had we possessed no animals, my mother opened only the top half of her bedroom window.

One night my mother was awakened by the thud of a smallish animal jumping on to her bed. That, as I have said, was a happening not in the least uncommon. On this particular occasion, however, she suddenly felt a sense of awful terror. The thing landed near the foot of the bed, then slowly worked its way up, until pressing down the bedclothes just below her neck. This visitation took place several times, but I am uncertain of the length of interval between. Whatever these were, the normal animal population would recurrently turn up in the middle of the night without in the least disturbing my mother's nerves. She was not only very used to animals and their ways, but also on easy terms with anything in the nature of the Occult, which, so far from inspiring fear in her, she was inclined to seek out. (Towards the end of her life, when she and my father were living near a vicarage troubled by poltergeist phenomena, my mother remarked that she would 'give anything' to have an opportunity to spend the night there, just to see what happened. I have no doubt whatever that she would have gone through with this had the chance arisen.) This latter side of her makes the terror she felt on several occasions at Stonehurst even more extraordinary.

'Next time I shall speak to It,' she said. 'I shall ask: What do You want? It makes me so frightened that sometimes I wonder whether my hair will have turned grey when I look in the glass in the morning.'

These manifestations must have come to something of a climax in the first half of 1914, the year of the outbreak of war; the less specific appari-

16

tions—supposed misty white shapes—probably spoken of earlier than that, indeed soon after we came to live in the house. I feel pretty sure that my mother was never given opportunity to put her question to the nocturnal visitant after she decided to do so, but am uncertain whether that was simply because we went to live elsewhere after the Regiment went to France.

Some parents would have tried to keep all this from a child of seven or eight. My father, left to himself, would probably have done so. My mother, on the other hand, regarded any such concealments as shutting off an essential aspect of life. Talk about 'ghosts' was never at all curtailed on my account, and did not in the least disturb me. I have fairly strong feelings about the 'atmosphere' of houses, but never, in fact, found that of Stonehurst in the least uneasy; though this was certainly a period of great imaginative activity—no doubt true of most children of that age — in which elaborate fantasies of all sorts occupied my mind to an extent that they seemed part of daily life.

There was a sequel to the Stonehurst ghost story. A year or more after leaving the house my mother met someone (probably another army wife, most soldiers finding themselves sooner or later in the Aldershot area), who knew the bungalow, and spoke of 'rather an odd woman' who had lived there. The 'odd' lady—who was not one of the family from which we had rented the house—used to breed schipperkes, small black dogs from the Netherlands, with sharp ears and curly tails, at that period fashionable as pets. When one of her schipperkes died, so it was reported, the dog's photograph was hung in her bedroom, its individual eating bowl placed below. It looks a little as if my mother's great affection for animals had made her in some subjective manner a receptive medium. The fact that she should have been frightened was not only unlike her, but unlike most (though by no means all) documented accounts of such hallucinations, which often include animal apparitions.

In spite of the comparative remoteness of Stonehurst, I used to see a fair number of other chilren, and remember (as opposed to a few years later) being conscious of a sense of attraction to little girls of my own age. The education of these—usually—officers' children was undertaken by Miss Judkins, an easygoing figure of slightly droll appearance, who lived in a cottage about a mile away, and did her rounds on a bicycle. Miss Judkins, adequate at instruction, was, I think, no more than that; my im-

17

pression being that most of what I learnt at this period was in consequence of books my mother read to me, or such that I read myself. That view may be unjust. Certainly I was sufficiently equipped to cope with the usual subjects when, in due course, I arrived at a day-school. It had been supposed that I should go to boarding-school at nine and a half. What interim state, if any, had been contemplated between Miss Judkins and a preparatory school, had we remained at Stonehurst, I do not know. I should have found the change a drastic one if I had gone direct from one to the other. As things fell out, the war turned all plans upside down.

II

Go, Bid the Soldiers Shoot

I have quite often come across persons of my own age, even a year or two older, both male and female, who say that as children they were scarcely aware of World War I taking place; beyond a dim memory of chocolate in short supply. Such is not my own experience. For me the impact of the war was menacing from the beginning. Within a few weeks of the Regiment's embarkation, the air was full of rumour of casualties— some true, some untrue—to be confirmed one way or the other later. The killed were often fathers of children who had come to tea, or subalterns remembered as chatting in the hall while they changed into tennis-shoes. Life seemed all at once geared to forces implacable and capricious, their peril not to be foretold. By the time we left Stonehurst I was approaching nine years old. Childhood, with its intensity of imaginative adventure that comes to an end with school—at least is greatly altered and modified there—had been allowed to linger on rather beyond its statutory limits. Mine had been on the whole rather a lonely childhood (though I never at all desired brothers or sisters), but not in the least an unhappy one. Now the condition was brought categorically to a close.

War was declared on 4 August, 1914. My father, a company commander, embarked on 12 August, and was engaged in the early open fighting of the campaign, before the armies settled down to trench warfare. He was never a great one for reminiscence, but I have heard him say that, during this early war of movement, the German infantry would advance shoulder to shoulder in the old close formation of the past; ac-

19

cepting fearful losses, but continuing to come on. The Welch suffered heavily too, and were in the Mons retreat. Long without food, my father entered a deserted farmhouse, and saw what looked like a bottle of white wine standing on a shelf. He took a deep draught. The liquid was olive oil.

My mother and I moved to London. Clara remained as an adjunct. We lived at different times in houses or flats of friends; furnished rooms; a boarding-house in South Kensington; in what order I do not remember. At the Glendower Place boarding-house, the chief excitement at meals was to see if the lady at the next table would remove with her teeth, as she sometimes did, the cork of the bottle of pills that was always beside her place. The furnished rooms, where we did not stay long, were almost next door to Mr Gibbs's day-school, which I now attended. This was a period when I was often taken to museums on Sundays: the Victoria and Albert, with its galleries of faceless figures in 18th century costume; the London Museum, with the prisoner in a rat-infested cell of old Newgate.

The youngest pupils at Mr Gibbs's, a well known establishment, wearing cherry-coloured caps, were six or seven years of age, and, though that was rare, boys could stay on until twelve or thirteen. Those who remained seem to have been well taught. Teaching was good in the lower forms too, though not at all intensive. Mr Gibbs, an attractive personality, showed that it was perfectly possible for a headmaster to be also a nice man. Games (more serious than knock-ups in the asphalt yard) were played at a sportsground in Barnes, to which a private bus travelled twice a week. I became aware for the first time of my own inability to play them; also of the unpleasantness of some boys—a necessary prelude to the unpleasantness of not a few men—but on the whole memories of Gibbs's are agreeable.

The war was not greatly rubbed in there, though I remember a faint sense of embarrassment at some end-of-term function, when a very small boy called Sandy Baird (later internationally known for his good looks) did a recitation (after he had slapped his knee several times) of John Oxenham's lines:

> What can a little chap do,
> For his Country, and for you?
> What *can* a little chap do?

20

Towards the end of the year my father went down with dysentery. He had always been victim of internal upsets, which he combined with more than a touch of hypochondria. Throughout life, offered a dish at his own table, he was liable to turn away with the words: 'I daren't, I daren't.' This time it was the real thing, and he was invalided to England. My mother, who believed all hospitals to be little less than slaughter-houses, where only the strongest could withstand the ministrations of the medical staff, soon extracted him. I am not sure where we lived when she got him out of hospital; possibly in a borrowed flat. On recovery, he was posted as brigade-major to a formation in one of the newly raised 'Kitchener' Divisions. It was made up chiefly of recruits from the Midlands, especially Birmingham; troops he subsequently regarded as the best he ever came across throughout his service.

Like Falstaff and his levies ('We'll to Sutton Co'fil' together'), my father was ordered to report to a Brigade Headquarters at Sutton Coldfield in the environs of Birmingham. One of his first duties was to pick from several candidates a staff-captain to serve under him. He chose a temporary officer of The Gloucesters, Thomas Balston, within a year of his own age (then thirty-four), who possessed earlier Territorial experience with the lawyers' unit, the Inns of Court Squadron. The Division moved fairly soon from the Birmingham area to Yorkshire; Brigade HQ at Leyburn in Wensleydale.

I went up to Yorkshire for the summer holidays of 1915. August was as cold as winter. The steep dark wooded slopes, rocky tree-shaded streams, a dramatic even sinister country, has always remained in my mind. Brigade staff was housed in a small requisitioned hotel; I suppose for fishermen in normal times. Before the rest moved in, my mother and the staff-captain (whom she never found very sympathetic) undertook some of the initial domestic arrangements for living there. I must have come in contact with Balston at Leyburn, but cannot remember him at that period. He was to play an important part in my subsequent life.

Tom Balston's early arrival in these Memoirs raises a question of how best to deal with such recurrent figures. Are they just to be mentioned, then picked up again in a later volume, like the unfolding of a novel's plot, or the Second Act of a play? Alternatively, is it better to anticipate the Writer's personal narrative, and briefly summarize his lifetime relations with those making an early appearance? There is something to be

21

said for, and against, both methods. A mixed chronology is perhaps preferable; each case treated on its own merits. Balston, belonging essentially to my opening years of working in London, is in most respects identified with that period. Others, whose character and doings began to react on my own from the moment of first contact, may require another approach. Nevertheless, a word should be said at once to establish the significance of Balston's appointment as staff-captain, in order to prepare the ground for a figure who, if not in the least exotic, was also far from ordinary.

Tall, spare, with short thick black hair that stood up like a flue-brush, Thomas Balston had a jerky nervous manner, literary interests, a great obstinacy of purpose. A good staff-officer, he got on pretty well with my father in principle, though after the war each would complain about how difficult the other had been to work with. This is credible in each case; Balston, as subordinate, probably having the worse time. They must have had something in common, because, in an unintimate way, they remained friends for years; both neurotic, though in very different ways. One of their shared tastes was in illustrated books; Balston luring my father away from the Nineties to the pre-Raphaelite Sixties, a genre in which he was never really at home.

Balston was, of course, far the better educated of the two. He was, among other things, a pioneer collector of Staffordshire china figures, a form of popular art on which he wrote a book. He also produced works about his own family (a branch of the Maidstone papermakers), and studies of the Martin brothers: John Martin, painter of *Belshazzar's Feast, The Destruction of Sodom*, and similar dramatic biblical scenes; Jonathan Martin, who burnt down York Minster; the arson of the latter undoubtedly appealing to an anarchic strain in Balston himself.

In accounts of his own life, Balston always insisted on the bad terms existing between himself and his father, whom he represented as thoroughly unamiable, not least in being well off, but too cantankerous to spend anything on his children. Balston had more or less paid for his own education by scholarships: at Eton (of which his great-uncle had been headmaster); and later at New College, Oxford. He would also speak without enthusiasm of his several brothers and sisters. Before the war he had kept himself by tutoring, and literary hack work, but his ambition had always been to be a publisher. This he eventually achieved, becoming a director of the house of Duckworth; in consequence of which, a dozen years after this wartime interlude, I myself was employed there.

After Wensleydale, the Division moved south to Salisbury Plain. My father's brigade was stationed round Codford, where a kind of shanty town had grown up, sheds and booths set about between torrents of mud traversed by duckboards. We lived at Boyton Cottage, dower house of Boyton Manor, the local 'big house', then let to Colonel (later Sir Martin) Archer-Shee, who was commanding a battalion of the Gloucesters. A lively Tory MP, Colonel Archer-Shee was half-brother of the naval cadet falsely accused of stealing a postal-order; theme of Terence Rattigan's play, *The Winslow Boy*. Mrs (later Lady) Archer-Shee was American. On visits to their house I saw the four volumes of *Battles and Leaders of the Civil War*, an illustrated symposium which first aroused an interest I have never quite lost in the War between the States; rekindled on discovery of the distant Powell cousins (noted in the Appendix) who fought for the Union, and at least one of whom had Confederate brothers-in-law. From Boyton Cottage, in 1916, then ten and a half, I finally set out for boarding-school.

2

From time to time various preparatory schools had been considered, a runner-up being one on the south-east coast (a great place for such establishments), but somebody told a story about the headmaster forcing a boy with a sore foot to play football, with some dire result (nothing much short of loss of a leg would surely have been noticed), and, the rumour telling against the place, I was sent elsewhere. The school to which I went, also in Kent but inland, had been recommended by a fellow Territorial adjutant, by then killed in action. At least eighty per cent of the boys were sons of regular army officers, a good sprinkling of the fathers being generals.

At this period—even if I sometimes toyed with the idea of becoming a painter of huge subject pictures, or illustrator of historical novels in the manner of Cruikshank or Phiz—I quite seriously supposed that I should myself in due course enter the army. As the war showed no sign of ending, this seemed logical enough, and (with the navy) was the normal goal of most of the boys at the school. (In this connexion, I have often been impressed in later life by the distinguished military records achieved by boys remembered at school as possessing not the least physical toughness.) My own concept of a soldier's life was a purely romantic one; not at all encouraged by my parents, who—if inclined, then and later, to sheer off the more tricky problem of what on earth I *was* to do for a living—no doubt saw the army, even at that stage, as an inappropriate calling. My father (owing to his impatience with other forms of professionalism, hard to imagine as anything but a soldier) was well aware of the disadvantages of army life; indeed, like most soldiers, chronically grumbling about military conditions; the circumstances of which, however courageously stood up to, were always intensely unsympathetic to my mother. I persisted until the age of about fourteen—when the incongruity of any such ambition dawned even on myself—in supposing that an army career lay ahead. The nature of the school, as such, did not therefore strike me as at all exceptional.

Before becoming a pupil, I was taken by my mother to see the school. It had been built for that purpose, conceding no architectural or decorative feature to attract the eye. We had tea with the Headmaster, in his sixties, recently retired, but returned to take charge again, both his sons being now in the forces. Although rather notably lacking in all literary appreciation, he strongly resembled the photographs of Kipling towards the end of his life; that hanging on the stairs of the London Library always a disagreeable reminder of the Headmaster's sparse grey hair, drooping tobacco-stained moustache, abnormally thick spectacles, eternal old thick tweed suit, worn whatever the climate. Cutting a loaf of bread at tea, he barked out: 'Crust or crumb?' The phrase was unfamiliar to me. He looked enraged.

After tea we were taken over the premises. In the gymnasium the junior boys were marching round. The Headmaster called one of them out, and questioned him. The boy, just about my own age, good-looking, dark, rather plump, gave his replies in a quiet manner. He was Henry Yorke (later the novelist, Henry Green), who was to be a close friend for many years. Indeed, being brought in touch with Yorke is the only outcome of any interest to be connected with the school. This preview of Yorke was one of those curious foreshadowings not uncommon in life. Yorke's own theory as to why he had been pulled out from the rest of the small boys doing gym was that comparative plumpness disposed the Headmaster to

24

show him off to parents as an example of how sumptuously the boys at the school were fed.

In the event I caught whooping-cough, so arrival was delayed until about mid-term. That had the advantage of leaving only about seven or eight weeks to go, but—fellow new boys by now more or less acclimatized to surroundings still unfamiliar to myself—was otherwise an uncomfortable introduction to boarding-school life. At ten and a half I was also rather old for a new boy. There were certain advantages in being bigger and more experienced, these offset by a loss of childhood's curiosity, and protective forgetfulness. By then I had become aware of the amenities of home life, particularly in wartime.

Even for prep schools of the period mine would rank high in any competition for dearth of cultural enlightenment. By this stage of the war, competent teachers hard to come by, there was an ever rolling stream of assistant-masters and mistresses: the males likely to be ancient, shiftless, wounded, gassed; the females (at this school uniformly charmless), often scarcely qualified academically to do the job at all. Two fairly doddering veterans dug out of retirement (both, I believe, Old Harrovians) were agreeable, and liked my essays. One of them (nicknamed 'Spook', not without reason) was celebrated for having once shouted to a hesitant batsman: 'Damn you, boy, always run a catch!'

The drawing-master, Mr Corke, also stands out as a well wisher. He was reputed once to have spat in the coal-scuttle; whether in aesthetic exasperation, I do not know. Those who showed enthusiasm were allowed to draw pretty well whatever they liked, but the normal routine was freehand rendering of formal groups composed of white cubes, cones, and cylinders; alternatively, copying, with much cross-hatching, timbered cottages and ruined towers illustrated in a book designed for that purpose. It was rather as if the policy of art instruction veered between Chirico and Girtin.

The Headmaster taught classics, mathematics, and a language that passed for French. He had cranky ideas about instilling the principles of arithmetic, in consequence of which my own mathematical capacity, at best frail, never wholly recovered; though the subject was well taught at Eton, the change for the better staggering me when I went there. I firmly believe in the value of Latin (quite apart from Stendhal's tenable view that 'le latin est bon parce-qu'il apprend s'ennuyer'), but the classical syl-

25

labus of the top (Headmaster's) form might have been judged a little old-fashioned by Dr Arnold himself. The whole of Saturday morning (three or four hours on end) was consecrated to turning complicated English sentences of five or six lines in length into Latin prose. In the course of one of these sessions the Headmaster went so far in commendation as to remark: 'If I'd had you earlier, I could have done something with you'; but the regret was his rather than my own.

There were frequent and remorseless promptings that the men in the trenches were having a worse time than ourselves. In the music hour we used to sing *The School at War*, a song with words by Cyril Alington, headmaster of Eton; the tune (somewhat recalling *The Londonderry Air*) composed by A. M. Goodhart, my future Eton housemaster.

> We don't forget you in this dark December.
> We sit in schoolrooms that you know so well;
> And hear the sounds that you so well remember,
> The clock, the hurrying feet, the chapel bell. . .
> We don't forget you in the wintry weather;
> You man the trench, or tramp the frozen snow.
> We play the games we used to play together,
> In days of peace—that seem so long ago.

Among these not specially striking poetic images, I used for some reason to find a certain beauty in 'dark December'; also in the lines of another verse, which went:

> Who lie our Country's debt of honour paying,
> And not in vain, upon the Belgian shore.

Later I came on 'the rain and wind beat dark December' in *Cymbeline*, and in Dryden's *Annus Mirabilis*:

> To swell those tides, which from the Line did bear
> Their brim-ful Vessels to the Belg'an shore.

This final phrase turns up again in Spenser's *Faerie Queene*:

Then shall a royal virgin raine, which shall
Stretch her white rod over the Belgick shore.

Had Spenser's phrase stuck in Dryden's head, through Dryden filtering down to Alington, somehow catching my own ear, by some mysterious magic, at the age of ten?

Orwell, Connolly, Waugh, Betjeman, Jocelyn Brooke, to name only a few, have pungently described the disenchantments of schooldays of that date, so that in the case of my own preparatory school there seems no point in rehearsing once again a subject already exhaustively treated. Nothing picturesquely horrible ever happened to me there, though I should be unwilling to live five minutes of it again. At the same time I do not wish to appear less competent than my contemporaries in making creep the flesh of the epicure of sadomasochist school-reminiscence. A single small side-dish will suffice in adding to this generously laid out feast.

The Archer-Shee postal-order case being prototype of an endemic category of school row, a boy at my prep school was similarly accused. Though such things are hard to judge, he was a boy who might have been supposed particularly unlikely to have done anything of the sort. Two senior boys, officious and half-baked, reported him. In consequence the Headmaster administered thirty-two strokes of the birch. The whole school was assembled to hear the victim's cries from the Headmaster's classroom (down two or three steps from the big schoolroom), where afterwards it was found that, in the course of this flagellation, the boy had urinated on the floor. His schoolfellows were forbidden to speak to him until further notice.

Some weeks later it turned out that a slip had been made. The boy in question had neither stolen, embezzled, nor forged. He was, in short, totally innocent. The Headmaster was put under the humiliating obligation of making public amends in the presence of the whole school (once more assembled in the big schoolroom), and (his father being on active service) the boy's mother. After recapitulating in an ungracious manner whatever shreds of explanation were available to excuse such a miscarriage of justice on the part of one set in authority, the Headmaster observed: 'Of course the licking doesn't matter in the least. What's important is that there remains not the smallest imputation of dishonesty.'

27

Henry Yorke, as opposed to Balston—almost literally carrying a spear when the curtain goes up on him—enters the stage with a speaking part. Close friends of early years are apt to be less easy to 'rationalize' to oneself, therefore less easy to describe, than those known more casually, and Yorke, in any case a somewhat enigmatic personality, is a forcible example of that. As Henry Green, he wrote an autobiography (*Pack My Bag*, 1940), which takes him to the age of about thirty-five; a book, at once reticent and revealing, that gives his own account of our preparatory school, and much else besides.

Pack My Bag opens with the arresting statement: 'I was born a mouth-breather with a silver spoon . . .' This metaphor perfectly hits off one side of Yorke; the grotesque physical image invoked possessing a comic potentiality certainly recognized by him in offering an economic and moral definition of himself. The silver spoon refers to coming from a family reasonably categorized by him (in a press interview) as aristocratic; a landowning younger branch that had—by no means always the case—superlatively kept its end up.

Yorke was the youngest of three brothers. His father, a classical scholar who had made a prosperous career in business, was half-Dutch, an odd mixture of reserve and rather crude teasing (an amalgam Yorke to some extent inherited), not only characteristic of that generation, but perhaps also evidencing the Netherlands blood; which was laced with equally grand Austrian and Portuguese. These foreign strains were reflected in Yorke's own appearance, and (like George Orwell's quarter-French ancestry) should be taken into account in relation to temperament and approach to writing. His mother (a Wyndham, brought up at Petworth, accordingly regarding all other residences as small), in contrast with her husband a sparkling talker, had an inimitable style in anecdote, in which sporting vernacular would be deliberately decorated with the brilliantly pedantic phrase.

If one side of Yorke found the silver spoon a handicap to respiration, another accepted it as understandably welcome; and coming to terms with opposed inner feelings about his family circumstances, his writing, his business activities, his social life, was something he never quite managed to achieve to his own satisfaction. To say this is, of course, to look ahead. *Pack My Bag* constantly emphasizes an interior tumult that re-curred throughout Yorke's life. When we were young I had no idea how deep these troubles must have lain. Then—and later—he always seemed pretty successful in whatever he put his hand to—writing, business, life in general—but success is not the criterion of whatever alleviates the stresses that his own self-examination suggests.

The eldest brother had preceded Yorke at our preparatory school, the other going elsewhere. Both elder brothers were unusually good at work and games, and Yorke records how his own fallings-short were invariably contrasted by the Headmaster with the eldest's glowing achievement. This brother died at the age of about sixteen, while he was at Eton. Yorke himself, if no dazzling star, was perfectly competent at the normal rou-tines of school life, a skilful fisherman, and later to play billiards for Ox-ford. Nonetheless (even if left unspoken by anyone but the Headmaster), there was a tendency for him to be treated at home with affectionate but slightly amused acceptance that he was not quite the performer the other brothers had been at his age.

This situation is not to be exaggerated. When such a motif is set down on paper it can acquire an altogether undue weight. Yorke's family per-fectly recognized that he had a line of his own, but (as *Pack My Bag* shows) his talents were not easy to define—and he was himself the worst possible salesman of them. No one, least of all his relations, could be alto-gether blamed for not immediately grasping the nature of his gifts. To myself, as guest in the house, he always seemed on the easiest terms with his own family—ragging his father in a manner I should never have dreamt of using towards my own—but he would often complain of ten-sions at home, and was certainly obsessed by a parental 'myth', especially where his father was concerned.

I do not remember when we first made friends at our prep school; not immediately; possibly only after moving into one of the two dormitories containing twenty or more boys. In these big rooms (in one of which an alcove for washing-basins was called Port Arthur from the Russo-Japanese War of 1905) both Yorke and I—like professional narrators of the Orient—were recruited, during the half-hour after lights-out when talking was permitted, to entertain the company by telling stories. This folk-type of group culture was surprisingly popular. The stories were usually re-hashes of popular novels, or serials running in magazines; in neither case works specifically intended for boys, though no doubt tending to possess a detective or thriller basis. I occasionally offered a concoction of my own; here too (as with Shakespeare) derivative elements probably traceable. I remember establishing some sort of status for the narrator—a blow struck for art and letters—by refusing to continue if too much whispering, or other interruption, took place. All this sounds as if at an early age I had decided to become a novelist. That was not so; although, sitting on the radiators of the gym, Yorke and I did begin to write a novel together (a thriller), but it progressed no further than the first half-page of an exercise book.

Yorke, who himself never possessed the smallest relish for military mystique, had been sent to the school on the recommendation of an uncle by marriage, a general. I can't remember how he saw his own future at that age, but feel sure that he spoke of it—as of most things—altogether dogmatically. As a boy he was an unremitting talker, especially if not at ease, a compulsive flow, hit or miss in content, but, as often as not, funny, perceptive, entirely individual. He records that while growing up he would sometimes produce for the benefit of strangers in a railway carriage narratives of pure fantasy about himself. As a small boy he had an exceptional command of the mature phrase, but was otherwise a fairly conventional schoolboy, daring only in his spoken objectivity. When we were about eleven I was astounded in this respect by Yorke remarking: 'The fact is that both my parents are extremely selfish.'

He was always interested in words, repeating unfamiliar ones (e.g. hirsute) over to himself, laughing at them, discussing them. We must have been about twelve or thirteen (I don't think I was yet at Eton, though Yorke may have been) when we found, in an out of the way sitting-room in the Yorkes' country house, two volumes of Rabelais. The name even then conveyed unspeakable obscenities, and we set to work at reading them forthwith. Neither then, nor later, have I been able to make much headway with the great satirist, but at the time he seemed something of a milestone in varieties of literary experience.

Yorke, though he constantly reiterates the tyrannous nature of the Headmaster, relates that he was on the whole happy at our prep school. He writes of the Headmaster: 'We respected him until in my case I at least went further and came to reverence him.' The literary device of speaking collectively is open to objection, but (even if not my own view)

Old Boys might well concur in the Headmaster being owed respect; even (Old Boys being what they are) reverence. What I find an interesting paradox, in this Kiplingesque praise of a famous man of little showing, is that (though coming to his work seriously only in middle life) I am a great admirer of Kipling; while Yorke found him wholly unreadable.

Yorke went to Eton at the end of the summer term of 1918. I stayed on two more terms. We used sometimes to exchange letters.

4

In 1917, my father was sent as instructor to the Staff College, then quartered at Clare College, Cambridge. The University was housing mostly officer-cadets. I can't remember where my mother and I had been living while my father was in France, but now we went to Cambridge, undergraduate furnished rooms at 4 Great St Mary's Passage. It was winter, Cambridge some of the time under snow. At Clare was an old college butler, Phipps (with grey side-whiskers), with whom we became friends. He gave me (presumably from the college cellar) a half-bottle of port to drink on my twenty-first birthday. This was certainly preserved, and consumed, but, ungratefully, I cannot remember the circumstances of doing so, nor the wine's year and shipper. I did not live at Cambridge again until I was myself sent on an army course there in 1941.

After some months at the Staff College, my father returned to France again (on the staff of the 25 Division); was then posted to the War Office. It must have been about this time that my parents took a house in St John's Wood. I remember air-raids on London after we went to live there; a bomb dropped on the pub at Lord's Cricket Ground, which was just round the corner.

Back at school, the Headmaster's form were construing Livy one November morning—he had just objected to the word 'voluptuous' as translation for some epithet applied to Capua, on grounds that boys did not know what the term meant—when at the back of the classroom the door opened. The Headmaster's wife ('Ma Baboon', her physiognomy to the life) came hurrying down the two or three steps. She went up to her husband, and began simian mumblings in his ear. The Headmaster removed his wire spectacles, contracted his eyes, closed the small bluebound teaching edition of Livy. The news had just come through that an Armistice had been declared. He announced that there would be no more work that day. Instead, the morning was divided into playing football, and, for the top form, cutting wood in the miniature labour camp adjoining the Headmaster's garden. In the afternoon we played football again. That evening I was reading a book in the big school-room. The Headmaster tramped in. He had experienced an afterthought. There would be prep after all, notwithstanding the Armistice. Otherwise, he said, the next day's work would be disrupted.

The following term, the Easter one, I sat for the Common Entrance Examination for Eton. Some weeks later, having just slipped a cartridge into the breech of a .22 rifle, I was lying prone on the mats of the rifle-range. The Headmaster would sit behind those shooting, registering with field-glasses the area of hits on the target. Suddenly he addressed me.

'You've taken Middle Fourth.'

A feeling of indescribable wellbeing flowed through me; a sensation I have experienced on one or two subsequent occasions on hearing good news. Middle Fourth, far from a triumph of scholarship, was a perfectly respectable level to achieve. My body had to remain a few more weeks where it was; the real me had already moved into another, and preferable, condition of life.

Until my late twenties I used to have a recurrent—if not very frequent — dream that I was back at my preparatory school. One night this dream took the shape of the Headmaster lying on a sort of chaise-longue; myself standing beside him. I don't know whether I had become a boy again, but he was speaking in the harsh tone he was accustomed to use when angry. Instead of answering him, I took one side of the piece of furniture on which he lay, and shook it. He protested. I continued to shake it with increasing vigour. The Headmaster's protests became weaker; then ceased altogether. I examined him. He was dead. So far as I can remember, dreams of the school never recurred after that night.

III

The Wat'ry Glade

My mother's eldest paternal uncle had been at Eton, and her sole maternal uncle (the unfortunate DRJ, who lost his reason and who figures in the Appendix of this book), but I doubt if she knew where any of the Welles family were educated, that process having taken place a long time before even in the case of her father, youngest by twenty years. My Welles grandfather had, in fact, gone to Westminster, then at the lowest ebb of its history (characterized to me by a former Westminster headmaster as 'the period when the older boys extinguished their cigars on the younger ones'), but, ominous as that sounds—my grandfather unlikely to have done the bullying—no legend survives of atrocious schooldays. DRJ had won the Prince Consort's German Prize (an Eton award of some distinction), so that leatherbound sets of Goethe and Schiller (with similarly ornate 'leaving books' presented, as was then the custom, by devoted friends) may have fixed that uncle's school in her mind.

In any case such matters as schools—and jobs—belonged to a man's world with which, unless forced by circumstances to do so, my mother greatly preferred not to traffic. She possessed a good deal of sound practical sense, a strong will (much stronger than my father's), grasp of the ordinary run of business that might come her way (renting a house or suchlike), but would otherwise strenuously avoid anything she regarded as a male sphere of influence. She was, for instance, entirely without curiosity as to the nature of my father's work at any given moment—about which he himself certainly went out of his way to make a tremendous mystery—and she would never, in the manner of some army wives, have indulged in a military technicality as the simplest manner of phrasing her husband's current employment. Schools, in her eyes, came under this essentially male heading; perhaps additionally so, as she had never attended one herself.

My father always wanted me to go to Eton, chiefly because he felt a mess had been made of his own upbringing, and Eton's name would rule out any such imputation in the case of his son. That it was to be regarded as an expensive school was not minimized by either of my parents; the fact always impressed on me that I was lucky to be sent there. As things turned out, I think I was, but my parents' attitude raises one of the many aspects of Eton myth, and, without embarking on an extended apologia for the school, a word may usefully be said in modifying some of these legends.

Eton then consisted of about eleven hundred boys; seventy with scholarships called King's Scholars (abbreviation 'KS', colloquially 'tugs'), the latter living in a separate building designated College; the rest, in houses of about forty boys each, called oppidans (town-dwellers). Every boy had a room to himself (collegers a cubicle their first year); a comparative privacy, which, combined with the size of the school, allowed for a never less than perceptible minority opinion on most matters. Pop, a self-elected body of about twenty-eight boys (of whom at least six were members *ex officio*) exercised an overall authority as prefects, and possessed certain privileges. Election to Pop, based overwhelmingly on athletic distinction, was generally regarded as the summit of school ambition, though Sixth Form (the top ten collegers, and top ten oppidans, the Captain of the School always a colleger) also commanded a lesser prestige.

It is perfectly true that Eton was among the more expensive schools (even then, I think, not the most expensive), but compared with other public schools the margin (anyway for one boy) was not astronomic. Three hundred covered everything. There was always a fuss if my own bills for a single half (term) reached a hundred pounds. It was often said that the trimmings to these bills were formidable. Had that been so, I should certainly not have remained at Eton. Some parents, it is true, would have preferred to spend the margin on themselves; others, like my own (who always lived very simply, often somewhat uncomfortably, during army dislodgements) preferred to send a son to Eton. I recall no sense

34

of inferiority on account of many boys' parents being richer and grander than my own, though of course many were. Indeed, the first powerful impact of snobbery and money was brought home to me, not at Eton, but at Oxford.

The supposed difference of background between oppidans and collegers is often exaggerated. It was not at all uncommon for brothers to be on these different sides of the school; for example, Yorke's father and eldest brother—who could not conceivably be described as coming from dim circumstances—had both been collegers. George Orwell is sometimes instanced as unhappy in being sent to a school where a good deal of money was in the offing, while his own parents were hard up; but Orwell had won a scholarship at Wellington—actually spent a term there—a school of high reputation, designed for the sons of soldiers unlikely to be rich. Nevertheless, both he and his parents unhesitatingly switched by choice to Eton.

Another legend is that 'no one did any work'. Until reaching the 'specialist' stage, the tutorial system made anything like real idleness hard to come by even for the most determined. This system was that the master who set the exercise was in close touch with the 'classical tutor'—usually also housemaster—who supervised the same exercise outside regular school hours; Lower Boys at Eton (in my day) working longer hours than German boys of the same age.

The so-called 'block system' disposed that boys of similar intelligence were taught together, in some degree irrespective of school seniority. If a boy was bad at Latin, but good at mathematics, he was taught with the dull Latin boys, the bright mathematicians. In 'school order' these might be two forms above, or two forms below. Boys who failed in examinations at the end of the half were likely to be got rid of. After passing what was then called the School Certificate, boys judged to have reached the limit of their capacity were, as at most schools, sooner or later shunted off into some relatively undemanding backwater; but I never heard this offered as explanation by a claimant to have 'done no work'.

This system gave a certain fluidity to the mixing of age-groups, but it should not be assumed that, because boys overlapped in their time at Eton, they necessarily knew each other there. The school was too big for that. A few instances will illustrate this. My brother-in-law, Frank Pakenham (now 7th Earl of Longford), almost my twin in age, went to Eton at twelve and a quarter (myself at thirteen and a half), and, far senior to me in the school, was known to me by sight only because his house was opposite mine. (We never ran across each other at Oxford; exchanging a sentence for the first time in about 1930, straightening our white ties before a looking-glass, having both arrived too early for a dance.) Orwell, two and a half years my senior, illimitably higher in the school, I did not even know by sight; and another subsequent friend, John Heygate (author of the Eton novel, *Decent Fellows*, and about the same age as Orwell) was known by sight only because, as junior Sixth Former, he led their procession into chapel. On the other hand, drawing, or intellectual interests (described later) brought me into touch with David Talbot Rice (Byzantinist), Oliver Messel (artist and stage-designer), Billy Clonmore (now Earl of Wicklow), and several more, who were two years or more older than myself.

I don't think Orwell and Heygate ever met in later life, but Orwell told me that they were once the two Sixth Form praepostors on duty at a birching by the Headmaster. Heygate had included such an occasion in *Decent Fellows* (1930), and Orwell, rather characteristically, took amiss that the college praepostor was described as 'pretending to look out of the window'; finding in these words a veiled sneer at himself. Cyril Alington, the Headmaster, who had a good deal of swagger and sense of the dramatic occasion, belonged very much to an Edwardian type of culture, though not averse from such frivolities as writing detective stories. The Provost, Montague Rhodes James, a shrouded but powerful eminence in the wings, biblical scholar and antiquary of distinction, was also author of the fictional ghost stories (notably *Whistle and I'll Come to You*) that are still remembered as in a class by themselves for a particular brand of eerie horror.

I went to Eton in the summer half of 1919. There were only a few boys in Middle Fourth, and the two forms below, so that all three were combined under the instruction of an Eton master of some fame, 'Bunny' Hare, who normally took only the dregs of the school. A veteran of great charm (if a trifle grubby), Hare had taught dull boys for centuries without having ever been known to lose his temper. I am glad to have encountered this historic figure, and feel no regrets at making a start among the lowest of the low. I had been placed a shade beneath my academic standard, and was given a 'double-remove' at the end of the half.

In the summer, the alternative was offered of cricket or rowing. Having always detested playing cricket, I had no hesitation in becoming a Wet Bob. Only in later life did I come to understand that much of the tedium I have always found in games derives almost as much from lack of competitive spirit, as inability to run, or catch a ball. At my previous school I had been in the rugger XV, once won my weight at boxing, achievements I do not put forward as stunning athletic triumphs, but (since certainly no skill was involved) because they suggest a certain sturdiness vis-à-vis contemporaries. In terms of muscle, I remember noticing at about fourteen that I was less strong, after puberty developing a lighter physique; perhaps becoming a rather different sort of boy. To round off, here and now, my athletic career at Eton (that is, a statement of what was in most of the school's eyes one's social status, in my case an extremely modest one), I captained the second House-football XI ('always a good type of boy does that', Hubert Duggan used to say), and rowed for the House in bumping fours; the latter a less sympathetic form of aquatics than, with a couple of friends, taking a gig up to Queen's Eyot, having tea there, and gently paddling downstream on a Thames summer evening.

As a Lower Boy, even halfway up the school, badness at games did not greatly worry me; when more senior, it undoubtedly raised a barrier between oneself and more athletically proficient contemporaries, with whom one would otherwise have been on easier terms. (When in the army, just returned from a 'course' to the Division Headquarters where I was serving, I asked a corporal how the rugger was going. 'We haven't had any rugger, sir,' he said. 'No one took much interest in organizing the rugger after you went away'. Such are the paradoxes thrown up by total war.)

I could not have been more fortunate in my Eton house. A. M. Goodhart's was not merely a 'bad' house, but universally agreed to be far the 'worst' house in the school. Its record at every branch of sport was unimaginably low; its only silver trophy, the Lower Boy Singing Cup. Tolerant scepticism was the note struck. This was partly due to chance—the particular boys who happened to have been sent there—partly to the eccentric character of Mr Goodhart himself; in certain respects a typical schoolmaster; in others, an exceptional example of his profession.

Then in his fifties, Goodhart somewhat resembled photographs of Swinburne's friend, Watts-Dunton; the same high forehead, walrus moustache, look of slightly unreliable benevolence, an awareness of being always prepared for the worst, and usually experiencing it. With the Eton master's uniform, black suit and white bow tie, he was old-fashioned enough to retain the starched shirt and cuffs of an earlier generation; often remarking that in his own time at Eton (in College) a boy who did not put on a clean stiff shirt every day was regarded as an 'absolute scug'. On the other hand, Goodhart equally deprecated modern extravagance in demanding all sorts of special clothes for sport; asserting that for the Wall Game (which, as an acknowledged star of all time, he would still sometimes play) an 'old tailcoat' was looked on as wholly appropriate.

Goodhart's sentences always began with a curious little purring sound, much parodied, but almost impossible to reproduce, far less describe; best indicated perhaps by a favourite quotation of his (from the *vers de société* of Frederick Locker-Lampson) referring to a racehorse of Lord Rosebery's:

> And the winnner of the Derby
> And the Guineas
> Proudly whinnies,
> When e'er the Opposition takes a fall.

Goodhart might be said to have whinnied before quoting the aphorisms, to which he was addicted, like 'Genius develops in solitude, Character in the stream of life.' One can hardly believe he took this from Stendhal's *De l'Amour* (On peut tout acquérir dans la solitude hormis le caractère), possibly both drawing the opinion from a common source. He would give impersonations of Mr. Gladstone: for example, the statesman remarking to fellow-guests at a dinner-party: 'It is monny yee-ars since I ot a Brazilian knot—or, indeed, a knot of onny kind.' Goodhart was also inclined towards uttering apparently contrarient statements like: 'Boys come in from football hot, and rather cold.'

Classics were the subject Goodhart taught, but his real interest was music. When the day was over he used to compose in his study, which was situated at the end of a passage lined with boys' rooms. There were several bathrooms in the house by the time I went there, but only a few years before hip-baths used to hang outside every door. Riotous members of the House would sometimes emerge at night—having made sure the

THE
UNIVERSITY OF WINNIPEG
PORTAGE & BALMORAL
WINNIPEG, MAN.   R3B 2E9
CANADA
DISCARDED

night-watch was on the upper floor—take one of the baths from the wall, and bowl it against their tutor's study-door; disappearing round the angle of the passage, to be found fast asleep when enquiries were instituted. By my day a quieter mood characterized Goodhart's pupils.

The Captain of the House when I arrived there was Arthur Peel (later Earl Peel), an unusually tall boy with a slight stutter, who messed (had tea) with the Captain of Games, R. W. E. Cecil (now Lord Rockley), for the second of whom I fagged. This Cecil (a perfectly agreeable fag-master) is to be distinguished from Lord David Cecil (the writer), for whom I also fagged later. Peel made a good impression a day or two after the opening of the half by his manner of having a kindly word with the new boys. The following half, when I fagged for Peel, he gave his fags the run of two or three shelves of quite readable books. Among these I found Alec Waugh's *The Loom of Youth*; greeted on publication two or three years before as a work of unspeakable depravity, owing to its references to public-school homosexuality. By the time I read the novel it was accepted, anyway by boys, as a reasonably accurate treatment of the 'romantic friendship', that might take in some cases physical form.

It was always said that Goodhart had wanted to marry a celebrated lady pianist, who had become wife of another Eton housemaster. Certainly he was always very attentive to her, when she sometimes came to sing-songs held in his drawing-room on the private side of the house, though it is not easy to imagine him as a married man. Naturally enough, he preferred goodlooking boys to plain ones, but not to excess, and one would suppose him a repressed bisexual. A touch of kinkiness was added by a fervid preoccupation with ladies' shoes (a fancy said to presage masochism), which Goodhart made no attempt to conceal. On the contrary he would from time to time hurry round the house after prayers, bearing with him for the admiration of his mostly indifferent pupils some huge volume illustrating *Feminine Footgear through the Ages*, or some similar saga of the Boot and Shoe.

Goodhart's encouragement of music included a hymn sung at house-prayers every evening, which he accompanied himself on a harmonium. The hymn was chosen by the Captain of the House (a limitation put on the frequency of *All Things Bright and Beautiful*), but one night Goodhart forgot to give out the hymn's number, and began singing and playing solo. Music has never held a great part in my life, but the Saturday night

39

sing-songs were a welcome change from the self-conscious attitude towards singing prevalent at my former school.

Goodhart's choice of what was sung, as of everything else, was eclectic. He had a great liking for the then popular song, *The Japanese Sandman* ('Just an old secondhand man/Trading new songs for old', or something to that effect); also for a Swahili hunting call that went *Aah—keelongula*, an invocation he would make us sing over and over again. One night—a carol suggests the Michaelmas half—when *Good King Wenceslas* was being sung, the verse was reached:

> In his master's steps he trod,
> Where the snow lay dinted:
> Heat was in the very sod
> Which the saint had printed.

At the moment when the third line was sung, Goodhart (perhaps not without all *arrière-pensée*), looking up from the piano, observed a boy, Elmley, I think (now Earl Beauchamp), laughing. When the sing-song was over, he told the boy, whoever it was, to wait behind. When the rest had left the room a confrontation took place.

'Why were you laughing, etc?'

The boy, not attending to what was being sung, had by then entirely forgotten the reason for his own amusement. He was completely mystified.

'I don't understand, sir.'

'You understand perfectly well, etc.'

The boy continued to show utter incomprehension, Goodhart growing increasingly angry. At last he burst out:

'You were laughing at the word *sod*. Do you know what it means?'

The boy gave some noncommittal reply. Goodhart was foaming by now. 'It is in vulgar use as short for sodomism—*the most loathsome form of dual vice.*'

I can't remember how this misunderstanding was eventually cleared up, but all ended relatively happily; though there was a certain amount of discussion throughout the House afterwards as to what Goodhart himself regarded as among the less loathsome forms of 'dual vice'. As housemasters went, he was no more obsessed about homosexuality than most,

40

the problem never far from the minds of any of them; one without conceivable solution—but then what sexual problem can ever be said to have been solved? About a year before my arrival several members of Goodhart's had been sacked, at least one for sending an indiscreet note to a younger boy. I remember during my second half hearing an elder boy spoken of as being 'gone on' someone, and finding no difficulty in grasping the general implications; nor, for that matter, in understanding those aspects of *The Loom of Youth*. At the same time there were probably a few boys who passed through the school with scarcely an apprehension of the underground love affairs, or more brutal intimacies, that took place; boys having a keen instinct for what could be suitably spoken of in front of their own kind.

Certainly romantic passions were much discussed, but—on the romantic level—I should have thought physical contacts were rare, though contemporaries indulged at times in more knockabout performances together. I felt no disapproval, but never knew of these except by hearsay. The masters might look on the subject as one of unspeakable horror; the boys behaved much in the manner of public opinion as to homosexuality today; ranging from strong disapproval to unconcealed involvement. In between these extremes of sentiment existed an abstinence that was as much due to fastidiousness as morals; a sense that, at best, this was a very makeshift release for those who had other objectives in view.

An early incident suggested to me that such goings-on were not always taken too seriously by grown-up people. Out for a run with another boy one winter afternoon, we were making for the open country beyond the railway arches that link Windsor with the main line. Men were working at the top of the viaduct. One of them shouted something. We yelled back that we could not hear. He repeated his words, now borne down wind: 'It's a cold day for sodding.'

A rather different sort of unconcern about youthful vices struck me a year or two later in a biography of the Emperor Napoleon I (translated from French) that I found in School Library. The author said that one reason why Bonaparte had not liked the military academy of Brienne had been on account of the 'impurity' there; the 'nymphs of Brienne' being famous. The word 'nymph' used by a serious historian in this sense seemed altogether more lighthearted than the attitude of Goodhart and the other Eton masters.

41

When, at the invitation of a boys' society there, I went down to Eton some years ago, a housemaster gave me dinner. Several boys were present at the table. In the course of conversation the housemaster remarked of some extraneous (non-Eton) figure: 'He's homosexual, isn't he?' No one round about seemed to regard the words as at all daring.

2

Peel (just below Sixth Form), and R. W. E. Cecil, eminently respectable figures, were members of the House Library, a body usually between four and six in number, amounting to self-elected house-prefects. In the middle age-group of most houses there inclined to occur a cluster of fairly rackety boys, from whom the house-tutor might expect trouble. In this respect Goodhart's was no exception, but, about three-quarters way up the House, the mixture was seasoned by two or three boys with intellectual interests, notably David Cecil, Robert Gathorne-Hardy, and Eric Dance; the last slightly older than the others, and, unlike them, in the House Library.

David Cecil, as a boy, was remarkably little different from the well-known author and critic he is now, his demeanour very grown-up (he behaved with great forbearance when I let his fire out), his interests already directed to literary matters. Gathorne-Hardy was later secretary to the American man of letters, Logan Pearsall Smith (employment in which he was followed by Cyril Connolly), about which he wrote an amusing book. Dance possessed quite unusual talents as an actor, though for some perverse reason his family would never allow him to go on the Stage, where he would certainly have made a name. Like several other gallant but unmilitary types known to me, Dance, serving in the Far East, met his death during the war.

These three were the hard core of something that made Goodhart's rather different from the run of the mill Eton house, even 'bad' house. They were, for example, foremost as organizers of Goodhart's House Dramatic Society. I was not personally involved in its productions (only just arrived, and without the smallest gift for acting), but, through the shows put on, had opportunity to see at an early age—among other works— Marlowe's *Doctor Faustus* (somewhat cut, but Helen of Troy played in the Elizabethan manner by a boy), *The Importance of Being Earnest* (I had already read *Lord Arthur Savile's Crime*, *Dorian Gray* soon after), and *Arms and the Man*, the only Shaw play I have ever found free from all tedium.

In principle, Lower Boys (a status lasting not less than three halves, nor more than seven) were not supposed to take Extra Drawing, but Goodhart approved of small boys who were interested in the arts (a type that often developed into the sort of boy he liked a great deal less), so that by exerting pressure I was allowed, from my second half, to attend the Studio, the scene of all but routine drawing lessons. The Eton Drawing Schools nowadays are a complex of red brick buildings set at one end of a rather cheerless open space, the whole looking like a military cantonment in India. The many rooms give greatly improved accommodation for instruction, posing models, holding exhibitions; premises in all respects more luxurious than in my own day. No doubt such changes were overdue, inevitable, beneficial. My nostalgias for the past are by no means automatic, but in this particular case I cannot help feeling regret. In fact not to insist that a great deal has been lost would be, on my own part, to betray an institution for which I always felt a deep affection.

The old Studio in Keate's Lane, at one end of a low-roofed house across the front of which trailed a purple wistaria, consisted of two moderate sized sky-lighted rooms opening into each other, which had probably once been part of the house itself. These rooms were always in a state of comfortable disorder; piled up with pictures, plaster casts, oddments of silver, china or glass, suitable for forming 'still life' compositions. Among the casts were a miniature Belvedere Apollo, and an impressive head of Mirabeau (pockmark on chin), the latter drawn at one time or another in charcoal on blue-grey paper by everyone who came to the place.

Over this nook of the Latin Quarter—Du Maurier's, or even Thackeray's—magically reconstituted among the byways of an English public-school, presided Sidney Evans, a drawing-master who might himself have been a hearty British artist in the Paris of the *Trilby* period. Bluff, good-natured, absolutely sure of himself (for instance, when a model looking like a retired burglar suddenly began to rave in the middle of a sitting of the School Drawing), Evans belonged to an Eton dynasty of some antiquity; among which his aunt had been the last 'dame' to reign over a boy's boarding-house. Evans himself combined a matter-of-fact manner with a

43

tolerant, by no means badly informed approach to painting. His own pictures were somewhat in the tradition of Sickert and the Camden Town Group, but he had that facility for pastiche that can be a handicap to developing one sort of talent, useful to those who teach. It was from Evans, when I was still a Lower Boy, that I first heard views on Matisse and Picasso, painters whom he might regard with a certain degree of scepticism, but—unlike many of his age half a century ago—did not declare fit only for the gallows or the madhouse.

In winter, after lock-up and tea, one would go round to the Studio, a retreat from surrounding school life so pleasant that even the holidays were scarcely in competition. It was nothing less than a disaster for me that Sidney Evans retired before the end of my time at Eton, his place taken by a master, who had formerly taught French, and possessed not a spark of Evans's charm and attack.

I have conveyed perhaps too idyllic a picture of Eton by this early introduction of the Studio. If the immediate impact was in general one of great relief, there were adjustments to be made. Two or three years passed within the House itself before I settled down with sympathetic companions; for two halves messing by myself, an eccentricity that would probably not have been allowed at another house. The balance of too much implied glamour is redressed by Goodhart's letters to my father; the Eton tradition being a longish end-of-half progress report from housemaster to parent. The ups-and-downs of this sequence—from Goodhart's point of view a fairly consistent movement down—give a somewhat chilly impression of their subject, though one I can hardly call unjust.

I had got off to a good start from the point of view of work, partly due to having been placed too low, and, throughout my time at school, Goodhart would quite often bestow a leatherbound book inscribed with some such precept as 'Improve the Best'. He was very generous in these gifts to his pupils. The first Goodhart communication (July, 1919) is entirely commendatory: 'He seems to be very happy here and gets on well with the other boys, no doubt because he is modest & unassuming and unselfish and goodtempered . . . He certainly has character.' This approving tone continues for two halves; but a year later (July, 1920) a warning note is struck: '. . . quiet but effective industry . . . gentleness and sense of humour . . .' but 'He does not make friends very easily and I am at a loss to know the reason, but I could not wish for a more conscientious pupil.' In

44

December of the same year, when Confirmation took place (I remember Alington saying in one of his talks on this subject that temptations 'didn't get less as you grew older'), things were still all right, but only just: 'He is a thoughtful and serious-minded boy though not very responsive at first.' There were still saving graces (March, 1921): 'He is a little apart from the other boys but I think they respect him', and (December, the same year): 'He will always have a good influence in the house owing to his sensible views and high principles.'

The clouds that had been threatening this hitherto comparatively sunny landscape now (August, 1922) become darker. The nature of the path downhill will be touched on later. 'He is a little different from the other boys and I feel that his quiet reserve and dignity may prevent him having any strong influence upon others when he gets to the top of the house. I hope this may not be so but I sometimes fear that they may regard him as superior and coldly critical. That is only an impression that may prove wrong . . . He is the sort of boy that grown up people, as I know, find an attractive companion.'

This condition of things, however regrettable, had come to be pretty well accepted by the following December: 'Anthony has plenty of power even if misdirected at times. [This rather sinister comment refers, I think, merely to some school routine, such as concentration on biographies rather than constitutional history.] You will see that Mr Marten speaks favourably of his work & advises that he should try for a Balliol scholarship next half and matriculate that way . . . I don't think he gets on very easily with other boys in the house. It may be due to his moodiness, which Mr Bell mentions & a way of speaking which may give offence to some because it seems to imply a cold superiority or frame of mind too judicial. It may of course be simply due to shyness.'

Henry Marten (later Provost of Eton), senior history master, could claim a goodish record among his specialists for scholarship winning. He was an instructor of an inspired kind, stylized, dramatic, humorous in his own way (though without any profound humour), every word and phrase ringing home effectively. He belonged to a great and compelling tradition of teaching, but, in any modern sense, was a man without down-to-earth contacts with human personality that must in the last resort be needed to understand history; e.g. homosexuality to him was just 'beastliness'.

E. A. Bell—who seems to have complained, no doubt justly, of my own

moodiness—also an excellent teacher of history, was an altogether different type from Marten, as well as being younger. A fat bespectacled little
gnome in his late thirties, he too used dramatic methods of his own, humour of quite another kind, a form of instruction that was much less formal than Marten's. When a boy said: 'But that was a matter of luck, sir',
Bell replied: 'If you haven't got luck, you might just as well go away and
hang yourself.' When I was up at Oxford, Bell attended an undergraduate
luncheon party (I was not myself present), where he got so tight that
some of his former pupils had to put him to bed for the afternoon. I
never came across him again after this Oxford visit. In due course he became a headmaster, and turned to Moral Rearmament.

The Goodhart letters continue into my penultimate half, like a dog
with a bone, to worry away at my isolated condition (April, 1923): 'It so
happens that he is rather aloof from the others in the house—though he is
a great friend of my captain Duggan of which I am glad.' This was Hubert Duggan, of whom more later, but it may be remarked right away
that such an axis might not always have met with Goodhart's approval;
Duggan having been associated with fairly turbulent elements, when less
high up in the House. In fact there may have been a touch of apprehension commenting on this association, which in any case undermined the
thesis of my friendlessness.

In my own memory the situation seems to have been no worse than
that I got on well with some, less well with others; a situation that matu-
rity has left altogether unchanged. Goodhart's view, understandably, rests
on observation made within the *House*, rather than within the *School*.
There was no bar to knowing boys in other houses (though Lower Boys
were not allowed to enter them unless fagged there), so that friends were
always available outside the House, even if one was dependent on its fellow members during winter evenings, when lock-up was at five. Life in
the House, and life in the School, were for most boys rather a different
business; a contrast naturally emphasized among the minority that disliked games. For the first year or two, as Goodhart's letters indicate, my
contacts were no more than the commonplaces of schoolboy life. About
1922—the beginning of the period when the letters become less well disposed—various things happened which may well have made me seem different, not so tractable as at an earlier period.

IV

The Grove of the Evangelist

I cannot sort out with absolute precision where my parents lived throughout my first three years at Eton. In general I associate holidays with 1 Melina Place, St John's Wood, the first house where they had their own furniture again, since all had gone into store after leaving Albert Hall Mansions. At one moment Melina Place was let, no doubt while we were at Camberley, where my father (student now, instead of instructor) was attending the Staff College course. There was also a period, possibly before the Staff College, possibly after, possibly both, when he was back with his regiment, then stationed in Ireland, where the 'troubles' preceding the Treaty and Irish Civil War were in full swing. During this Irish interlude my mother and I were certainly at Melina Place.

The group photograph of 1920 Staff College students shows an almost solid phalanx of World War II generals; among the army-commanders, Major B. L. (Field-Marshal Viscount) Montgomery. My father did not care for his fellow-student—'His jokes . . .' he used to say—and would have been stewed alive in later days rather than refer to the Field-Marshal as 'Monty'. He did not by any means always denigrate successful contemporaries, for some of whom, like Alanbrooke and Dill, he early prophesied brilliant careers. In fact he pointed out the former to me once when lunching at his club (The Rag), saying: 'You'll hear more of the young fellow looking at the papers over there—he's called Captain Brooke.'

As a child I saw little of my father, but fully accepted my mother's

propaganda to the effect that he was greatly to be admired. She genuinely regarded him, anyway in their earlier days, as a man of enormous
intelligence; among the two or three most remarkable in the country. He
was certainly unusual, possessing various *aperçus* and powers of expression that in most men would have led to some sort of personal philosophy
of life. In him, they seemed merely to serve as cause of a perpetual inner
conflict and anxiety. He was himself dimly aware of this paradox. It was a
conflict he never contrived to resolve. His temperament could not be
called a happy one; age and disappointment finally imposing an overwhelming cantankerousness. His perplexities were expressed by a self-
consciousness that made it impossible for him to perform the simplest act —
buy a newspaper, make a routine telephone call, express a casual opinion
at a social gathering—without putting all his weight behind whatever he
said. That might take the form of elaborate charm, heavy irony, loss of
temper that almost approached insanity; any of these states likely to be
used vis-à-vis individuals who had not the smallest notion why such
strong feelings had suddenly been conjured up.

Basil Hambrough, a friend somewhat older than myself (of whom I
shall speak, when I come to the 1930s), had been a subaltern in The
Welch Regiment before transferring to the Welsh Guards at their formation in 1915. I once asked if he remembered my father. Hambrough
thought for a moment. 'I seem to see something going wrong at an exercise, and a fellow standing in the middle of the road speechless with rage —
almost literally foaming? Would that have been him?' That was the picture to the life. This lack of self-control never went further than saying
regrettable things, but these were often regrettable enough. The state was
likely to be followed by dreadful depression and inertia; no doubt psycho-
logically definable as a condition. The lethargy, he would complain, was
inherited from his mother. Alternatively, he would enjoy bursts of great
cheerfulness, when everyone else had to fit in with his mood. He would,
for instance, sit happily for hours going through his book collection (never
reading much, but looking at the pictures); these buoyant patches not to
be entirely relied on, confidences offered during them always liable for
use as damaging evidence later. My father kept his favourite books locked
up, but inevitably forgot at times to turn the key; in consequence of
which I glimpsed at a comparatively early age a couple of volumes
of Havelock Ellis's *Psychology of Sex*, and a certain number of illus-

48

trated books which art did not always salvage from the realm of erotica.

My mother, coping skilfully with my father's framework of nerves, in general able to bring about peace after an outburst of temper, never seemed to suppose that her married life might be other than it was. She had chosen that state, and was perfectly prepared to take its disadvantages. In the last resort she was in command, but things rarely came to that. She too had an uncommon way of looking at the world; expecting little from it, though not at all in a cynical way. Only the company of her own family (perhaps one or two very old friends) giving her any pleasure, she would try to avoid so far as possible all other human contacts. She and I, in memory, seem to have been much alone at Melina Place. We got on well together, but I was often bored while growing up; a common enough element in most accounts of boyhood. Neither of my parents was suited by temperament to organizing the life of an adolescent; nor was that particularly easy for the sort of adolescent my housemaster's letters describe.

St John's Wood (Swinburne's 'Grove of the Evangelist', district of his Marlborough Road brothel), was only just emerging from Victorian disrepute as bower of love-nests and houses of assignation. There was also some tradition of writers and painters in the neighbourhood; in the later 19th century, chiefly prosperous Academicians like Landseer and Alma Tadema. By the time we went to live there blocks of flats had already begun to disfigure the outskirts, but a wide area still consisted of Regency villas with gardens (dwellings designed for keeping a mistress), their structure by then likely to be in need of repair, but of extraordinary quiet and charm for London of that day.

Not at all large, 1 Melina Place was somewhat rambling, with a kind of annexe of two rooms, one above the other, built out into the small garden. These (my mother's bedroom and sitting-room) were reached from the main building through a ground-floor bathroom; the bathroom, even more eccentrically, leading on the other side into the dining-room. In the garden stood one of the pear trees supposedly deriving from the orchards of the Knights Hospitallers, mediaeval landlords of the Wood, to which they gave the name of their patron saint; the fact that the whole estate passed into the hands of the Crown at the time of the Dissolution of the Religious Houses precluding certainty as to the long pedigree of these fruit trees.

All this history was a recommendation in my eyes, also the tradition of *louche* goings-on; the latter by no means at an end, as newspaper scandals from time to time indicated. It seemed inconveniently distant from familiar London, but there were compensations for that. Literary life was brought closer soon after our arrival in Melina Place by Arthur Machen taking a house at the end of its *cul de sac*. I did not know then that Machen's short story, *The Bowmen* (September, 1914), had given birth to the legend of the 'Angels of Mons', but Beardsley had designed the cover for his Keynotes Series novel, *The Great God Pan*, and his then fame as a writer of eerie tales is exemplified by John Betjeman's line in *Summoned by Bells*: 'Arthur Machen's *Secret Glory* stuffed into my blazer pocket'. We never knew this mysterious neighbour, but the occasional sweep of an Inverness cape, surmounted by a black broadbrimmed hat, with the sound of a throaty cough, made him seem all a bohemian author should be.

At Melina Place life began to take on a more coherent shape, and, though likely to be more solitary, I greatly preferred London to the country. At places like Camberley there would be a certain amount of company of my own age; a world of tennis-parties, not particularly congenial, but to which there seemed no alternative. I greatly desired a vibrating social life—which I imagined full of every sort of romantic possibility—but nothing of the kind seemed available in that part of Surrey. In London was always a whiff, however faint and far, of a kingdom of art and letters that lay beyond the hills; the painters and writers now putting into practice those 'experimental' movements that had—a fact so often forgotten — gone as far in all revolutionary directions by 1914 as they were ever destined to go. I used to draw, read, wander about the London streets, occasionally stay with school friends, or accompany my parents abroad. We had a bound set of *Punch* (from the beginning to 1900), and I knew by heart the drawings of Leech, Tenniel, Keene, and Du Maurier.

In the summer of 1920, *The Beggar's Opera*, by John Gay, was revived at the Lyric Theatre, Hammersmith; costumes and sets by Claud Lovat Fraser. This was an exciting experience for far more persons of my own age than I was ever aware of at the time. The style of Lovat Fraser (a war casualty, who died soon after his great success) was pillaged by imitators so immediately, so freely, that its originality is now hard to appreciate. That his art, especially in lesser designs, is not without a touch of whimsy, must be admitted. The implications of irony, disillusionment, cruelty, that add force to Bakst's Russian Ballet décor, for instance, are toned down to what is at times no more than a goodnatured cynicism. Nevertheless, Lovat Fraser brought about something of a minor revolution in his own line. The influence of *The Beggar's Opera* quickly entered every branch of daily life. When (possibly still a schoolboy) I was first taken by an Eton friend, John Spencer, on a round of nightclubs, among them that inconceivably squalid haunt, The Forty-Three, at least one of the tarts present was wearing a bedraggled version of the close-fitting bodice and flat hoops of a Beggar's Opera whore.

If Lovat Fraser's decorations opened up new ideas, so too did Gay's libretto. First produced in 1728, its wit and economy of language remained —and remain—altogether untarnished after two hundred and fifty years. The Opera's mood was perfectly adjusted to that of the Twenties; sentiment that seemed about to spill over into sentimentality (*cf.* Michael Arlen), suddenly cut short by a call to order demonstrating the absurdity, savagery, pointlessness of life; for example in such scenes as Macheath's idyll with the whores who betray him. I cannot remember when I first saw the show—fairly early on, I think—but I was already old enough to find some of the songs at once sexually and romantically exciting in a way that was altogether new.

Macheath:	Were I laid on Greenland's Coast,
	And in my Arms embrac'd my Lass;
	Warm amidst eternal Frost,
	Too soon the half year's Night would pass.
Polly:	Were I sold on *Indian* soil,
	Soon as the burning Day was clos'd,
	I could mock the sultry Toil
	When on my Charmer's Breast repos'd.
Macheath:	And I would love you all the Day,
Polly:	Every Night would kiss and play,
Macheath:	If with me you'd fondly stray
Polly:	Over the Hills and far away.

When, some years ago, I saw another revival of *The Beggar's Opera*, efforts had been made to bring tone and tunes into line with fashions of today. Much was lost. The point Gay makes is that Highwayman and Whore, Procuress and Turnkey, Fence and Footpad, seriously ape the elegance of the *beau monde*. Peachum and Lockit, coming to blows, seizing each other by the throat, retain their mutual formality of speech. The failure to update satisfactorily the characters and scenes was, in fact, an ironic comment on today's absurdities and humbug, no less profound, but from which even memory of form and elegance had faded.

This fervour of mine for Lovat Fraser's work linked up with an odd encounter of the Melina Place period. For Christmas or birthday present, my mother, as I have said, was likely to give my father some addition to his book collection, possibly a Nineties volume suggested by himself. As I grew older, and learnt something of his book-collecting interests, which I usually shared, such items (for example, a chalk drawing by Conder) were often bought at my instigation from shops visited or catalogues studied; book-catalogues arriving at the house in shoals. They remain one of my favourite forms of reading (more calming than wine-lists), and were in those days extremely educative.

A secondhand-book catalogue turned up one day emanating from an address, rather a peculiar one, in St John's Wood itself: 'The Bungalow at 8 Abercorn Place.' This was a street not much more than ten minutes' walk from where we lived. I cannot remember how contact was first made with the bookshop, but certainly my father was away, probably serving in Ireland. My mother may have ordered a book from the catalogue, which the bookseller, noticing the distance was small, had brought round himself by hand. Anyway, relations were opened up by my mother with the occupant of The Bungalow, and she herself visited the focus from which these books were sold. It turned out to be just the sort of unusual nook for which she had a *penchant*; for, without strong intellectual or aesthetic interests, as such, she had a certain taste for the out of the way and eccentric.

The houses in Abercorn Place, characteristic 19th century stucco residences with basements, turned out to have small gardens in front; slightly larger ones at the back. Access to the basement was gained by an area, but, at 8 Abercorn Place, if you crossed the little front garden and went down the area steps, you found, instead of a kitchen door at the end of the passage, a narrow alley leading past the house itself to the back garden beyond. On the far side of this grassed yard stood a miniature two-roomed wooden bungalow. How it first came to be built there I never discovered. From this strange place the bookseller who had sent out the catalogue conducted his business; in principle, entirely by correspondence.

'There's something odd about him,' my mother reported, after her first visit. 'I didn't at all dislike him—with his deep voice—but there's something odd.'

There certainly was something odd. This was Christopher Millard, a man considered odd by people far more inured than my mother to odd manners of living.

The standard account of Christopher Sclater Millard (b. 1872) is given in the opening pages of A. J. A. Symons's book, *The Quest for Corvo*, which briefly outlines the career of this prodigal son of an Anglican canon. Millard had been educated at Bradfield (he sometimes talked of the Greek play the boys performed there), and Keble College, Oxford; the latter suggesting that he too was originally destined for the Church. At an early age he developed a hero-worship for Oscar Wilde, though they never met; Millard becoming (under the pen-name 'Stuart Mason') historian of Wilde's three trials, and bibliographer of his works. He had earned a living by teaching, working in bookshops, acting as clerk in the War Office (during the war), and assistant editor to the *Burlington Magazine*. Setting up his own bookselling business had been made possible by a legacy of £100 a year left him by Wilde's friend, Robert Ross, to whom Millard had been for a time secretary.

I do not remember my first visit to The Bungalow at 8 Abercorn Place, nor how often I used to drop in there; perhaps a couple of times a holiday. Listening to Millard's talk about books, authors, people he had known, was a great enhancement of life at the time. Millard transacted his business, entertained his friends, lived his life in one of the minute rooms; in the other, he slept. There was an exiguous kitchen-bathroom. The whole place must have been dreadfully cold in winter. Books were everywhere: on shelves; on tables; stacked on the floor; stored away in boxes; all neatly arranged, because Millard was intensely methodical.

Tall, greyhaired, handsome in a rugged way, with the deep musical voice my mother had remarked, Millard had an appearance and personality to make him an impressive even overawing figure. I was at an age when thirty seems the threshold of declining years, and, in one sense, he seemed more than fifty, which must have been about his age when we met; in another sense, he appeared far younger, because he was the first grown-up person to treat me in conversation on absolutely equal terms. The melancholy of his demeanour was accompanied by a complete ease of manner. Although steeped in the Nineties, he was entirely without the mannerisms that Nineties relics subsequently encountered (Arthur Symons, Ada Leverson the Sphinx) displayed in one form or another. On the contrary, Millard always talked with a directness refreshing compared even with the affectations of my own generation.

Millard always wore an old tweed coat, flannel trousers, a faded blue-grey shirt. The elegance with which he carried off these ancient garments somehow gave no hint of the grim poverty in which he lived; the extent of which I had then no idea. He was much too undaunted to allow any such suspicion to take shape; and, in fact, one always imagined that he was doing pretty well out of his business. Sometimes, no doubt, he did do reasonably well, but his system of bookselling was designed to suit his own convenience, rather than the humdrum exigencies of the trade. He existed most of the time in the most frugal manner, but, after disposing of an expensive item from his catalogue, would celebrate with some sort of bust in the way of food and drink.

The catalogue-covers describe Millard's goods as 'Modern Books, Belles Lettres and First Editions'. Apart from the occasional MS, picture, bibliographical rarity, a pound or two is usually the price, sometimes even less. From the only catalogue that remains to me I should estimate the value of his stock at about £500; a rough and unprofessional guess. He liked to print 'unsolicited testimonials' at the back of these catalogues. One client wrote: 'It seems to be the habit to congratulate you on the books you sell. The only comment which occurs to me is that they are damned expensive.' That delighted Millard—and was not far from the general view of his terms—though now the books seem ludicrously cheap in most cases. I wish I had kept the rest of the catalogues he sent me.

In the course of these visits to The Bungalow I infected Millard with my own Lovat Fraser enthusiasm. He used to write to me sometimes at school on this subject, and about other books that he thought of interest. I fear (though I am not sure of this) that I may have preserved only the letters that contain specific information about Lovat Fraser items. One of these (22 February, 1922) says: 'It wasn't till I went to the Leicester Galleries show that I was badly bitten by the Lovat Fraser craze'; another (15 March, 1922): 'You say you "expect" I know . . . but I assure you I know very little about Fraser's work save from what you tell me.' In the end, as for Wilde, Millard compiled a Lovat Fraser bibliography.

There were often interesting items at The Bungalow. Millard showed me the manuscript of *The Ballad of Reading Gaol* (for some reason in transit there), written in purple ink, inscribed across the top in Wilde's hand: 'For those who live more lives than one, more deaths than one must die.' On another occasion, two framed drawings by Simeon Solomon, female classical figure in chalk on tinted paper, were propped up against a stack of books. They were said to have hung in the Wildes' drawing-room at 16 Tite Street. Millard also had on offer at one time a full-length portrait of Wilde in oils, showing him as a young man wearing a frockcoat. This picture had been refused (something unlikely to happen today) by the National Portrait Gallery. 'I should have thought they might have been able to find space for it in the lavatory,' Millard said.

Millard (20 February, 1922) refers to 'six of Max Beerbohm's letters (1895-96) to a married woman with whom he seems to have been having an affair. I have promised not to catalogue these last . . . It's a sordid business selling books, but very amusing.' These Beerbohm letters are perhaps of the same lot described (5 April, 1922) as: 'Very interesting, about 20 or 30 of them'. In view of the usual judgment that Beerbohm was not very active in the field of sex, it would be interesting to know if Millard's surmise was well-grounded.

Millard himself was, of course, homosexual; had, indeed, been in prison at least twice for getting the wrong side of the Law. Once, when we were having tea at The Bungalow, he said very casually: 'You know, you're a great temptation.' Although by then school had made me thoroughly familiar with the idea of such things, the implications seemed altogether absurd in the circumstances. I made some light remark in return, passing the words off as a joke. I don't remember Millard's comment being more than momentarily embarrassing at the time, nor was it an embarrassment to future visits. Looking back, it seems to me strange that I took the remark with such complete lack of seriousness—otherwise it would certainly have discomposed me—and, so far as I can remember, thought no more about it. Nothing of the sort was ever spoken again.

This hobnobbing with Millard occupied, I suppose, at most a period of eighteen months, perhaps less. At fifteen or sixteen—in fact well into one's twenties—incidents that take up a few weeks or months seem of far greater extent in memory. In due course my father came back to London. I do not know how he was employed. He may have been at the War Office again, though there seems no record of that. Nor can I remember whether he ever saw Millard. I think some brief meeting did take place; possibly Millard coming to tea. Certainly I used often to talk about books seen at The Bungalow.

By this period Tom Balston (my father's former staff-captain) was a comparatively frequent guest at Melina Place. He had been working in publishing for some years, and was now installed as a director of Duckworth's. There may already have been suggestions that I should join the firm. Balston had persuaded my father to become a member of a rather shadowy institution called the First Edition Club, founded and run by A. J. A. Symons, author of the Corvo biography mentioned earlier. I don't think the First Edition Club ever played much part in my father's life. Even if able to cope, as individuals, with its members, he would not have been at all at ease with them *en masse*. Nevertheless, he certainly went there once or twice, and it may have been in those surroundings that Millard's name cropped up.

Balston told my father that Millard had been in prison, and that he thought it unwise that I should frequent The Bungalow. This was a tiresome thing to do, though in line with the way people behaved at the time; Balston himself suffering an obsession that he would be blackmailed, and everlastingly telling stories of men or women who accosted him in the park in order to ask the way; a form of nervousness that suggests a deep-rooted fear of sex. Edith Sitwell used to say that she always saw Balston's gold spectacles flashing under the peaked cap of a Salvation Army officer (he was, in fact, a fanatical atheist), and these inhibitions may excuse such interference in someone else's life.

My father (speaking of the matter, if it had to be adumbrated at all, in comparatively reasonable terms) told me I must cease to see Millard. It fell out that this injunction exactly coincided with his own posting to a new appointment outside London. Quite how I should have otherwise dealt with the Millard problem, I do not know. I was unwilling to drop the visits; at the same time their imputations were painted in such forbidding light that I felt a trifle intimidated; although such menace as might

56

have existed was already past. Balston himself represented in my life another important link with a more inviting world. I was brought face to face with the difference between schoolboy sentiment and sensuality—something with which to tease the masters—and the whole force of society lined up to threaten a reputation. It was hard to experience no misgiving.

The whole Millard business is an example of my parents' appreciation of certain more exotic aspects of social life, and the arts, at the same time lack of comprehension—perhaps deliberate refusal to understand—where such approaches were likely to lead. In some respects this inability to formulate a coherent point of view may have been a good thing, forcing me to think for myself. It caused at the same time confusion of mind while I was growing up.

As matters turned out, the move from London made the break with Millard natural enough. One of his letters (5 April, 1922) shows that no suggestion of an awkward severance took place: 'I was passing Melina Place a few days ago and saw furniture vans outside, to my regret. I looked in to see if your mother was at home by any chance, but found she was out: she very kindly wrote to me the next day . . . If the "candle" is available for the enlightenment of a non-Etonian, please put me down as a subscriber, a subscription implying that the paper will be sent to the subscriber until one of the three expires.' I am glad to think that my mother, who understood things by instinct rather than by other means, behaved as she did.

Millard's last sentence refers to *The Eton Candle*, a magazine (subsequently listed by him in one of his catalogues) to which I shall return. I never met Millard again. He died in 1927. By then I had already come to work in London, but not yet found my feet in a world where Millard might be met. That period belongs to a later stage of these memoirs, but Millard's history, so far as I am concerned, may be appropriately rounded off with some of the stories I used to hear of him after his death.

Millard had worked on the *Burlington Magazine*, which C. J. Hope-Johnstone ('Hopey' or 'Hope-J' of many anecdotes of Augustus John/Bloomsbury provenance) had at one time edited. I am not sure whether they were on the magazine contemporaneously. Hope-Johnstone, a figure every bit as eccentric as Millard, though in a different genre, said: 'He was the sort who couldn't resist, when out on a country walk, leaping the hedge and raping a ploughboy. I remember talking about him with Clive Bell in the *Burlington* office one day. Clive said he'd rather have a female gorilla than the most beautiful boy alive.'

Another of Millard's affiliations in this latter stage of his life was The Varda Bookshop, which must have come into being about 1926. In terms of bookselling, The Varda Bookshop was a venture at least as out of the ordinary as The Bungalow at 8 Abercorn Place. Its small premises were situated a few doors down the street, where High Holborn curves south into Shaftesbury Avenue. Millard merely looked in there from time to time to give professional advice to Varda, who presided over the bookshop named after her.

Varda, who had not long before been billed (no misnomer) as 'The Beautiful Varda' in one of C. B. Cochran's shows at the Pavilion Theatre, productions renowned for their lavish stagings and the good looks of the cast, owed her name to an odd circumstance. She had been married for a short time to a Greek surrealist painter, Jean (Janko) Varda, a lively figure sometimes described in those days as the 'uncrowned king of Cassis', but not the marrying sort. On parting company with her husband, she had somehow managed to appropriate to herself (though christened 'Dorothy') his surname without prefix.

As well as beauty, Varda possessed a sharp and witty tongue. 'The only woman I know with a male sense of humour', Constant Lambert used to say. Lambert lived in one of the two small flats (the other inhabited by Peter Quennell) above The Varda Bookshop. This gift—or burden—of astringent wit was not always appreciated by those in contact with Varda, especially in the world of the Theatre. She did not follow up her appearances at the Pavilion (where she had been only required to walk across the stage), and the question of what to do with her life became one she was herself never tired of discussing in an entirely objective manner.

Among those who attempted to solve this problem was Michel Salaman, who set Varda up in the bookshop. Salaman, usually type-cast as a rich foxhunting art-fancying friend of Augustus John at the Slade, was all those things; also romantic, able to enjoy a joke, happily married, father of a lot of children. His notion was that having a bookshop to look after would allow a margin for intellectual life (regarded by Varda herself as a necessary element in anything she did), while regular employment might modify a too wayward manner of life.

Salaman did this out of a disinterested admiration for beauty and wit, combined with his own kindness of heart. This is far the most interesting aspect of the whole Varda Bookshop enterprise. If Salaman had been 'keeping' Varda, there would have been nothing much to it, but (so far as anything sexual can be certain in this world) she never became his mistress. This may seem extraordinary—in a sense both parties always seemed surprised about it themselves—but there it was. One effect of their platonic relationship was that Salaman and Varda always remained on good terms.

As impresario of The Varda Bookshop, Salaman proved no more successful than C. B. Cochran, where finding a permanent niche for Varda was in question; but for a time the shop was a place where friends bought their books and congregated for a gossip. Varda herself was by no means always available to serve her customers, if something better to do offered, when a stand-in of one sort or another would be nominated. This was occasionally Lambert, who complained that he always struck a day when all the lunatics in London had been let out to buy their books. One afternoon, when a friend was understudying Varda in the shop, a customer asked if they had Shelley's *Prometheus Unbound*. The works of the Romantic School were then not much in fashion, and the proxy replied: 'No, but I'm sure I've seen a bound copy on the shelves.'

Millard (by some arrangement of which I am ignorant) used to drop in from time to time to instruct Varda in the art of bookselling, and bring some order into this chaos. He and she seem to have got on well together, though the clash of temperaments must have been considerable. Varda, when I asked her about him, seemed chiefly impressed by Millard's strong views about the preservation of health, a subject on which he was something of a crank, it appeared, though I never remember that arising. One evening, after shutting up the shop, Varda and Millard had gone into a baker's, where he wanted to buy a loaf of bread. Whoever served him had blown into a paper-bag to open it. Millard was outraged. 'When you've quite done spreading germs and disease, etc.' Even Varda, no stranger to rows, was taken aback.

The Varda Bookshop died not much more than a year later than Millard. Perhaps it was better that his unique personality should remain an isolated vignette of my growing up; rather than remembered as one of the thousand strange facets of that early London life when I came to it.

V

The Game and the Candle

At Goodhart's, I eventually settled down to mess with Denys Buckley and Hugh Lygon. Lygon (younger brother of Elmley, who had by then left), fairhaired, nice mannered, a Giotto angel living in a narcissistic dream, was a year older than Buckley and me. He left after a couple of halves to travel abroad before Oxford; his place at tea taken (perhaps not immediately) by Hubert Duggan, also a year or more older; by then Captain of the House. That combination—Duggan, Buckley, myself—is my most remembered Eton life, out of school hours, or the Studio. Once, when the three of us were walking down town (probably on our way to Tap, a permitted pub, where we made a point of always using the inner room, to prevent any suggestion growing up of its being reserved for Pop), a small boy in jackets, afterwards identified as named Laycock (later Major-General Sir Robert, who arranged for Evelyn Waugh to be transferred from the Royal Marines to the Royal Horse Guards), muttered 'Goodhart's bloody trio.' Duggan was delighted. 'Excellent' he said. 'Excellent. That's what we are. Goodhart's bloody trio.'

Hubert Duggan's demeanour at school—though not in later life—contributes something to a character called Stringham in my novel. On the other hand, Buckley bears no resemblance whatever to Templer, represented as the Narrator's other companion at tea. Templer (if such things must be established) is—again only at school—a trifle like John Spencer, a friend at another house, always dressed in the latest mode. Spencer was one of the several temperamentally unmilitary figures known to me who died in action; major in the Welsh Guards, serving in the Middle East.

Denys Buckley (son of a judge, himself now Lord Justice Buckley) is one of the few incontrovertibly well behaved friends of my early days. Equipped with dark good looks, quick at his books, not at all bad at games, Buckley neither indulged in bad behaviour, nor was particularly interested in it in others. He accepted good behaviour as a natural way of life, not something imposed from the outside. In another house he would probably have ended in Pop. As it was, he was committed to being a component of Goodhart's bloody trio. At the same time Buckley was not in the least self-righteous. I remember my astonishment at coming into the House Library one afternoon to find him smoking a cigarette while he worked—an incredibly risky thing to do—and his own laughter at my surprise.

Hubert Duggan had an elder brother, Alfred, who was at another house. They were of Irish-Argentine stock, their father—both were never tired of reiterating—having died of drink in his early thirties. Their mother, an American beauty and heiress, was by then second wife of Lord Curzon (Marquess Curzon of Kedleston), a public figure celebrated not only as a member of the Government, but, since his Oxford days, prototype in the popular imagination of an aloof and pompous English aristocrat. Curzon deliberately propagated this 'image' of himself. The Duggans were well disposed towards him, saying that (provided his own opinion was not called into question) he was perfectly able to appreciate a joke; and only possession of a modicum of humour could have seen him through some of his elder stepson's goings-on.

When—thinking of Hubert Duggan's appearance—I wrote that Stringham looked like Alexander the Great receiving the children of Darius, as represented in Veronese's picture in the National Gallery, I assumed that Alexander was the central figure in crimson. I now find this is thought to be Alexander's favourite general, Hephaestion; indeed the National Gallery's handout allows no demur on the point, stating the identity as a fact. Goethe too supposed that, when he saw the picture then privately owned in Italy. Others disagree with this judgment, and I am with them, until convinced by overwhelming iconography.

Plutarch says that the Persian group mistook Hephaestion for Alexander, because he was the taller (Lemprière states they were in any case very much alike); and the point is whether the figure in crimson (pointing

61

with his *left* hand) is indicating the true Alexander, or saying, like the Duke of Wellington: 'If you believe that, you'll believe anything.' Veronese's central figure seems to me clearly intended as the focus of the picture. The features are not altogether unlike frescoes, presumably traditional, of Alexander in the Naples Museum and House of the Faun at Pompeii, which Veronese's taller and more heavily moustached personage in armour does not at all resemble.

Anyway, Veronese's man in purple, with slightly receding dark curly hair, is the one like Hubert Duggan. This may be checked by reference to a photograph in Harold Nicolson's *Curzon: the Last Phase*, in which Duggan, in hunting clothes, stands by his stepfather under the colonnade of Hackwood. His short upper lip (faintly scarred), and the shape of his forehead, also recalled portraits of Byron; though it was his brother, Alfred, who inclined to a consciously Byronic stance. As with all persons living very much in the moment, Hubert Duggan's qualities are hard to convey. In some ways unexpectedly tough, in spite of indifferent health, he had wit, a strong vein of melancholy, a kind of natural dash and elegance, altogether untouched with 'showing off'. Without being good at games he could keep his end up (he used to say of himself 'a cricket cap was on his head, his step was light and gay'), and he was a stylish rider in point-to-points. At school he spent a lot of his time reading (though exiled in the wilderness of Army Class), would quite often introduce books hitherto unknown to me, but he never in the least became part of the Eton (or Oxford) intellectual world.

I did not know Alfred Duggan at Eton. He belongs to my Oxford period, but he may be introduced at this point, if only on account of his characteristic exit from the school. Shorter, more thickset than his brother, Alfred was far more rackety than Hubert at his most exuberant. His hook nose, and (when sober) somewhat assertive manner (when drunk he became genial) made him a trifle Napoleonic. Notwithstanding being always in trouble, Alf was very much his mother's favourite.

Towards the end of his time at Eton, Alf Duggan had formed the habit of leaving the house by an unfastened window between the hours of lock-up and prayers; a period he would spend with a girl from the town, with whom he had established some sort of relationship. To avoid identification as a member of the school, he would naturally change from tailcoat and white tie into ordinary clothes. Inevitably these absences were no-

ticed. His housemaster, rather an unpleasant man, instead of simply tax-
ing him with the offence by circumstantial evidence, locked the door of
Duggan's room, so that he was forced to come down to prayers in a
lounge suit, thereby drawing everyone's eye to him. It might be added
that, as a Roman Catholic, Duggan would not have been compelled to attend house-prayers (an option in which Catholics varied), but probably,
like his brother, he preferred not to seem 'different'. The end would have
been, of course, the same without the housemaster's piece of petty sad-
ism; prelude to a series of similar involuntary displacements.

The Duggan brothers, under the resplendent wing of Lord Curzon, and
affluent international connexions of their mother, moved—not entirely
without protest—in a decidedly grand world. Alfred, although professing
himself a Communist in those days (given to singing the *Internationale*, a
tune for which tone-deafness presented no handicap), was not at all indifferent to smart society. His undoubted abilities were then thought to
presage a parliamentary career, even his stepfather apparently sharing the
view that Alf would end in the Cabinet, and accepting wild oats as established ingredient of great men in their youth. In the event, it was Hubert
Duggan (who used to grumble about his mother's efforts to turn him into
a conventional young man) that went into the House of Commons,
thereby to some extent fulfilling her ambitions for her sons.

In both the Duggans—sentiments no doubt also deriving from their
mother—was always a suggestion of hostility towards the 'great families'.
Probably domestic life with the Marquess was enough to impart a touch
of that prejudice into the heart of the deepest-dyed traditionalist. Certainly the brothers were fond of emphasizing that they had not a drop of
English blood. This sense of being in some degree alien was, paradoxically, more observable in Hubert than Alf, in spite of the latter's frequent
toasts (breaking the glass) to the Irish Republic and Social Revolution.
That may have been because Hubert was primarily in revolt against his
home life, rather than the human condition; while Alfred, adored by his
mother, preferred to express rebellion on a wider front.

The grandiose life surrounding the Duggans certainly did not exclude
all dissatisfactions with the *beau monde*, even all lack of social precarious-
ness. I remember my own surprise when Hubert Duggan angrily dis-
sented from my describing as amusing Maugham's comedy, *Our Betters*
(1923), which satirizes Americans married into aristocratic (mainly Brit-

ish) families. The satire may not be of a very subtle order, but it must have got home at Carlton House Terrace and Hackwood.

Hubert Duggan's emergence from a group of fairly insubordinate boys in the middle of the House, to become its captain, somehow specially suited his needs. Trouble-making contemporaries gone, he was left with Buckley and myself, companionable, but without his own prestige of age. He liked the sort of responsibilities that devolved on him, and, even at Goodhart's, it was possible to ameliorate and reform rules and customs, without at the same time allowing the House to become a bear-garden. For a time Duggan seems to have 'realized' himself in a way he never quite managed again, so far as I know. He did not finish the course at Eton. His health went wrong (he was tubercular), and he left school earlier than intended. There was a long visit to Argentina. We corresponded, but did not meet again until my third term at Oxford.

2

The Studio, under Evans, apart from being a pleasant place to sit and draw, provided common ground for boys of all ages to meet. Although working from the same model was not to be over-presumed on in relation to wide gaps in school seniority, there was a sense of community within, where, irrespective of school status, everyone was aspiring to be an art student. This was not the world of Duggan or Buckley; nor, for that matter, of Henry Yorke. The diarist-narrator of *Blindness* refers, in the school sequences, to grotesque self-portraits pinned on the walls of his room—I remember something of the sort—but Yorke could not really draw; these burlesques executed only to exacerbate public opinion in his own house.

I cannot exactly recall the earliest stirrings of the Eton Society of Arts, but, when the Society was formed, the Studio became its centre for Saturday evening meetings; thereby bringing in there several boys not necessarily associated with drawing, though likely to have some claim to practise one or other of the arts. Some of the members were also contributors to the magazine produced not long after the Society's inception, *The Eton Candle*, to which Millard had referred. The clearest method of considering both the Society and the magazine is perhaps to give a list of the former's foundation members, saying a word about each—and what happened to him later—rather than attempt to deal with everything that pertains to these interwoven matters in a more chronological fashion.

The foundation members of the Eton Society of Arts (list dated February, 1922) were as follows:

W. S. Evans, *President.*

B. C. de C. Howard, *Vice-President.*

H. V. Yorke, *Secretary.*

H. M. Acton.

W. M. Acton.

R. Byron.

A. F. Clutton-Brock, KS.

H. Lygon.

A. D. Powell.

R. L. Spence.

C. S. Anderson.

C. E. Minns, KS.

Evans was, of course, ultimately in control. The other names, apart from officers of the Society, might be expected to run alphabetically—school order would certainly have been regarded as too stuffy an approach—but, in fact, the gradation probably followed Brian Howard's own whim as Vice-President; settled as if he were captain (in Eton phraseology 'Keeper') of some game, choosing members of a team for special aptitudes; the number eleven perhaps settled on for the reason that a printed list pinned to the wall would resemble precisely that. The list did not, of course, represent anything like the total of boys in the school addicted to the arts. There was, however, a kind of homogeneity of membership, though one hard to define; some individual always seeming to run counter to any generalization attempting to cover all members of the Society. It would at least be true to say that everyone there had been prepared to come out in the open as belonging to a newly formed association bound to excite a good deal of ridicule among the boys; unlikely to be very popular with a fair number of masters.

On the one hand, inclusion avoided masters' pets, conformists already belonging to established societies approved by the authorities, members of which were likely to be in any case higher up in the school than most of the Arts Society. On the other hand, Arts Society membership rose above (anyway in our own eyes) devotees of art and letters of too seedy a bearing, or too abject a pi-ness; of which there existed in the school a fairly considerable underworld. It was, indeed, something of an embarrassment to the Society that the uninstructed were often unable to tell the difference between such outcasts and ourselves. In terms of school order, membership stretched from a boy just below Sixth Form, to one who had only just reached the lower remove of Upper School. A suggestion of raffishness, here and there observable in the list, was not looked on amiss.

Brian Howard and Harold Acton (now Sir Harold) were most active in the foundation of the Society; certainly in influencing the shape it took. Howard did not do Extra Drawing, consequently was not a frequenter of the Studio in the ordinary way, though he had at least on one occasion entered a picture (mildly 'modernistic' in design) for some drawing prize. I never liked Howard, nor found his performances in poetry or painting of interest. He seemed to me the essence of that self-propagation for its own sake which has nothing whatever to do with creative ability. At the same time, if some of his antics were likely to obstruct, rather than encourage, an interest in the arts at Eton, his self-confidence and sophistication were both startling in a boy of that age. It was overwhelmingly Howard's drive that brought the Society of Arts and *The Eton Candle* into being; something that must be fully acknowledged. If things had been only a little different, he might have developed into a prodigious ad-man.

A volume of documentation on Howard has been compiled by Marie-Jacqueline Lancaster, a mordant act of piety ruthlessly subtitled *Portrait of a Failure*; Harold Acton's *Memoirs of an Aesthete* offer a vignette of an old friend at once reliable, bantering, in the last resort sympathetic; but Cyril Connolly's squib, *Where Engels Fears to Tread: From Oscar to Stalin. A Progress. By Christian de Clavering* (Howard's middle names were 'Christian de Claiborne') remains not only the funniest comment on Howard's pretensions (to some extent, it must be admitted, on Connolly's too), but also, without falling back on moral judgments, conveys the best picture of Howard's style. ('I can always sell my Gris.' 'But what will you do then?' 'Oh, write—paint—don't fluster me.')

In the manner of the Twenties (belaboured by Wyndham Lewis, himself a claimant in the same line, not without all reason), Howard supposed himself a 'genius'. Like the Actons and the Duggans, he was American on his mother's side. His father's origins, enigmatically imprecise, seem to have been largely American too. The surname 'Howard' had been adopted in preference to that of 'Gassaway'; the latter understandably regarded as having too richly Dickensian a ring for an art-dealer and professional critic.

Tall, a dead white face, jet black wavy hair, full pouting lips, huge eyes that seemed by nature to have been heavily made-up, Howard had the air of a pierrot out of costume. He was immediately noticeable among any crowd of boys, but I never came across him at school until the Arts Society was under way. There was something of Bloch (in *À la Recherche*) about him, but a far more aggressively violently behaved Bloch, prepared to make a scene on the smallest provocation; less well educated too, for in spite of modish intellectual fireworks in conversation, Howard found difficulty in passing into Oxford at a time when the University's scholastic requirements were not excessive.

Once their son was up at Oxford, Howard's parents are said to have exercised some influence in persuading him to abandon intellectual ambitions and friends in favour of the more socially advantageous world of hunting and steeplechasing. Howard courageously took on the physical hazards of these pastimes, and it is hard to feel that much pressure was required in making the change. He had brought off a triumph at school with *The Eton Candle*. Competition in that sort of line at Oxford was keener. Howard's equipment would have been put to considerable strain to attempt anything of the kind. As it happened—university generations varying in such respects—an eminently available cluster of young lords arrived to get to work on in Howard's second year; an objective he successfully attained. The rest of his career (told in Mrs Lancaster's book) does not make cheerful reading: notoriety as giver and disrupter of parties; nomadic homosexual wanderings over Europe; lowly duties in the ranks of the RAF during the war; drink in excess; drugs of the hard sort; suicide in his early fifties.

My prep school friend Henry Yorke, the Arts Society's Secretary, had entered Eton at the same level as myself, but, arriving two halves before, was a couple of forms higher up. We did not see very much of each other at first, but began to meet more later on, and were sometimes taught together. We used to talk a lot about books, Yorke's literary tastes already beginning to diverge from my own. I don't think he ever went through a Nineties period, though in due course he became much addicted to George Moore. I remember enjoying *Lewis Seymour and Some Women*

(Moore's first novel, *A Modern Lover*, published in 1883, revised with the new title, 1917), a book anticipating some of the Nineties tone. Yorke may have produced Moore's novel in the first instance, but I chiefly remember laughing with Hubert Duggan (its possible originator) about a long conversation there between a man and a woman, which turns out to be taking place while they are in bed together.

Quite early on, Yorke was accustomed to take the line that he did not like Shakespeare (not a good sign as a rule), one characteristic of a standpoint equally uninfluenced by convention or fashion. At Oxford, perhaps before, he had a passion for Carlyle (an author tolerable to myself only in small doses), and (a taste I have never acquired) Doughty's *Arabia Deserta*; both indicating a congenial leaning towards obscure diction. Yorke was later a Jamesian, traces of that influence to be seen in his own work. His preference for an 'experimental' approach in his own writing was not (like Joyce's) founded on a wide range of reading, and general interest in styles of every sort. On the contrary, Yorke was extremely eclectic in the books he read. He had begun writing a novel at Eton, its nature unrevealed, though the fact admitted; an undertaking not regarded overseriously by relations and friends.

The 'experimental' element of *Pack My Bag* brings Yorke up against the problem (observable in Gertrude Stein's 'straight' autobiographical works) of how, if writing 'experimentally', to make the reader reasonably clear about the facts of the autobiographer's own direct experience, while at the same time forgoing literal description. Yorke, aware of this dilemma (solved by Gertrude Stein by switching to a perfectly normal style), does not always maintain the manner of his novels; hovering between what at times threatens to become *faux-naïf*, even whimsical, and comparatively uncomplicated sequences, such as that chronicling his own love of fishing. He does not mention Eton by name in *Pack My Bag* (in *Blindness* the school is called Noat), transposing Eton institutions, which are examined in some detail, as if at another school. The subjectiveness of such matters as his own relations with boys at his house, or the circumstances of the Society of Arts vis-à-vis the rest of the school, do not lend themselves to this metamorphosis, which is apt to become merely obfuscating.

Yorke complains in *Pack My Bag* of having allowed himself to become Secretary of the Arts Society, of which he speaks rather condescendingly;

asserting that no one would have bothered with such things, if they had been in a position to make their mark in the school by more conventional paths. This seems not only a kind of ingratitude towards what was a considerable enhancement of school existence, but an attitude altogether surprising in Yorke himself, who throughout life—when he had much else on his plate—toiled away in his spare time at writing novels that were unlikely ever to bring him more than *succès d'estime.* Again the deep split in his feelings is revealed; half a despising of the arts; half a dedicated writer. It would also be hard to guess from *Pack My Bag* that its author, as a boy and young man, was a gifted witty companion, refreshing in many of the ways he looked at life; rather than the figure presented thus as eternally hesitating between a stuffy conventionality, and scarcely less tiresome revolt against convention.

Harold and William Acton (both at the same house as Alfred Duggan) belonged to a ramification of the Shropshire family of that name that had become Italianized; one of its offshoots virtually ruling the kingdom of the Two Sicilies in the 18th century. The two Actons, brought up largely abroad, familiar from childhood with the arts as a professional adjunct of everyday life, viewed the Eton scene very differently from the average boy there. Their father (represented by his sons as a formidable figure, fighting duels in middle age, and behaving somewhat oppressively to his children) had been intermittently a painter, but his energies were chiefly devoted to La Pietra, the splendid Renaissance villa outside Florence where they lived. I paid a visit there at fifteen, when travelling in Italy with my parents; then fifty years later saw the garden altogether changed by the yew hedges that had grown up.

The Acton brothers looked unEnglish, totally unschoolboyish, an impression increased by talking with them; their manner dramatic, formal, courteous, seasoned—especially in the case of Harold—with a touch of impishness. Harold Acton's high forehead, eyes like black olives, slightly swaying carriage, created an ensemble perfectly to fit the conventions of the Chinese artist who later painted him in Chinese dress. William, no less unusual, was more heavily built, in fact quite muscular, exuding energy, words pouring from him in a torrent that made almost a language of his own.

William Acton (a shade younger than me, his brother a shade older) had not yet arrived at Eton, when I first met Harold at the Studio, on one of my earliest evenings there. We must both have been Lower Boys. Acton was showing Mr Evans a book of Picasso reproductions; probably my own introduction to the painter's name, certainly to his work. While Evans turned the pages, Acton remarked that the previous evening the Headmaster, dining with his housemaster, had been taken round some of the boys' rooms after dinner. In Acton's room he had picked the Picasso *cahier* from the bookshelf, and glanced through it.

'What did the Headmaster say?' asked Evans.

Acton gave one of his most impish laughs.

'He smiled rather sourly, sir.'

Evans laughed heartily at that too. The drawings (Picasso's early 1900s period) included the drypoint of Salome kicking up her leg high before Herod. Even a sour smile did credit to a headmaster of that day.

Harold Acton (as will be seen in connexion with *The Eton Candle*) made his début as a poet, but soon moved on to other forms of writing; appropriately becoming historian of the Bourbon kings of Naples. His two volumes of Memoirs (to which his book in memory of Nancy Mitford might be regarded almost as an extension) are written in an easygoing style that sometimes cloaks a good deal of shrewd objectivity on the subject of individuals mentioned there. With regard to his own contemporaries in general, he makes the sage observation that, so far from being a flight of frivolous butterflies, as sometimes labelled, they were a collection, most of them, of hardheaded and extremely ambitious young men. Acton found a life sympathetic to himself teaching at Peking University; leaving China to serve in the Intelligence branch of the RAF. Afterwards he returned to La Pietra. He offered to leave the villa to Oxford, but the University was unprepared to take on administration.

William Acton's painting at Eton tended to vary between 'still lifes' severe as Cézanne's, and costume designs more exotic than Bakst's. At Oxford, he too, rather unexpectedly, rode in the hunting-field, and at 'grinds' (university point-to-point racing)—for excitement rather than social reasons—totally disregarding headlong falls. One of these falls took the form of descent from his own second-floor window in Meadow Buildings at Christ Church; a mishap that did permanent interior damage. In moments of self-fantasy Willie Acton would say that he wanted to join a British cavalry regiment, though even he regarded that as an unattainable end. In fact, he became a professional painter, producing among other work a series of portraits of fashionable beauties; naturalistic heads on classical busts (sculptural ones) against a surrealist background of ribbons and seashells.

Since the fall from the window Willie Acton's health had never been good, and, when war came, he saw it through in the ranks of the Pioneer Corps; resolutely rejecting all efforts to transform him (natural employment for a painter) into a Camouflage Officer. In 1944 he was sent to Italy as interpreter for Italian prisoners-of-war. Rundown and depressed, he was found one day dead in his bath.

Robert Byron, in certain respects every bit as flamboyant a personality as the Actons or Howard, was also in quite another mould. His character is more of a riddle. I never knew him at all intimately, but he was a close friend of Yorke. His house at Eton, nearly as exotic as Goodhart's, accomodated Clonmore, Oliver Messel, his cousin Rudolph Messel, John Spencer, and several others with claims to unconventionality and raffishness.

If Byron's personality and aims are not easy to express in a line or two, there is no doubt about his uniqueness. A connexion with the Poet's family has been suggested, but there seems to have been no ascertained kinship. His father was a civil engineer. As the cards fell out—in his own case rather characteristically—Robert Byron, although not at all keen on Lord Byron's poetry or legend, found himself from the outset of his career associated with Greece, where his surname was one to stir the blood.

Stocky, very fair, his complexion of yellowish wax, popping pale blue eyes, a long sharp nose, Byron looked thoroughly out of the ordinary. His husky insistent manner of speaking demanded immediate attention, a way of talking that could be attractive, even when protesting, which it usually was. He was energetic, ambitious, violent, quarrelsome, with views in complete contrast with those of the typical precocious schoolboy of the period. Anti-Nineties, the very words 'intellectual' or 'good taste' threw him into paroxysms of rage. He was in any case habitually in a state of barely controlled exasperation about everything.

Byron drew with facility (his subtly pornographic frescoes chalked on the walls of The Hypocrites Club at Oxford are, alas, no more), but he may not have been one of those to frequent the Studio. It would have been in his manner to operate independently, to enter (like Howard) for prizes, without participation. I am unsure about this. Byron's vitality was

71

of the kind other people live off. What appeared on the surface undoubtedly hid much that was unguessable beneath. There was a great deal of toughness, mental and physical, both camouflaged by wild buffoonery and exotic behaviour. Always hard up, Byron was also always generous, while making the most extraordinary supposed economies, like finding some purveyor of grotesque tweeds, who would tailor for him suits of unheard-of cheapness. Not at all averse from going out of his way to make himself agreeable to rich or influential people likely to be of use, Byron would always be the first to draw attention to any such comparative genuflexions on his own part; at the same time prepared to have a blood row at a moment's notice with anyone whomsoever, no matter how inconvenient to his own interests.

Like Yorke, Byron was anti-Shakespeare ('Hamlet that emotional hoax') and in due course his passion for all things Byzantine overrode any other consideration, where art or antiquity was concerned. ('Americans are expending £1,000,000 to convert the most picturesque quarter of old Athens into a pillared playground for cats, that they may unearth yet another shoal of those inert stones which already debar persons of artistic sensibility from entering half the museums of Europe'.) If taken *au pied de la lettre* Byron's literary judgments are as unreliable as those on painting and archaeology, but a determination to be always on the lookout for a new approach—anyway one individual to himself—makes a great deal of what he says worthy of attention; if only for the light cast on his own personality. At school, and as an undergraduate, he used to express horror of 'abroad' and 'foreigners', but his life was largely spent making adventurous journeys, and his best book, *The Road to Oxiana* (travels in Persia and Afghanistan), makes plain that his blend of persuasiveness and aggression was as successful dealing with alien persons and situations as with his own countrymen. In those days passports contained the question: 'Any special peculiarities?', and a square frame was provided for a photograph of the passport-bearer's wife. Byron filled in: 'Of melancholy appearance' for the former, and (resulting in the document being withdrawn) sketched an imaginary picture of the latter within the frame.

In Byron's books an obsessive repugnance for cliché sometimes leads to overwriting; complicated mosaics of private reference, or semi-facetious pedantry, piling up in a manner to obscure the issue. This is particularly true of *The Station* (from which come the quotations above), a visit to

Mount Athos in a party that included David Talbot Rice and Gerald Reitlinger. When Byron's style comes off there are splendid images and literary parallels, but it is a hit-or-miss method. D. H. Lawrence (in his days of reviewing for *Vogue*) gave a word or two of condescending but authentic Laurentian praise to *The Station*. One regrets that the two of them never met. The impact would have been considerable.

Byron's ambitions undoubtedly extended beyond a mere wish to be known as a writer, action and power playing a prominent part in his inner needs. Quite apart from the Victorian Revival advocated by him (and Harold Acton) at the meetings of the Arts Society, Byron carried in him something of the genuine 19th century Englishman—a type even in those days all but extinguished in unmitigated form—the eccentricity, curiosity, ill temper, determination to stop at absolutely nothing. Notwithstanding the old-fashioned Britishness of his nature, Byron might have found easier expression of his gifts in another country. We do not much run here to the d'Annunzio type, the writer who is also a man of action (Malraux, Koestler, Mishima, Mailer), personalities drawn to politics, striking public poses, but also desiring to excel in the literary field; in contrast with the dyed-in-the-wool politician, always attracted to the over-imaginative approach, rather than the humdrum banalities of true political life. Disraeli is perhaps our sole notable example at both levels; with Orwell in a different manner. It is somewhere there that I think Byron belonged.

If the Continent could better have accommodated Byron's mixture of intellectual tumult, near-nihilistic aestheticism, muted but never silent political gropings (sometimes Right, sometimes Left), he would have had to submit to some 'philosophy' (perhaps not in America), another loathed word and concept. He also possessed the Continental yearning towards the formation of a group or school round himself; from time to time trying, never with success, to organize some cohesion among his Eton (later Oxford) associates. Byron remained a friend of Yorke and Harold Acton, to some extent kept up with Howard, but after early London days (when Duckworth's published *The Station* in consequence of my knowing Byron) I never saw a great deal of him. The comparatively elaborate production requirements for his subsequent works on Byzantine art (collaborating with Talbot Rice) caused the books to go elsewhere. Byron was an author not easily satisfied. He wrote in my copy of *The Station*: 'Tony, with bitter remorse for his sufferings, Robert.'

73

By the time the war came, Byron was working (doing well, it was said) with an oil company. Unhappy at failing to get himself into uniform—though the Services would have exacerbated him beyond belief—he joined a news-section of the BBC. His varied connexions, reputation for enterprise, nervous energy, would certainly have brought a more picturesque job sooner or later; even if his employment was not already 'cover' for something adventurous. When, in 1941, he sailed for Egypt as special correspondent, the ship was sunk on the voyage by enemy action.

Byron had by no means finished all he was likely to do in life. The force of his personality, quality of his talk, his powers of extensive imagery, taste for the macabre, can be caught only in snatches from his writings. Explosions were frequent. When someone tediously enquired what he would like best in the world, Byron snapped back: 'To be an incredibly beautiful male prostitute with a sharp sting in my bottom.' This love for the perversely grotesque would have taken pleasure in the prophetic nature of a passage he wrote about himself in *The Station* a dozen years before his own end. The monks of Athos had told a story of one of their deacons, drowned at sea, later found whole in the carcase of a shark. Byron comments: 'Having long arranged, in the case of natural and accessible death, to be buried in a mackintosh and manure the garden, I was appalled by this prospect of leaving my vile body, not even digested, in the body of a fish.'

If the two Actons, Howard, Byron, all represented flamboyance in the Arts Society, Alan Clutton-Brock, a colleger, was more staid. Through his father, a professional art-critic, he was closely associated with painting; both father and son appearing together in the pages of *The Eton Candle* when published. In due course Clutton-Brock (whom I barely knew) became himself an art-historian, trustee of the National Gallery, Slade Professor at Cambridge. Like Harold Acton, he served during the war as an officer in the RAF Intelligence Reserve. While undertaking these duties a situation occurred which parallels one in my novel that has been condemned for being too coincidental. Mrs Lancaster's book recounts how Brian Howard, posted to Clutton-Brock's RAF station, was employed there serving teas. I had not heard of this surprising reunion of two members of the Eton Society of Arts, when I wrote of Stringham turning up as a waiter at the Narrator's Divisional Headquarters.

Hugh Lygon, named earlier as messing with Buckley and myself, was younger brother of Elmley. They were sons of Lord Beauchamp, then Leader of the Liberal Party in the House of Lords, who, like Lord Curzon, was celebrated for his own brand of pomposity; indeed, considered by the Duggans (and Yorkes, who were neighbours) an unsurpassed exponent of that propensity. Lygon made no pretensions to practise the arts, not a *sine qua non* of the Society's membership, but a usual condition, and, judged by its standards, arbitrary, if not exactly easygoing, he was not very obviously eligible. It is possible that his inclusion was to be accounted for by a *tendresse* (probably unvoiced) felt for him by one of the more influential members, like Howard or Byron.

Amiable, not at all intellectual, Lygon continued to move in The Hypocrites world at Oxford (to be touched on later), and suffered from poorish health after he went down. He tried various occupations, farming, working in a racing stable (racing finally engrossing him professionally) but seemed unable to settle down. While travelling in Germany, perhaps suffering from sunstroke, he had a fall and died in his early thirties.

Roger Spence (at the same house as the Actons) was one of the essentially well-behaved members of the Society. Son of an Indian Army colonel, Spence, tall, dark, quiet, always a little worried in demeanour, had appointed himself a kind of unofficial guardian of the Acton brothers, especially Harold; a buffer between them and unappreciative elements in the school. He used to draw at the Studio; possibly did *plein air* studies too. Spence's integrity and sober bearing made him (in Goodhart's phrase) respected by the other boys. When *The Eton Candle* was published, Spence was business-manager; that side of the magazine accordingly conducted with cool efficiency.

In those days bound for the Diplomatic Service, Spence (who lived rather a retired life at Oxford) passed the examination, but (private means in theory needless, in practice still desirable) decided he had not enough money for the career. To the suprise of his friends he went into the army. I don't think we met between Oxford and 1941, when we ran across each other in one of the entrance halls of the War Office, where I was then on probation for employment. At first sight, Spence's shoulder seeming to reveal no more than two pips, I supposed that, after fifteen years as a regular soldier, he was no more than a lieutenant like me. The Oxfordshire and Buckinghamshire Light Infantry wear minute insignia of rank. One of the apparent stars was a crown. Spence was a lieutenant-colonel.

75

We saw each other from time to time during the war. Towards the end of it, or soon after, Spence was appointed brigadier on one of the Inter-Allied Staffs. The long hours demanded of this sort of staff-work, accompanied by a good deal of nervous strain, are murderous. Spence died, it has been credibly suggested, from overwork. He was in his early forties, and had never married. Doing his duty, behaving well, being quietly agreeable, seem entirely to have engaged his life.

Colin Anderson (at the same house as Henry Yorke) was a refutation of Yorke's opinion that membership of the Arts Society necessarily aroused conventional disapproval, because Anderson, in spite of this association, was elected to Pop; thereby certainly adding to the Society's prestige. Large, sandyhaired, quiet voiced, the only member of undoubted athletic distinction (Byron possessed certain claims as a long distance runner), he used to draw at the Studio. Family connexions took Anderson (now Sir Colin) into the shipping world, where he became youngest President of the Chamber of Shipping. He was also Chairman of the Contemporary Arts Society, a trustee of the National Gallery and the Tate; forming a notable collection of pictures himself, among them (tribute to the Victorianism of the Arts Society) Holman Hunt's *The Awakening Conscience*. Anderson and Yorke, though somewhat amphibiously, were the only two members of the Society to become 'businessmen'.

Finally, the other colleger on the list, Christopher Minns. By then within sight of Sixth Form, he was at the same level of the school as Cyril Connolly, who speaks of Kit Minns (*Enemies of Promise*) as a friend; a boy who refused to be bullied. (Incidentally, Orwell uses the name 'Minns' in *Coming up for Air*.) This Connolly affiliation is not without interest, because it shows Minns as prepared to take on the Arts Society, regarded by Connolly as too dubious in character to get mixed up with. At the time I had no idea that any likelihood existed of Connolly's membership, but from what he himself wrote later, he seems to have toyed with the possibility.

Minns, dark skinned, very quiet, scarcely spoke at all at meetings. I could not imagine why he was there, unless nearness to Sixth Form was regarded as an impending benefit for the Society. Then, only the other day, Harold Acton revealed to me that Howard had a 'crush' on Minns. Acton's recollections of Howard's asides on these warm feelings bring their speaker convulsively to life: 'He *definitely* has a certain something

76

. . . So subtle, of course, *you* wouldn't see it . . . still waters run *deep*, my dear . . . Pure Hymettus *honey*, my dear . . .' Minns seems to have been altogether unaware of having inspired this passion.

The *Old Etonian List* showed C. E. Minns as having died in 1961. Wanting to complete the potted biographies of all the Arts Society's foundation members, I wrote to his brother, Francis Minns, in College a few years after this period. Francis Minns filled in the story. Their father had been in the Indian Civil Service, like Orwell's. Kit Minns went up to King's, Cambridge, after Eton, passed top into the Diplomatic Service, but after a few years, not liking the life, resigned. There was no row. He simply found official superiors, regular hours, routine duties, not to his taste. The rest of his life was spent in a somewhat desultory manner doing odd jobs: journalism of a rather nondescript kind; 'selling strange drinks to clubs for wine-merchants' (his brother's definition of one interlude); a certain amount of teaching. Minns married, had children, but as member of the Arts Society with undoubtedly the highest academic qualifications of a conventional sort, his days were passed comparatively in the shadows.

Such, then, are the individual stories of my fellow foundation members of the Eton Society of Arts. A leaflet enclosed in *The Eton Candle* announces the subjects of some of the Saturday evening discussions: Post-Impressionism; the Decoration of Rooms; Colour as applied to Decoration; Oriental Art; Spanish Painting. They all sound fairly ambitious. I do not remember anything whatever about them, except that Byron, speaking on the Decoration of Rooms, once advocated a black ceiling, grey walls, white carpet. From time to time notabilities like William Rothenstein and Roger Fry (neither of whom seemed very sparkling) came down to speak on art. All this was stimulating, but inevitably a moment came when members with views to put forward had said everything they had to say; distinguished speakers from the outer world had been already heard, or were unwilling to put in an appearance. Some of the livelier members left for the university. Mr Evans retired. I do not remember how soon all this happened, but those who replenished the ranks, especially the new President, never quite achieved the old spirit. It was suggested—and carried—that puppet-shows should be staged. Puppets have never been much in my line; I therefore resigned.

From the start Howard had been anxious to turn the Society of Arts

77

into a prestige-gathering association; wanting writing-paper with a heading, and other outward and visible signs of established status. My own instincts were always against such things. I felt—puritanically, probably also naïvely—that the arts should be pursued for their own sake; if by a persecuted minority, so much the better for those dedicated to them. If the Society ceased to be despised and rejected, anyway relatively speaking, it would, before we knew where we were, become a body of which membership was an athletic privilege. Had not Pop itself once been known as the *Literati*? In this difference of opinion no doubt lie the seeds of many age-old disputes.

Looking back now, the Eton Society of Arts seems essentially the group expression of certain individuals rather than a general need for the school. So far from Yorke's implications of hatred and derision, my own enquiries suggest that, among contemporaries and near-contemporaries, only a few boys had ever heard of the Society and its activities. With regard to its 'Victorianism', something that took place at Eton at this period should be mentioned, as indicating how necessary it was to draw attention to the fact that, because things were Victorian, they were not necessarily bad.

On the walls of Eton chapel are intermittent mediaeval frescoes. In the 1840s, during certain renovations, some of these were barbarously painted over, but, before being entirely blotted out, the question came up for discussion. The Prince Consort was consulted on the matter (the objection was mainly that the pictures represented saints, regarded as papistical), and made the sensible suggestion that the neo-gothic stalls which were proposed for the restored chapel should be arranged on some sort of a pivot or hinge, so that they could be swung away from the wall by those who wanted to inspect the frescoes. Unfortunately this good advice was not followed.

It was, of course, absurd that rare mediaeval paintings should be concealed by 19th century woodwork, and, fashion having changed about church decoration (for that matter, about saints), the gothic stalls were swept away, so far as the walls were concerned, though to some extent this same style of decoration remained at the west end of the chapel. The removal of the stalls was not an improvement. College chapel looked a great deal more imposing when the stalls were in place. The frescoes are altogether insufficient to provide a coherent mural, and efforts to eke them out with bits of tapestry have not been successful. As so often, the Prince Consort was perfectly right.

A month after the Arts Society's foundation *The Eton Candle* was published in March, 1922. The magazine, quite a handsome production, bound in pink cardboard, with superlatively wide margins to the page sold at half-a-crown. The cover was boldly inscribed *Volume I.* The tradition of magazines edited by boys—usually known at that time as 'ephemerals', since they appeared on one day only, probably the Eton Festivals of the Fourth of June, or St Andrew's Day—went back a long way. At the end of the 18th century, and in early years of the 19th, Etonian magazines had appeared edited, for instance, by Canning, Praed, and Gladstone, while boys there. Nothing outstanding had been attempted since those days; certainly nothing of the kind now contemplated—which was to sound the trumpets of Modernism echoing through Eton's wat'ry glade.

A feature of *The Eton Candle* was its Old Etonian Supplement of writers and painters. This aspect was not unique, Praed's magazine including a few contributors who were already at the university. The OE painters represented in *The Candle* (only one of whom could be regarded as in the least *avant-garde*) were an irretrievably *pompier* crowd, but Modernism was loudly proclaimed by the names of Osbert Sitwell and Aldous Huxley; the second of whom had been employed at Eton as an assistant-master the half before I arrived. The *bonne bouche* of *The Candle*'s Old Etonian Supplement was an 'unpublished' poem by Swinburne, to whose 'illustrious memory'—in spite of a lengthy opening article by Howard insisting on the pre-eminence of free verse—the magazine was dedicated.

Inevitably, the OE Supplement swamped the schoolboy contributions, of which by far the major part consisted of poems by Howard himself and Harold Acton. What remained at the literary end was fairly typical of juvenile *belles lettres* of the period; the graphic arts being represented by a promising if unadventurous *Nature Morte* by William Acton, and a not very interesting drawing (influences of Beardsley and Lovat Fraser unconcealed) of my own. The latter had been felicitously captioned by Howard (off the cuff) *Colonel Caesar Cannonbrains of the Black Hussars.*

The Swinburne lyric of four stanzas, entitled *Love*, had been handed over to Howard by Edmund Gosse, then at the height of his fame as man of letters of the Old Guard. I have a high regard for Swinburne as a poet, but to say that they are not Swinburne at his best is a very considerable

79

understatement. They are, in fact, so awful that, on rereading them after many years, I had serious doubts that Swinburne could ever have written the lines. Nevertheless, Mr John S. Mayfield, the American authority on Swinburne, confirmed that *Love* was one of the four poems privately printed by the forger, Thomas Wise (with whom Gosse had always remained on friendly terms), in 1918; and that they also occur (without reference to previous publication or printing) in the Bonchurch Edition of Swinburne's Collected Works.

What were Gosse's motives for producing—like a rabbit from a hat—this Swinburne item for a schoolboy magazine? People, especially people like Gosse, usually have a good reason for performing conjuring tricks of that particular kind. From the moment when Wise produced the privately printed edition of these verses, there is a dubious air about the whole undertaking. Did Swinburne ever write them at all? It is an interesting question. Gosse, as it happened, turned up at Eton about this time as judge, or one of the judges, of the Loder Declamation Prize; an occasion treated as a show that non-competitors could watch. After the grander recitations had taken place, two Lower Boys in jackets who were in for the final of the junior prize, read from the Bible. One of them was Alan Pryce-Jones, my first sight of the later editor of *The Times Literary Supplement*, on which I was to work after the war. Gosse, the essence of self-assured self-satisfied literary men, made several sagacious remarks about not stressing prepositions when reading aloud.

A copy of *The Eton Candle* was acquired by Balston (probably sent him by my father on my own behalf), who was sufficiently impressed by Harold Acton's poems there to publish a collection of them the following year, with the title *Aquarium*. By that time Acton was an undergraduate at Oxford. Millard listed *The Eton Candle* in his catalogue. Howard went to see him, and thought him '*very* sinister'. Millard wrote (5 April, 1922) that Howard reminded him of 'Scott-Moncrieff whom I knew at about the same age when he was at Winchester.' *The Candle* might be said to have cast its flicker beyond Eton High Street.

VI

Arcades Ambo

At some stage towards the inauguration of the Arts Society, and *The Candle*, Howard asked me to tea in his room, a form of hospitality not unique to himself, but with distinct implications of style. After issuing the invitation, he added as an apparent afterthought: 'Connolly may be looking in'.

I was impressed. Connolly was in Pop, and—although to walk arm-in-arm with Connolly would not, in snobbish terms, have rated anything like as high as with the Captain of the XI, Keeper of the Field, or Captain of Boats—to run across him in this informal manner would nevertheless grade as a manifest social success. I hardly expected such heights, nor, in the event, was there any sign of Connolly at tea, taken tête-à-tête with Howard, who may genuinely have credited the possibility. Neither Howard nor I knew at the time that any hope of such patronage had gone overboard through Howard's too vainglorious display on the mantelpiece of Connolly's Pop-headed postcard accepting a previous invitation. This was the only occasion when I nearly came across Cyril Connolly at Eton; no contact between us ever taking place there.

I knew him, of course, by sight. It was impossible not to notice Connolly as he passed in the street, or loitered in School Yard. He looked like no one else. Even so, his personality made no very definite impression until one afternoon when I was walking back from the tree-shaded playing field called Upper Club. The picture remains a clear one in my mind. Connolly himself mentions that, after becoming a member of Pop, he experimented in wearing a dinner-jacket (instead of blazer or tweed coat)

81

with flannel trousers, 'a fashion that was not followed.' In this guise I first took him in as a formidable entity. Arm-in-arm with another colleger (one not in Pop), he was strolling towards the elms of Poets' Walk. Connolly was laughing and talking a lot. I felt conventional misgiving at the dinner-jacket as an innovation in school dress.

In later life, when—in Praed's apt phrase—Connolly had matured into an 'Eton boy grown heavy', his outward appearance was not in a general way unlike that of Sainte-Beuve or Edmund Wilson (fellow-critics he admired, especially the former), the same used-up sulky expression of men burdened with too many books to review. There was also some suggestion—an identification he himself would have welcomed—of a beardless uncarefree Verlaine. When younger, Connolly's features are not so easy to describe. He speaks of his own 'ugliness', and it is true that, when news broke of the Pop election, Hubert Duggan rather brutally enquired: 'Is that the tug who's been kicked in the face by a mule?' Nevertheless, if Connolly's face was not in the common or garden sense his fortune, it was certainly one of his several means of imposing a fascination on people.

One searches for some parallel in similar facial contours. They were of the kind required for admission to the Pavlovski Guard, recruited (in memory of Tsar Paul) only from applicants with retroussé noses. Puck of Pook's Hill comes to mind (drawn by H. A. Millar, illustrator of *Little Folks*, and the E. Nesbit books), but, in Connolly's case, amused malice took the place of the hobgoblin's air of age-old understanding. A comparison with Socrates has also been made (I remember the suggestion greatly irritating Henry Yorke), and to come suddenly on a sculpted head of the philosopher in a museum might easily call Connolly to mind. If antiquity is to be invoked at all, the lineaments were perhaps more those of the formal masks worn in Greek drama—Comedy or Tragedy equally suited—an expression at once mocking and uneasy. The antique mask analogy would not, I think, have displeased Connolly himself.

Since the days of an 18th century forebear who had served with my own great-great grandfather in the Marines, the Connollys had been soldiers and sailors; usually attaining respectably senior rank. Connolly's father had retired as only a major, but was also an authority on conchology, and had compiled a cookery-book. He and his wife were estranged. Sea shells and gastronomy might have been thought to offer a life-line, but relations were not warm on his son's side; though perhaps rather less hostile in private than publicly proclaimed. Very little is said about the author's parents in *A Georgian Boyhood* (satirically titled sub-section of *Enemies of Promise*), a wonderfully vivid account of upper-class schooling of the period. Unlike most records of its kind, *A Georgian Boyhood* develops a coherent narrative, with a beginning, middle and end. In fact the 'plot' is so good that a summary far from does justice to its many subtleties, but some outline is required to understand the Connolly myth, one which regulated all its creator's subsequent standpoint and career.

A bright little boy, an only child, is sent to a preparatory school specialising in winning scholarships. The headmaster's wife, dominating, capricious, prone to favouritism, worshipping success, induces in the boys a combined burden of ambition and guilt. Among the other pupils are Eric Blair (later to be known as George Orwell); and, for good measure, Cecil Beaton (now Sir Cecil, photographer and designer). Connolly and Orwell become close friends. Both win scholarships to Eton. (The age ratio all important in schooldays, was: Orwell b. 23 June, Connolly b. 10 September, 1903; Orwell, taking the examination a year before Connolly, therefore always three forms above him at Eton.)

After a novitiate of comparative hell in College, the hero emerges in the ascendant. Beyond all reasonable expectation, he is elected to Pop; also gaining the blue riband of history scholarship, a Brackenbury at Balliol. But life is over. Oxford falls short; London shorter. After the Eton triumphs, all is anti-climax, dust and ashes. The rest of existence is spent in a state of suspended animation, idleness and apathy inhibiting any true release of intellect and talent.

The Connolly myth, therefore, is that of the oppressed hero who wins through, only to find the Fates have stacked the cards against him. The circumstances are, of course, special ones—it might not unreasonably be asked, who on earth is interested in the particular customs of Eton or any other school—but in a sense the circumstances of all effective autobiographers are special, only a few individuals possessing the powers required to assemble and assess their situation; as Connolly himself says: 'writers who can analyze their own environment.' Such autobiographers, however esoteric the backgrounds, are almost always worth reading, but not all are able—or even desirous—to express the story, as Connolly does (while always reserving to himself the right to treat

83

his own life as a joke) in terms of Greek tragedy or a Hardy novel.

Factually true, the Connolly myth cannot be accepted in all its implications. In school terms, Connolly does not at all exaggerate the extent of his achievement, though perhaps overestimating the executive powers of Pop, which chiefly rested with individual members holding specific offices. That is not to discount the prestige of the body as a whole, probably as high as ever in the school's history. For a boy without athletic distinction to be elected was not unknown, but Connolly's handicaps as a starter in the race included not only being outside Sixth Form (a status likely for any colleger in the running, simply because that meant the top ten of the seventy), but not even among the next half-dozen collegers, who enjoyed certain minor privileges.

Where the myth burgeons into overelaboration is in Connolly's insistence on his own unproductivity. Even if the work produced was not, on the whole, the sort for which he himself would have most wished to be remembered, *Enemies of Promise* is a remarkable book; *The Unquiet Grave* has many admirers; much of the literary journalism retains its sparkle; *Horizon* was something of a beacon during the war; the *Letters to Noel Blakiston* have a stamp of their own. Evidence, in fact, points to Connolly enjoying his journalism more than he would ever admit. His neuroses ('cowardice, sloth, vanity, *Angst*', on all of which he was never tired of harping) certainly led him to refuse jobs and cut appointments, but that was in a sense a form of action; greater firmness of purpose often required to turn down some offer from an editor, or the BBC, than resignedly to accept.

Conviction of his own 'genius', that virus of the Twenties, had infected Connolly, too, at an early age. He wanted, in his own words, to be 'Baudelaire and Rimbaud, without the poverty and suffering.' He would also quote with ironic regret the bitter law laid down by his sometime master, Logan Pearsall Smith: 'You can't be fashionable and first-rate.' Something of a prodigy of assorted literary knowledge as a boy, a natural writer, an acute (if limited) critic, a gifted satirist, Connolly was not a poet or novelist. Novels, in any case, came a bad second to poetry in his literary affections, and his ruminations in print as to how they should be written reveal profound lack of appreciation of what it feels like to be a novelist.

By the time I was at Oxford the Connolly myth was already pretty well established in his own mind, even if other people still saw 'promise' that he had himself ostensibly (anyway in retrospect) already jettisoned. One speculates as to what might have happened had a few additional black-balls found their way into the Pop ballot-box; a bloodyminded Balliol don taken against the Connolly interpretation of history. In the latter event, Connolly might well have found himself—King's, Henry VI's sister foundation, more traditional for a colleger—an undergraduate at Cambridge, with its different ethos. Would the plea then have been—like Scott Fitzgerald's failure to make the Princeton football side or achieve an army posting overseas—that (Pop and the Brackenbury missed by a hair's breadth) not success, but dire disappointment, had paralysed the will?

In one of the letters to Blakiston, Connolly writes: '. . . just as one imagines Narcissus looking into the pool, not with vanity but with troubled curiosity and flower-like absorption . . .' I suspect that any alteration in the mere narrative shape of the Connolly myth would have made little ultimate difference to its dramatic overtones, their inspiration deriving not so much from the author's relative success or failure in early life, as from a passionate interest in himself. True interest in yourself is comparatively rare, sharply to be differentiated from mere egotism and selfishness; characteristics often immoderately developed in persons not in the least interested in themselves intellectually or objectively. Indeed, not everyone can stand the strain of gazing down too long into the personal crater, with its scene of Hieronymus Bosch activities taking place in the depths.

In self-inspection, Connolly could endure more than most. Not unnaturally, he tends to concentrate on specific areas below, in preference to others not necessarily less worth analysis, but from his chosen angles he can be absolutely ruthless in drawing attention to what many persons would be very willing to leave concealed. The sheer intensity of this self-interest makes everything Connolly writes about himself interesting; even when, as in some of the later book reviews (much of his literary criticism being a branch of autobiography), touches of self-fantasy from time to time obtrude.

As a writer, he paid for this gift of self-examination by possessing no deep interest in other people as such, unless they were immediately orientated on himself. Even then, those concerned were likely to be romanticized or denigrated, without too much attention being allowed to their circumstances. This did not prevent brilliant flashes of caricature like Brian Howard as de Clavering or Ian Fleming as Bond 'striking camp'. A lack of interest for individuals in what might be called the Proustian sense was perhaps characteristic, too, of the whole of the Arts Society. There were several champion egoists among them, but none capable of taking his own machinery to pieces, and scrutinizing its workings, in the Connolly manner.

Yorke had leanings in that direction, *Pack My Bag* making confessional references to physical and moral cowardice, parsimony, snobbishness, sexual shyness, and so on. These glances lack Connolly's objective treatment; an agonized self-consciousness being something different from self-revelation treated clinically yet understandingly. One of the most peculiar aspects of autobiography is the way in which some authors are acceptable in their sexual and suchlike intimacies (Proust masturbating in the lavatory), others are without great interest in those rôles, at worst only embarrassing. At first sight, the simple answer seems to be that some write 'well', others less well; but in the field of self-revelation the altogether uninstructed can produce a masterpiece of apt expression; the seasoned writer, at times a cliché. I can find no literary explanation other than that only certain personalities are appropriate to dissection; others not.

Connolly, like Yorke, though in a different vein, is inclined to insist that what he thinks supplies the rule for what those around him thought, but he always writes with clarity, whereas Yorke will often blur the picture with deliberate obscurantism. Connolly's current assessment of an individual or way of life (even books and authors) was inclined to move up and down like mercury in a thermometer, he himself at times scarcely able to keep up with the speed of his own quicksilver's rise and fall. Nevertheless, any Connolly rating, even when it readjusted yesterday's estimate, was likely to be invested with its own kind of force; if only desperate fear that he might himself be in some way inconvenienced and bored, rather than benefited and amused.

A Georgian Boyhood emphasizes two overwhelming factors in what its author calls 'the background of the lilies' (emblems on Eton's coat of arms), both elements examined by him with much understanding: first, the 'monastic intensity' of life as lived in College; secondly, the 'romantic' preponderance of all Eton education. To the former, Connolly brought his own natural intensity of feeling (his 'sloth', as has been remarked, almost as much an expression of a strong personality as participation could be), a condition which so to speak doubled the intensity dose. The pres-

My mother.

My father.

AP with Pekoe, early in 1906, at Gravesend.

AP with Pekoe, Christmas 1908, in Holland Walk, Kensington.

Funeral procession of King Edward VII, 1910; Capt. Philip Powell
(Welch Regt., adjutant 13th London Regt.), behind top-hatted figure on
left; Lt. Col. the Earl of Longford (commanding 2nd Life Guards escort),
right of kilted attendant of late King's dog, Caesar.

The bungalow (called here Stonehurst), near Bordon
Camp, Hampshire.

AP on Jock, *ca.* 1913, at Stonehurst.

1 Melina Place, St John's Wood.

AP aged twelve; first
passport photograph.

Thomas Balston, as
staff-officer, *ca.* 1916.

A. W. A. Peel and R. W. E. Cecil, with Lower Boys who
fagged for them at Goodhart's. AP front row left.

Electioneering for an Eton master, 1923: Robert Byron
extreme right; Hubert Duggan, on box holding reins;
John Spencer, sitting in cab; AP at back, face hidden.

AP at Eton, just before fifteenth birthday.

Colonel Caesar Cannonbrains of the
Black Hussars: drawing by AP in
The Eton Candle, 1922.

Hypocrites Club fancy-dress party, March 1924, given by John (The Widow) Lloyd, and Robert Byron: *back row:* Harold Acton, in army cap, and resembling mask: *second row:* AP in helmet, with sword; Arden Hillard, as nun; John Lloyd, holding programme; Robert Byron, in top-hat, with stick: *sitting:* S. G. Roberts, Lecturer in Tamil and Telegu, known as 'Camels and Telegraphs', in white coat.

Hypocrites fancy-dress party: *back row:* John Spencer, with curly cigarette holder: Elmley, in cocked hat; Hugh Lygon, in cap, with pistol;
Robert Byron, in top-hat, extreme left; Romney Summers, extreme right,
in Regency costume: *third row:* David Talbot Rice, holding bottle: *front
row:* Graham Pollard, wearing sailor hat; E. E. Evans-Pritchard, in burnous.

Henry Yorke (Henry Green),
at Oxford.

Denys Buckley, at
Old Boys' match.

Eric Blair (George Orwell),
College Wall Game team.

Cyril Connolly, as an undergraduate.

Alfred Duggan, at Oxford.

Maurice Bowra, *ca.* 1928.

AP in the Mont Cenis Pass, autumn, 1924, with Romney Summers' Vauxhall.

AP and Matthew Ponsonby, 1926, at the Ponsonbys' house, Shulbrede Priory, Surrey.

The Elms, Melton Mowbray, Leicestershire.

surized romanticism also stimulated something already within him, Eton education merely indicating the channels that a purely personal romanticism should best take.

'Monasticism' was an unavoidable condition of College. If there were an understandable feeling among the rest of the school that these seventy clever boys formed a race apart (the differentiation rather 'intellectual' than 'social'), that separateness was certainly not rejected by College itself, where oppidan friends seem to have been much more instinctively discouraged than *vice versa*. Some oppidan houses were, of course, far tougher than others, but certain of the brutalities that Connolly records— a poor advertisement for self-government by learned persons—seem to me preparatory-school bullying unlike in kind, rather than degree, what went on in the rest of the school. At the same time, these hardships suffered collectively produced an indestructible corporate feeling, of which Connolly himself possessed a strong sense. He contrasts friendships in College (not necessarily those of a sexual slant) with the easy casualness of oppidan relationships. One can see what he means, and the *Letters to Noel Blakiston* show how these College friendships continued into Connolly's later life.

No doubt all public schools of the period attempted to inculcate at least some of the 'romantic' influences Connolly so well describes—Homer metamorphosed into a pre-Raphaelite poet, Plato seen as a great headmaster, Greek homosexuality merged into heroic comradeship—but Eton, historically and architecturally, was unusually well placed to indoctrinate the romantic mystique; her antique towers, beside the still unpolluted Thames, offering a dreamlike sanctuary for the antithetical deities presiding over that particular romantic vision: Honour and Discipline; Success and Sacrifice; Death and Victory; in a school of eleven hundred boys, after four and a half years of war, eleven hundred killed, fourteen hundred wounded. If the prizes offered were splendid, the oblation was no less unstinted.

Those who resisted these pressures often ended up more deeply imbued than the conformists, and it is part of Connolly's thesis that he had thrown himself into school life so wholeheartedly that there was no disintoxication from its opium dream. On this myth of personal experience he superimposed another of personal aspiration: self-identity with Palinurus, pilot of Aeneas voyaging to Italy after the sack of Troy. Palinurus, overcome by sleep at the tiller, and falling into the sea, gained the shore, but was murdered for his clothes by the savage inhabitants of that coast. I found a reference to Palinurus in *Marmion*, but too late to enquire from Connolly whether he knew of this comparison with Pitt.

> With Palinure's unalter'd mood,
> Firm at his dangerous post he stood;
> Each call for needful rest repell'd,
> With dying hand the rudder held,
> Till in his fall, with fateful sway,
> The steerage of the realm gave way!

Connolly's Palinurine symbolism is never altogether clear, but Scott's is certainly a larger claim than he could have made for himself. I take his own meaning to be, broadly speaking, that as a young critic he had undoubtedly led the way in trying to get rid of what was out of date, also in drawing attention to new writers. This elaboration of his own personal myth—in the manner of extended myths—runs somewhat counter to the version earlier propagated, the frustrated creative writer who has taken only unwillingly to criticism; but there seems no other explanation. As Palinurus was never ritually buried ('the unquiet grave'), his shade had to wait the prescribed time to cross the Styx. Here the image of a restless dissatisfied soul can be accepted. Even if Connolly was not actually murdered by the literary barbarians on whose coast he was cast, his presence there was associated with drowsiness. There was also a case for regarding his critical raiment as having been to some extent pillaged, especially in relation to the immediacy with which he had appreciated the importance of American writers like Scott Fitzgerald (then scarcely at all known in England), and, to a lesser degree, Hemingway.

That Connolly missed some of the credit for these reconnaissances was largely his own fault. The account of the situation of English writing at the beginning of *Enemies of Promise*, in many ways acute, is also far less adventurous in tone than Connolly's early reviewing. He gets bogged down in self-pity about the difficulties of a writer's life—his King Charles's Head—showing some uncertainty whether it is better for a writer to be a success or a failure. There are hedgings of bets, and genuflections to Bloomsbury. Scarcely anything is said of trails he had once begun to blaze. There is, I think, a reason for this loss of confidence.

Arcades Ambo

Connolly inscribed my own copy of *The Unquiet Grave* with a four-line portrait of himself:

> An artist he of character complex;
> Money he loved, and next to money, sex.
> No roses culled he from the Muses' garden;
> Neurosis held him in the grip of Auden.

The unserious tone of the verse embodies in the last line an important and interesting confession. After Connolly had written a good deal of *Enemies of Promise* (of which he would sometimes talk before it was finished) he came in contact with the Left Wing poets of the Thirties. Little as Communism—the great *trahison des clercs* of the Thirties—accorded with Petronian hedonism he was carried away. It was, indeed, a moment when, for a while, W. H. Auden and his troop swept all before them; briefly extinguishing almost everything else in their literary age-group. This flavour is particularly noticeable in *Enemies of Promise* towards the end of the critical pages, where the author's newfound Left Wing enthusiasms form a kind of superstructure that sits somewhat awkwardly on the book's original foundations.

Connolly (compared with, say, Orwell) had no flair whatever for politics, and, as the years rolled by, changes took place in many viewpoints; not least in those of Auden and his associates. Accordingly, *Enemies of Promise*, so far as it expresses political opinions, shows its author as marooned on an island of somewhat vicarious commitment; an uneasy Prospero whose spells, in which he himself only halfheartedly believes, have become vitiated by the passing of time. *The Unquiet Grave*'s inscription suggests that Connolly—aware of so much about himself—was aware of that too.

Much admired when it appeared during the war, *The Unquiet Grave* seems to me a far less effective work than *Enemies of Promise*. Some of its *obiter dicta* date back to a Commonplace Book kept by Connolly since his earliest days, which 'with a view to publication', was shown to me, perhaps as far back as 1927, when first at Duckworth's. It was characteristic of Connolly that, after handing over the Commonplace Book for publisher's reading, he added: 'If your firm doesn't like it, make some excuse when you give it back to me. Say the Autumn List is already full, or

something like that. Not just that they don't think it good enough to publish.'

The Unquiet Grave's self-portrait, more impressionistic than *A Georgian Boyhood*'s, less unguarded than the Letters, emphasizes the author's
love of pleasure, sensual and intellectual. That pleasure was as much
in *expertise* as in the thing itself. Connolly loved the concept of being
scholar, dandy, bibliophil, gourmet, connoisseur. He knew more than the
average about many things, but aspired to know all there was to be
known about everything. This desire to lay down the law could result in
howlers about such matters as marks on china or silver. Friends who produced (for attribution) a bottle of Australian champagne in a napkin were
told it was Krug 1905 (or some such vintage); in consequence, losing their
nerve, and assuring Connolly that he was miraculously correct.

That did not mean Connolly lacked all knowledge of wine. On the contrary, he could talk convincingly on the subject, and I drank some of the
best claret I have ever tasted in his house. At the same time I have seen
him apparently altogether unaware that he was drinking something specially good. What was at fault was the claim to omniscience. He could be
very generous (especially in giving presents), but could show himself less
than grateful for generosity in others. Superlatively competitive, he had
to give a one-man performance. Somebody else's anecdote or artefact was
always a challenge. He was jealous, rather than envious; whatever was in
question, he must always go one better. Unlike such good talkers as Constant Lambert or Maurice Bowra (anyway up to a point), Connolly had
no great liking for being entertained by talk, and as a rule himself no flow
of conversation. His flair was for the unexpected comment or elaborate
set piece.

What, in short, was the point of Connolly? Why did people put up
with frequent moroseness, gloom, open hostility? Why, if he were about
in the neighbourhood, did I always take steps to get hold of him? The
question is hard to answer. The fact remains that I did; though never
coming under his sway to the extent he expected of friends; unless—for
which he was prepared in certain cases—he was the one to submit. He
was rarely at ease with an equal relationship. I never avoided being under
slight suspicion of not accepting all his sides with equal seriousness. Nevertheless, I knew well that, if it suited Connolly to flatter, I was an easy
victim. He was a master of flattery; flattery of the best sort that can seem

on the surface almost a form of detraction. There was undoubtedly something hypnotic about him.

In Connolly's collected literary criticism it is rare to look up a given subject, and find nothing of interest. Some point is almost always made, if only a subjective one. Logan Pearsall Smith used to advocate the principle of limited literary objectives, rather than taking in writers perhaps not sympathetic to the critic himself, and Connolly inclined to accept that lesson. His own personality, pervasive, mutable, is less easy to pinpoint than his writing. He was one of those individuals—a recognized genus—who seem to have been sent into the world to be talked about. Such persons satisfy a basic human need. Connolly's behaviour, love affairs, financial difficulties, employments or lack of them, all seemed matters of burning interest. He had, so to speak, taken the sins of the world on himself. Some rebelled, refusing to be drawn into the net of Connolly gossip. They were few in number, and perhaps missed something in life. From the moment when he burst through the Pop-barrier (no doubt before that too, on a smaller scale), he was the subject of profuse anecdote; his interest in himself somehow communicating its force to other people.

Connolly—like others of his generation—recalls Laertes' comment that 'the canker galls the infants of the spring'; and, as Hamlet remarked of Laertes himself, 'To divide him inventorially would dizzy th' arithmetic of memory.'

2

It was through Connolly that I first heard about George Orwell. At Eton, Orwell's face eludes me. Looking at photographic groups of boys in College, I can remember—anyway by sight—most of those sitting round about, in many cases their names. Orwell himself I do not remember; nor even the name 'Blair, KS', spoken aloud or seen on lists. This is strange because his platoon in the Corps—one of two made up of collegers—was in the same Company as Goodhart's; so that for at least two halves we must have seen each other hurrying across Cannon Yard on the way to Monday morning parades. By that time Orwell was in Sixth Form, myself just in Upper School, a large gap therefore stretching between us. Nevertheless, it seems best to speak of Orwell here, while Eton is surveyed, rather than leave him to a later period. He was, in his way, very much an Etonian, however greatly in apostasy, but was of course altogether uncompromised by Oxford.

When *Down and Out in Paris and London* appeared in 1933, a painter friend, Adrian Daintrey, recommended the book to me, adding: 'You'll never again enjoy *sauté* potatoes after you've heard how they're cooked in restaurants.' I read Orwell's book, and was impressed by its savagery and gloom, but cannot claim to have marked down the writer immediately as one we should hear a great deal more of; still less, that here was someone who would become a close friend. A year or two later, seeing *Keep the Aspidistra Flying* in a secondhand bookshop, I bought it. Again I liked the novel for its violent feelings, and presentation of a man at the end of his tether, rather than for form or style, both of which seemed oddly old-fashioned in treatment, as did many of the views expressed in the story.

I spoke of the book dining one night with Connolly in about 1936. He was then married to his first wife, Jean Bakewell, an American, and living in a flat in the King's Road, Chelsea. By that time I too was married. Connolly revealed—something of which I had no idea—that Orwell was one of his oldest friends. They had recently been in touch again, and Connolly gave a sobering account of Orwell, his rigid asceticism, political intransigence, utter horror of all social life. Connolly emphasized Orwell's physical appearance, the lines of suffering and privation marking his hollow cheeks. The portrait was a disturbing one. Connolly was at the same time enthusiastic about Orwell. He urged me to write him a fan letter. This I did, thereby making my first Orwell contact fifteen years after he had himself left Eton.

Connolly's picture of a severe unapproachable infinitely disapproving personage was not altogether dispelled by the reply I received to my letter. Orwell, with his first wife Eileen O'Shaughnessy, was at that time running a small general shop near Baldock in Hertfordshire. His answer, perfectly polite and friendly, had also about it something that cast a faint chill, making me feel, especially in the light of Connolly's words, that Orwell was not for me.

I was so sure of this that, when opportunity arose of meeting him in the flesh, I was at first unwilling to involve myself in so much frugal living and high thinking; more especially in wartime, when existence was uncomfortable enough anyway. This was in 1941. I was on leave from the army. My wife and I were dining at the Café Royal. An old friend, Inez Holden, came across to talk to us from a table on the far side of the room. I had first met Inez Holden (then very pretty) with Evelyn Waugh in 1927. She was a writer, author of several novels, and miscellaneous journalist, but was at that time doing war work in an aircraft factory, operating the house-cinema. She said that the man and woman with her were George and Eileen Orwell, suggesting that we should join them after we had finished dinner.

To make the evening rather more of an occasion, as one did not 'go out' much in those days, I had changed into 'blues', patrol uniform, an outfit with brass buttons and a high collar. I felt certain Orwell would not approve of such a get-up. It was no doubt bad enough in his eyes to be an officer at all; to be rigged out in these pretentious regimentals, at once militaristic and relatively ornate, would aggravate the offence of belonging to a stupid and brutal caste. Notwithstanding these apprehensions—made light of, I admit, by my wife—we moved over in due course to the Orwells' table. Orwell's first words, spoken with considerable tenseness, were at the same time reassuring.

'*Do your trousers strap under the foot?*'

As the uniform had belonged to my father, they were indeed 'overalls' (rather than trousers), though I was not wearing the regulation spurs on the heels of the wellingtons beneath.

'Yes.'

Orwell nodded.

'That's really the important thing.'

'Of course.'

'You agree?'

'Naturally.'

'I used to wear ones that strapped under the boot myself,' he said, not without nostalgia.

'In Burma?'

'You knew I was in the police there? Those straps under the foot give you a feeling like nothing else in life.'

His voice had a curious rasp. I thought at the time that its note was consciously designed to avoid vocables that could possibly be regarded as 'public school'; though equally the tone made no concession whatever to

93

any other 'accent' known to me. When, later, I commented in print on
Orwell's way of speaking—suggesting the delivery was intentionally to escape any class-label—a postcard arrived from Orwell's former 'classical
tutor' at Eton, A. S. F. 'Granny' Gow (by then a Cambridge don), saying:
'Well, G. O. had little need to "avoid consciously a public school tone"
for he croaked discordantly already in 1917 when he reached Eton.' Gow
(who also briefly taught me Greek), a classical scholar of distinction, and
authority on A. E. Housman, had also been a good friend to Orwell.

Connolly and Beaton, both from the same preparatory school, shared
this slight rasp (in Connolly's case approaching what might be called
Duke of Windsor cockney), but Orwell's way of speaking has twice at
least been brought back to me when talking with former forestry officials
from India and Africa. The intonation perhaps derived from Orwell's father, who had been in the ICS, possibly a recognisable official delivery,
something occasionally suggested in descriptions of Kipling who could
have picked it up. Nevertheless, however he talked, Orwell had, as it
were, resigned from the world in which he had been brought up; while
never really contriving to join another.

Tall—as has been more than once remarked, closely resembling Gus-
tave Doré's Don Quixote—Orwell also looked uncommonly like Cézanne's portrait of Monsieur Choquet, the painter's friend in the Custom
House. The deep grooves in Orwell's cheeks, of which Connolly had spoken, were at once apparent on either side of his mouth. He wore a narrow moustache, neatly clipped, along the lower level of his upper lip.
This moustache, as long as I knew him, was always a bit of a mystery to
me. I never had quite sufficient courage to ask about it. Orwell's approach to life was always strictly controlled, so that this feature must
have possessed some special meaning for him. Perhaps it was his only remaining concession to a dandyism that undoubtedly lurked beneath the
surface of self-imposed austerities—a side momentarily revealed by the
enquiry about strapped-down trousers.

Indeed Orwell, in certain respects, was far closer to the moral concept
of a 'dandy' than Connolly, who liked talking about dandyism as a philosophy, but was himself burdened with the essentially undandyish trait of
intermittent lack of social self-assurance. Orwell's contemporaries at
school even speak of a tendency in those early days towards the mannerisms of a P. G. Wodehouse hero, the moustache—in itself somewhat un-

Wodehousian—possibly partaking of this 'dandyism à rebours' in Orwell's nature. Perhaps, on the other hand, it had something to do with the French blood inherited through his mother, which caused him to resemble the Cézanne portrait, or one of those fiercely melancholy French workmen in blue smocks pondering the meaning of life at the zinc counters of a thousand *estaminets*.

Certainly this last image was the nearest Orwell ever achieved in the direction of even faintly proletarian appearance. It was the moustache that provoked thoughts of France, because nothing could have been more English than his consciously tattered old tweed coat and trousers of corduroy or flannel, an outfit that always maintained exactly the same degree of shabbiness, no worse, no better. In much the same manner as Millard, Orwell always looked rather distinguished in these old clothes.

'Does it matter my coming in like this?' he asked, before entering the room at a party we were giving, when we lived in Regent's Park.

The question is an example of the unreality of much of Orwell's approach to life. By that time he and I knew each other well. The clothes were the clothes he always wore. Why should I have invited him, if I thought them inadequate? It was hardly to be expected that he would turn up in a brand new suit. Did he half hope for an unfavourable answer?

'Yes, George, it does matter. They won't do. You can't come in. We'll meet another time.'

In justice to Orwell, some of his suppositions regarding social behaviour were so strange that he might not have been surprised had I replied in those terms. I am certain that denial of entry on such grounds would, on his side, have made little or no difference to our friendship. It would merely have confirmed his worst suspicions; perhaps even pleased him a little to find his views on the tyranny of convention so amply justified.

A year or two after the meeting at the Café Royal, when I had been posted to the War Office, Orwell and I arranged to lunch together. For some reason we failed to make contact at the small but very crowded Greek restaurant in Percy Street he had suggested for luncheon. Each thought the other had not turned up, and ate alone at a table. On his way out, Orwell passed me.

'Come back and sit for a moment,' he said. 'I ordered a bottle of wine. I'm afraid I've drunk most of it, as I thought you weren't going to arrive, but there's still a drop left, as I couldn't get through it all.'

Wine, at that period of the war, was hard to obtain and expensive. It was characteristically generous of Orwell to have provided it, when beer would not have seemed at all close-fisted. At that time he was employed in some BBC news-service, not in want, but certainly not particularly well off. None of his books had yet begun to sell. With all his willingness to face hard times—almost welcoming them—Orwell was by no means a confirmed enemy of good living, though always tortured by guilt when he felt indulgence was overstepping the mark. This sense of guilt is, of course, generally attributed to Orwell's 'social conscience'. He himself, at least by implication, would have ascribed such feelings to that cause. My own impression is that guilt lay far deeper than roots acquired merely by politico-social reading and observation. Guilt had, I think, been implanted in him at an early age, no doubt inflamed by the preparatory school experiences, shared with Connolly, about which Orwell himself wrote in *Such, Such Were the Joys*. He may—like Kipling, for whom as a writer he possessed a vigorous love/hate—have contrasted those grim days with a happy early childhood; for, although Orwell himself was inclined to imply that he had been brought up in a home of Victorian severity, his sister's memories suggest that, on the contrary, he had been rather 'spoilt.'

When, in the latter years of the war, my wife and small son, Tristram, were living at Dunstall (her uncle, Lord Dunsany's house, which we had been lent) at Shoreham in Kent, George and Eileen Orwell came down for the day. Going for country walks, Orwell would draw attention almost with anxiety to this shrub budding early for the time of year, that plant growing rarely in the south of England. He was, it is true, very fond of flowers, but there was something about this determined almost scientific concentration on natural history, or agricultural method, that seemed aimed at excusing the frivolity of mere ramblings. 'Interesting to note the regional variation in latching of field gates,' he would remark. 'Different sometimes, even in the same county.'

In this was something of Connolly's love of *expertise*, and also some of Connolly's omniscience. Guilt, naturally enough, harassed Orwell in matters of sex.

'Have you ever had a woman in the park?' he asked me once.

'No—never.'

'I have.'

'How did you find it?'

'I was forced to.'

'Why?'

'Nowhere else to go.'

He spoke defensively, as if he feared condemnation for this 'cold pastoral', as Connolly used to call such *plein air* frolics. It was a Victorian guilt, and in many ways Orwell was a Victorian figure—though of very different sort from Robert Byron, to whom I have also applied the label. Like most people 'in rebellion', he was more than half in love with what he was rebelling against. What exactly that was I could never be sure. Certainly its name was legion, extending from the turpitudes of government to irritating personal habits in individuals.

For example, Orwell complains (in the essay *How the Poor Die*) that English hospital nurses wear Union Jack buttons. This used to puzzle me, because, even at the period of which he wrote, if—in an access of chauvinism—you had wanted to sport a Union Jack button, I do not believe you would have been able to procure one for love or money. The button in question probably indicated the hospital at which the nurse had qualified; some such insignia resembling the design of the flag. To see such a badge as an emblem of flaunting jingoism comes near a mild form of persecution-mania. Many of Orwell's prejudices seemed equally to belong to this world of fantasy. That may be unjust. Mental and moral surroundings are subjective enough. It is largely the way you look at things. At least no one would deny the nightmare world envisaged by Orwell round about, if a true one, was drastically in need of reform.

'Take juries now,' he would say. 'They're mostly drawn from the middle-classes. Some fellow comes up for trial on a charge of stealing. He's not wearing a collar. The jury takes against him at once. "No collar?" they say. "Suspicious-looking chap." Unanimous verdict of guilty.'

Orwell himself was not at all unaware of the manner in which his own imagination strayed back into the Victorian age, nor, for that matter, of the paradoxes in which some of his enthusiasms involved him. Indeed, he liked to draw attention to the contradictions of his own point of view. He was also fond of repeating that, if some formula for agreement were reached by the nations, world economics could be put right 'on the back of an envelope'; but never revealed how this solution was to be achieved.

To his Victorianism he constantly returned, both in conversation, and, so far as possible, in life; the latter chiefly represented by the places he inhabited. He was delighted, for example, with the period flavour—certainly immense—of a small house in Kilburn, where, during the war, he rented the basement and ground floor. Its terrace had been built about 1850. The house conjured up those middle-to-lower-middle-class households (Orwell put himself in the lower-upper-middle-class) on which his mind loved to dwell; particularly as enthroned in the works of Gissing, whom he regarded as England's greatest novelist.

'They would probably have kept a Buttons here,' he said, enchanted at the thought.

We dined with the Orwells in Kilburn one night, prior arrangements being made (in the Jorrocks manner, himself employer of a Buttons) for sleeping there too, owing to the exigencies of wartime transport. The sitting-room, with a background of furniture dating from more prosperous generations of bygone Blairs, two or three 18th century family portraits hanging on the walls, might well have been the owner's study in a country house.

'When George went to the Spanish war,' said Eileen Orwell, 'we panicked at the last minute that he hadn't enough money with him, so we pawned the Blair spoons and forks. Then some weeks later his mother and sister came to see me. They asked why the silver was missing. I had to think of something on the spur of the moment, so I said it had seemed a good opportunity, Eric being away, to have the crest engraved on the silver. They accepted that.'

I never knew Eileen Orwell at all well. My impression is that she did a very good job in what were often difficult circumstances. At the same time it was, I think, an exception for her to tell a story like that. She was not usually given to making light of things, always appearing a little overwhelmed by the strain of keeping the household going, which could not have been easy. Possibly she was by temperament a shade overserious for a man falling often into a state of gloom himself. Orwell might have benefited by a wife who shook him out of that condition occasionally. He was fond of emphasizing his own egoisms.

'If I have a dog, I always think my dog is the best dog in the world,' he used to say, 'or if I make anything at carpentry, I always think it's the best shelf or bookcase. Don't you ever feel the need to do something with your hands? I'm surprised you don't. I even like rolling my own cigarettes. I've installed a lathe in the basement. I don't think I could exist without my lathe.'

The night we dined at Kilburn I slept on a camp-bed beside the lathe. There was just about space. It was an unusual, though not entirely comfortless room, and by that stage of the war one had become accustomed to sleeping anywhere. At about 4 a.m. there was a blitz. The local anti-aircraft battery sounded as if it were based next door. The row the guns made was prodigious, even by normal blitz standards. Orwell came blundering down in the dark.

'I'm rather glad there's a raid,' he said. 'It means we shall get some hot water in the morning. If you don't re-stoke the boiler about this time, it runs cold. I'm always too lazy to leave my bed in the middle of the night, unless like tonight there's too much noise to sleep anyway.'

The bad health that prevented Orwell from taking an active part in the war was a terrible blow to him. He saw himself as a man of action, and felt passionately about the things for which the country was fighting. When he heard Evelyn Waugh was serving with a Commando unit, he said: 'Why can't somebody on the Left do that sort of thing?' As a sergeant in the Home Guard he always spoke with enjoyment of the grotesque do-it-yourself weapons issued to that force, ramshackle in the extreme, and calculated to explode at any moment. Goodness knows what Orwell would have been like in the army. I have no doubt whatever that he would have been brave, but bravery in the army is, on the whole, an ultimate rather than immediate requirement, demanded only at the end of a long and tedious apprenticeship. It is possible that he might have found army routine sympathetic. He was not without love of detail, in fact was very keen on detail in certain forms. His own picture of military life was apt to be based on Kipling.

'Did you ever handle screw-guns?' he asked me.

At the time the phrase struck me as scarcely less obsolete than the pikes issued—and strongly recommended—at the beginning of the war, when invasion seemed likely to take place. I found that was incorrect, and screw-guns were indeed used in Burma and elsewhere. In the Spanish Civil War Orwell had served with a force designated POUM, chiefly Anarchist, which he joined not on account of special political affiliations, but because that unit seemed to offer the best chance of getting into action. Wounded in the throat, in danger of being arrested, perhaps executed, by the Communist Secret Police, he had to get out of Spain in a hurry. I once enquired how discipline was maintained in such an army. 'You appealed to a man's better nature,' Orwell said. 'There really wasn't much else you could do. I took a chap by the arm once, when he was being tiresome, and was told afterwards that I might easily have been knifed.'

Orwell was in his way quite ambitious, I think, and had a decided taste for power; but his ambition did not run along conventional lines, and he liked his power to be of the *éminence grise* variety. That preference was no doubt partly owed to a sense of being in some manner cut off from the rest of the world; not allowed, as it were by an irresistible exterior influence, to enjoy more than very occasionally such few amenities as human existence provides. This did not prevent his strong will and natural shrewdness from making him an effective negotiator. Indeed, his genuine unworldliness—in the popular sense—was used by him with considerable effect when handling those who were rich or in authority. He would somehow unload on them the whole burden of his own guilt, until they groaned beneath its weight. He was not at all afraid of making himself disagreeable to persons whom he found, in their dealings with himself, disagreeable. 'If editors, or people of that sort, tell you to alter things, or put you to a lot of trouble,' he used to say, 'always put them to trouble in return. It discourages them from making themselves awkward in the future.'

It is interesting to speculate how Orwell's life would have developed had he survived as a very successful writer. The retirement to Jura, even at the preliminary warning signs of financial improvement, was probably symptomatic. Orwell, I suspect, could thrive only in comparative adversity. All the same, one can never foresee the effect of utterly changed circumstances. Prosperity might have produced unguessable alterations in himself and his work. It would inevitably have invested him with more complex forms of living; complications which, in accordance with his system, would have to be rationalized to himself, and weighed in the balance.

Orwell's gift was curiously poised, as suggested earlier, between politics and literature. The former both attracted and repelled him; the latter, close to his heart, was at the same time tainted with the odour of escape. He once said that he could not write a line without a specific purpose. On the other hand, so far as day to day politics were concerned, he could never have become integrated into any normal party machine. His reputation for integrity might be invoked; his capacity for martyrdom relied on; his talent for pamphleteering made use of. That was all. He could never be trusted not to let some disastrously unwelcome cat out of the political bag. With literature, on the other hand, in spite of an innate 'feeling' for writing and criticism, he always had to seek the means of attacking some abuse or injustice to excuse himself. This did not prevent books from being, in my opinion, his true love.

In his own works Orwell returns more than once to the theme that, had he lived at another period of history, he would have written in a different manner. I do not believe this to be a correct judgment. I find his talent far removed from that objective sort of writing which he saw as an alternative to what he actually produced. His interest in individuals—in literature or life—was never great. Apart from various projections of himself, the characters in his novels do not live as persons, though they are sometimes effective puppets in expressing their author's thesis of the moment. Orwell had a thoroughly professional approach to writing, and a finished style. His critical judgments are sometimes eccentric, and his dislike for all elaborate methods of writing, whatever they might be, seems to me an altogether untenable form of literary puritanism.

He was easily bored. If a subject came up in conversation that did not appeal to him, he would make no effort to take it in; falling into a dejected silence, or jerking aside his head like a horse jibbing at a proffered apple. On the other hand, when Orwell's imagination was caught, especially by some idea, he would discuss that exhaustively. He was one of the most enjoyable people to talk with about books, full of parallels and quotations, the last usually far from verbally accurate.

The adoption of a child, the sudden death of Eileen, the world wide success of *Animal Farm*, the serious worsening of his own health, all combined within the space of a few months to revolutionize Orwell's life. The loss of his wife, just after the much contemplated acquisition of the baby, especially created a situation that would have caused many men to give in. No doubt some arrangement for re-adoption could have been made without too much difficulty. That would have been reasonable enough. No such thought ever crossed Orwell's mind. He had enormously desired a child of his own. Now that a child had become part of the household, he was not going to relinquish him, no matter what the difficulties. In fact one side of Orwell—the romantic side that played such a part (using the word differently from, say, Walter Scott's romanticism, or the romanticism of Eton education, though no doubt all romanticism has a somewhat similar root)—rather enjoyed the picture of himself coping unaided with a small baby. Let this point be made clear; Orwell *did* cope with the baby. It may have been romanticism, but, if so, it was romanticism which found practical expression in that way. This was characteristic of him in all he did. His idiosyncracies were based in guts.

He would still go out at night to address protest meetings—'. . . probably a blackguard, but it was unjust to lock him up . . .'—and the baby would be left to sleep for an hour or two at our house, while Orwell harangued his audience.

'What was the meeting like?' one would ask on his return.

'Oh, the usual people.'

'Always the same?'

'There must be about two hundred of them altogether. They go round to everything of this sort. About forty or fifty turned up tonight, which is quite good.'

This mixture of down-to-earth scepticism seasoned with a dash of self-dramatization formed a contradictory element in Orwell's character. With all his honesty, ability to face disagreeable facts, refusal to be hoodwinked, there was always also about him a touch of make-believe, the air of acting a part. Connolly mentions that at their prep school he, no doubt Orwell too, used to read the poems of Robert W. Service (chiefly memorable for the verses about Dangerous Dan McGrew), and Sir Anthony Wagner (herald and genealogical scholar, now Garter King of Arms) told me that, when he was Orwell's fag in College, Orwell, on his departure, presented him with Service's *Rhymes of a Rolling Stone*. 'He was a kind and considerate fagmaster,' said Wagner, 'but he did not talk much.' The parting gift is not without interest in consideration of Orwell's character.

Orwell came to see me in London one day when our younger son, John, was lying, quiet but not asleep, in a cot by the window. I went out of the room to fetch a book. When I returned Orwell was assiduously studying a picture on the wall on the far side of the room. John made some sign of needing attention. I went over to the cot, straightening the coverlet, which had become disarranged, my hand touched a hard object. This

102

turned out to be an enormous clasp-knife. I took it out and examined it.

'How on earth did that get there?'

For the moment the mystery of the knife's provenance seemed absolute. Orwell looked away, as if greatly embarrassed.

'Oh, I gave it him to play with,' he said. 'I forgot I'd left it there.'

The incident, infinitely trivial, seems worth preserving because it illustrates sides of Orwell not easy to express in direct description: his attitude to childhood; his shyness, part genuine, part assumed; his schoolboy leanings; above all, his taste for sentimental vignettes. Why, in the first place, should he want to burden himself, in London, with a knife that looked like an adjunct of a fur-trapper's equipment? Echoes perhaps of Dangerous Dan McGrew? Why take such pains to avoid being found playing with a child, a perfectly natural instinct, flattering to a parent? If some authentic masculine sheepishness made him hesitate at being caught in such an act, why leave the knife behind as evidence? It was much too big to be forgotten.

I think the answer to these questions is that the whole incident was arranged to create a genre picture in the Victorian manner of a kind which, even though he might smile at the sentimentality, made a huge appeal to Orwell's imagination, and way of looking at things. He was, so to speak, playing the part of a strong rough man, touched by the sight of a baby, but unwilling to confess, even to himself, this inner weakness. At the same time, he had to be discovered for the incident to achieve graphic significance.

Orwell would not, I think, deny that sentimental situations had a charm for him. I can imagine him discussing them in relation to another favourite theme of his, 'good bad poetry', and 'good bad novels'. In his own books Orwell is too practised a writer to be betrayed into presenting sentimentalities in their crude form, though he is fond of showing them, so to speak, brutally in reverse; for example, his taste for such episodes as lovers' assignations ruined by forgotten contraceptives or the curse.

In due course the trouble with Orwell's lung became so serious that he had to take to his bed. It was fairly clear that he was not going to recover; only the length of time that remained to him in doubt. 'I don't think one dies,' he said to me, 'as long as one has another book to write—and I have.'

During these last months he married Sonia Brownell, first met by him some years before, when she had been on the staff of Connolly's magazine, *Horizon*. In spite of the tragic circumstances of Orwell's failing condition, marriage immensely cheered him. I saw a good deal of him when he was in hospital. In some respects he was in better form there than I had ever known him show. There was now and then a flicker to be seen of the old Wodehousian side.

'I really might get some sort of a smoking-jacket to wear in bed,' he said. 'A dressing-gown looks rather sordid when lots of people are dropping in. Could you look about, and report to me what there is in that line?'

War shortages still persisted where clothes were concerned. Nothing very glamorous in male styles was to be found in the shops. Decision had to be taken ultimately between a jaeger coat with a tying belt, or a crimson jacket in corduroy. We agreed the latter was preferable. It was a small concession to an aspect of human frailty that Orwell had for years strenuously denied himself. Sitting up in bed now, he had an unaccustomed epicurean air—only, unhappily, his conviction that an unwritten book within preserved life proved untrustworthy. I have often wondered whether he was buried in the crimson coat.

The Orwell myth, now substantially launched in a shape scarcely amenable to modification, presents on the whole a tortured saint by El Greco (for whom Orwell would certainly have made an admirable model), a figure from whom all human qualities have been removed. Periodically fierce arguments rage as to precisely where he stood politically. I am not here concerned with that side of him, although it is worth remembering that it took courage—in that now largely forgotton post-war period, when Stalin was still being held up by the Left as a genial uncle—to fire an anti-Communist broadside like *Animal Farm* that placed a permanent dent in the whole Marxist structure; especially courageous on the part of a writer, himself of the Left, laying his professional reputation open to smear and boycott, which those he so devastatingly exposed hastened to set about.

VII

The Close and the Quad

Early in 1922, my father posted to Headquarters Southern Command, we moved to Salisbury, there inhabiting at different times two furnished houses: 16 The Close, just within St Anne's Gate; 35 The Close, on the green opposite the Cathedral. Even at that period much of Salisbury was already marred by unsightly building, though far less than today, a few of the streets then comparatively unspoilt. The Close remained—and remains—a precinct of immense beauty, a quiet dignity not easily rivalled. Unfortunately quiet dignity in architecture does not stave off adolescent gloom. The muggy climate, somniferous social ambiance, my own inability to keep myself amused in conventional ways, made the city a powerful toxin to inflame that endemic distemper of growing up, during late holidays from school, and early Oxford vacations. In fact Salisbury represented—still recalls when I pass through its now traffic-infested streets—unfathomable depths of adolescent melancholy and boredom.

My father used to say: 'Of course, you're not the sort of chap who likes to take a gun, and get a bit of rough shooting.' This was patently true; but, if it came to that, neither was he. I see now, possessing the tastes I did, I might have been even less conveniently placed had my family been firmly rooted in a country setting, where hunting and shooting were taken as a matter of course. Indeed, the burden such pastimes can be to those not by nature addicted to them is suggested by Yorke's autobiography (often his attitude is ambivalent, my own would probably have been likewise), but such conclusions are hard to arrive at when you are young.

105

I have only hunted two or three times in my life, spending most of the day falling off, but my father had been issued with a horse for his job, which I used sometimes to take out hacking. Proceeding on one of these solitary rides along a wet macadamized road on the outskirts of Salisbury, buses passing from time to time, I was once run away with, but managed to avert disaster.

'Girls', a subject in which I had begun to feel an interest, seemed all but non-existent round about, anyway in the form I conceived they should take. There must have been girls in Salisbury, but where were they? Again my own lack of enterprise was probably to blame. I remember a few girls, of course, but none filled the bill; even tennis parties seeming mostly to consist of majors, colonels, and their wives.

As in London, I used to spend most of the holidays reading and drawing. I wish I had kept some record of books consumed at various ages. At twelve or thirteen I read some of Compton Mackenzie's *Sinister Street* with a certain excitement, but did not manage to finish the novel, wherever I came across it. There were English Literature prizes at school, which involved reading the poems of Keats and Matthew Arnold with some attention. The claims for bohemian life already instilled by *Trilby* were increased by the novels of W. J. Locke (though I remember very little about them): *The Morals of Marcus Ordeyne* (1905), *The Beloved Vagabond* (1906), *The Joyous Adventures of Aristide Pujol* (1912). About the end of the time that I was at school *The Morning Post* ran a John Galsworthy Competition. I won it. I still possess the prize, a pocket set of Galsworthy's Collected Works (leather, 7s 6d each), volumes damaged by damp when our house in London was left unoccupied (and bombed) during the war, but *The Man of Property* still comparatively intact, inscribed: 'A. D. Powell, with the wonder and admiration of John Galsworthy'.

At Salisbury a steady stream of books, mostly novels, were obtained— by my mother at my instigation—from Boots Circulating Library, where the librarian (Miss Wickens) was a keen purveyor for relatively highbrow clients. One day in School Library I came across a magazine (I suppose *The Criterion*) which contained a long account of James Joyce's *Ulysses*. I was very interested by what was said—I certainly did not handle the book itself until at least three or four years later—but this interest seemed quite separate in itself; causing, so to speak, no conversion or repentance as to middlebrow reading matter. Such forms of intellectual

106

double-harness are perhaps characteristic of literary self-education. Constant Lambert used to say that, in thirty years' time, Michael Arlen would be indistinguishable from Aldous Huxley (my father described *The Green Hat* as the best novel he had ever read) and it would not be impossible to trace period resemblances, but, when *Antic Hay* came out almost the same week as I went up to Oxford, I was prostrated by its brilliance. Huxley's novels, even the early ones, seemed disappointing when reread in middle life, but now the originality of *Antic Hay* is apparent to me again; though the note goes flat when erudite frivolity is abandoned to teach a moral lesson. In those days I was quite unaware that from time to time a moral lesson was being taught by the author.

When I left Eton, at the end of the summer half, 1923, I was ready to go, though life had been pleasant enough in the House Library, with Buckley, by then Captain of the House, and several other friends outside the House; though none of these played much part in later life. I spent a day or two in Oxford for the Balliol Scholarship examination; in that way matriculating for the college. The *viva* on this occasion was my first contact with Kenneth Bell, subsequently my Balliol history tutor. 'You're the fellow who liked *The Beggar's Opera* so much', he said; but I do not remember what question in the papers could have elicited this conclusion. At Eton, the July Examinations took place. From the results of these the marks of all Specialists were brought down to a percentage; everyone then arranged in order, no matter what their subject. I came 9th in the school, and 3rd oppidan, thereby winning an Oppidan Prize, regarded as a laurel of reasonable distinction.

An encounter that took place my last half should be recorded; perhaps as a mystic example of persons suitable for inclusion in novels instinctively offering potential novelists an opportunity for looking them over as appropriate material. A young woman known to my parents—possibly she had worked as a secretary in the War Office—was passing through Eton by car. As a friendly gesture, she called on me. She had a man with her, not himself an Old Etonian, but who behaved rather as if hoping to be taken for that. Why the girl and the man knew each other, I have no idea, but, years later, I was able to identify the girl's companion as Evelyn Waugh's model for Captain Grimes. I feel grateful to fate that I was thus—almost magically—privileged to meet Captain Grimes in the flesh.

My father, between spasms of grumbling about school bills, and occasional resistance to attitudes of mind inevitably acquired at Eton, had taken a fair amount of vicarious pleasure in my being there. When, rather tentatively, I first raised the possibility of proceeding to a university, he was less well disposed; remaining always suspicious of Oxford, and everything for which the academic principle might be supposed to stand. The relationship of father and son is never less than exacting, but there is no avoiding for either this particular climacteric brought on by the years; the metamorphosis of boy to man. I may myself have handled that critical period without special adroitness, but my father's exceptional dislike for any change or development in life, his own or anyone else's, did not lessen the strain of a traditionally delicate evolvement. Not at all hostile, anyway in certain moods, to learning as such, he always feared the uncertainties, the unsheltered regions, that the world of the mind opened up. At the same time, although my own condition may have presented a problem—in a sense a trickier one than appeared on the surface—I suspect he would have found things at least as trying, if not more so, had my obvious goal been the army. Certainly nothing seemed to gratify him less than my attainment during the war of comparatively appropriate military employments. He was never able to make up his mind whether success or failure in a son was the more inimical. As Balston remarked later: 'It's an entirely unphilosophic mind.'

Chiefly on Balston's recommendation, Balliol was singled out as the most fitting college; my father half-fascinated, half-repelled by its reputation for arrogant brilliance. Balston himself had been up at New College, which he stigmatized as 'only teaching you to brush your hair the right way'; an imputation additionally prejudicial since his own stubbly crop of black bristle was permanently standing on end. (I remember Balston once remarking that he might be in Oxford, 'if I can stand a New College bedroom in winter'; and, such was my then hardihood, being unable to grasp climatic implications that became clear enough in a few years' time.) Marten, my Eton history tutor, himself a Balliol man, supported the proposition. The usual syndrome of Dreaming Spires, Lost Causes, Zuleika Dobson, Sinister Street, together with the general drift of most of my friends, made me prefer the idea of Oxford to Cambridge, but I did not feel strongly as to which college harboured me. Balliol's effortless superiority sounded as good as anything else.

Balliol's great days were, in fact, by then long over, but a certain puissance still clung to the name. Rising above a deliberately imposed discomfort and drabness, the College retained a distinct character of its own. The architecture, in comparison with so much today—not least in Oxford—that is incalculably more hideous, now seems a perfectly acceptable if uninspired example of academic neogothic taste. The immediate impact, when I came up for the exam, was a little dispiriting. In domestic administration the rest of Oxford is probably now as uniformly austere, but at that period Balliol stood out in bleakness. When almost every other college provided commons (bread, cheese, beer) for luncheon in each individual undergraduate's rooms—dinner in hall of quite high if simple standard—Balliol lunched communally, its food (unless specially ordered for a private meal) at best indifferent. I remember my astonishment when Connolly, taking an empty place beside me at lunch one day, after giving his order to the scout, added: 'And lots of potatoes.' No doubt he was experiencing one of those urges towards compulsive eating he himself refers to, but the Balliol potatoes were usually far from tempting.

The best thing about Balliol was a tradition of tolerance. Everyone did what he preferred. There was little or no pressure—as at some smaller colleges—as to playing games or other types of conformism. No one was expected to live the same sort of life as other members of the College simply because they were members of the College; and many Balliol men, even of the same year, never exchanged a word with each other during their Oxford residence. At the same time there was plenty of college-spirit for those who liked college-spirit. It was not forced on those who did not.

My Oxford generation was the first of that decade to inhabit a university untinged by the ex-soldier and his ways. Persons who had been 'in the war' might seem a million to us, yet only the previous year there had been undergraduates in residence liable to speak of hall as 'Mess', and otherwise indulge in obsolete barely decent locutions derived from military service. Such jargon was naturally deplored by the more sophisticated ex-campaigners, but even these latter were inexpungibly branded by war-service in the eyes of the oncoming waves of schoolboys. This 'age-gap' of the Twenties was a chasm to make all subsequent ones of its sort seem inconsiderable. Men and women grown up before 1914 were not only older, they were altogether set apart; and thus they remained throughout life. You never caught up with them. This was true, broadly speaking, whether or not they had been actively involved in hostilities. It was particularly true (though, paradoxically, within this category sometimes superficially obscured) of the younger men, those nearer in age to my own lot. These relatively youthful war veterans had, on the one hand, known a world already disappeared; on the other, were keenly conscious (their juniors too, but only feeling their way) of new still undefined forms of existence, which, come what may, they were determined to explore and exploit.

Evelyn Waugh (*A Little Learning*) speaks of three hundred a year as an average undergraduate allowance for that period. In his own case, he says, a scholarship, with various additional subventions from home sources, made this sum up to about fifty pounds more. I was in much the same case. I had a basic three hundred; my father (not without all protest) showing himself, when it came to the point, open to putting up fifty pounds more for foreign travel during the Long Vac. It would probably be true to say that most Etonians at Oxford had four hundred; a few, fifty or a hundred in addition to that. On the whole undergraduates who graded (in Oxford terms) as 'very rich' were not Etonian; most Eton parents, however well off, holding strong views about discouraging extravagance in their sons; any extra money being provided with a view to keeping a horse, rather than for lavish entertaining. It was for some time inexplicable to me why, living in London later, a whole year on three hundred seemed less gruelling than Oxford (which I left without debts) for six months on the same amount. I now see that (apart from paying college bills) one was stockpiling all sorts of necessities in the way of clothes that had to be only gradually renewed.

Among the many notices from undergraduate societies offering membership, letters from tradesmen soliciting custom, and other such communications pouring in on the freshman, I found myself receiving (through whose offices I do not know) cards for evenings at the house of the Slade Professor (Sir Michael Sadler), at which some notability in the arts would from time to time speak. I am surprised now by the comparative lack of interest I took in these invitations. This indifference seems explained by a kind of intellectual recession undergone while I was at Oxford. Perhaps something of the kind is less uncommon than might be expected; the potentially bright schoolboy, pressures of school relaxed, becoming a slightly dazed undergraduate. Up to a point, I suppose, I continued to pursue interests possessed at school, but they seem to have lost much of their former force; a falling off of intellectual vitality that was characteristic, it now seems to me, of my three years at the University.

I had at least the good sense to attend the Slade Lecture at which Sickert spoke, though I remember only a little of what he said. Tall, grey-haired, crimson in the face, wearing a thick greenish loudly-checked suit, he chatted in a conversational voice, humorous and resonant, while he flourished a cigar. His personality filled the room. Half a century later, I learnt that (his second wife having died three years before), Sickert was still sunk in the deepest depression. No one could have guessed that. On the contrary, he appeared in the best of form, delivering his direct no-nonsense art criticism to an audience of not much more than twenty, most of whom, like myself, probably had little idea what good stuff they were listening to; what safeguards against swallowing whole the doctrines of Bloomsbury (of which I was equally uninformed), by then beginning to dominate the critical scene so far as painting was concerned.

No one I had known at all well at school came up to Balliol that year, and even at other colleges there were few close friends. Hubert Duggan was convalescing in Argentina; Henry Yorke and Denys Buckley—both within a couple of months of my own age, but starting university life a year later—were still at Eton. Others, known less well but as equals, like Harold Acton (Christ Church) and Robert Byron (Merton), arrived the previous year, were rather grand personages now in their own Oxford world. Even some of the Eton friends of my own year (not of the Arts Society sort) seemed increasingly grown up, with more coherent plans than my own for Oxford life; which were indeed non existent.

When (having spent some weeks of that summer staying in a French household in Touraine) I came up to Balliol in October, 1923, A. L. Smith was Master of the College. He was well spoken of, but I never saw more of him than to attend, with a batch of other freshmen, a routine tea party at The Lodgings. Smith died the following year. He was succeeded as Master by an ambitious politician, A. D. Lindsay (later Lord Lindsay of Birker), with whom I also had little contact, beyond being taken by him for one term in Political Theory. I found him unsympathetic as a theorist and a man.

Balliol was a college that insisted on certain academic standards, rusticating undergraduates who failed to pass History Previous (the first stage of the History School, which I was reading), an examination held at the end of two terms. The tutor to conduct me through History Previous was C. G. Stone, known as 'Topes'. In principle regarded as a 'good man', Stone, then in his late thirties, was rather unusually deaf, with an illimitable stutter. To these two obstructions in communication between us he added inability to read my already regrettably illegible handwriting. An awareness of these barriers made him seem shy and gruff. In spite of intermittent difficulties in conveying the substance of my essays, he perfectly caught the opening sentence of the first, which began: 'The close of the Dark Ages fell on Christmas Day in the year 800, when Charlemagne was crowned in Rome as Emperor of the West.' Stone articulated a comment: 'Don't start your essays with that sort of metaphorical clearing of the throat.'

A week or two later I forgot some textbook required. Stone managed to get out: 'You must try and remember you are no longer a schoolboy.'

I found such admonitions galling at the time, but the former made me think about writing in a way I had never done before. Christmas Day in the Dark Ages had seemed, if not the happiest day in the epoch (as in the Workhouse), at least the most picturesque. I now saw in a flash the importance of structure. Stone's words did nothing but good. His particular brand of donnishness was in any case suitable foundation for a very different sort of tutor—one possibly best not encountered at first onset—Kenneth Bell, by whom I was taught for several terms after surmounting the first History School hurdle.

Kenneth Bell was one of the two outstanding Balliol dons of that era; the other being F. F. Urquhart, always known as 'Sligger'—not 'Sligger Urquhart', as now sometimes altogether incorrectly rendered, either Sligger or Urquhart—was Dean of the College; responsible, with the administrative support of a Junior Dean, for undergraduate discipline. Urquhart and Bell (judged to be on not specially good terms with each other) were a contrast in every respect: Urquhart, then in his middle fifties, mild, monkish, whitehaired, withdrawn, elusive in manner; Bell (as a Balliol undergraduate Urquhart's pupil) still under forty, wartime Gunner major with an MC, militarily moustached, bluff in demeanour, apparently a hearty of hearties, but in fact full of unexpected powers of discrimination.

It is convenient to speak of Urquhart first. In earlier days as a don he had gained the reputation of operating an undergraduate salon. By the time I came up to Balliol anything to be so called had fallen into abeyance. Callers in the evening were not discouraged (lemonade always on offer), but Urquhart was usually alone. There might be a single other visitor; more rarely, one of the quieter College dining-clubs could have closed their evening with a visit. The term 'Sliggerite', for an habitué, was almost always attached to those of an earlier Oxford generation than my own. I was on good terms with Urquhart, who tutored me (not very effectively) for a term or two, but was never in the running for being a Sliggerite; feeling even unable to face the alleged rigours of the châlet in Switzerland, where he conducted annual reading-parties.

At least half-a-dozen Oxford dons possessed claims to run a salon; no doubt as many at Cambridge, because, when reviewing my book *A Question of Upbringing*, two Cambridge papers said that the don there called Sillery was obviously modelled on a wellknown Cambridge figure. Nevertheless, Sillery has time and again been 'identified' with Urquhart. Here seems an opportunity for stating that Sillery and Urquhart, apart from both being dons, were persons of altogether different sort. Perhaps it is tedious to labour the point. I do so only for the sake of truth. Urquhart (of some university fame, social rather than academic) has undoubtedly been portrayed in more than one novel about Oxford. Had I wished to do so, I could have offered my own projection of an unusual personality. Such was not my aim, and Urquhart, far from being (like Sillery), a talkative power-seeking Left Winger, was a devout Roman Catholic, hesitant in manner, conversationally inhibited, never pontificating about public affairs, nor addicted more than most dons to the habit of intrigue. Somebody once said with truth that a typical 'Sligger remark' was, after a long pause: 'Have you ever noticed how, the higher you get in mountainous country, the more the sheep begin to resemble goats?'

At noisy college festivals Urquhart was likely to slip away early to his rooms, while Bell remained to get tight. At one of these dinners (the year before I came up) a disaster had nearly taken place on this account. Urquhart had reappeared in the quad, probably on account of the row that was being made, and Bell, in a burst of high spirits, threw some coal at him from an upper window. It was not immediately clear who was responsible for this bombardment, and, by the time Urquhart (more probably the Junior Dean) reached the place from which the fusillade had been launched, undergraduate friends (including Alf Duggan) had concealed Bell under the bed, or otherwise disposed of the body. Had they not done so there might have been serious consequences for Bell, possibly loss of his Balliol Fellowship—finally removed in quite other circumstances.

Drunken uproariousness was only one side of Bell, the avatar in which he was a beer-swilling devotee of the college boat. In another, he was the great promoter of Balliol's 'clever men', champion of any undergraduate he thought intelligent, especially one in difficulties of some sort with the authorities. Bell's support was not in the least limited to those of academic promise as such. The undergraduate in question might easily belong to a type Bell could be expected to reprobate. He approved of success ('A man says: "I was married in a tailcoat and a bowler hat, and, by God, my son shall be married in a tailcoat and a top-hat" '), but he recognized that there were different sorts of success. He was prepared to stand up for ability concealed by an awkward manner, rackety behaviour, absurd clothing.

Bell's own pupils were expected to work hard. He was a most stimulating teacher, but it was best to go in the first of the three morning sessions, during each of which four undergraduates would in turn read aloud their essays. Like all who function on nervous energy, Bell, at the start, would give unsparingly of himself, pouring out acute comment; some of the fire dying down by the third hour of the morning. He had his own views on history, but liked to be amused and surprised by what his pupils wrote; especially, for example, in attacking highminded muddleheadness, and the clichés of the Whig historians.

Bell paid attention not only to history, but to the manner in which an essay was written. 'But what a portentous length!' he would protest, at the end of a long screed by an over-diligent student. He was always anxious to show that history was about people, human beings, not a cluster of well arranged political and economic theories. Somebody (possibly myself) made some priggish judgment on the policies of the Holy Roman Empire. Bell commented: 'Yes, that may well be true—but we shall never know what Charles V felt like in the early morning.'

If I had been made to think of the structure of writing by Stone, Bell carried the lesson much further. The price his pupils paid (myself will-

114

ingly enough) was that he taught history for itself, not as medium for ac-
quiring a good degree in the Final Schools. The History syllabus, as laid
down, was obviously impossible to cover with any thoroughness in three
years. Bell took the line that is was better to know some of the conspec-
tus well, rather than attempt superficial acquaintance with the whole. His
methods (and their results) exemplify an eternal antithesis in education—
and almost every other branch of existence—the inner good, as opposed
to the immediate practical advantage.

Kenneth Bell's own career ended rather sadly. In the early years of the
war his marriage broke up. In those days official academic attitudes towards the sex-life of dons were very different from what they were to become. The fact that Bell had left his wife for another woman (who died
tragically only a few months later) was not countenanced by Lindsay,
who, as Master of Balliol, was instrumental in having Bell's Fellowship removed from him. That was, of course, Bell's daily bread. A man like Bell
was able to find other employments (he made a new career for himself, in
due course becoming a parson), but Balliol had been his whole life. The
College was in the end the loser. Kenneth Bell was in his way rather a
great man.

3

Three or four days after arrival in Oxford, one evening after hall, I was
sitting in my room (on the second floor of the Garden Quad) wondering if
it were too early to go to bed, when the door began to open very slowly
and jerkily. A figure stood on the threshold, supporting itself by a hand
on the door-knob, the body visibly trembling, the face of ghastly pallor. It
was Alfred Duggan. He was all but speechless with drink. Words came at
last, but only with great effort.

'Can you—lunch with me—Hypocrites—Friday?'

'I'd like to very much. Won't you come in?'

Duggan smiled kindly, but did not answer, or enter the room. Very
slowly, very jerkily, the door closed again. The sound of much staggering
and crashing came from the staircase. I was flattered by the visit, and the
invitation. I had, of course, heard of The Hypocrites Club. There would
be no great difficulty in discovering its whereabouts. I did not know Dug-

gan at all well. We might have met a couple of times when he had driven over to Eton (a car in those days rather a dashing possession for an undergraduate) to see his brother. Once he had brought with him another Balliol Etonian of his year, John Heygate (later baronet), and the four of us had gone down to Tap. There was a slight sense of Hubert Duggan being determined not to be high-hatted by his elder brother. Heygate barely spoke. In due course I was to know Heygate well, but—in the Balliol manner—I don't think we ever exchanged a word during our overlapping Oxford period. He was not of The Hypocrites world.

The Hypocrites Club has often been decribed; two or three rooms over a bicycle-shop in an ancient half-timbered house at the end of St Aldate's, not far from where that long street approaches Folly Bridge, a vicinity looked on as somewhat outside the accepted boundaries of Oxford social life. The Club had been founded by a group of Trinity and Oriel men, relatively serious and philosophy-talking, so the legend ran, an orientation of which traces still remained at the stage of its evolution when I lunched there with Duggan. David Talbot Rice, and John 'the Widow' Lloyd, had been among its foundation members, and the former may have been responsible for bringing there Acton, Byron, and more frivolous elements. When I first set foot in the Club transmogrification had gone a long way, though still short of the metamorphosis, on the whole regrettable, into a fashionably snobbish undergraduate haunt; before final closure by the authorities, ostensibly for being outside the University licencing area, but in effect for rackety goings-on.

The Hypocrites was staffed by a married couple called Hunt, with an additional retainer, Whitman. Mrs Hunt did the cooking (simple but excellent), her husband and Whitman acting as waiters. Hunt was clean-shaven, relatively spruce; Whitman, moustached, squat, far from spick and span. Both Hunt and Whitman were inclined to drink a good deal, but, in their different ways, were the nearest I have ever come across to the ideal of the Jeevesian manservant, always willing, never out of temper, full of apt repartee and gnomic comment. Evelyn Waugh (intermittently a prominent Hypocrites member, though excluded at this period for having smashed up a good deal of the Club's furniture with the heavy stick he always carried) had been served with a drink one evening just before closing time.

'But, Whitman, I told you, when you asked, that I did *not* want another drink.'

'I thought you were joking, sir.'

I can't remember who else were guests at Duggan's luncheon-party, but, among other members of the Club present, were John Lloyd (called 'the Widow' possibly on account of a shaving preparation styled *The Widow Lloyd's Euxesis*), a great mainstay of The Hypocrites, and joint host, with Byron, of the fancy-dress party given there the following year; Graham Pollard, of revolutionary bearing and sentiments, already earning a living while an undergraduate by selling rare books; E. E. Evans-Pritchard, the anthropologist, grave, withdrawn, somewhat exotic in dress. Pollard lived over the main gate at Jesus, where he later asked me to tea to see his books. He said that, judging from the finger marks, he concluded *Love and Pain* to be his scout's favourite volume of Havelock Ellis, whose works he also possessed. With John Carter (a colleger I had known slightly at school, who had gone on to Cambridge) Pollard was to be the first to expose the Wise forgeries.

I recall some difficulty (soon mastered) in getting through a pint of the Club's dark beer, powerful for one still unaccustomed to alcohol. Duggan himself was inclined to drink a pint of burgundy out of a tankard at lunch. He may have done so that day. His head was not specially strong, and he was often tipsy, though an amusing companion when not overdoing his Byronic swashbuckling in such ways as playing poker for absurdly high stakes. Duggan used to hunt, and ride with the Drag, thereby making one of the few links (in my first year) between sporting spheres of Oxford life, and the very different crowd, its character not easy to define, that made up The Hypocrites Club.

This was about the peak of the social division in the University (in a sense, the larger world too) crudely covered by the labels 'aesthete' and 'hearty'; both only very relative terms to distinguish certain antithetical attitudes of mind and body. A Ninetyish aestheticism of a musty sort was by no means defunct in Oxford of those days, but on the whole, with one or two exceptions (another subsequent anthropologist, Francis Turville-Petre, could scarcely be excluded from the category) aesthetes of a type unrevised since the turn of the century were not Hypocrites material. The Club was equally far from the soberly dressed, well behaved undergraduate intelligentsia (L. P. Hartley, David Cecil) of a year or two before.

At one end of the scale at The Hypocrites, Harold Acton—while himself making fun of the old-fashioned aesthete—might reasonably be so classed by the undergraduate-in-the-High; at the other, Talbot Rice and Elmley (both Secretaries of the Club at different periods), with many more, could not have been less aesthete-like. Nor were Byron and Waugh that sort of aesthete, though both (especially Byron) affected a style of dress that probably so denoted them at their respective colleges; clothes being the touchstone of public opinion where 'aesthetes' were concerned. Alf Duggan was inclined to wear a very neat suit of dark green plus fours (as for a smart shooting party), which Hubert Duggan used to call 'my brother's little green suit'. Byron once said: 'Alfred, you ought to wear *black* plus fours.' 'Surely not,' said Duggan. 'I should look like Oscar Wilde at his worst period. I know I'm getting too fat. Will anyone do a week's starvation with me? I've tried it before, and the only trouble is you don't want to start eating again.'

A tennis-blue once turned up at The Hypocrites, but in a general way games-players would be as rare among guests as members. With the exception of Duggan, I can remember no early intermingling of Hypocrites types with the Bullingdon (hunting, plus an admixture of golf) such as took place later, in the way that there was overlapping with the Union or OUDS. Another link with a different sort of Oxford was Romney Summers, recently down from Brasenose (where he had rowed), a preeminently 'hearty' college, where Summers retained several friends.

Redfaced, beefy, with a lot of charm, and passion for social life, Summers had been unable to tear himself away from Oxford, continuing to occupy rooms in King Edward Street. Not enormously rich in the wider sense, he was very comfortably off for a young man (his father dead, mother living abroad), combining fast cars, bridge-playing, large parties at Commem, with Hypocrites life. He was one of the two or three in my first year who would give dinner-parties for, say, thirty guests (sometimes one would literally not know the host by more than name), a form of hospitality that—like a particular kind of party in London later—withered away completely after about a year. Summers was one of the greatest time-wasters I have ever known; the whole day over before he had accomplished a twentieth part of what he had intended to do when he got up in the morning.

In the main sitting-room of The Hypocrites stood an upright piano, which Byron (occasionally others, but predominantly Byron) would play, contorting his features into fearful grimaces, while he sang Victorian ballads in an ear-splitting alto.

> Rose a nurse of ninety years,
> Set his child upon her knee—
> (*f*) Like summer tempests came her tears—
> (*fff*) Like summer tempests came her tears—
> (*ppp*) 'Sweet my child, I live for thee.'

About three weeks after I had been in residence at Balliol, Alf Duggan arrived in my room, this time about ten o'clock in the morning. His manner was brusque. He said: 'I was in London last night, and omitted to take any precautions about my bed not having been slept in. The scout reported me. I was sent for by Sligger. I've just seen him. I told him I lay drunk on your floor all night. Will you confirm that, if Sligger asks you about it.' He went away without further words on the subject.

Duggan used to talk a good deal about his 'mistress' (a night-club hostess), whom he would visit in London from time to time. Absence from rooms in college at night was normally covered by arranging for a friend to untidy the bedclothes, and urinate in the chamber pot, the night before; thereby giving an impression that the owner had risen early, and (when the scout called him with a jug of hot water) was already up and abroad. Alternatively, it was possible to climb into college before dawn, though by that method Balliol was a college not particularly easy of access. In due course I was sent for by Urquhart, and questioned. I corroborated Duggan's story. Urquhart accepted it, but I felt I was not making the best of impressions as a freshman.

VIII

Cymbals in Naxos

Among Balliol freshmen of my first year (not, like Anthony Russell, and one or two others, already known at school) were Matthew Ponsonby, Arden Hilliard, Peter Quennell, and Pierse (then more usually 'Piers') Synnott. Ponsonby (who has now inherited the peerage his father, the Labour politician, Arthur Ponsonby, was given about this time) was brother of Elizabeth Ponsonby, already something of a gossip-column heroine of what came later to be looked on as the *Vile Bodies* world of London. Ponsonby himself liked parties, but had none of his sister's taste for publicity, even if he could be rampageous at times (pulling down about thirty feet of ivy in the Garden Quad one night; then, as the Junior Dean appeared, expostulating: 'The vandals! Look what they have done!'), but was best known as a sympathetic friend, and great recipient of confidences. This made him an expert on the interior life of the College, but, immensely goodnatured, altogether without ambition, he liked the information entirely for its own sake. He told me recently that he was blackballed for The Hypocrites, something hard to believe, but, if true, certainly due to a misunderstanding, as he had many friends there, even if his life seemed to be chiefly concentrated within Balliol.

Ponsonby was friend of Arden Hilliard (son of Balliol's bursar), who had come up to Oxford from Winchester with a Balliol Exhibition and an unmanageable burden of good looks. Handsome, nice mannered, mild in demeanour, Hilliard, at first meeting, conveyed not the smallest suggestion of his capacity for falling into trouble. The variety of ways in which

120

he got on the wrong side of the authorities during his period of residence (prematurely cut short) was both contrarious and phenomenal. He was one of the nicest of men, in certain moods content to live a quiet even humdrum existence; at other times behaving with a minimum of discretion, altogether disregarding the traditional recommendation that, if you can't be good, be careful.

Prudence was even less known to Hilliard than to Alf Duggan, though Hilliard was entirely without Duggan's taste for swagger. Nevertheless, one evening (on his way to The Hypocrites fancy-dress party) he passed through the main gate of Balliol dressed as a nun. After going down there were periods of farming before becoming a captain of infantry during the war; later an erratically charted course that had something of Jude the Obscure in reverse; erstwhile scholar who transformed himself into a rustic swain. A vignette that remains in my mind of this early Balliol period is of being woken up one night to find Hilliard and Ponsonby standing by my bedside. Without a word, one of them held out a brimming glass of sparkling burgundy. I drained it, equally in silence.

The attitude of the University authorities of those days towards the question of 'women' (they were indifferent to homosexuality) is shown by an incident involving Ponsonby and myself. We were returning to Balliol one night (dead sober), when in the High we met a waitress called Nelly, on her way home with another girl, who also worked at The George. Nelly, rather a famous Oxford figure, was known as much for her niceness and good nature in the restaurant, as for her prettiness. We talked to the girls for a minute or two, wished them goodnight, and returned to college. The following day Ponsonby and I were both sent for by the Proctors. 'You were seen talking to women at a quarter to twelve last night in the High.' A Proctorial spy had followed us, enquired our names at the Balliol gate, then shopped us. We were not fined, but given a stern warning.

Although I associate Ponsonby mainly with life in Balliol, he introduced me to several friends from other colleges, including Roger Fulford (future royal historian, better known to me after coming down), who had sustained a considerable rôle in Evelyn Waugh's life at Lancing, owing to their being new boys the same term, and the only two allowed to speak to each other. Fulford was at Worcester, then rather a hearty-dominated college; Trinity, which housed Bobbie Cross and Marcus Cheke, also at

121

the time rather stuffy. These last two came up my second year. Cross, lively, with strange slit eyes claimed to derive from Red Indian blood (his father, surgeon-colonel of The Life Guards, had married a well-off American lady), was tubercular, went down early, and died young. Cheke, tall, thin, very fair, recalled in appearance, as well as name, Sir Andrew Aguecheek, as usually played; and was in due course knighted. He looked like a Cruikshank drawing, especially when he would sometimes wear a lavender frockcoat inherited from a great-grandfather, and ride a bicycle, which, if not a penny-farthing model, was of equally vintage type. Neither Cross or Cheke belonged to any conventional brand of 'aesthete', nor were they Hypocrites frequenters.

As Trinity was next door to Balliol, Trinity men who, as Balliol guests, overstayed the closing at midnight of college gates, could be lowered home by certain windows. The most convenient place to effect this defenestration was a guest-room, usually unoccupied; but one night, when Cheke and Cross were being helped through the window by several Balliol friends, it turned out that someone was sitting up in bed there. Whoever it was took the intrusion pretty well, the light being turned on only for a few seconds. His identity was never ascertained with absolute certainty, but everything pointed to the disturbed sleeper being the College Visitor, Lord Grey of Fallodon, a former Foreign Secretary.

During my first year, Pierse Synnott (denounced by Lindsay as a 'gilded popinjay') was inclined to join in Balliol escapades of this sort, though I think The Hypocrites was not much in his line, even if he occasionally went there. Towards the end of the year Synnott put all dissipation behind him, committing himself to Greats and a Double First; prelude to becoming *haut fonctionnaire* at the Admiralty. He had good contacts with dons (Roman Catholic affiliations with Urquhart), and it was through Synnott that I met Maurice Bowra. I feel pretty sure too (perhaps through the Bowra connexion) that in Synnott's rooms I first examined *The Waste Land*.

Peter Quennell, arriving at Oxford with an already respectable reputation as poet, also on easy terms with celebrities like Gosse and the Sitwells, was somewhat alarming in his freshman sophistication. His pale yellow hair, attenuated features, abstracted demeanour, seemed all a young poet should be; an appearance that could mislead those who did not expect a businesslike attitude towards literature, and down-to-earth

approach where the opposite sex was concerned; the second of those particularly rare in the Oxford circles here described. In fact the only occasion when I ever met an 'undergraduette', while I was up at the
University, was when a girl from one of the women's colleges sprained
her ankle one afternoon in Quennell's company, and I helped assist her
through Balliol quad. Balston (at the recommendation of Edith Sitwell)
came up to Oxford with the aim of securing Quennell's name for the
Duckworth list; in which it eventually figured much later with a first
brief handling of the poet Byron. Quennell did not frequent The Hypocrites. I remember him lending me Turgenev's *Sportsman's Sketches*, the
unadorned style of which was then rather above my head.

Quennell's poetic exterior as an undergraduate led to an outstanding
example of the birth of legend. During wartime military liaison duties it
came my way to attend a dinner-party given for King Haakon of Norway
and the Crown Prince Olaf. Prince Olaf (now King of Norway) had come
up to Balliol my second year. I had not known him there, but was presented at this dinner as a fellow Balliol man. After dinner the Crown
Prince talked of Balliol days. He said: 'And do you remember that fellow
Quennell, who used to walk through the quad holding a lily in his hand?'
I admitted that I had never had the good luck to witness such an occasion. The Crown Prince was plainly surprised. 'Yes, I assure you—' turning to those round about he demanded attention: *'The man walked
through the quad holding a lily! Would you believe it?'*

Quennell was rather justifiably indignant when I told him the story, because, far from walking Piccadilly (more literally Balliol quad) with a
poppy or a lily, his fullblooded tastes had brought an abrupt end to an
Oxford career. On several occasions he asked me to undertake the offices
required for masking an absentee's bedroom, but one night—like Alf
Duggan—Quennell omitted to detail a friend for these duties. Lindsay
sent him down.

Synnott once remarked: 'Connolly and Quennell have a complex that
they are the two great men of Balliol.' Whether or not that were true, the
view (before Quennell's withdrawal) was not wholly unreasonable; Connolly having exchanged his school impetus for a strangle-hold on Urquhart; Quennell with already published works, and more in the offing.
The Hypocrites was uncongenial to Quennell, though he probably appeared at the Club at one time or another; to Connolly The Hypocrites

was not even to be thought of. Connolly was no less further removed from such everyday Oxford spheres as indicated by the names of the Union, OUDS, or Bullingdon. Even by Balliol standards he lived a life apart; one more resembling the 'correct' intellectual undergraduates of two or three years before, but without their smooth social gambits.

I do not remember where I first met Connolly at Oxford; possibly in Urquhart's rooms; possibly with Synnott. A good idea of what might be called the 'Urquhart end' of Balliol (its livelier side, for there was a stodgy one too) is suggested by the Connolly/Blakiston Letters. This nook of the College included Patrick Balfour (now Lord Kinross, traveller and journalist), and was penetrated by rays from Maurice Bowra and his constellations; the latter to be considered in due course. Connolly and Blakiston, together with Synnott and Henry Yorke (by then arrived at Oxford) were to be of the châlet party, which I refused. Certainly Yorke did not go either. The *Letters* indicate the manoeuvring that would take place over such matters; Connolly forcing his will on Urquhart; Urquhart's reprisals by unexpectedly inviting all sorts of people Connolly regarded as bores. Vis-à-vis Urquhart (from whom he is generally believed to have extracted a more or less regular subsidy), Connolly occupied a far more commanding position than the casual don/undergraduate relationship implied by the term 'Sliggerite'.

One summer afternoon in my first year, Connolly asked me to come on the river with him. On the way down to where a canoe was to be hired, he enquired: 'Do you like adventures?' Uncertain what exactly he meant (probably still rather awed by his school prestige) I gave a tempered reply in favour of adventure; one not to be taken as involving anything too wholesale. When we were afloat Connolly directed the boat up a side stream, where flowed some mild rapids evidently already known to him. The adventure consisted in paddling violently against the current, so that the stones were at last surmounted while travelling upstream.

The incident illustrates a side of Connolly not widely recognized; the fact that, although the first in any company to become bored, he retained keen pleasure in certain childish activities. This taste for canoeing against rapids is referred to in the *Letters* (together with one for cutting sticks, and throwing them as assegais); and, fifteen years later, staying with Connolly, and his first wife, Jean, in a small house they had rented in Sussex, he repeated (this time my wife the passenger)

124

his performance of paddling a boat upstream against some minor hazard.

In my second year there came up to Balliol a future friend, of whom I never saw a great deal at Oxford, but often visited later, who, up to his death in 1969, would read the proofs of my books, never without making improvement. This was Wyndham Ketton-Cremer, who, like Quennell—in a manner more traditional, less sophisticated, though scarcely less assured—arrived with already some name as a poet. An odd mixture of shyness, humour, obstinacy, shrewd judgment, literary sensibility, love of country life, Ketton-Cremer was always well behaved. He never seemed to need the mildest form of saturnalia. To the end of his days an additional glass of sherry before dinner, one of port after, represented the height of his indulgence. At Balliol he did not always avoid rowdy companions. His friend John Bowle (historian and Marlborough crony of John Betjeman), with others, would sometimes become impatient at Ketton-Cremer's staidness. One longed for him to get drunk, swear, fall down, break a window, even if he remained (as he always did) uncommitted as to sex. No such outbreak ever took place. Probably he knew what was best for himself.

In his early twenties Ketton-Cremer inherited Felbrigg (a mansion now in the National Trust) near Cromer in Norfolk. The house had come down to him in a curious manner. Original seat of the Wyndham family in the middle 1400s, the estate passed in the 18th century into the hands of owners who took the name of Wyndham, without Wyndham blood. These pseudo-Wyndhams going downhill, the house, with all its contents, was sold in the 19th century to a Norwich merchant called Ketton. Ketton's son died without issue, but his daughter had married a Mr Cremer (Wyndham Ketton-Cremer's grandfather), who was himself half a genuine Wyndham. Accordingly, house, portraits, furniture, in the end passed back to one of Wyndham blood in the female line.

Ketton-Cremer has left his own inspired account of Felbrigg—a grey stone Jacobean façade, the parapet surmounted with high lettering: GLORIA IN EXCELSIS DEO; the back parts of the building, dark red brick of about 1680—a book remarkable for its power and depth of treatment. Here he lived as squire, undertaking a thousand local duties; as author, producing works—notably *Horace Walpole* and *Thomas Gray*—which, in unshowy brilliance, put him in the top class of historical biographers. Ketton-Cremer was also keenly interested in contemporary writing. His suggestions, when reading my own proofs, sometimes indicated that, anyway inwardly, he was not as innocent as some might suppose. Even in his younger days (when not without schoolboy good looks), a tie-wig would have completed Ketton-Cremer's outward appearance; while latterly a full-bottomed peruke seemed almost positively demanded.

To round off these Balliol fragments: Alfred Duggan, although he escaped retribution on the occasion when he had supposedly passed out on my floor, was, like Quennell, sent down a term or two later for spending a night out of college. At this period Duggan's stepfather, Lord Curzon, was Chancellor of Oxford University, a circumstance that may have played a part in the sentence being reduced from total dismissal to mere rustication. Possibly Smith was less inflexible in such matters than Lindsay. By the time Alf Duggan returned to Balliol, Hubert Duggan had come up to Christ Church, and (at his own wish) gone down; the two brothers never being at Oxford simultaneously.

On his reappearance in Oxford, Alf Duggan was at first in a somewhat chastened mood, working hard, drinking comparatively little, not gambling at all, apparently a changed man. Then, for some minor offence like not attending enough roll-calls, he was 'gated' (confined to college from nine in the evening) during a week when some party was taking place which he particularly wished to attend. To do this it was necessary to leave Balliol by some route other than the main gate; later return by climbing in.

In consequence, Duggan asked me to lower him from his first-floor window, which looked out on to St Giles. There was some difficulty in finding suitable tackle for this operation, eventually effected by use of a long woollen Old Etonian scarf. Just as Duggan was suspended from the window, the scarf split in two, causing him to land with a heavy bump on the pavement. He seemed none the worse, threw back the other half of the scarf (which, repaired, survived to keep my younger son, John, warm during an upstate New York winter at Cornell), and proceeded on his way. Unfortunately Duggan drank too much at the party to make feasible climbing back into college. This time his exit from Oxford was final.

Alfred Duggan's subsequent story was an unexpected one. It has been told before, but is worth recalling. For twenty years (during which we met briefly not more than a couple of times) he existed as a spectacular drunk. All sorts of attempts were made to cure him. None had the smallest effect. During the war he pulled himself together sufficiently to serve in the army for a year or two, taking part in the Norwegian campaign. Then, after the war, in his late forties, he made a tremendous effort of will, not only giving up drink, but opening for himself an entirely new career.

In 1950, when I was editing the novel-review pages of *The Times Literary Supplement*, a publisher asked that a first novel by an unknown writer should not be overlooked on the grounds of belonging to an obsolescent genre of literature. The author was called 'Alfred Duggan'. I remarked how strange that I should have known someone of that name; the last man on earth to attempt an historical novel. The book was clearly well done, and went out for review. Only appreciably later did I learn that the unbelievable—as so often—had taken place. Alf Duggan had begun a new career.

Although Duggan's novels do not attain Kipling's mastery of character and situation, they are seen through the eyes of a contemporary in the same manner as Kipling's historical stories, and have a similar accuracy of detail as to daily life of the period, such as correct descriptions of armour. The sense of conviction with which they are written gives narrative force, and they are in some way entirely individual to Duggan. After establishing himself as a writer, and something of a local archaeologist, he married, settling in Herefordshire, whose feudal past offered a perfect background for the historical imagination. Visiting him there a few years before he died in 1964, one felt that those, like Kenneth Bell and Lord Curzon, who had seen promise, were proved not so very far wrong.

2

On my first or second Sunday in Oxford, I had been taken to a morning gathering, regularly given at his rooms in Beaumont Street, of an odd fish called George Kolkhorst. Kolkhorst (who for some reason encouraged his friends to address him as 'Gu'g') held an unexalted position in donnish hierarchy as Lecturer in Spanish. He was fairly well off; an income believed to be derived (though grave doubts have been cast on this legend) from shares in the Lisbon tramways. At these Sunday morning parties, Kolkhorst, who spoke in a reedy voice, always articulating with great care, used to wear a silk dressing-gown, and eyeglass hanging from his neck by a broad black ribbon. Sherry or madeira was dispensed in small glasses. In a little secret book Kolkhorst would record from time to time his own epigrams; hatched with herculean effort. The Widow Lloyd once referred to him as Mr Turveydrop, but the name, coming to Kolkhorst's ears, caused little bad feeling as he seemed unversed in Dickens.

Just as The Hypocrites had been taken over by Acton, Byron, and their friends, Kolkhorst's Sunday mornings were similarly invaded; though I think that was a Byron enthusiasm which Acton did not share. Even within the host's own Oxford terms of reference some of the more faithful Kolkhorst frequenters were of an extraordinary dimness. John Betjeman (who came up my third year, and I met at Oxford only once) has impishly stated that Kolkhorst and Bowra were in rivalry. This pronouncement is not to be taken too seriously, Bowra moving in a donnish empyrean, compared with the seedy salon of Beaumont Street. Nevertheless, each would speak disparagingly of the other: Bowra always referring to Kolkhorst as 'Kunthorse'; Kolkhorst, to 'that fly in the ointment on the seats of the mighty', or the 'Twelfth Man of the Upper Ten'.

Among other people met for the first time at this *après midi de Kolkhorst* was Evelyn Waugh, then (having come up in a by-term) technically in his third year, and a famous Oxford figure. I was introduced by Clonmore, who said: 'I'm glad to see you put on a suit for Sunday, Evelyn.' The suit in question was dark blue double-breasted, the coat open. Small, rather pink in the face, his light brown wavy hair not far from red, Waugh nodded severely, at the same time giving utterance to a curious little high-pitched affirmative sound, a mannerism that always remained with him. He showed no disposition to chat. His air then—and when we met in Oxford later—was of a man disillusioned with human conduct, a man without ambition, living a life apart from the world. This was in any case what one was inclined to feel in one's third year, but Waugh (as described in *A Little Learning*) had consciously withdrawn from earlier University activities of a popular sort, undergraduate journalism, the Union, the OUDS.

I do not remember where I next came across Waugh (possibly with Quennell, with whom he had pre-Oxford acquaintance), but that was quite soon. We never knew each other at all well as undergraduates, though always on good terms. I was invited at least once, if not more, to an 'offal' luncheon at Hertford, where about half-a-dozen of Waugh's cronies, mostly from his own college, would eat 'commons' in his rooms. These lunches were highly enjoyable, without any of the self-consciousness apt to attend more pretentious undergraduate luncheon-parties. Waugh himself seemed to enjoy them. His moods were always unpredictable. He could be disagreeable to persons he took against, weaving grotesque fantasies about them, but he was the most generous and compelling of hosts; though innate melancholy was never far away.

At this date Waugh did not at all identify himself with Oxford's rank and fashion as conventionally understood; in fact (as the opening pages of *Decline and Fall* indicate) he was, if anything, hostile to the smart ethos of the Bullingdon or anything resembling that. His own earlier celebrity had been at a level on the whole inimical to the nihilistic side of Hypocrites life and culture, which was not well disposed to what was regarded as more commonplace undergraduate activities. *The Cherwell*, edited by John Sutro, himself a Hypocrites figure (and non-stop professional mimic of exceptional talent), was recognized as rising above the humdrum. Waugh was a contributor, doing the magazine's illustrated headings. Some of my own drawings appeared in *The Cherwell*, as well as a few reviews, but, although invited on one or two occasions, I never managed to participate in Sutro's other offshoot, the Railway Club.

It was still relatively an Age of Innocence for most of those concerned with this aspect of the Oxford scene, one greatly to alter in the next two years; become less rackety, more political, more snobbish. So far as *Brideshead* presents a naturalistic picture of the University of that epoch (some contemporaries, myself not among them, think it does), the novel is closer to the times when Waugh used to come up to see old Oxford friends (of which he has left a pungent account in the Diaries) during his purgatorial interlude of schoolmastering.

When not suffering from melancholy, Waugh had extraordinary powers of improvising—and carrying through—antics on so extensive a scale that (as his biographer, Christopher Sykes, suggests) a great professional comedian seems to have been lost in him. In those days he had the gift, by no means universal, of being intensely funny when drunk. The sessions he devoted to ragging ('mocking', to use a Waughism; another favourite Waugh term, 'zany') were likely to take certain routine forms. One of these was 'mocking Marples' (an undergraduate whose only foible, so far

129

as I know, was to keep in his window a bowl of goldfish); or, under Urquhart's sitting-room that looked out on St Giles, singing—to the tune of *Here we go gathering nuts in May*—the (certainly unjust) jingle: 'The Dean of Balliol lies with men'. It was chiefly at crowded gatherings where he was likely, if in good form, to be putting on some sort of performance, that Waugh and I saw each other at Oxford; tête-à-tête meetings not taking place until my early days of working in London.

Hubert Duggan came up to Christ Church in the summer term of 1923; and immediately took a dislike to Oxford. This attitude was in contrast with his brother's, for, although Alfred showed no capacity for adapting himself to the rules of the University, he thoroughly enjoyed being there. Hubert, on the other hand, fell into deep depression at once. No aspect of undergraduate life, drunk or sober, appealed to him. Unlike Alf, variously prepared to hunt, play poker, drink at The Hypocrites, impress his tutor with an essay, Hubert—who spoke highly of girls in Argentina—had no taste for any of those things. He went down at the end of the term; later joining The Life Guards. While he was still at Oxford we used to see a good deal of each other, but, after going down, he disappeared, naturally enough, into the *beau monde*; which swallowed him up, producing perhaps no great happiness.

While Hubert Duggan was still at Oxford, we were both involved in an absurd, and not very creditable, incident that began by an Eton friend of Duggan's driving over from Sandhurst with another cadet. We may all have met at Reading, as halfway house, and lunched in the neighbourhood. As well as the two RMC cadets, Duggan and myself, the party included Byron (who possibly wished to study some architectural feature of Reading), with another Oxonian, identity now forgotten. The penultimate stage of the excursion was dinner in or near Camberley, to which we finally returned with the Sandhurst couple. No doubt a fair amount was drunk. After dinner it was decided that the visiting party should take a look at the Royal Military College. This venture was a hazardous one, Sandhurst regulations (in precise contradistinction to Oxford's) being comparatively liberal about 'women', but rigorously severe as to 'drink.'

The RMC consisted of two buildings, the Old and the New, to some extent separate from each other in administration, so that cadets who saw us assumed that we were also cadets from the other building. A dance was in progress—a weekly affair—and couples were moving in and out from the ballroom to the grounds. Byron, who never did things by halves, threw himself into this adventure with his usual enterprise. He had somehow become possessed of a roll of lavatory paper, and, stationing himself at the door of the ballroom, handed a few sheets to every couple as they left the room. I saw this happening momentarily, but Duggan and I, both relatively sober, were in some manner occupied elsewhere; perhaps saying goodbye to the Etonian friend, who, foreseeing trouble, had decided to lock himself in his quarters. The other cadet had disappeared. I do not know what arrangements had been made for a rendezvous to return to Oxford—perhaps the car had been hidden—but, when Byron appeared there, it turned out that he had—not without all reason—been thrown in the Sandhurst lake.

On the homeward journey, still dripping torrentially, his teeth chattering because it had turned rather cold, Byron, in his exacerbated voice, though sometimes unable to speak with laughter at the thought of all that had happened, described how he had been put on 'a sort of gun-carriage', trundled down to the lake, then quite gently propelled into the water. He suffered no after-effects from this immersion. The other cadet, less prudent than Duggan's friend, or less lucky, allowed himself to be seen in a supposedly intoxicated condition, for which he was courtmartialled and sacked.

Quite a long time after this happened, I was told that two versions of the incident had taken shape in Sandhurst legend: one, that a raiding party of several hundred Oxford undergraduates had come over, and, after a pitched battle lasting several hours, been repulsed; the other, that the whole story was absolutely imaginary, an invention that had somehow grown up over the years, a neurotic fantasy, perhaps a solar myth.

A final vignette of my first year: I went round to Hubert Duggan one morning, probably between nine and ten o'clock. On entering his sitting-room, I saw the bedroom door was open. A middle-aged man, wearing a grey homburg, was standing by the bed talking to Duggan, who had not yet risen. I thought possibly a tradesman had come to deliver some goods, measure the window for curtains, possibly press that a bill should be paid. A don, wearing a hat, would be unlikely to be holding a conversation with an undergraduate in bed at that hour. As the two continued to talk, I decided to return later in the morning. By the time I came back Duggan was up and dressed.

'I overslept this morning,' he said. 'When I woke up, who should be standing by my bedside but the Chancellor.'

The man in the grey hat had been Curzon.

3

My first Long Vacation I planned as a Grand Tour of Europe. I have forgotten who my companion was to be in the first instance, but he fell through for one reason or another; as did a substitute. Somebody said that Archie Lyall, then in his second year at New College, intended to visit the capitals of Central Europe that summer. We had briefly met in my first term. It was arranged that we should travel together; a rendezvous fixed in Venice, as Lyall wanted to start a week or two earlier. An untypical Wykehamist, in middle life a quirky Falstaff without the same high spirits, he was less *outré* in those days; though signs of the later Lyall were already apparent. We got on pretty well during the trip, but rarely ran across each other afterwards. Most of what I know of his subsequent career comes from a little privately printed Memoir, produced after his death in 1964, by friends (among them Ketton-Cremer), who greatly valued him as an eccentric figure.

Lyall was to have been a barrister, but, never managing to settle down to the Law, wrote several travel books, and—said to be a useful manual—*A Guide to the 25 Languages of Europe*, a handbook at which he had begun to work during our travels together. When the war came (possibly before that too) he was employed on various more or less secret missions; in due course served with SOE; a legal training caused him to be appointed judge in some ramification of the Allied Military Government. When that was over Lyall worked intermittently as a film actor, consequence of a talent-scout seeing him making faces in a restaurant. I last met him in connexion with his hobby of collecting limericks (perhaps bawdy verse in general), as I had recorded some of Constant Lambert's, which Lyall wished to transcribe. At that period, the early 1950s, married to a Jugoslav lady, he was living comparatively lavishly in South Kensington. The marriage did not last. At the end Lyall seems to have become rather a sad nomadic figure; among other qualifications, authority on the brothels of Europe and the individual characteristics of their respective ladies. This proficiency was acquired at a stage later than our tour, which included no such investigations.

From Venice, Lyall and I took a train to Trieste, arriving after midnight. Hotel porters, names on their caps, were waiting at the station. We chose one with some familiar designation like 'The Royal' or 'The Bristol', and were conducted to a vehicle. It was soon clear that our hotel was not in the centre of Trieste. The car entered the suburbs, bumping along over tramlines. Then the tramlines terminated. The outskirts of the city were left behind. Now it was dark tree-lined roads. These went on interminably. We began to feel some trepidation, but there was nothing to be done. Finally the car stopped before the high gates of what appeared to be a small park. They were opened. The car proceeded up a winding drive. At the top of the slope, sure enough, was an hotel. Very tired, we turned in without further enquiry.

The prospect of sun and sea outside the window the following morning made all worth while. We were at Miramare. Close by, overlooking a sparkling Adriatic, stood the little Victorian castle of the Archduke Maximilian, briefly Emperor of Mexico. Below its neogothic turrets the water was of an incredibly blue transparency. Rocks and marine vegetation, absolutely clear in its depths, recalled—seemed to embody—those other contrasted blues of Manet's melancholy soldier, glancing down at his rifle.

In due course we returned to Trieste, a town I am always glad to have visited as scene of Svevo's *Confessions of Zeno*; a novel with the barest descriptions of its setting, yet somehow well conveying the background, with the harbour's long sloping promenade. Then a gruelling train journey took us to Belgrade. The company in the carriage was reasonably amusing, two ladies (an Austrian *Gräfin*, now Jugoslav, her rather flirtatious blonde friend), and a baron (his visiting card revealed him) of indeterminate origins, travelling in cosmetics. As the taps on the train ran dry the following morning, the Baron shaved in beer. He is responsible over the note in *Lyall's Languages* to the effect that confusions can arise for the phrase 'public house' (in Great Britain, an inn; on the Continent, a brothel), and is to some extent model for Count Bobel in an early novel of mine, *Venusberg* (1933).

Belgrade, untidy, down-at-heel, without attempt at being planned as a town, was in those days also not without all Comic Opera allure. Along the river bank, the *cafés-chantants*, opening at ten o'clock in the morn-

133

ing, if not earlier, were filled with pretty Serbian girls and topbooted officers, white tunics, red breeches, long swords. At night, mysterious arch-
ways led to courtyards where an audience of about a dozen middle-aged
men would be listening to gipsy music. One wanted that sort of thing
more than museums in those days. From Belgrade, through the monotonous Hungarian plain, we travelled by Danube to Budapest. It meant sitting up all night, but the cost was only about fifteen shillings in English
money. On the boat a man addressed me in an unknown tongue; then
added incredulously 'Sprechen Sie nicht bulgarisch?' To one of these Da-
nubian trips (we went by river also to Vienna) I owe another *Venusberg*
character, Count Scherbatcheff, a White Russian.

Budapest was lively, flashy, full of propaganda about the Transylvanian
lands gone to Rumania; showing far less than Vienna the ravages of war,
where some of the many beggars still wore tattered grey uniforms.
Prague, the final capital of the trip, the weather dull, somewhat disappointed by the extent of drab modern buildings that overlaid the ba-
roque. Here Lyall was to prolong his Czechoslovakian visit with friends. I
proceeded home, arriving in London with a last half-a-crown to pay the
taxi.

That autumn, 1924, my father was sent to Finland as staff-officer to
the major-general heading a British Military Mission (which included a
sailor and airman), requested in an advisory role by the Finnish Government. Accordingly, I spent two Oxford vacs at Helsingfors (the Swedish,
rather than Finnish name, Helsinki, then in general English use); thereby
experiencing a new entirely unfamiliar mode of life that was certainly a
contrast with Salisbury or Camberley.

Venusberg, again, recalls some of these Finnish interludes, though
much of the novel's background, especially the political circumstances,
are altogether imaginary, with no bearing on what was happening in Finland at the time; nor, for that matter, in the neighbouring Baltic States,
not yet overrun by the USSR. The town described in *Venusberg* is a mixture of Helsinki (where we lived in an hotel facing a 'modernismus' railway station on the far side of a wide square), and Reval (as Tallin was
still apt to be called), the Estonian capital across the Gulf of Finland,
where I spent a weekend. The architectural admixture of this ancient
Hansa city, with the modernity of Helsinki, apparently produced an ap-
proximation to Riga, capital of Latvia, which I did not visit.

Finland, ruled for six hundred years by Sweden, possessing a Swedish-Finn 'ascendancy' class not without all parallel to the Anglo-Irish (including descendants of soldiers of fortune with names like Ramsay or Fleming), was absorbed by Russia after the Napoleonic wars. In theory Finland was to remain a semi-independent grand duchy, with its own political institutions, but throughout the 19th century an increasing policy of Russification resulted in much unrest there. In 1919 Finland became independent, following civil war in which the Swedish-Finn, General Mannerheim, defeated the Bolsheviks. After independence, a strong nationalist movement curtailed Swedish-Finn influences in all branches of the country's life, in favour of those exclusively Finnish; a process under way when we were there, though not yet run its full course.

Most Finns detested the Russians, Tsarist or Soviet, but their social life, to a considerable extent Scandinavian, had inevitably been influenced too by Russian domination. One entered a social world, familiar in Russian novels, of which there was no precise English equivalent: diplomatic; official; military; professorial; everyone knowing everyone else; no one at all rich; everybody inhabiting flats. Dinner-parties took place at the mid-Victorian hour of five-thirty in the afternoon—sometimes advanced to six-thirty as concession to foreigners' taste for dinner at a late hour—and, if the occasion did not merit a white tie, the older generation of men would wear (rather than the modern dinner-jacket) a black tie and black waistcoat with a tailcoat. The considerable colony of White Russian refugees augmented the sense of living in a 19th century Russian novel or Scandinavian play.

Finland then had a Prohibition law, only thin beer allowed, though something stronger was almost always available at parties. The triennial ball given by the nobility—that is to say the Swedish-Finn gentry, a class living very modestly—took place on one of my visits. After the President had arrived, a fanfare of trumpets announced the entry of General Baron Gustav Mannerheim (to whom I was presented in the course of the evening), an impressive figure. He had been lieutenant-general in the Tsarist army, and, having some turn for writing, his memoirs are worth reading; especially the ride through Central Asia. At this ball the mazurka (forbidden under Russian rule) was danced, a more complicated Sir Roger de Coverley, attractive to watch.

At the invitation of the Military Mission's interpreter, Captain Hameen-Antilla (later, I believe, a general), I spent a weekend at Viborg (Viipuri, now annexed by the USSR), an old border fortress with a castle. Hameen-Antilla's regiment, The Karelian Guard, was stationed there, and (to celebrate some national event) a big party was taking place. We dined in Mess at five or five-thirty, prelude to one of the longest jollifications I have ever attended. First was a theatrical entertainment at the town-hall; then dancing until midnight in another part of the same building; after which a second show took place in the theatre. When the later performance was over, dancing continued until dawn. We walked back at six through the streets of Viborg after an enjoyable party that had taken up just about twelve hours.

These Finnish visits brought vividly alive the societies described, on the one hand, by Strindberg and Ibsen; on the other, by Dostoevsky and Chekhov. For that reason alone I have always been grateful for them. They were also a useful education in learning that one's own country's ways of doing things are not necessarily everyone else's; and (being deplorably bad at languages) I became something of a master of broken English, an asset when serving as liaison officer with the Allies sixteen years later.

The shortcomings of insularity, to which the Finnish trips were a stimulating antidote, are illustrated by a story told me by one of their distinguished professors, an anthropologist. On his first visit to England, many years before, he had paid a visit to a fellow don, at which university in the United Kingdom I do not remember. The Finn was wearing the galoshes habitually used against the snow and slush of the northern winter. He left these overshoes in the hall. After their talk, his host accompanied him to the front-door. Seeing his guest's galoshes lying side by side, he took a run, giving a kick that sent them far up the passage; at the same time explaining: 'We don't wear those beastly things here!'

When the Mission's tour of duty was at an end, we travelled back over Sweden, Norway, and Denmark, to Hamburg, where the streets were littered with the torn posters and scattered pamphlets of a recent election. Hindenburg had just become German Chancellor.

Foreign travel during this undergraduate period seems best handled collectively, before reverting to termtime Oxford. Romney Summers was always planning elaborate journeys, many of which never took shape, and he spoke of driving his car to Vienna that summer, the Long Vacation of

1925, with an old friend of his, Geoffrey Allen. Summers suggested I should join them. This was a chance not to be missed. We met at Dinard, then almost an English seaside resort (where it took Summers six days to galvanize himself into moving; at the end of which the hotel accidentally sent my luggage back to England, its return occupying another three days), and set off across France for the Swiss frontier.

Allen had been at Goodhart's, but, two or three years older, and leaving early, had been known to me only by sight. Preferring not to attend a university, he had gone into the family business, which had to do with advertisement hoardings. His elder brother, Bill Allen, had come down in tradition as a great ragger of Goodhart (after making some prevarication, and being told to report to his housemaster immediately, he had turned up wearing only one sock), but Geoffrey Allen was not at all obstreperous. Although an agreeable companion for that sort of trip, he was less interested in art and letters than perhaps anyone I have ever met; entirely unimpressed by the whole notion of that side of life. In him intellectual energies were directed to such fields as buying the ideal suitcase or picnic basket, regarding either of which his advice was always worth having.

The only incident I remember on the journey east across France took place in a small provincial restaurant, where several young Frenchmen at the next table had spent the whole meal having a row about money. On the way out, Summers said in a friendly voice, as if in farewell greeting: 'Don't argue about tuppence, or I'll have you publicly buggered.' This valedictory comment was politely acknowledged. We were taking a route through Valais and Grisons, a part of Switzerland then not much explored, country of mediaeval castles. These cantons had only recently admitted motor vehicles, and were to vote on this experiment in two years' time. It was not uncommon to travel for several miles behind a haycart, the peasant deliberately refusing to steer a foot or two towards the side to allow a car's passage.

In Vienna (Austria exceptionally cheap on account of the exchange) we stayed at Sacher's; not the grandest hotel, but with romantic archducal traditions that had something in common with those of Rosa Lewis's Cavendish Hotel in London. Sacher's was, of course, more *de luxe*, less eccentric, than the Cavendish, but Frau Sacher roamed about the place in somewhat the Rosa Lewis manner, and gave us each a slice of her famous chocolate cake. On the return journey Allen went back by train (possibly because he did not trust Summers to get him home on schedule), Summers and I setting out this time for the Italian passes. Entering northern Italy, we crossed its bare mountain plateau, in the middle of which a huge gilt angel has been surrealistically set up, memorial to the victory of Vittorio Veneto. Our exit was by way of the Mont Cenis, where autumn's first fall of snow had taken place, and we were warned to keep an eye out for bandits.

Towards the end of that same year, 1925, a few weeks before my twentieth birthday, my father took some leave in Paris. I accompanied my parents there. On that vacation Marcus Cheke, cramming French for the Foreign Office examination, was living in Paris with a French family. Cheke's diplomatic career was an unusual one. He had always liked appearing at fancy-dress parties as an ambassador in stars and ribands, but was never regarded by his friends as a very serious candidate for the Diplomatic Service. Nevertheless, he passed, though too low to be offered a place. Failing to become a regular diplomat, Cheke (whose father was a retired Gunner colonel) took the comparatively unusual step, for someone in his circumstances, of settling down as an honorary attaché at British legations in Europe. He was in Portugal when the war came, and was there absorbed into the regular Foreign Service. He rose in due course to be Deputy Marshal of the Diplomatic Corps; then Minister to the Holy See. In the latter post a great favourite with the Pope, he had some name for pomposity in the former. Cheke's manner in middle life (he died in his fifties) could certainly be stilted, but I think there remained underneath some of the uncertainty and love of comedy of his undergraduate days, and that he was simply acting out a vast diplomatic fancy-dress party that had become his whole career.

In Paris, Cheke and I used sometimes to go out together. One afternoon he took me to a place he knew in the Avenue des Champs-Elysées, combination of tea-shop and dance-hall, where you could take tea (or a drink), and foxtrot all the afternoon. Everyone was dancing-mad at that epoch, the *thé-dansant* all the rage. We had no one to dance with—the place (as also Cheke) was of the utmost respectability—but the scene was enjoyable to watch from a table. Amongst a predominantly French clientèle, a tall greyhaired man was clearly wearing a London-cut suit. This middle-aged rather elegant Englishman was dancing with a small decidedly pretty girl, obviously French. Whenever the couple passed our ta-

138

ble the girl cast unmistakable *oeillades* in my direction. I felt elated by this notice—my then inexperience with the opposite sex was beyond belief—and I could not think why anything of the sort should be happening.

Finally it was time to go. Cheke retiring to the *Messieurs*, I was left standing in the large foyer, or anteroom, to the dance-floor. Suddenly I noticed the girl of the *oeillades* also standing by herself on the other side of the room; her partner no doubt absent for the same reason as Cheke. With an enterprise I should almost certainly have lacked a few years later —what Surtees calls, in another connexion, 'the daring pleasure of youth undaunted by a previous fall'—I went quickly across the hall, and, in halting French asked if we could meet. The girl smiled, and said: 'Ici, demain.' We parted before Cheke or the greyhaired Englishman returned.

That night, dining with my parents at the hotel, I could hardly believe what I had done; though the incident was confirmed in my dreams. The following day I said that I was again going out with Cheke, with whom I should also be dining. In the afternoon, overwhelmed with apprehension, I turned up at the *thé-dansant* place at five o'clock, or whatever the appointed hour. A minute or two later the girl arrived. She was undoubtedly pretty. We found a table. The girl said at once that she was called Lulu, and worked at Zelli's; well-known *boîte de nuit* of that era. I grasped for the first time that I had picked up a tart. What on earth else I supposed could possibly have brought about the situation in which I found myself is hard to imagine, but, at the time, such was not what I had thought or intended.

We had something to drink—Lulu a grenadine, myself a *fine*—and danced a bit. She told me she was twenty-six. Certainly she looked no more. I felt far from sure of myself, and ordered another *fine*; which Lulu rightly deplored. Obviously we could not stay at the dance place for ever, though I was not altogether anxious to move on to the next stage of the adventure. Finally a taxi was summoned, and Lulu gave the address of a *maison-de-rendezvous* on the slopes of Montmartre. By this time the unwontedness of the occasion, the two *fines*, most of all the unhappy gift of seeing oneself in some sort of perspective, had removed almost all the right feelings of crude sensuality. The preparatory traditions of the bedroom did not help. The best to be said was that total fiasco was evaded.

Afterwards we dined in a small crowded restaurant known to Lulu, and not far away. This dinner was really the most enjoyable aspect of the whole episode. Lulu, a great talker, made jokes about a couple at a neighbouring table: the man, not a Frenchman, with a beard ('certainement bolchevik'), and his vis-à-vis, a lady with a straw-coloured bob ('une femme troublante'). After dinner we kissed goodbye: Lulu making for Zelli's; myself for my parents' hotel. I felt considerable nervous exhaustion, though in principle better able to face the world.

IX

Skins: Thick, Thin, and Changing

In the summer term of my first year at Balliol, Synnot brought Maurice Bowra, then Dean of Wadham, to my rooms in college. I had, of course, already heard of this famous young don, but without gaining much idea of what he was like, nor why he was famous. Noticeably small, this lack of stature emphasized by a massive head and tiny feet, Bowra—especially in later life—looked a little like those toys which cannot be pushed over because heavily weighted at the base; or perhaps Humpty-Dumpty, whose autocratic diction, and quickfire interrogations, were also paralleled. As against that, the short ringing laughs likely to accompany Bowra's comments were not at all characteristic of Humpty-Dumpty's rather sour resentment, though their tenor could be equally ominous.

Bowra possessed a considerable presence. As a don, he habitually wore a hat and suit; the last, during festive seasons like Commem, sometimes varied by flannel trousers, light grey, though never outrageously 'Oxford' in cut. My memory of the suits is of different shades of brown, but some say they tended, anyway later on, to be grey; whichever colour, they were very neat, always seeming a trifle tight over the outline of a figure essentially solid rather than plump.

This exploratory call went off pretty well. Conversation turning to the poet Byron (rather a favourite topic of Bowra's), he remarked that, in his hearing at the Gilbert Murrays' recently, a visiting notability had asked: 'Are you interested in incest, Professor Murray?', to which the Regius

141

Professor of Greek had rather brusquely answered: 'Only in a very general sort of way.'

After the Balliol meeting I was to some extent included in the Bowra *monde*—or rather one of them, for there were not a few—a world which partook of various others in Oxford, avoiding the extremes of either 'hearty' or 'aesthete', although in itself a little apart from any of the worlds of which it might be said to partake. Immensely generous, Bowra entertained a good deal at Wadham; in my own experience, always undergraduates. I can never recall meeting a don in his rooms. No doubt that was simply a matter of segregation. The dinner-parties were of six or eight, good college food, lots to drink, almost invariably champagne, much laughter and gossip, always a slight sense of danger. This faint awareness of apprehension was by no means imaginary, because the host could easily take offence (usually without visible sign, except to an expert) at an indiscreet word striking a wrong note—anyway one personally unpleasing—in dialogues which were, nevertheless, deliberately aimed at indiscretion. Bowra's reaction was likely to be announced a day or two later.

'What so-and-so said the other night has just come back as Bad Blood.'

The rooms themselves were simply furnished, with few pictures; what pictures, I cannot remember. Later, at the Warden's House, there was a drawing of Bowra himself by Henry Lamb, which almost certainly dated from a visit to Pakenham (now Tullynally) in the early Thirties, when he and the Lambs (Henry and Pansy) had been staying with the Longfords (Edward, 6th Earl, and his wife, Christine) at the same time. The larger surfaces of wall to be regulated in the Warden's House underlined this taste for austere interior decoration; a characteristic worth mention as reflecting Bowra's energetic practical nature, concerned with action, rather than amelioration of his own surroundings; an aspect of himself in contrast with his other—if you like 'poetic'—side, and one he would perhaps have preferred more evenly balanced.

The impact on me, as an undergraduate, of Bowra's personality and wit is one not easy to define, so various were its workings. If the repeated minor shocks of this volcano took many forms, their earliest, most essential, was a sense of release. Here was a don—someone by his very calling (in those days) suspect as representative of authority and discipline, an official promoter of didacticism—who, so far from attempting to expound tedious

142

moral values of an old-fashioned kind, openly praised the worship of Pleasure.

Of course everybody who had got as far as the Nineties at school was familiar with 'older people' (in my own case, Millard), who represented, even recommended, a romantic paganism, but Bowra went much further than that. He was totally free from anything approaching Oxford 'aestheticism' of the Kolkhorstian order. Everything about him was up-to-date. The Bowra innovation was not only to proclaim the paramount claims of eating, drinking, sex (women at that early stage somewhat derided, homosexuality and autoerotism approved), but to accept, as absolutely natural, open snobbishness, success worship, personal vendettas, unprovoked malice, disloyalty to friends, reading other people's letters (if not lying about, to be sought in unlocked drawers)—the whole bag of tricks of what most people think, feel, and often act on, yet are ashamed of admitting that they do, feel, and think.

In the field of personal hates—Bowra made no bones about these—was his suggestion of the Bête Noire Club. Subscribing members of the Club were each allowed one name to put on its list, to be circulated to all other members, who, irrespective of whether or not they personally had anything against the individual concerned, would secretly persecute him on every possible occasion. Not only was the Bowra gospel sustained with excellent jokes, it was seasoned with a sound commonsense and down-to-earthness, distinguishing it not only from pretentious high-thinking, but also from brutal pursuit of self-interest divorced from all good manners. 'You don't get the best value out of your selfishness, if you're selfish all the time.'

Perhaps some analogy might be drawn between first coming in contact with Bowra, and an initiatory dip into the works of Nietzsche; although, so far as I know, Nietzsche's altar was not one where Bowra burned much, if any, incense. No modern philosopher, alone the Ancient Greeks, supplied all he loved and stood for. That, at least, was the impression he chose to give.

The Bowra delivery, loud, stylized, ironic, usually followed by those deep abrupt bursts of laughter, was superlatively effective in attack. I have heard it suggested that another alumnus of Bowra's school (Cheltenham), one a few years older than himself, was reputed to possess a somewhat similarly detonative form of speech—thereby suggesting a common Cheltonian source, probably a master there—but no details were available, and this rumour has never, so far as I know, been authenticated. It is rather the sort of thing people invent about a much talked-of personality like Bowra. Even if a foundation had already been laid, Bowra himself had undoubtedly perfected the mechanism, formidable, succinct, earsplitting, in a manner that could only be regarded as his own. Its echoes are still to be heard (1976) in the tones of disciples, who, in an unfledged state, came heavily under Bowra influence.

One felt immediately, on meeting him for the first time, that Bowra was a man quite different from any met before. This awareness was certainly true of myself, also I think of most other undergraduates, whether they liked him or not. Some very definitely did not. He was prepared— for an acutely sensitive man, as he himself always proclaimed, far too prepared—to make enemies. To any question about drawbacks in his own nature from which he had suffered, he had an invariable reply: 'A skin too few—yet one continues to go out of one's way to court hatred.'

I am, of course, speaking of the young Bowra. As in the Beerbohm cartoons of Old and Young Selves, there was modification—though not all that much modification—with increased age and fame. No doubt sides had been always hidden away from what was revealed to undergraduates, who were simply admitted to an astonishing vision of forbidden things accepted as a matter of course; and with appropriate laughter. Kenneth Bell used to say: 'The wall round the Senior Common Room is a low one, but there is a wall'; a remark not only metaphorically but literally true of Balliol. Bowra, most of the time, ignored this barrier altogether. I remember the unexpectedness of a sudden reminder of his own professional status, sense of what was academically correct, when, after a noisy dinner party at Wadham, someone (not myself) wandering round Bowra's sitting-room, suddenly asked: 'Why, Maurice, what are these?'

Bowra jumped up as if dynamited. 'Put those down at once. They're Schools papers. No indeed . . .'

A moment later he was locking away in a drawer the candidates' answers, laughing that such an outrageous thing had happened, but for a second he had been angry. The astonishment I felt at the time in this (very proper) call to order shows how skilfully Bowra normally handled his parties of young men. One used 'Maurice' as a form of address, but a note from him (usually an invitation) would always be signed 'CMB'.

Even in those early days it was from time to time apparent that Bowra

144

himself was not immune from falling victim to Bowra doctrine, a fact that he—anyway in later life—was far too intelligent not to recognize, and ironically to acknowledge. The showmanship, usually brilliant, was never in the least fraudulent, but only the more naïve of the spectators could fail to grasp that a proportion of it was purely defensive. There were less well fortified Bowra positions to be considered with the well fortified ones. The former sometimes proved vulnerable, not so much to deliberate assault, as to undesigned incursions on the part of disciples speaking too frankly; indeed speaking in the manner Bowra had taught them. They would, for instance, report back painful things other people had said about Bowra himself, which, very naturally, he did not always appreciate. Nevertheless, in spite of such occasional boomeranging, he would stick to his guns, and usually come out on top, or not far from that.

Bowra, less than eight years older than myself, must have been just twenty-six when I first knew him. The fact now seems altogether incredible. Certainly, as indicated, he navigated with perfect ease the waters dividing undergraduate and don. Beyond that stream was a flood not to be crossed; an intangible sense of experience, which—then and for ever—set those who had been 'in the war' apart. Belonging to the strange fascinating brood of survivors, Bowra had come up to New College not only older than the average pre-war or post-war freshman (and far more intelligent), but, with others of his species, already on familiar terms with sex and death. He often spoke of the former; of the latter, very rarely.

So far as sex was concerned, when I first knew him, Bowra always talked as if homosexuality was the natural condition of an intelligent man. I think it extremely unlikely that, as a don, he ever had physical relations with an undergraduate, but he would gossip much of such goings-on, and tease friends like Yorke and me for being 'heterosexual'. His stories about women were rarely obliging, but his own tastes began to run less consistently very soon after this period. He was certainly attracted by women in the course of his life, and actually engaged to be married more than once.

The war was another matter. When he spoke of army experiences it was always with mimicry and laughter. ('Got a boil on your cock, old boy, then crash along to the MO, who'll soon put you right with a Number 9'; or his own battery commander's commendation of *Artillery Training*: 'A book written by far cleverer men than me or you.') All the same, I am

145

sure that the comparatively short (though not unadventurous) time Bowra spent in the army played a profound part in his thoughts. I believe it possible that even at those Wadham dinner parties, when the uproar was at its height, not least on the part of the host, the days and friends of the war were never far away; a shadow falling like Cynara's.

There existed a Bowra system of social terminology which the neophyte had to pick up, and adhere to. That was not at all difficult on account of its convenient terseness, and manner in which it had been designed to cover most human types to be found at Oxford, and elsewhere. Indeed, its total adoption was hard to resist; one of the forms of power Bowra exercised. In this special phraseology, 'presentable' was not merely an important label, but *sine qua non* for being accepted into the Bowra system of things. There existed certainly Bowra acquaintances— kept well in the background—who never quite made the grade, yet were (Bowra being kindhearted as well as ruthless) still allowed some access to the sanctuary; but the status these occupied, even if low, never went so far as the very damaging absolute antithesis, 'unpresentable'. Those who had 'unpresentable' pinned on them were likely to be remorselessly barred.

'Able' (or 'able, I'm afraid') probably did not signify personal approval, but was at worst a fairly high commendation. 'Upright', also not lightly accorded, might be held in its way equally complimentary (if you cared about old-fashioned honourable dealings), but was likely to carry overtones a shade satirical, with also no guarantee of friendliness. 'Nice stupid man', hardly flattering to the object of its designation, was at the same time well disposed, and accorded relatively sparingly. 'Shit of hell', a status in the severest degree derogatory, was in practice inclined to imply, as well as hearty dislike, an element of uneasy suspicion, sometimes amounting to acknowledged fear.

Bowra made great play with these categories, which were an established part of his verbal barrage. There were other important phrases, such as 'make bad blood' (referred to earlier), and 'cause pain'. 'Bad blood' might be used in two different senses. Bowra would remark: 'I made splendid bad blood between so-and-so and so-and-so over such-and-such a matter the other night'; laughing at the thought of what he had brought about. He would also, as has been said, speak despondently of 'bad blood' made in relation to himself. This latter might be deliberate vilification, or a casual phrase later conceived as having snide bearing on

146

himself. 'Cause pain' was likely to refer not to specific attacks of his own, or other people, but the success or good luck of individuals, which brought pangs of envy or jealousy on hearing the news. 'Cause pain' may have had its origins in a favourite saying of the hero of R. L. Stevenson's *The Wrong Box*, also much quoted (and acted upon) by an Eton master, E. V. Slater: 'Anything to cause a little pain.'

These Bowra approaches to life, jocular yet practical, provoking both laughter and trepidation, are hard to preserve on paper. That is true of his—and all other—wit. Bowra's wit could be of the carefully perfected order (none the worse for that), set pieces produced with a flourish for social occasions, many examples of which remain on record; good talkers being apt to be remembered chiefly for their comparatively elaborate *mots*. Excellent as those could be, Bowra's throwaway lines, and comebacks, often surpassed them; thereby marking him out (which cannot be said of all good talkers) as a wit who neither required previous preparation for what he said, nor saved up all the best stuff for smart company. The ephemeral nature of such good remarks prevents them from passing into history, since they ornament conversations too trivial to remember or reconstruct: for example, someone (perhaps myself) commented on a story just told: 'On earth the broken wind . . .', to which Bowra added without a pause ' . . . in the heaven, a perfect sound.' On another occasion a recent graduate spoke of the uncertainty of some job put forward by the Oxford Appointments Committee's secretary, named Truslove; Bowra replying at once: 'How shall I my Truslove know?'

The Bowra world was one where there must be no uncertainty. A clear-cut decision had to be made about everything and everybody—good, bad—desirable, undesirable—nice man, shit of hell. This method naturally included intellectual judgments, and taste in works of art. In one sense, nothing is more expedient in approaching such matters than lucid uncompromising thought, well expressed; in another, the arts inhabit an area in some degree amorphous as their means of creation; in short, a good deal of latitude required for experiment. In the Bowra world there was little or no concession to uncertainty—latterly that was perhaps less true—and, when I first knew Bowra, he always seemed to show a slight sense of uneasiness at activities in art and letters of a too independent sort. That was, of course, within the sphere of Bowra being, in principle, always well disposed to what was *avant-garde*.

147

With all his intelligence and spoken wit, Bowra himself remained throughout his life curiously unhandy at writing. He was a capable, if rather academic and uninspired, literary critic. His comic poems were comic, no more. They possess no unique quality. Any field in which he did not excel was a distress to him, the literary one most of all; one of the reasons why, for young men who wanted to develop along lines of their own, it was better to escape early from Bowra's imposed judgments. There was a touch of something inhibiting. It was preferable to know Bowra for a time, then get away; returning in due course to appreciate the many things he had to offer.

2

Henry Yorke came up to Magdalen in my second year. He has left his own account of Oxford in *Pack My Bag*. He did not find university life sympathetic, though he disliked it less than had Hubert Duggan. This part of the autobiography, too, makes its author sound unnecessarily bleak, and again shows me that I underrated his neurotic pressures. Yorke mentions, for example, that when (in the manner of all sports secretaries) a visit was paid to ask if he wanted to play rugger, he replied that he could not do so, because he suffered from a 'weak heart'. This begins to suggest persecution-mania of a positive sort. Magdalen, a small smart self-contained college in those days, might in a general way be classed as 'hearty', but Yorke, quiet in demeanour and dress, with no reason whatever for being unpopular, was not in the smallest danger of being, say, debagged on the night of a bump-supper. If he possessed undoubted eccentricities, these were not of a kind to excite popular disapproval.

Legend (partly his own) has somewhat overstated the extent of these eccentricities; also Yorke's drinking, which, as an undergraduate, I should have thought on the whole more moderate than that of many of his friends. He did, however, make a point of watching a film every afternoon, and every evening, of his Oxford life; change of programme at the city's three cinemas making this just possible without repetition. He also, without exception if he had control of matter, ate fried fish and a steak every night for dinner. Another of his idiosyncrasies was to shave with ordinary washing soap.

Through connexions of his own Yorke had almost immediately registered as a Bowra friend, and we used obsessively to mull over together Bowra parties and Bowra lore. Yorke also had an introduction (probably through his mother, who must have been just about a contemporary) to Lady Ottoline Morrell at Garsington; a house to which he soon brought me too. Bowra was already a Garsington habitué, and great retailer of Garsington stories.

Garsington conditions have often been described, emphasis usually laid on the exotic appearance and behaviour of the hostess, both of which certainly had to be reckoned with. The worst perplexities always seemed to me to lie rather in the utter uncertainty as to what level of life there was to be assumed by the guest. A sense of 'pre-war' constraint—or rather what one imagined that to be—always prevailed, in fact probably more characteristic of contemporary Bloomsbury than the *beau monde* of earlier days. There was also, I can now see (Harold Acton's memoirs bear out), a war between the generations; young men from Oxford welcome as much to be overawed as encouraged.

At Garsington one more or less wild man was likely to be present, a bohemian exhibit (in Wyndham Lewis's phrase, an Ape of God), making appropriately bohemian remarks. To have these comments addressed to oneself, especially during the many silences that fell, was something to be dreaded. Alternatively, you might be caught out, in quite a different manner, by forgetting, say, the date of Ascot, or the name of some nobleman's 'place'. On the whole the legend of imposing intellectual conversation was the least of Garsington's threats. The arts, if discussed at all, were approached in a manner that—if such can be said without offence—might reasonably be called middle brow; though none the less alarming for that. It was like acting in a play—or rather several different plays fused together—in which you had been told neither the plot, nor your own cue: sometimes a drawing-room comedy; sometimes an Expressionist curtain-raiser; sometimes signs loomed up of an old-fashioned Lyceum melodrama.

On my first visit to Garsington the other guests were David Cecil (by then a don), and L. P. Hartley, who at that time had written only his first novel, *Simonetta Perkins*, a story of a middle-aged spinster, who fell in love with a gondolier. Leslie Hartley and I made no contact on this occasion, but subsequently, as a critic, he gave my early novels encouraging

149

notices, and twenty or more years later, as a country neighbour, we used to see a good deal of him. A somewhat Jamesian figure (a writer he much admired), Hartley had a mild manner that concealed a certain taste for adventure. This took the form of thoroughly enjoying extraordinary *con-tretemps* with members of his own domestic staff. He loved entertaining — and being entertained—and was the most generous of hosts, but would go out of his way to find cooks or butlers of literally alarming eccentricity. If he had kept a day-to-day record of some of the consequences of this hobby, it would make extraordinary reading. One of his favourite anec-dotes was of a cook who worked for him for a short time, mother of a small daughter. Some row took place, and the cook gave notice. Just be-fore her final exit she brought the little girl into Hartley's sitting-room, and said: 'Take a good look at him, Emily, an Oxford man, and a cad.'

Even Bowra was prepared to recognize that an invitation to Garsington was not a matter to be treated lightly. For the most experienced in salon life, it represented moving up to the front line; for a nervous undergradu-ate, an ordeal of the most gruelling order. Bowra, staying once in the house, coming down to breakfast early, had inadvertently eaten the toast (possibly Ryvita, even if toast, toast of some special sort) found in the toast-rack. A short time later Lady Ottoline arrived. She looked round the table. Something was wrong. She rang the bell.

'*Where is my toast?*'

Lady Ottoline's very individual way of speaking, a kind of ominous cooing nasal hiss—often imitated, but, like Goodhart's whinny, never al-together successfully—was at its most threatening. The parlourmaid (also a formidable figure, addressed by name, which I do not remember) fixed her eyes on Bowra.

'The toast was there when *he* came down, m'lady . . .'

Garsington was one of those educational experiences of which, like many of that date, one appreciated the value only much later. The visits belonged, I think, chiefly to my third year, by when Yorke and I had moved from our respective colleges to rooms side by side on the top floor of 4 King Edward Street, the corner house; lodgings in the robust music-hall tradition kept by the redoubtable redhaired Mrs Collins, who herself rarely appeared. In general, undergraduates remained two years in col-lege, and I do not now understand why Yorke went into rooms in the town after his first year. Possibly Magdalen was short of space, and glad for anyone to do that; Yorke's apprehension about being attacked may have also played some part.

Yorke and I used sometimes to give luncheon and dinner parties together at King Edward Street (perhaps two or three times a term), and one of these, which seemed an amusing experiment at the time, I now recognize as a piece of reckless tight-rope walking. We invited both Kenneth Bell and Maurice Bowra to dinner. There were several other guests, and the occasion appeared a great success at the time, even though Bowra, first to arrive, had commented without enthusiasm when he heard Bell was to be there. Throughout the evening, Bell, in his own bluff erratic manner, let fly a coruscation of amusing remarks; Bowra for once keeping relatively quiet. Such a dinner-table combination was not a very tactful one, both from general principles as to the unwisdom of mixing too strong personalities—overseasoning the dish—and, in this particular case, playing tricks with Bowra's own very delicate relationship with the other dons of that day; some of whom were inclined to raise an eyebrow at the ease with which he moved among undergraduates. Bell moved easily among undergraduates too, but in a very different manner. In fact the two of them belonged to such disparate categories of don that no great harm was done; but the risk had been great.

That dinner-party gave an opportunity to learn, which I did not take. Had I been quicker to comprehend its intricacies, later events might have been less gauchely handled; although, the way things fell out—so far as I myself was concerned—could have been for the best.

After returning from Finland, my father went back to his regiment, then stationed at Tidworth (a hutted camp on the Wiltshire/Hampshire border), my parents living for a time a few miles away at Andover, in a 'private hotel'. This residential hotel was a depressing spot. I spent one or more vacs there; also in furnished rooms in the town. One afternoon—I do not remember the season, but summer rather than winter—an obviously hired car turned into the short drive leading to the hotel, and stopped at the entrance. Out of the car stepped Bowra and Synnott. Synnott had perhaps been driving, but some memory remains of a chauffeur. Certainly Bowra was not at the wheel. They said they had dropped in to tea. My parents were out, but arrived back later, and were introduced.

It appeared that Synnott had been staying up for some weeks of the vac (probably in order to work for Greats), and, he and Bowra coming

151

over to this part of the country for a jaunt (possibly to visit the sights of Winchester), had decided to pay a call. I cannot imagine how they knew where I was living. This was an unprecedented excitement in the cheerless Andover day. When it was time to return to Oxford, Bowra put forward the suggestion (which may even have been represented as the object of the visit) that I should come back with them; stay for a day or two with Bowra at Wadham. It would make a change. Synnott, I feel pretty sure, was almost immediately on his way home.

I accepted this proposal in the manner one accepted so much at that age, just as something that happened—rather like being taken to Garsington, or the drive to Vienna—an adventure, more or less. I was very glad to get away from Andover even for a short time. I did not give much thought to what might be expected of me at the receiving-end; which was, I suppose, to make myself reasonably agreeable for a day or two; return home without overstaying my welcome. I remained at Oxford for two or three days, then came back to Andover; but, entirely owing to my own fault, the visit was not a success. This was due to a lack of discernment that goes with immaturity. There was also little to do in Oxford out of term (Bowra himself naturally occupied with his own academic duties during the day), and I was scarcely less bored pacing the High than back at the Andover hotel.

One evening, dining tête-à-tête with Bowra in his rooms, I spoke of how little I liked being at Oxford, and how I longed to get it over and go down. The lack of finesse in voicing such sentiments in the particular circumstances was, of course, altogether inexcusable. The concept that Bowra himself was a young man with a career still ahead of him, about which he no doubt suffered all sorts of uncertainties, even horrors, never crossed my mind. Bowra seemed a grown-up person for whom everything was settled. In a sense that made my gaffe even worse. One learns in due course (without ever achieving the aim in practice) that, more often than not, it is better to keep deeply felt views about oneself to oneself. In any case a litle good sense—a little good manners even—might have warned me that such a confession was not one to make to a slightly older friend, who, even then, was rapidly becoming one of the ever brightening fixed stars of the Oxford firmament. Bowra's own hospitality had no doubt played a part in inducing such plain speaking, but I make no attempt to put forward wine in extenuation.

Skins: Thick, Thin, and Changing

Such sentiments towards Oxford—though shared by Hubert Duggan and Henry Yorke—were uncommon for an undergraduate of my generation, most of whom regarded—still regard—those days as the happiest, etc. I do not in the least wish that I had never been up at Oxford. I owe an enormous amount to my three years there. Nevertheless, although reminiscence of the University has here largely been in the shape of chronicling rackety goings-on, a great deal of my time was spent in a state of deep melancholy. All this burst out at Bowra's dinner-table.

It took some thirty-five years for my relationship with Bowra to recover from that evening at Wadham. I was not put into anything like the worst disgrace possible, condemned to the unmitigated outer darkness to which some might be liable; especially those to whom the phrase 'treading on other people's corns' had been used—and not at the time understood—although Bowra himself did not merely tread on corns, he deliberately stamped on them, as most appropriate treatment. Beyond the adoption of a somewhat tarter form of address, and a falling off of invitations, no spectacular censure took place. We continued to meet while I remained up at Oxford, later sometimes running across each other in London.

Although I regret my maladroitness in causing this rift, I am not sure whether for my own good it was not just as well to be withdrawn from Bowra influence before the grip became all but irremovable. Probably disjunction would in any case have taken place, seeds of variance existing at the stage each of us was approaching, some sort of a temporary break inevitable.

The Bowra story, so far as I am concerned, may be brought to completion out of chronological order. In 1941, while I was awaiting a posting at the Intelligence Corps Depot at Oxford, Bowra lunched with my wife and myself at the Randolph. All went well, even if things were not quite on the footing they once had been. Professor Lindemann had just been raised to the peerage as Lord Cherwell.

'Don't mind that at all,' Bowra said. 'Don't mind that at all. Causes pain. You'd hardly believe the pain it's caused.'

In about 1948, we rented for the holidays a cottage in Kent. While there we met a young man who turned out to be an undergraduate of Wadham, of which Bowra was by then Warden. I asked him how he got on with the head of the house. His praise was abounding. He could not sufficiently commend a man of such distinction, for whom no member of the college was too humble to be noticed, none too geographically remote to be lost touch with after going down; understanding, amusing, hard working, the Warden was a don in a million. 'But', added the young Wadhamite, 'I've heard he's an absolute fish out of water when he's away from the academic world he's accustomed to.'

I cannot imagine any typification that would have annoyed Bowra more; nor, indeed, one that was on the whole less true, though I believe he did find himself not much at ease, towards the end, with certain academic developments in which he had to be involved. The words are, however, of interest in illustrating how easily one can make that sort of mistake at an early age (not necessarily only then), and by showing how profoundly Bowra threw himself into the Warden's rôle. This capacity for taking on with enthusiasm forms of life comparatively alien to those with which he was commonly associated (though in a sense perhaps still possible to call academic) was well illustrated by Bowra on Hellenic cruises.

Never to have seen Bowra on an Hellenic cruise was to have missed an essential aspect of him. The ship would contain close on three hundred passengers, of whom more than half might come from the United States. Bowra (now Sir Maurice) would from time to time lecture, and in general propagate, sometimes in an indirect manner, the archaeological sites to be visited. His lectures at Oxford were not—anyway in the eyes of his colleagues—regarded as Bowra's forte. Those he gave on the cruise were another matter. No one who heard him in the museum at Olympia (Centaurs and Lapiths) could be anything but richly stimulated; an experience really worth having. It might be supposed that a man by this time famous as a scholar, and personality, might have become a trifle unapproachable for the run-of-the-mill tourist. Nothing could have been further from that, nor from his former pupil's assessment of Bowra removed from a conventionally academic setting; at least one very different from Wadham. Bowra was just as likely to be seen at a table of delighted greyhaired matrons from the Middle West or West Kensington, as exchanging cracks with Mortimer Wheeler (or whatever might be snobbishly regarded as the tourist élite) over a *raki* at the bar.

In 1960 my wife and I went on one of these Hellenic cruises, which included putting in at Sardinia, Sicily, Malta, North Africa, as well as Greece. When, with the rest of the party, we met at London Airport, there was a second of wondering how things were going to go, so far as the Bowra relationship was concerned. The plane flew to Milan, then came a longish bus journey to Genoa. Bowra and I sat next to each other on the bus. We talked a lot. Old contacts were re-established. The dé-tente was complete.

At Malta, Bowra asked us (including our son, John, then fourteen years old) to dine with him at a restaurant he knew on the island. This restau-rant was situated on the higher levels of Valletta. We reached it on the way out by taxi; Bowra explaining that we could more easily return by public lift, which operated at regular intervals, grounding its passengers only a short way from the harbour, and our ship. We dined enjoyably, and strolled to the place of the lift. A notice indicated that we had missed the last descent by ten minutes, and were faced with a long and steep journey back on foot.

Four-letter words have been rather overdone of late years, but, when the ex-Vice-Chancellor of Oxford University, President of the British Academy, holder of innumerable honorific degrees and international lau-rels, expressed his feelings (and the feelings of all of us), it was intensely funny.

'Fuck!'

The monosyllable must have carried to the African coast.

On a second cruise that included Bowra the ship passed through the Dardanelles. As we sailed by the shore of Gallipoli, in a brief quite unem-phasized ceremony, a wreath was committed to the sea. Some days later I remarked to Bowra that, although the best part of half a century had passed, the moment of the wreath's descent to the waves had been mov-ing, even rather upsetting. I was not prepared for the violence of agree-ment.

'Had to go below. Lie down for *half-an-hour* afterwards in my cabin.'

After this second cruise, Bowra asked me to be his guest at the Wadham 'Dorothy' Dinner. We stayed with him in college. On the morn-ing we left, I was with him in the hall of the Warden's House, when an undergraduate (bearded) arrived to ask a question or obtain some permission. Bowra fired out a question in the old accustomed explo-sive manner. The young man did not at all react. One knew that an amused—even a naïve—reflex would immediately have achieved a favourable result, but no reaction was visible at all. The undergrad-

155

uate went away. 'I don't understand them at all nowadays,' Bowra said.

Later in the same year Bowra came to us for a weekend. It was during this visit that something (in addition to Gallipoli) convinced me how much the first war had meant to him. We took him to dine with neighbours. There was certainly plenty to drink, but that did not altogether explain what happened after dinner. Bowra insisted—he really did insist—on the whole party spending the rest of the evening singing 'There's a long, long trail a-winding' and 'Pack up your troubles in your old kit-bag'. Perhaps by then he did not often find himself in company where such behaviour was even conceivable. I suppose it is just possible that an evening might have ended in the same way in days when I had first known him, but I never remember anything of the sort; and in any case it would then have been somehow different.

Two additional cruise incidents should go on record. My wife had been dancing *The Blue Danube* waltz with Bowra, the sole dance he recognized, first of all (she reported) pawing the ground like a little bull entering the ring. When we were sitting together afterwards, speaking of invitations, domestic arrangements—some trivial matter, its subject forgotten—she let fall a quite thoughtless comment.

'But surely that's easy enough for a carefree bachelor like you, Maurice?'

Bowra was suddenly discomposed.

'Never, *never*, use that term of me again.'

He laughed immediately after, but for a second it had been no laughing matter; perhaps a sudden touch of what he himself, in the old days, had named 'creeping bitterness.'

The other matter arose one afternoon sailing past Samothrace. Kipling's name had cropped up. Bowra said: 'Have you ever played the game of marking yourself for the qualities listed in *If*—? It's a good one.'

We set about playing the *If* game at once. Rather unexpectedly Bowra knew the poem by heart. I now greatly regret that I did not immediately afterwards write down the attributes Bowra claimed (he was very modest about them), and also the correct system of marking. My impression is that you clocked up half a mark for possessing a quality in principle, another half for improving on the situation; that is to say, trusting yourself when all men doubt you, scoring additionally for making allowance for their doubting too. It is, however, possible that you were assessed for five out of each combined condition. The second system is less likely, because I seem to recall that Bowra gave himself a total of three-and-a-half out of a potential fifteen, or thereabouts. His own comments greatly augmented the pleasures of the game.

'Being lied about, don't deal in lies—that's absurd of course. Next one.'

We came to Triumph and Disaster.

'Can't say about Triumph. Never experienced it.'

'Maurice, what nonsense.'

But he was adamant. He had never known Triumph. All the same he had liked playing the *If* game, and was in very good form after it.

3

I once calculated that nine of my Oxford friends left the University (mostly sent down) by the middle of my second year. I can now bring the total up to seven only; even that number leaving a distinct gap. The names of two others may well have slipped my memory. To some extent in consequence of this elimination, my last year was passed in a comparative retirement. Perhaps, as I have said, that is often what a final year feels like.

By that time there had also been a shift away from the old sort of Oxford life represented by The Hypocrites. It would be impossible—to take a couple of lords as examples—to imagine undergraduates less snobbish than Elmley or Clonmore; but an influx of rather a different sort had followed them, resulting in something of an *entente* between the smarter 'aesthetes', and a 'hearty' world centred on the Bullingdon; while a sprinkling of rich Americans also showed preference for rather self-conscious little cocktail parties. These things are hard to map, but the old knockabout styles were at an end, replaced by attitudes perhaps no more ambitious (because plenty of ambition had been about before), but less happy-go-lucky.

Meanwhile Yorke had placed his novel, *Blindness* (1926), with a publisher; a stroke that demanded from certain people a sharp new assessment of the position of someone who might have seemed well on the way to posing the unanswerable question (set at the start by so many bright young men) of what, when it came to the point, was he going to do. A published novel could not altogether be laughed off. It also dignified our comparatively withdrawn life in King Edward Street. We used to talk a lot about Proust.

In the spring of my last year, 1926, Hubert Duggan, by then in The Life Guards, came up to Oxford to ride in a 'grind'. He brought with him a young American, of whom both the Duggans had sometimes spoken, usually with such phrases as 'he hangs round my mother, and helps do the flowers, that kind of thing'. This was Chips Channon, then in his late twenties. He did not come to the point-to-point, and, when we were alone together, Duggan explained that Channon was now more or less accepted as a friend by himself and his brother; adding that Channon had made himself very useful to Alf after the final sending-down from Balliol; and, Hubert Duggan admitted, had also been good at supplying books, etc., at the time of his own illness. I met Channon again when we came back from the grind. He seemed very friendly, easy to get on with, not at all what I had imagined from the picture painted by the Duggans of what a social climber was like.

I did not see Channon again until twenty years later; the icebound winter of 1947. Violet Wyndham (daughter of Ada Leverson, The Sphinx) gave a dinner-party, something by then rather rare in immediately post-war London. Channon was among the guests. Now a comparatively veteran member of the House of Commons, he was greatly changed from the *beau jeune homme*, who had received letters (which he says he destroyed, thinking them of no great interest) from Proust. I reminded him of our former meeting. The effect was almost startling. He began an impassioned attack on the Duggan brothers, speaking with great bitterness of the way they had treated him. I was prepared for Alf having given Channon a rough ride, and being unpopular, but his deep resentment of Hubert's behaviour surprised me. 'And their drinking!' Channon added. It was one of those spells when Channon was not keeping his Diary, so no record remains, as it might have done, of past vexations recalled by this conversation.

When the General Strike took place in 1926 the country was divided up into areas administered by Civil Commissions designed to deal with emergencies. Most of the personnel of these Commissions was drawn from the regular civil service, each including an army officer to act in liaison with troops stationed in the neighbourhood. One of these Civil

158

Commissions was situated at Reading, where my father was appointed liaison officer. The universities were more or less closed down during the
strike, and it was arranged that I should come over to Reading to work in
the Commission. I had a small office through which passed the letters
brought in, and sent out, by motor-post. This episode (apart from giving
some experience of what working in a government office was like) would
have possessed no great interest had not the Commission itself been
housed in Reading Gaol. The prison had been out of use even then for
many years. Those temporarily working there were shown round. Wilde's
cell was naturally the chief exhibit; the 'foul and dark latrine'. There
were two padded cells: one done up, walls, floor, ceiling, more or less like
a railway carriage; the other—merely for drunks—in rough matting.

During the summer term that year, my last at Oxford, I had to visit
London. It was arranged that Hubert Duggan and I should dine together.
He was then living in quarters at the Household Cavalry barracks in Albany Street, Regent's Park, only a short way from Chester Gate, where,
after I was married, we lived for years, both before and after the war. In
Duggan's quarters, that evening, took place the scene which suggested
the sequence in *A Question of Upbringing*, where Stringham puts off the
Narrator for dinner; and, at the time, it was indeed true that I grasped a
parting of the ways had come. The occasion represents the last moment
in the novel when Duggan might be said to have any direct bearing on
Stringham's doings as described.

After that evening Hubert Duggan and I scarcely met again before
running into each other during the war in White's Club (then accommo-
dating my own, which had been bombed), and having a talk. We were
both captains. 'Of course you don't get into the big money until you're a
major,' Duggan said. That was our last meeting. He died about a year
later. I found myself in the Albany Street barracks again on the day of my
demobilization from the army in 1945. It was there that you handed in
certain items of equipment, and were issued with various documents, before going down to Olympia to choose a civilian suit of clothes.

Before the Oxford Final Schools, a Balliol examination was held called
Collections. At this college try-out I was judged to have done reasonably
well. Kenneth Bell said: 'When you go up for your *viva*, they'll recognize
you're a fairly bright chap, and ask you about what you know.'

Schools took place; the day of the *viva* came. Nothing could have been

further from Bell's prophecy. I was long cross-questioned as to a period of
English mediaeval history (one with which in later life I should have been
glad to be familiar) at which I had hardly glanced. I had also been unwise
in choice of 'special subject' (primary documents to be studied); for some
inexplicable reason insisting on doing the Congress of Vienna, its material
largely in French, and—a language of which I was altogether ignorant—
German. All I can remember from it are unconvincing descriptions of his
love of natural landscape in Talleyrand's dispatches. There were all sorts
of alternative subjects that could have been advantageous; even the offi-
cially recommended English Revolution offering late 17th century background for subsequent interest in John Aubrey.

I took a Third without the satisfying conviction that I had never done a
stroke of work. On the contrary, I had worked quite hard, though without the least sense of direction. As things turned out, nothing could have
mattered less than a Third; but a good degree might have been important. Bell wrote: 'It will be all the same in four or five years' time.' It was
pretty well all the same then and there, even if I expected a Second. My
father—who had perhaps feared a First—did not seem greatly disturbed.
On the whole I was glad to go down, quite looking forward to entering
Duckworth's in the autumn, where I was to spend three years learning
the business of publishing.

Henry Yorke stayed on for a term or two, then decided he would not
take a degree. Instead, he planned to spend some time (in the event two
years) working as an operative in the family business at Birmingham. This
interlude of his, contemporary with some of my own first two or three
years in London, belongs chronologically to that part of the story, but, as
Yorke and I appear in this volume as contemporaries at preparatory
school, Eton, and Oxford, some immediate rounding off seems required.

Yorke usually defined his family's engineering firm as making lavatories
(with flushes creating unusually deafening uproar), though sanitary fit-
tings were subsidiary in the production to such equipment as beer-
bottling machines. His decision to work there has been represented (to
some extent by himself in *Pack My Bag*) as ideological, but I remember
no suggestion of that at the time—though there always existed deep and
secret recesses in Yorke's mind that were not revealed—the motive specifically given as wish to write a novel about factory life from first-hand
experience. In *Living* (1929), though trade unions are not mentioned, and

(for my own taste) the 'experimental' style threatens at times to become laboured, he brought this off with as great force and originality as has probably ever been achieved.

Whether or not it occurred to Yorke from the start that experience 'on the floor' would be ideal foundation for working as executive in the office, I do not know, but that certainly turned out. His remaining elder brother, traveller, scholar, student of esoteric beliefs, chose a path in life far from the world of business; Yorke himself becoming in due course head of the firm (from which he retired at the age of about fifty), while continuing to write his books.

This dichotomy of his life, as suggested earlier, was always something of an obsession with him. Speaking in *Pack My Bag* of his Oxford period, Yorke records: 'Though I am not a Jew a don compared me with Swann. This gave me great pleasure.' As Yorke differed from Swann in almost every essential respect, the comparison cannot be called an apt one, but what people think about themselves is at least as important as what others think of them, and this view of his own condition does underline Yorke's overpowering sense of being divided in two. It was of course true that his life was part business, part writing; but other writers (Kafka, Svevo, Wallace Stevens, Roy Fuller) have also experienced that combined state without finding on that account their nervous system corroded inwardly, or being in the least like Swann.

In one sense novelists are unsatisfactory critics of other novelists' work, because they always feel that they themselves would have written any given novel another way. At the same time they are probably the only individuals truly aware of the interior images that haunt the novelist's imagination. Yorke has the novelist's fascination with the casual phrase (especially that), the exceptional situation, the oddly adjusted human relationship. He has a deep interest in the eternal contrast between everyday life's flatness and its intensity. At the same time, there is always something in Yorke's writing—an unassimilated vein of feeling in which whimsicality and sentimentalism seem to be fighting it out with bareness of diction and moral austerity—that suggests better accommodation in poetry. So far as I know, he himself speaks only once of writing poetry; doing so when staying with a French family before coming up to Oxford. I never saw this, or any other verse, by him, but the images in his novels (especially if cut up into short lines), together with certain as-

161

pects of his temperament, strike me as those of a poet rather than novelist.

Throughout his life elements of a success-story were not lacking in Yorke's career, yet he never felt he had been a success; except perhaps briefly when his novel, *Loving* (1945), showed considerable improvement on earlier (and later) sales. To the last he was complaining that he had failed to achieve recognition, though he appears in standard works of reference on writers of his period; perhaps a small recompense for a life's work, but one writers of respectable distinction often fail to pull off. Certainly Yorke was disappointed. In the latter part of his life he withdrew from many people—myself among them—he had formerly known, becoming something of a hermit. There had never been any specific coldness or rift between us, or, for that matter, regarding many other friends he had ceased to see.

Towards the end of the 1950s (the moment dated by the new US Embassy being not yet quite ready for use), I went to a large party given by the American Institute in a house on the south side of Grosvenor Square. There were a few chairs round the walls, but almost everyone was standing up, and, acoustics being not of the best, the noise made by concentrated literary conversation was even more resonant than usual. A long way off I saw a hand feebly waving from a chair, but could not discern, from where I stood, who was sitting there. It turned out to be Yorke.

He began to speak excitedly. He was not in very good shape. We talked for a while, the row going on round about making his words hard to catch. In one of his old bursts of volubility, he began to pour out a lot of memories of the past experienced together: our prep school; how his uncle, the General, had shown him campaign maps of France; names of people we had known at Eton, whom he now never saw. In the end he was almost in tears of emotion. 'I'm not well,' he said. 'People say it's drink. It's not that. I'm not well. I think I'm going to die.' I felt rather upset after this encounter. It was the last time I saw him. He died in 1974.

Yorke's Memorial Service was at St Paul's, Knightsbridge. I was at the back of the dark church, with several empty pews behind me. Halfway through the service an old man with white woolly hair and a brownish-yellow skin came in. He might have been a Mexican by his appearance. He knelt down in the back pew, and began muttering prayers half aloud, as he told some beads. After a while, before the end of the service, he left. It was an incident Yorke himself would have greatly relished.

Looking back on my own coming down from Oxford, I am surprised at how little I remember about it, how vague are the circumstances in my mind. The occasion seems to have lacked all drama. At some stage that summer I went with Arden Hilliard for two or three weeks to Corsica (then relatively unexplored); an enjoyable trip though without great adventure. We crossed from Marseilles to Ajaccio, and toured the island. Bonifacio, on Corsica's southern tip, was then impressively unmodern. The town was entered by a narrow bridge, across which was probably not a house built later than the first half of the 17th century. Beyond these narrow African streets were the barracks of French colonial troops. Under a blazing sun, disregarding all considerations of shade, huge Senegalese in red tarbooshes took their siestas on the soft steaming asphalt of the parade-ground.

We returned to France by the northern port of Bastia, crossing to Nice. Hilliard and I were sitting in a café there a day later, when Hugh Lygon came in. Seeing us, he established at a table the girl who was with him, and made for where we were sitting.

'I'm staying at Willie Maugham's villa,' Lygon said. 'I've been stuck for the afternoon with this terribly boring Rumanian. May I sit and talk to you for a minute or two? She'll be all right on her own for a bit.'

The subjective interest I find in these words is that I felt not the smallest interest—as I should have done a few years later—at the possibility of hearing about Somerset Maugham and his house-party. Maugham seemed to me then an irretrievably third-rate author, and I could well believe that staying with him was boring, shunting his guests round, an unenviable way of spending a Riviera afternoon. I am now astonished at such simplicity, literary and social. Maugham has his failings as a writer, but stories like *Rain* and *The Outstation* are pretty good in their own genre; while the happenings at the Villa Mauresque always offered at least one good anecdote. In a month or two's time, enveloped in this fog of naïvety, I was to dive headfirst into the opaque waters of London life; forsaking all status as an infant of the spring.

APPENDIX

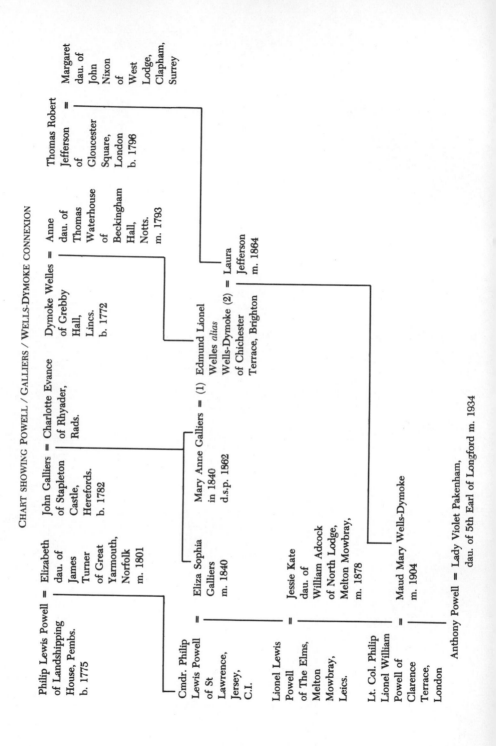

CHART SHOWING POWELL / GALLIERS / WELLS-DYMOKE CONNEXION

Philip Lewis Powell of Landshipping House, Pembs. b. 1775

= Elizabeth dau. of James Turner of Great Yarmouth, Norfolk m. 1801

John Galliers of Stapleton Castle, Herefords. b. 1782

= Charlotte Evance of Rhyader, Rads.

Dymoke Welles of Grebby Hall, Lincs. b. 1772

= Anne dau. of Thomas Waterhouse of Beckingham Hall, Notts. m. 1793

Thomas Robert Jefferson of Gloucester Square, London b. 1796

= Margaret dau. of John Nixon of West Lodge, Clapham, Surrey

Mary Anne Galliers in 1840 d.s.p. 1862

= (1) Edmund Lionel Welles *alias* Wells-Dymoke (2) of Chichester Terrace, Brighton

= Laura Jefferson m. 1864

Cmdr. Philip Lewis Powell of St Lawrence, Jersey, C.I.

= Eliza Sophia Galliers m. 1840

Lionel Lewis Powell of The Elms, Melton Mowbray, Leics.

= Jessie Kate dau. of William Adcock of North Lodge, Melton Mowbray, m. 1878

Lt. Col. Philip Lionel William Powell of Clarence Terrace, London

= Maud Mary Wells-Dymoke m. 1904

Anthony Powell = Lady Violet Pakenham, dau. of 5th Earl of Longford m. 1934

Origin of Species

The cathedral church of St David's in Pembrokeshire provides a convenient launching-pad. In the aisles of its choir recline two figures in armour, the vizors of their conical helmets lifted, their crumbled hands raised in prayer. The elder man is Rhys ap Gruffydd (1132–1197), 'The Lord Rhys', last effective native ruler of the South Wales kingdom; the other, his most enterprising son, though not the eldest, Rhys Grŷg (1169–1234), Rhys the Hoarse, lord of Ystradtywi and Dinefwr, approximately what is now Carmarthenshire. Both effigies are of the late 14th century. They seem to have been set up at this long period after the death of those they commemorate by the Talbot family (later earls of Shrewsbury), whose descent through a high-powered bastard line from Rhys the Hoarse apparently suggested this method of pegging out a claim to the overlordship of South Wales. With this same end in view, the Talbots also adopted (still use in the dexter quartering of their shield) the arms blazoned on the surcoats of these stone warriors; the *lion rampant within a bordure* of the South Wales kings.

The forerunners of The Lord Rhys, a shrewd fairly capable crew (one of whom ruled 'all Wales', seven or eight of the modern counties, regarded by their own inhabitants as 'Britain'), began in a relatively small way by intrusion into North Wales—Gwynedd, the Blessedland—of a chieftain called Gwriad, whose line (like those of the other eventual Welsh dynasties) came from Rheged, the Celto-British Cumbrian kingdom stretching from the Clyde to the Dee. Gwriad appears to have used

167

for staging-base the Isle of Man, where a 9th century cross inscribed with his name commemorates himself or one of his kin.

Gwriad hints at an enjoyable, if tenuous, continuity with late Roman times by reputed descent from Llywarch Hên, an historical 6th century magnate (by tradition a bard), who in turn is derived in 9th century genealogies from Coel Hên Gautepec, Old Coel the Protector (Professor Kenneth Jackson insists, 'the Skulking'), remembered in mediaeval rhyme as Old King Cole (the name Coelius or Coelestius erroneously seeming to connect him with Colchester), a Pennine ruler, possibly last *Dux Britanniarum*, whose government extended to—perhaps went beyond—Hadrian's Wall.

The territories of Rhys ap Gruffydd (of the St David's tomb) varied throughout his reign, but Deheubarth, the Southland, roughly comprised Cardigan, Carmarthen, with parts of Pembroke, Glamorgan, and Radnor. The Radnor cantref, Maelienydd (lying up against the Marcher lordships of the Border), was granted by Henry II at the Council of Oxford in 1177, making Rhys ap Gruffydd the King of England's 'liegeman'. From then Rhys ap Gruffydd abandoned his own title of king, being known henceforth as Yr Arglwydd Rhys—The Lord Rhys. This feudal negotiation brought about my own family's six-hundred-year domicile in Radnorshire.

The Lord Rhys (who instituted the first eisteddfod) came to New Radnor in 1188, with his son Rhys the Hoarse (of the other St David's tomb), when Baldwin, Archbishop of Canterbury, was preaching the Third Crusade in Wales. Accompanying the Archbishop was Giraldus Cambrensis, Gerald the Welshman, who noted in his *Itinerarium Kambriae* that the archiepiscopal party put up for the night *'cum apud castrum Crukeri quasi duobus a Radnoura millibus passuum proficisceremur'*— that is to say 'at Castle Crûgeryr when we had come about two miles [Welsh miles, in fact four] from [New] Radnor'. The name of this small motte-and-bailey fortress (pronounced in Welsh 'Creeg-error') means the Eagle's Mound or Crest. Crûgeryr will come into the story later.

The Lord Rhys, dissuaded by his wife from becoming a crusader, succumbed a decade later to the relapsing fever of bubonic plague. In contrast with the severe dedicated figure of the St David's tomb, he died excommunicate, having not long before incited several of his sons to chase from bed the Bishop of St David's (come to deliver a reproof) '*staminis tantum femorabilibusque indutum*'—that is, wearing only a woollen garment and drawers. The aggrieved ecclesiastical authorities caused the implicated sons to be scourged, and, as he was by then deceased, the fevered remains of The Lord Rhys were beaten too, like the corpse so treated for scientific purposes by Sherlock Holmes in *A Study in Scarlet.*

Whether Rhys the Hoarse was one of the sons involved is not clear, nor the extent of the lands he himself held in Radnorshire. Two of his descendants—presumably Lancastrians—were imprisoned by Edward IV for claiming through this forebear the 'Honour of Radnor', a seigneury representing about a quarter of the modern county. An energetic character, great patron of physicians (conceivably in an attempt to cure an asthmatic condition) Rhys the Hoarse died of wounds incurred storming Carmarthen Castle at the age of sixty-five. Like his father—and most Welsh princes—he left, with some dozen sons born in wedlock by several wives, twenty more by extra-marital unions. This last habit caused no dismay at the time, bastard lines recorded with equal care in pedigrees kept not so much for glorification as basis for land tenure and payment of bloodshed fines; some of the most ancient Welsh stock being in these styled 'labourer' or even 'pauper'.

Among the apparently legitimate offspring of Rhys the Hoarse was Llywelyn Ddireid, Llywelyn the Mischievous (the epithet, says Professor William Rees, implies a touch of impiety), a younger son, who—perhaps excluded by his exacerbating habits—appears to have cashed out of wider public issues at the time of the Edwardian conquest of Wales, settling on Radnorshire properties held in fee by his father and grandfather. He could be 'Llywelyn the Receiver' named in a Minister's Account for those parts in 1281, and is sometimes associated with Gwaeddel (or Wythel), a small manor or township, owned by certain of his descendants, at Gladestry, four or five miles from New Radnor.

Like most of the uchelwr (Welsh uppercrust) after the Edwardian conquest, the generations that followed Llywelyn the Mischievous continued to administer their own lands, now as royal officials. It was a remarkably tolerant situation for those days. One of his progeny appears on the Fealty Roll of the Black Prince, when instituted Prince of Wales in 1343; and this man's son, Llywelyn ap Philip, married the heiress of Crûgeryr, the little castle where the Archbishop had stayed a hundred and fifty years before. After becoming its castellan, Llywelyn ap Philip (from whose brother, incidentally, descended Dr John Dee, the Elizabethan man of letters and alchemist) is usually known as Llywelyn Crûgeryr. Much celebrated in bardic verse, he had some contemporary fame, and (probably after his death) the Heralds assigned him, from the name of his castle, the punning device of an eagle; to distinguish his many descendants from other branches stemming from The Lord Rhys.

2

Four miles along the road running north-west from New Radnor, the two green humps of Crûgeryr—all that is now left of the castle—stand menacingly on the high ground. Once these supported the bailey (tower), in which the defenders fortified themselves; the motte (enclosure), where the beasts were driven for safety from the surrounding fields. Probably built by *Advenae* (as Norman and other adventurers were called by the Welsh chroniclers), never more than a wooden structure, the castle's prototype is illustrated in the Bayeux Tapestry. Llywelyn Crûgeryr himself, when not at war, is likely to have lived domestically in the still inhabited house, Llanevan, lying deep in fields on the far side of the highroad, under the slopes of Radnor Forest.

To what extent the castle was designed for long-distance defence is argued, but its situation certainly provided a convenient observation post to command Radnor Forest (forest here used in the mediaeval sense of a chase for hunting deer, rather than a tract of trees), where the apprehended trespasser forfeited a joint of his finger. Whether the silhouette of mound and tower suggested an eagle's beak and crest, or the name came from the wonted soaring of eagles overhead, I do not know. The landscape to the west—a kind of chessboard or tactical table over which Crûgeryr still seems to brood—offers a breathtaking expanse of open country; line after line of low hills, ever fainter in outline, merging into late Turner sunsets of illimitable skies.

In the early 1400s, Owain Glyndŵr brought civil war to the country, harrying the Marches and the South. This brilliant, mysterious, it seems legally wronged, but—for Wales—disastrous figure might in Welsh terms (by his mother's lineage from The Lord Rhys) almost have been regarded as kin. The 'irregular and wild Glendower' captured New Radnor, hanging the garrison on its walls, and 'defaced' Crûgeryr; the last term used by the Book of Golden Grove, which also records that one of Llywelyn Crûgeryr's sons killed three hundred of Glyndŵr's men.

Llywelyn Crûgeryr's grandson, John ap Ieuan ap Llywelyn, evidently Yorkist, may have been accorded 'denization' (English citizenship before Henry VIII's Act of Union), from the wording of certain royal grants, the date of one of which (appointing him Mayor of Gladestry and Serjeant of Radnor Foreign) suggests a Bosworth connexion. Like several of his close relations, John ap Ieuan ap Llywelyn (who died in 1499) is celebrated in a personal ode by Lewis Glyn Cothi (roughly contemporary with Villon), liveliest and most charming of the Bards, if not the greatest.

> Bont Llyr Cruc Eryr i dan goron. Loegr
>   Bont legat kerdorion.
> Bont bric dar dros Gymaron.
> Bont gwraid Maeffyueid yw Iohn.

> Under the Crown of England isn't John the Lear of Crûgeryr?
> Is he not the legate of musicians?
> Is he not the oak over Cymaron?
> Is he not the root of Radnor?

The ode goes on to praise John ap Ieuan ap Llywelyn for his generosity, wide possessions (Cymaron another Radnorshire castle), his bright armour, the nine varieties of wine he brought to the country. Lewis Glyn Cothi was of course singing for his supper, but it must be agreed as incontrovertibly smart to be compared with King Lear a century or more before Shakespeare standardized the story.

One of the sons was rewarded for services to 'Arthur the Prince deceased', first Tudor Prince of Wales, but on the whole the chronicle sinks to transactions in land, quarrels with neighbours, fines in the Ecclesiastical Courts for keeping mistresses—gone the days of princely harems—a sentence for the last including *tres fustigationes*, wisely commuted by payment of 3s 4d. Howel ap John (son of the Lear of Crûgeryr) had a son called, in the old-fashioned manner, Clement ap Howel, but Clement's son, Roger, in the new mode, stuck to his father's suffix, remaining

Roger ap Howel, or more usually Roger Powell; establishing the surname.

Roger Powell was involved in legal squabbles regarding a Gladestry property his grandfather had mortgaged. He won his case, but never recovered the land; not uncommon in those days when up against powerful opponents. In this case the daughter of the defendant (a distant cousin) had married Sir Gelly Meyrick, who inherited his father-in-law's estates. Meyrick, steward of the Welsh properties of Elizabeth's Earl of Essex, was the public-relations man responsible for mounting a special performance of Shakespeare's *Richard II* on the eve of the Essex rebellion. He was executed with his master in 1601. A letter dated the following year in the Salisbury Papers says: 'Prosser is said to be one of those that killed Mr Powell of Radnorshire to pleasure Sir Gelly Meyrick'. There were, of course, many Mr Powells of Radnorshire, but Roger Powell's undated will (proved 1594) suggests haste. Although litigation had taken place many years before, a claimant to some of the Gladestry lands (awarded to him in law) might still have been felt better out of the way.

At the time of this unlucky lawsuit, Roger Powell was living just over the Herefordshire border in the parish of Brilley; its churchyard, with those of the adjacent Radnorshire parishes of Clyro and Llowes, to become thick with Powell graves during the next two hundred years. At Llowes, a Powell is said to have built (probably rebuilt on an old foundation) a house up in the hills, The Travely, where one branch of the family lived from the first quarter of the 17th century to the 1860s. In spite of the apparently Welsh 'tre', the name derives from the de Travelys, lords of Pipton, three miles distant. These Norman *advenae* were possibly the same stock as the de Traillys, tenants of the Bishop of Coutances in Normandy, some of whose feudatories certainly settled in that area of the Welsh March. If the names have indeed the same root, this upland homestead (in which some of the 17th century house and farm buildings survive) commemorates the Norman village of Trelly, a few miles from Coutances. Set eight or nine hundred feet up, looking across the valley of the Wye towards the Black Mountains, the Back of Beyond is no empty figure of speech to describe The Travely's situation.

Two lines descend from Thomas Powell (1636–1680) of The Travely: the elder one continuing to live there; the younger, tanners (almost as common a local industry as farming), inhabiting Bronydd (or The Vron), a house at Clyro; the parish of which the diarist, Kilvert, was curate in the

1860s. After two generations of tanning, Thomas Powell's great-grandson, William Powell (1715–1762) was appointed an officer of excise. Posts in the Excise much sought, this suggests local pull, possibly with the Harley Earls of Oxford, powerful landowners in the Marches, to whom the excise officer's eldest son, also William, became steward.

This second William Powell (1742–1799) of The Broadheath, Presteigne, Radnorshire, seems to have done pretty well out of his stewardship. His wife's parents were tenants of Stapleton Castle, near Presteigne (though technically in Herefordshire), a former Mortimer stronghold, 'slighted' during the Civil War, within the ruined ramparts of which a 17th century house had been built. Stapleton Castle will recur, but with this William Powell° I am not directly concerned, being descended from his younger brother, Philip.

At the convenient age of twenty-one, Philip Powell (1746–1819) became heir to his uncle or great-uncle by marriage, the Revd Philip Lewis, who left him Tyncoed (The House in the Wood) at Disserth, about twelve miles from Clyro, where it still stands in its clump of trees. The extent of the inheritance is hard to assess, but, in land deals transacted later on, a parcel of about eight or nine hundred acres changed hands, apparently about half the property. Most of that was likely to be bare up-

---

°William Powell of The Broadheath (a house in which Charles I by tradition spent the night in 1645), reputed an enormously fat man, into whose waistcoat five ordinary men could be fitted, owned property in different parts of Radnorshire, which included Bryncoch (now Frôn Goch) on land close to Crûgeryr. This turned out to have an odd significance. William's youngest son, Thomas Joseph Powell (1787–1855) married Henrietta, daughter of Thomas Howells, wool-manufacturer and Quaker, of Hay, Brecon, just across the Wye from Clyro. Howells had visited America on business soon after the War of Independence, interviewed General George Washington, but refused the First President's offer of land at a cheap rate near the new capital named after himself. No doubt in consequence of this trip, Howells's son-in-law, Thomas Joseph Powell, sailed with his family to Baltimore in 1817, staying some years in Virginia, finally, after many tribulations, settling in the wild frontier country of Ohio. With the proceeds of the sale of Bryncoch, which he had inherited, he bought 1080 acres at White Eyes Creek (named after a local tribe of Indians), Coshocton, Ohio, about a quarter of which property his direct Powell descendants still (1976) farm. Strong Abolitionists, many of the Powells served with the Union army during the Civil War. Thomas Joseph Powell's nephew, the Revd John Powell, also emigrated to Ohio; Powells spreading to many other Middle West States, and as far afield as Texas and Florida. An American literary connexion (though no shared blood) is established by Henrietta Powell's brother, Joseph Howells, becoming grandfather of William Dean Howells, novelist, and friend of Henry James.

land pasture of no great value, in a country of large holdings, famous for its dearth of rich estates.

> Alas, alas, poor Radnorsheer,
> Never a park, nor ever a deer,
> Nor ever a squire of five hundred a year,
> Save Richard Fowler of Abbey Cwm Hir.

All the same the inheritance must have been acceptable, and probably explains why, at a period when marriage beyond the confines of the immediate neighbourhood was exceptional, Philip Powell went as far afield as Pembrokeshire for a wife. In 1774, at Haverfordwest (where in December, 1939, as second-lieutenant, I joined a Territorial battalion of The Welch Regiment), he married Alice Moore, one of three orphaned daughters. She brought with her a house called Muslick (or Musslewick) at Marloes, a parish on the county's western shore; the unWelshness of the name characteristic of Pembrokeshire. Muslick (in mediaeval times inhabited by a Flemish chieftain, descendant of immigrants settled there by Henry I) was in existence as late as 1920. Now only a few humps of grass at the top of the cliff indicate where once its windows looked out over the mulberry-coloured rocks and bottle-green seas of St Bride's Bay.

At the time of his marriage Philip Powell must have given the impression of making a goodish start in life. It is unlikely that anyone bothered much about the entry—less than six months before the wedding—of an illegitimate birth, attributed to him as father, in the parish registers of Disserth; where he had immediately become a churchwarden on inheriting Tyncoed. Similar slips had befallen his father and grandfather, not to mention more remote ancestors. If any discerned in this an unfavourable omen, they were right. In a year or two's time Philip Powell plunged into a ferment of disaster: rows with relations and business associates about money and land; pressure of unpaid debts; accusations of physical assault; bankruptcy; commitment (though released on the same day) to the Fleet; lawsuits that dragged on for at least twenty years.

A veil—a small corner only lifted by myself—was discreetly drawn over Philip Powell, and his goings-on, by those who came after. My father must have felt this in his bones. Certainly he knew nothing whatever of his great-great-grandfather, not even that they both bore the same christian name. So far as human personality can filter through legal phraseology Philip Powell's temperament sounds a troublesome one, his head full of grandiose schemes for making money. What form, if any, these took, I do not know. Like the Man from Shropshire (another county of the March) in *Bleak House*, litigation may have been unavoidable in terms of a complicated inheritance; the choppy economic seas of the period doing the rest.

In consequence of this débâcle all the Radnorshire property seems to have been sold, but some at least of Alice Powell's dowry salvaged from the wreck; the latter circumstance causing a change of scene for the Powell family. When, in 1796, a local grandee recommended their eldest son, Philip Lewis Powell (1775–1832) for a commission in the Marines, the Powells were living at Muslick, the house on the west coast of Pembrokeshire.

The Corps of Marines (not yet Royal), in which commissions had been regulated by patronage rather than purchase since the middle of the 18th century, included a fairly high proportion of Welsh officers, on the whole impecunious. In *Mansfield Park*, Fanny Price's father, no doubt a Welshman, was a lieutenant of Marines; rather an unsatisfactory person, though less so than Mr Micawber, also a halfpay Marine officer. The Army List of 1798 shows Philip Lewis Powell next to Keats's much hero-worshipped Jennings uncle (one day senior), and about a year behind William Connolly (later major-general), Cyril Connolly's great-grandfather. Among the three Marine colonels (relatively senior naval officers probably thus graded to augment pay) were Horatio Nelson, and my wife's great-great-uncle, Thomas Pakenham.

Duty must have carried Philip Lewis Powell to Great Yarmouth, then a major port of the country, where, in 1801, he married Elizabeth Turner. She came of a hardheaded race of East Anglian bankers, mayors, and town-clerks, flavoured (like the American Powells) with a touch of Quaker. Her father was dead (deceased fathers-in-law already showing signs of becoming a pattern for Powell bridegrooms); her brother, Dawson Turner, FRS, botanist, antiquary, patron of Crome, Cotman, and Blake, a figure in the intellectual world of the period, who deserves a biography one of these days. The Turners must have found a job for this new brother-in-law in their county, because on marriage Philip Lewis Powell retired from the Marines, and his children were baptized at Old

Buckenham, where he was living when (suggesting not absolute lack of cultivated interests) he subscribed to the several volumes of Blomefield's *History of Norfolk*.

Later—possibly after his detrimental father died—Philip Lewis Powell returned to Pembrokeshire; a house called Landshipping. It stands on one of the little peninsulas that jut out into the upper reaches of Milford Haven, where the narrowing waters flow between open fields and hanging woods. A former mansion of the Owens of Orielton, Landshipping had been damaged by fire at the end of the 18th century; gaunt ruins standing beside the still inhabited parts of the house, which is sometimes shown on old maps as 'Llanshippen', as if commemorating the cell of a Celtic saint called Shippen. Etymological questions are always to be approached with caution, but the name seems simply to signify the quay where cargoes were landed. This derivation is borne out by local obituaries, which speak of 'Philip Lewis Powell, Esq., agent to Sir John Owen'; suggesting charge of the small local colliery, where some years before the enterprising baronet had installed one of the newfangled steam-engines. Landshipping, in a state of utter decay when I saw the place forty or more years ago, has since been commendably restored; the house renovated, the ruins, shaded by trees, providing a gothic embellishment to a garden sloping down towards the sedge and marshy flats of the Haven.

Philip Lewis Powell, a man who had lived respectably (even with a certain style, being rumoured to have driven his own coach from Norfolk to Pembrokeshire), was looked on by his immediate descendants as the main progenitor, almost only begetter of the line. He may never have been rich, but he had avoided the lamentable embarrassments of his predecessor. Since he left nothing to speak of in the way of money (such land as he possessed sold to provide dowry for his daughters), his five sons had to be content with their father's blessing, together with some token like a gold watch or bunch of seals. The Honourable East India Company maintained a depot at Haverfordwest, and three of them had entered the Company's service. Of these, one (ensign of Madras Native Infantry), while employed in the great Survey of India, was blown up in an accidental explosion at the age of seventeen; another (lieutenant of Bombay Native Infantry) died in camp at the age of twenty; the third, my great-grandfather (bearing the same names as his father), of the HEIC's Naval Service, survived to marry and produce a son.

176

This second Philip Lewis Powell (1805–1856) served a year's training as 'volunteer' in the Royal Navy; an experience that left some tradition of tears on leaving home at the age of twelve, and, in the robust Marryat style, being thrown overboard as the most effective method of learning to swim. Before retiring from the HEIC on account of ill health in his middle thirties, he commanded an East Indiaman ship of war; then withdrew with his family to Jersey, where he ended his days. After his death an exercise-book filled with his verses was found, of no striking talent, though one couplet is worth quoting, as illustrating those maternally aligned pinings emphasized by Kipling as so typical of Anglo-Indian exile.

> I wish I were the weeds that wave
> In winter by my mother's grave.

Although, when he left the sea, Commander Philip Lewis Powell abandoned Wales for the Channel Islands, he reverted to type to the extent of marrying back into the Radnor/Hereford border; his wife's parents (though of different family from his great-uncle William Powell's in-laws) also living at Stapleton Castle. She was called Eliza Sophia Galliers, a name suggested, without supporting evidence, as being of Huguenot origin. It seems to have come down from Shropshire, but the family had been in the Presteigne area for at least two hundred years, and by then accumulated a good deal of Welsh blood.

There is a slightly adventurous air about the Galliers family, of whom there were about a dozen brothers and sisters. Their mother, something of a matriarch, born locally and apparently illegitimate, died in Paris at an advanced age. A Russian general married into the family, and Eliza Sophia's sister, Charlotte Florentia, was wife of Major William Sidney Oates, an Englishman serving in the army of the kingdom of the Two Sicilies. Mrs Oates became in due course lady in waiting to the last Queen of Naples; famous in life for her heroism at Gaeta; in literature, for championship of M. de Charlus in his hour of need at the Verdurins.

Commander Philip Lewis Powell, *my paternal great-grandfather*, married Eliza Sophia Galliers in 1840. In the same year her sister, Mary Anne Galliers, married (as his first and childless wife) my *maternal grandfather*; a relationship made clearer by chart (page 166). This circumstance, eventually bringing together my parents, offers a suitable moment to turn to my mother's family.

3

If the Powells knew little, and cared less, about their annals, that was not equally true of the Wells-Dymokes, who were not at all disinclined to congratulate themselves on selected aspects of their lineage. The form 'Welles' or 'Wells', alternating as late as the 19th century, was not due to shaky spelling (an insufficiency from which I myself suffer through paternal heredity), but to individual preference for a conscious archaism. 'Welles' implied descent from the once powerful Lincolnshire family of that name, prominent in the Wars of the Roses; a derivation possible, but unproved. My mother's predecessors, small landowners and parsons living for several generations in the Horncastle/Spilsby area—where the Wolds merge into Fen—seem to stem from 'Thomas Wells of Horncastle, Gent., deceased', named in 1652 as one of the Royalists of the county sequestrated under the Commonwealth. Like some of the Powells, he may have been a tanner. Owing to the Wells taste for 'Thomas' as christian name, I have never established with certainty whether descent from him is direct or collateral.

The pivotal figure of the story is a later Thomas Wells (1702–1781), rector of Willingham-by-Stow, a parish near Gainsborough on the Nottinghamshire border of Lincolnshire, about forty miles distant from Horncastle. The Revd Thomas Wells married Elizabeth, daughter of Robert Dymoke of Grebby Hall, a union that resulted in all sorts of subsequent repercussions. Grebby, a small property near Spilsby (the house described in a Lincolnshire handbook as 'Late Georgian: the whole a local builder's job') can never have been in the least grand, but is said to have been in Dymoke ownership since the reign of Edward III. I cannot vouch for that. It was the inheritance of a cadet branch, the main Dymoke estate being Scrivelsby Court, a larger affair, though not at all excessive in size, near Horncastle.

Lincolnshire records quite often chronicle intermarriage between the families of Wells (or Welles) and Dymoke, the most flashy example— through which Elizabeth Dymoke brought her Wells children undeniable blood of the mediaeval house of Welles—being Sir Thomas Dymoke's marriage to Margaret Welles, sister of Richard, 7th Lord Welles; both brothers-in-law being beheaded together at Stamford in 1471 after the Kingmaker's Plot. The Revd Thomas Wells's bride possessing the surname of Dymoke was therefore normal enough, but certain additional prestige was undoubtedly added by the fact that Elizabeth's brother, called like his father Robert, was through cousinship next heir to Scrivelsby—together with the office attached to the manor of Scrivelsby, that of King's Champion. To explain all this involves, I fear, a few rather technical genealogical details. I will try to abridge the longest of long stories, without leaving as unintelligible the strong feelings later aroused.

Robert Marmion, a Norman of some standing, appears to have married the niece of Scrivelsby's Domesday tenant. Anyway, for that reason or another, Robert Marmion was living at Scrivelsby in 1115, where his particular branch of the Marmion family continued for several generations, ending with four daughters. One of these Marmion daughters married Thomas de Ludlow, and their granddaughter, Margaret de Ludlow, married Sir Thomas Dymoke (d. 1381), who took over Scrivelsby, where the Dymokes remain to this day; though the mansion (burnt down in the mid-18th century, and rebuilt in gothic style) has now been demolished except for its gatehouse.

So far, so good. We are merely confronted with a reduced but still relatively intact estate, never bought or sold since the Conquest; rare, certainly, but not unique. In the case of Scrivelsby there was, however, a complicating factor. In the Middle Ages, castles and manors were held (ultimately from the King) by rendering certain feudal services, usually the provision in time of war of a stated number of knights suitably equipped, an obligation later commuted for money payment. In the case of Scrivelsby a more exceptional tenure was adumbrated. In 1328 (to make a cross-reference, approximately the date of Llywelyn Crûgeryr's birth) an official body called the Court of Claims found Scrivelsby manor 'held of the King by Grand Serjeanty *videlicet* of being armed on the day of the King's Coronation for the defence of the King's estate'.

This office of King's Champion was stated to derive from the Marmions, who were alleged to have been Champions to the Dukes of Normandy. Since Philip Marmion (last male Marmion to own Scrivelsby) had been father of four daughters, there was sharp contest as to which of these coheiresses transmitted to her husband the Champion's office. In

179

1377, the Dymokes won the case; Sir John Dymoke the first to perform the ceremony of throwing down the glove at the coronation of Richard II.

This was all very well, but a document happened to exist (dated 1291) to the effect that Philip Marmion held Scrivelsby *'per baroniam'*. That legal phrase implied a straightforward feudal tenure—sometimes (as will be seen later) argued to establish an hereditary peerage—with no proviso as to such matters as 'coming to the King's Coronation armed cap-à-pie with Royal arms delivered by the King, seated upon the King's chief charger, offering himself to make proof for the King against all opposing the Coronation'.

The domestic archives of the dukes of Normandy adduce no evidence to substantiate the claim that the Marmions were at any time under such an obligation. It is more than possible that the Norman dukes employed a champion (the comparative commonness of 'Champion' as a surname attesting such henchmen in far less exalted households), but, if that were so, retainers of more down-to-earth combative ability are likely to have been appointed, rather than magnates in the Duke's own social class (the Marmions being supposedly related to the Conqueror) in a dukedom where the ruler (until established as King of England) was regarded as essentially *primus inter pares*.

Nostalgia for the past seems to recur in cycles. The 14th century was one of these epochs of Romantic Revival: Froissart: tournaments: even in their way the anachronistic tombs of The Lord Rhys and his son at St David's. In short, it looks very much as if the whole business of King's Champion might have been a put up job; a poetic fiction at which Richard II himself possibly connived. After the persistence of six centuries this fancy for a Golden Age of Chivalry (if that does explain the Champion's office) has acquired a romantic patina of its own, recording a mood perhaps even preferable to a mere bureaucratic continuation of coronation routine.

The history of the Dymokes in their rôle of King's Champion is not to be gone into here, but—so far as the Wells family is concerned—attention must be drawn to the fact that when (about 1291) Scrivelsby was inherited by Joan Marmion, a younger branch of the male Marmions was still going strong elsewhere. These latter Marmions, flourishing well into the second half of the 14th century, became 'barons by writ', that is received a summons to the King's Council (as opposed to their earlier *'per baroniam'* land tenure); a process regarded in the legal doctrine of a later age as creating an hereditary peerage (one transmittable through daughters in default of sons), though not so looked on by historians today. This survival of a junior Marmion male line (while Scrivelsby passed to the Dymokes through a female of the senior Marmion line) was to cause controversy centuries later.

So too was another matter. Sir Edward Dymoke, a 16th century head of the family (who not only discharged the delicate triple assignment of successively acting as Champion to Edward VI, Mary, and Elizabeth I, but also, in his Fenchurch Street house, lodged the visiting Ambassador of Muscovy and suite), married the sister—and eventual heir—of the first and last Lord Talboys. In addition to the peerage from which he took his name, Lord Talboys also held (according to 19th century peerage doctrine) the *de jure* barony of Kyme. When he died the Talboys barony expired, but the children of his brother-in-law, Sir Edward Dymoke (from one of whose daughters, incidentally, George Washington descends), became coheirs to the Kyme barony. This circumstance was also to occupy the attention of the Wells family later on.

4

Robert Dymoke (1699–1736), whose only sister married the Revd Thomas Wells, was in Holy Orders like his brother-in-law. The Dymoke cousin to whom he was heir presumptive (Champion at the coronations of George I and George II), a relation thirty years older than himself, had never taken a wife. As things turned out, the sitting Champion died in his ninety-second year (within eighteen months of being required to ride into Westminster Hall for the third time to throw down the glove for George III), but—as the head of the family entered his seventh decade—Robert Dymoke must have felt that Scrivelsby, and the Champion's office, were (to use a colloquialism) in the bag.

That was not to be. In Lincoln town, on the northern corner of the junction between Bailgate and Eastgate, stood The Angel, a well reputed tavern. On the west side of the Exchequer Gate lay the Chequer Well. One January night in the year 1735, after some civic banquet or private relaxation (a contemporary letter reports) 'poor Parson Dymoke coming back from the Angel in liquor', on his way towards the Cathedral precincts fell into the Chequer Well. Neighbours, who might otherwise have leant a hand, ascribed his shouts for help to vinous exuberance.

The Revd Robert Dymoke's remains lie in Lincoln Minster. A Latin inscription, reciting his many qualities, adds REGIS CAMPIONIS HAEREDIO PROXIMI—though in practice a clergyman, if King's Champion, delegated the ceremony to his closest lay relation. The tribute ends with an exclamatory lament: EHEU! QUANDO PAREM INVENIET VERITAS NUDA. I have sometimes pondered the words. 'Alas! When will naked truth find his equal?' Could that be an Augustan pleasantry on the part of his relations, or even the Dean and Chapter; an arch reference to Truth, a naked lady, residing at the bottom of a well? Whether or not any such conceit was intended, Robert Dymoke dying unmarried, Grebby Hall devolved upon his sister and heiress, Elizabeth, wife of Thomas Wells.

During the next generation no one seems to have bothered much about the Dymoke connexion. The nonagenarian Champion was in due course gathered in, and another Dymoke cousin inherited Scrivelsby. This new lord of the manor had been a hatter in Fenchurch Street (his business—to which one of the Revd Thomas Wells's sons was apprenticed—no doubt occupying the premises where the Muscovite Ambassador had been entertained), felt being a great Lincolnshire product; an example of the erroncousncss of the notion that grew up towards the end of the century that the old feudal families did not go 'into trade'. Within a few months, the hatter-Champion himself dying, his son (riding the vintage charger that had carried George II at Dettingen in 1743) officiated at the coronation of George III.

By this time great changes had begun to take place in the manner in which people thought of the past. Ancient titles, estates long handed down, had always been acceptable, but a Romantic Revival now was under way more powerful than any of the 14th century. The Middle Ages were imaginatively transmuted by historical novels and verse into a tapestry of ruined castles, ivied abbeys, knights errant, wronged maidens, sinister monks, seductive pages; while, in a more scholarly field, serious researches began to take place among the cadastres and cartularies of manor and monastery.

The Wells family, tucked away in Lincolnshire, might easily have remained unaffected by these trends of the historical imagination, had not the Revd Thomas Wells's heir (a Doctor of Divinity who extended Wells incumbency of Willingham-by-Stow to nearly eighty years) begotten one of those troublesome sons—no doubt recurrent at all periods, but somehow rather characteristic of the 18th century—and named him 'Dymoke'.

Dymoke Welles (1772–1832), establishing his approach early in life by reverting to the archaic spelling of the surname, settled down to being a problem. Colleges still possessing strong county associations, he was first sent, like his father, to Lincoln, Oxford. The two previous Wells generations had been Cantabs, and, after a year or so at Oxford, Dymoke Welles too migrated to Trinity College, Cambridge; taking a degree at neither university. He then proceeded to Gray's Inn, but was never called to the Bar. These are marks of a doubtful starter. Family uneasiness must have been confirmed, when, at the age of twenty-one, he eloped with Anne Waterhouse (apparently just nineteen), one of the two daughters of a neighbouring Nottinghamshire squire.

All I know of Anne's father, Thomas Waterhouse of Beckingham Hall, is that he served his year as Sheriff, and kept a pack of harriers. His wife, also Anne, has left more trace. Mrs Waterhouse came from the Derbyshire family of Hurt (the Sitwells, who changed their name from 'Hurt', linking on a long way back), and, as a girl, is alleged to have received a proposal of marriage from Nelson.° She was a friend of John Wesley, a Lincolnshire neighbour, who, not long before his death, sent her a copy of what he calls 'Thomas à Kempis' Christian Pattern'. Wesley's letter refers to 'my dear Miss Waterhouse, who, I think, will (in spite of that deadly enemy the Gay World) be wise above her years'. I take this daughter to have been my great-grandmother, who—the Gay World having triumphed—ran away with Dymoke Welles.

°Anne Hurt was a few years older than the victor of Trafalgar, who is certainly on record as friend of the husband, Captain Thomas Massingberd, RN, of her other daughter, Elizabeth Waterhouse. Captain Massingberd's mother (also Elizabeth) let rooms to Lord Byron at 16 Piccadilly. The Poet was a distant cousin, descended, like Thomas Waterhouse, from the Nottinghamshire family of Rosell. Mrs Massingberd of Piccadilly (herself in chronic financial difficulties) acted as go-between with moneylenders when Byron was under age. Two of Byron's letters have passed down to me, one of which asks that 'Miss Cameron' should be given her 'clothes and trunk', as he had parted with her. Byron had rescued this young lady from a brothel, passing her off as a relation. She caused some consternation by miscarrying at a Bond Street hotel while dressed as a boy.

At the close of his life Dymoke Welles wrote of his wife with deep affection, but in most respects he was a less than ideal husband, who sounds not altogether unlike Philip Powell. He appears to have lived anyway some of the time at Grebby (where the existence of an illegitimate family was hinted), and there are suggestions of obscure money-making schemes. At one moment he stood for Parliament (Beverley in Yorkshire), but was not returned. This parliamentary failure may have stimulated ambition to get to Westminster in another manner.

One of the consequences of historical research prompted by the Romantic Movement was the coming into being of an industry devoted to the seeking out of heirs to those mediaeval 'baronies by writ of summons' referred to earlier. Claims taken to the House of Lords resulted in the bringing out of abeyance not a few peerages unheld for centuries, sometimes in the interest of a claimant lacking an acre of the barony's original land. This legal practice (which continued well into the 20th century) is now regarded as a misunderstanding of mediaeval usage, summons to the King's Council not then necessarily envisaging an hereditary peerage; still less that the title should continue through a succession of landless coheiresses. At the same time, it is understandable that descendants of 'barons by writ'—informed by reputable lawyers that they possessed colourable claim to a peerage—should have a shot at reaching the House of Lords by that means.

Disraeli's novel *Sybil* devotes some amusing passages to Mr Hatton, scholar and antiquary, whose knowledge of mediaeval documents makes him a powerful figure of an entirely new kind.

'If the Whigs go out tomorrow, mark me, they will disappoint all their friends . . . Perhaps they may distribute a coronet or two among themselves; and I shall this year make three; and those are the only additions to the peerage which will occur for many years. You may rely on that. For the Tories will make none, and I have some thoughts of retiring from business.'

The baronet, to whom Mr Hatton explains this situation, demurs that peers may be created from 'good families', naming one he himself considers deserving of this honour. This provokes a characteristically Hattonian (or rather Disraelian) comment:

'A very good family indeed; but I do not make peers out of good families, Sir Vavasour; old families are the blocks out of which I cut my Mercuries.'

Mr Hatton is pictured as operating in the 1830s, but, so far back as 1814, the main line of the Dymokes had set out to establish their right (through the manor of Scrivelsby being stated in the parchment of 1291 as held *'per baroniam'*) to the barony of 'Marmyun of Scrivelsby'. This, if ever there was one, appears an instance of wanting to have your cake and eat it, Scrivelsby—as has been described at some length—celebrated for centuries as held, not as a fief of one of the King's barons, but by the 'King's Champion' tenure; although—to be fair to the Dymokes—there was no particular reason, on the face of it, why the lord of that manor should not be at once King's Champion and a peer of the realm. The Dymokes still owned a very fair proportion of the lands which (together with a strong sword) constituted in mediaeval eyes the chief elements in fitting a man to advise the monarch in council. The genealogist who compiled this case, Thomas Christopher Banks, sounds remarkably like the model for Disraeli's Mr Hatton.

Another circumstance should not be forgotten. It was one calculated to fire a Dymoke (or a Wells, if so descended), who possessed any imagination. Had not Walter Scott, whose writings were evoking a romantic hurricane throughout Europe, chosen the name 'Marmion' as prototype of the great nobleman of high romance? Proud and sinister, melancholy and fearless, Lord Marmion's path is a shambles of slain enemies and seduced nuns; the latter sometimes disguised (like Byron's poor Miss Cameron) in the garb of a page. The period in which Scott places the poem—rather splendid in its way—is that of Flodden (1513), but the fiefs attributed to its hero-villain—Fontenay-le-Marmion in Normandy, Lutterworth in Leicestershire, Tamworth Castle in Staffordshire, and, of course, Scrivelsby in Lincolnshire—were the actual holdings of the historical Marmions.

> They hail'd him Lord of Fontenaye,
> And Lutterward, and Scrivelbaye,
> Of Tamworth tower and town.

This gothic mirage was altogether too much for my great-grandfather, Dymoke Welles; discernible at all levels as a man of romantic temperament. He saw himself, by descent through a female but senior line—the principle no different from that by which, earlier at Scrivelsby, the Dymokes had supplanted the Marmions—not only as rightful King's Champion (for which office there had more than once been counter-claimants in the past), but also heir to two quite separate mediaeval baronies, those of Marmion and Kyme. He might possess only three hundred acres, but these, inherited from a long way back, had formerly been part of the Marmions' extensive Lincolnshire lands. A peerage in the 19th century represented considerable practical assets as foundation of a political career; one of its privileges, at the very least, immunity from arrest for debt. Given his character, Dymoke Welles must have found the temptation irresistible; worth having a try, if only for the hell of the thing.

My great-grandfather put in a claim to the barony of 'Marmyun' in 1819 (apparently thereby spiking the Dymoke family's guns in this respect), followed up by another, to perform the office of King's Champion at the Coronation of George IV; in fact, the last occasion when the ceremony took place. Neither was successful; the latter presumably turned down out of hand—since after all the office went with the manor, or so it looked, if it went with anything—the former dragging on for years; never, I think, argued to a finish. Before any such termination, something else happened to settle matters. Dymoke Welles was not a rich man. The costs of genealogical corroboration and lawyers' fee were ruinous. It seems not unlikely that there were also hare-brained financial projects. For one reason or the other, probably on account of both, Dymoke Welles (again resembling Philip Powell) went bankrupt.

Some sort of recovery was made, because Dymoke Welles's eldest and second sons (both of whom were childless) owned Grebby, some of the lands of which (remaining in the family until 1900) passed on to my grandfather, though his next brother had sold Grebby Hall. The latter sale was possibly to pay the expenses of a further venture to reach the House of Lords on the part of the second Welles brother (named 'Dymoke' like his father), who, in 1839, petitioned the Crown to terminate in his favour the abeyance of the barony of Kyme. At one moment during the proceedings, Lord Redesdale (kinsman of Nancy Mitford), an advocate eminent in peerage cases, exclaimed in court that the case had been proved. There were, however, a great many Kyme coheirs, and one of them—a member of the Lister family, also descended from the Dymokes—

put in a counterclaim. Without Mr Hatton's expert guidance one would hesitate to pronounce on so technical a question, but, I have to admit, the Listers have the air of tendering a sounder case. Neither party proceeded further.

To round off this account of the genealogical escapades of my mother's family: her own father (its last male representative), on his second marriage in the 1860s, changed his name from Welles to Wells-Dymoke. The Heralds advocated that spelling, and (perhaps rather lightheartedly, heraldically speaking) allowed him to take, undifferenced, the arms of Dymoke, with an additional crest for the double-barrel. On my grandfather's part these formalities were not without all practical basis. The termination at Scrivelsby of the senior male line was approaching. If there were a tussle as to the heir-at-law (which seemed probable) he did not want to be left out. In the event—not without a measure of indetermination as to where the inheritance lay—all was finally disposed; and, as has been said, the Dymokes remain at Scrivelsby.

Speaking of quite another sort of champion, quite another sort of title — middleweight boxing at Princeton—Hemingway's narrator in *The Sun Also Rises* says: 'Do not think that I am very impressed by that as a boxing title, but it meant a lot to Cohn.' In somewhat the same manner, do not think that I am very impressed by these claims to baronies by writ, and attempts to dislodge from their home the male line of the Dymokes after five hundred years—but they meant a lot to the Wells family of that date.

Family Phantoms

A certain air of fatigue, of enervation, attends the children of Dymoke and Anne Welles. The former, in addition to being a difficult husband, may also have been a trying father. In immediate ancestry the Waterhouse sisters (Mrs Massingberd and Mrs Welles) were last representatives of a surprising number of local lines (Waterhouse, Eastland, Hawksmore, Rosell, and others), become extinct after a respectable run of generations. Indeed, both sides of the family—if the concept is not an imaginary one — give the impression of exhausted race; possibly a commoner condition at the social level of these obscure squires than a somewhat higher one, where existence was brisker. Only a kind of inner tiredness can explain the eternal potterings of my mother's father.

Goodnatured, easygoing, by all accounts without outstanding vices of any kind, Edmund Lionel Welles *alias* Wells-Dymoke (1814-1892) contrived—unlike his father—to be called to the Bar. There the matter rested. His most energetic endeavours were represented in early years by service with the Royal Cumberland Militia, in which he rose to the rank of captain. Far from military in his tastes (unlike my Powell grandfather), he had doubtless been roped in by his brother-in-law, Roland Pennington, of the Fifth Fusiliers (Northumberland's regiment), a Peninsular veteran; one of the first up the ladders at Badajoz, and wounded several times. Captain Pennington had run away with my great-aunt, Georgiana Welles; married—like her parents—at Gretna Green.

My mother, deeply devoted to her father, but possessing a good deal of realism in her manner of looking at things, used to say he had 'lived his life' with his first wife. Their house, The Grange, West Molesey, has now disappeared in a housing estate. He was fifty when she died. Lionel Welles was on good terms with his Galliers in-laws, becoming godfather to his nephew, Lionel Powell (named after him), and with Mary-Anne often visiting her sister married to King Bomba's dragoon. The Welles photograph albums are full of foreign friends, by no means all Neapolitan. This *penchant* for foreigners made my grandfather anxious to entertain a member of the Chinese Legation to dinner; and the children, looking down over the banisters, always remembered the button indicative of rank surmounting the Chinese diplomat's hat.

My grandfather, who enjoyed making scrapbooks, and was attached to conceits like 'Forewarned is fore-harmed', or 'If you eat till you're cold/You live to grow old', retained to the end of his days locutions modish in his youth, like 'old 'ooman' or 'yaller weskit'. He also bought pictures in a mild way, his leanings those displayed at the Wallace Collection—Watteau, Lancret, Teniers, minor Netherlandish masters— but, lacking eye for a winner, was apt to be satisfied with barely tolerable copies. He had his daughters painted by Richard Buckner, a fashionable artist of the early to mid Victorian years, exhibitor at the RA, though never himself an Academician. The three little girls, wearing frocks specially chosen not to 'date', fill the large ably composed canvas.

Buckner, not a bad performer, deserves a Memorial Show one of these days. George Du Maurier had a peculiar animus against him, writing in *Trilby* (set in the 1850s): 'These were the days of Buckner's aristocratic beauties, with lofty foreheads, oval faces, little aquiline noses, heart-shaped little mouths, soft dimpled chins, drooping shoulders and long side ringlets that fall all over them—the Lady Arabellas and Lady Clementines, Musidores and Medoras! A type that will perhaps come back to us someday! May the present scribe be dead!' Buckner does not make my mother and my aunts look in the least like that in the Seventies. Du Maurier's anti-Buckner feelings break out again later in the novel: 'Little Billee was no tuft-hunter . . . Hideous old frumps patronized him and gave him good advice, and told him to emulate Mr Buckner both in his genius and his manner—since Mr Buckner was the only "Gentleman" who ever painted for hire; and they pronounced him in time equal success.'

Militia exercises in Cumberland may have brought my grandfather into touch with his second wife, Laura Jefferson. It was at this marriage, with renewed hope of children, that he changed the surname to Wells-Dymoke. The Jeffersons, tough quarrelsome North Countrymen from a *Wuthering Heights* world of the Borders, were 'statesmen' (minor gentry or well-to-do yeomen who farmed their own land), living round about Carlisle. An untrustworthy inscription in Sebergham church connects with some armigerous Yorkshire Jeffersons, but (Percy tenants in the 16th century) they could have been Roundheads passed over in the Visitations by a Cavalier herald.

The Jefferson men were famous for their bad tempers. The family was much intermarried with local Grahams. When Laura Wells-Dymoke's Jefferson and Graham grandfathers were twin churchwardens at Sebergham, the vicar noted (1802) in the parish register: 'Notoriously memorable.' During the latter part of his life her father, Thomas Robert Jefferson, was on speaking terms with so few of his innumerable relations that cousins (none on the Welles side) played little or no part in my mother's childhood. Thomas Robert Jefferson started life as a doctor, but appears to have practised only as a young man; possibly switching later to some form of business. He lived in a largish house in Gloucester Square, Bayswater, well supplied with portraits of himself, including a marble bust. Watching the coronation of George IV, he had been close to the door at which Queen Caroline had tried to force her way into the Abbey, and he remembered her, very red in the face, being turned away by officials.

There was a strain of madness in the Jefferson family. I do not know from which side it came.° In my grandmother, this took the sublimated form of hypochondria, but her sister (married to a soldier), childless, was painfully melancholy. She finally went over the edge, as did their brother —

°Laura Jefferson's Scotch maternal grandmother, Margaret Ramsay, was said to be of the Highland family, Ramsay of Bamff, descending from the 1st baronet's marriage to a Blair of Balythock. I have never traced this line, possibly illegitimate; as her brother (a major-general) seems otherwise unlikely to have allowed himself to be left out of the *Baronetage* as a potential heir. A 17th century scarf, cap, and gloves, came down to my mother through the Jeffersons and Ramsays, who appear to have bought them from another Ramsay cousin. These seem to have belonged to Alexander Ramsay of Bamff, physician to James I and Charles I, the second of whom he attended at Edinburgh in 1633. Sir Douglas Ramsay of Bamff, 11th bt., told me that in Scotland such items were often the portion (no money available) of a younger son; later passing about within the family. In the 18th century several of these Ramsays of Bamff were physicians at Fort St George in India; the connexion perhaps through one of them.

always referred to as DRJ—who (by tradition after a row with his father about a woman) was withdrawn from circulation in his twenties.

DRJ, contemporary at Eton and Balliol with Swinburne (alas, no legend survives), from his place of involuntary retirement used to write his Wells-Dymoke brother-in-law long friendly rather pompous letters ('Where modern manners are concerned, I belong to the old school, etc'), in one of which he asks to be sent immediately a rifle and bayonet. When he died at some considerable age he left behind him as his most treasured possession a small painted walnut casket full to the brim of trifles that had taken his fancy: tie-pins topped with miniature violins, oars, tennis racquets, the head of Garibaldi; cameos; medallions; printed cards facetiously recommending *A Certain Remedy for Jealousy, A Cure for Deceit, The Importance of Punctuality*; fragments that had shored him against his ruins through a long seclusion from the world.

Laura Jefferson looks attractive in a quiet way at the time of her marriage. She was not without liveliness of fancy, one of her turns being to read aloud a paragraph from the newspaper, substituting for the real ending some fantastic climax of her own. Fussing about her health—which left my mother with a quite exceptional detestation of all medical matters —led to a good deal of changing house: 28 Montagu Square (where my mother was born); Bryanston Square; Tunbridge Wells; Onslow Square; finally, 13 Chichester Terrace, Brighton; scene of most of my mother's stories of her girlhood.

The Wells-Dymokes could be called a happy family, even if scarcely qualifying under Tolstoy's much quoted—perhaps rather meaningless— opening sentence of *Anna Karenina*: 'All happy families are alike but an unhappy family is unhappy in its own way.' The Wells-Dymoke way, a little subdued in tone, proved none the worse for that. The parents got on well together, if somewhat absent-mindedly. My mother would describe how, given a present, her father would scarcely look up from his desk: 'Yes, dear, thank you very much indeed—put it on the table.' Owing to their father's age, their mother's rigidly established ill health, the sisters went about more on their own when they 'came out' than was usual at that time. Nevertheless, when there was no party or dance, they would be quite content to stay at home, one of the family reading aloud or playing the piano.

Even Aunt Vi (who later lived a comparatively adventurous life chang-ing soldier husbands in India and elsewhere) agreed that none of the sis-ters found the tenor of Brighton existence at all boring. Aunt Vi used to be called 'Miss Wiolet' by their butler, Moore, a retainer waggish rather than sententious, and one of the last to transpose (in the Dickensian man-ner) the letters 'V' and 'W'. He died at a moment when his employers in-herited two unprepossessing busts (some public figure, and possibly an additional representation, in some inferior material, of Thomas Robert Jefferson), which were broken up and put as chippings on Moore's grave. The footman, James Gomme, a superlatively good cook by nature, later came to my parents in that capacity; surviving until my own childhood.

My mother, without any profound feeling for music, was at the same time skilled enough at the banjo, then all the rage, to get laudatory no-tices when she gave amateur performances at the Pavilion; the Prince Re-gent's marine residence at Brighton having by then become a concert hall. She had a fair number of proposals of marriage (engaged at least once before the final one), and told me (the action would have been un-characteristic) that she once gave a too insistent suitor a black eye. She was by far the brightest of the three sisters, the only one (Aunt Cicely dy-ing in the attempt) to leave offspring.

2

Some years after my Wells-Dymoke grandfather's second marriage in 1864, my other grandfather, Lionel Lewis Powell (1848-1911) was setting up as surgeon at Melton Mowbray in Leicestershire. Lionel Powell had passionately desired to go into the army, but that was not to be. Partly because he was only child of a widowed mother (eight years old when his father died); partly, I imagine, because during the last years of purchase there was not enough money to lay out on a commission—anyway not enough to support one in England, the Indian army meaning permanent exile—he had to abandon that ambition. Military inclinations remained to the end of his days, which the Volunteers (later Territorials) had to sat-isfy.

Of my grandfather's qualifications as a medical man, I will say no more than that my mother—much attached to her father-in-law—used to declare that she would have gone to any lengths to avoid being treated by him. As I have remarked, her own mother's nervous anxieties about health had set her daughter against medicine in all forms; a prejudice increased by later interest in Christian Science. Whatever his skill, Lionel Powell did not do at all badly so far as earning a living was concerned; in achieving that, happily combining business with pleasure. Next to the army, my grandfather loved above all things foxhunting. Melton, acknowledged world centre of the sport, not only provided the amenities of three famous packs, but, when he was not himself following hounds, assured by the regular spills of the hunting season an unfailing succession of battered patients at the door of the surgery. What remained of the week was devoted to the Leicestershire Volunteers.

My grandfather (just remembered by me on a visit to London not long before his death) possessed, I think, a good deal of charm. He certainly went down well with the Melton hunting *monde*, long notorious for a social life as fast as its fastest runs in full cry. Hearty, extrovert, altogether unburdened by intellectual interests—though perhaps not unscarred by melancholy—my grandfather loved that sort of life and its rough pleasantries. One of his favourite practical jokes was to thrust a walking-stick suddenly between the shins of the companion strolling beside him; safely catching the victim, as he heeled over, just before reaching the ground.

Like my Wells-Dymoke grandfather, Lionel Powell too—a fearful heredity to come down from both sides—detested 'business' of all kinds. As my mother's trustee (before becoming her father-in-law, in fact at the time of her projected marriage) he found himself obliged to accompany her (by then an orphan) to interview lawyers about financial matters. On the way to the solicitor's office he unluckily noticed a man selling penny-whistles, a musical instrument certainly now obsolete at that price, one of which he immediately purchased. There was no particular harm in that, had he not persisted in playing the whistle throughout all the lawyer's efforts to clarify complicated matters connected with former wills, marriage settlements, and legal arrangements regarding my mother's unbalanced uncle. I still preserve a letter from the same long-suffering solicitor intimating—quite kindly—that, however much trouble was saved by that method, professional etiquette forbade a lawyer to accept from a co-trustee of a Trust forty-nine blank cheques (which he returned) signed by my grandfather, the said trustee.

193

Having devised for himself a reasonably ideal bachelor existence, Lionel Powell did not marry until his thirties, when he took for wife Jessie Kate Adcock, only child of a brother officer of Leicestershire Volunteers, a captain of an older generation. William Adcock (1821-1890), one of the fourteen children of a Melton farmer who also seems to have operated a brickyard, had risen from small beginnings on the Lincoln/Leicester border. Starting from scratch in the brewing and wine trade, he had accumulated an unspectacular but acceptable pile; in due course marrying the daughter of another wine merchant, James Digby of Spalding. I do not know whether she was the traditional boss's daughter.

Patron of local artists, pioneer of amateur photography, a rough-and-ready caricaturist who could depict convincing impressions of himself and his future son-in-law attending tipsy Volunteer carousals, William Adcock was by no means a nonentity. Unfortunately, where buying pictures was in question, his guesses were as wide of the mark as those of his near contemporary, Lionel Wells-Dymoke; though each displayed a quite different taste of the period. William Adcock liked the contemporary German school of his day, represented in England by such genre painters as Walter Dendy Sadler (best known for *Thursday*, monks fishing, often erroneously called *Tomorrow will be Friday*), but, even in the light of renewed interest in genre painting, nothing memorable was passed on from his collection. In fact the only picture of any merit that hung on the walls of my Powell grandparents' house was the portrait of a horse and dog, with a view of Melton in the background, by that admirable artist, J. E. Ferneley; bought, I think, by my grandfather, rather than his father-in-law. My grandmother disposed of it after his death (to an itinerant dealer for a tenner) on the plea that she was hard up; probably more from a kind of innate spite towards her children.

My father, chiefly I think from snobbish reasons (he was only eight when his maternal grandfather died), always spoke disparagingly of William Adcock, hinting at inverted sexual tastes; at which my mother would laugh reprovingly, and say *she* always heard it was illegitimate children. I have no reason to credit either imputation. At that period, in that sort of not very enlightened society, anyone interested in the arts was likely to be thought of shaky moral tone, especially an unusual man making his way up the social scale rather too rapidly in local opinion. William Adcock built for himself a very grim residence in dark red brick, North

194

Lodge, situated in one of the less attractive districts of Melton; a town in any case famed for foxhunting rather than architectural beauties.

At North Lodge took place one of those Surtees-type incidents without which no Melton reminiscences would be complete. The house had been let for the hunting-season to some brothers called Flower. One evening after dinner, 'Peter' Flower made a bet that he would ride his favourite hunter up the main staircase to the first floor; then down again. The wager was taken. Horse and rider reached the first floor successfully. There the horse decided to remain. For two days the animal refused to descend the staircase. In due course, at a cost of between two and three hundred pounds (then a respectable sum), a scaffolding had to be erected, an opening breached in the wall, some sort of a platform contrived, before the hunter, now more famous than ever, could reappear at a Kirby Gate meet.

Before leaving William Adcock I should put on record an item that seems to concern his shade. In my later twenties—possibly at the seaside — I was having my fortune told (cards or palmistry) by a professional fortuneteller. She asked if I were a musician.

'No.'

'I thought I saw you playing the piano. Is it a typewriter?'

'Yes.'

'You are a writer? You have exceptional feeling for what people are like. People are all round you, and you describe them.'

I bought my first typewriter with the proceeds of my first novel, which would date this incident as after 1931.

'I see a dead relation of yours—he might be a grandfather—standing behind you. He is looking after you. He has a beard. Looks a bit like King Teddy.'

This description conveyed nothing at the time, even the whimsical designation of Edward VII taking a moment to grasp. My Powell grandfather wore a Kitcheneresque moustache (photographs, it is true, did turn up years later showing him for a very brief period with a full beard as a young man), and, although towards the end of his life my Wells-Dymoke grandfather sported a small white tuft under his lower lip, neither was to be thought of in his life as a bearded man; certainly not in the manner of the monarch named. Then Polly Hubbard, cook to my Powell grandparents for some fifty years, afterwards with my parents in London, offered an explanation of this enigmatic vision. William Adcock, it seemed, had indeed been noted for his resemblance to the then Prince of Wales; a similar beard and tendency to embonpoint. On one occasion passengers waiting for the train at Melton Mowbray railway station, under the misapprehension that the Prince was advancing along the platform towards them, had removed their hats to my Adcock great-grandfather. This supposed likeness had been altogether unknown to me. William Adcock was twenty years older than his royal double, but beards can produce an artificial affinity.

If North Lodge was a fairly horrific residence, so too was that of my Powell grandparents. Originally denominated The House, the name was thought too pretentious by my grandfather, who rather unimaginatively rechristened his home The Elms. Owned (perhaps built) as a hunting-box by an early impresario of Melton as a foxhunting centre, William Lambton (father of the better known Ralph Lambton much celebrated in the Surtees novels), there were some fifteen to twenty bedrooms, excellent stabling, and, although in the middle of the town, an acre or more of garden surrounded by a high wall. The facade from the garden side was not too bad; the interior, a seat of deep depression.

No doubt the guests for whom The Elms had been in the first instance intended were expected to spend most of the time in the saddle, or in bed. There was little accommodation downstairs for the entertainment of a large house-party. The entrance from the street was by a front-door in a wall. This led into a long glass-roofed tunnel, at the end of which a second door gave on to an inky-dark passage-hall. To the right of the hall was a sunless dining-room of no great size; to the left, a small room used by my grandfather as a consulting-room. Beyond the consulting-room another door, veiled by a velvet curtain of immense weight, marked the only downstairs lavatory (possibly two more on floors above), a windowless cell, comparatively spacious, where the visitant was immediately assailed by an absolutely overpowering oriental scent—musk, attar of rose, frankincense, sandalwood, myrrh, aloes, cassia—what combination of all the perfumes of Arabia is impossible to say, but unique in its intensity. On the far side of the stygian darkness of the hall was the door of a drawing-room with french-windows that faced the garden. In the drawing-room, frame to frame, hung watercolours judged—wrongly—by my great-grandfather to have shown promise. The sliding-doors at one end of this room were kept permanently closed, thereby insulating a portion as a kind of boudoir for my grandmother, where she used for ever to recline.

If the Wells-Dymokes could be classified as a happy family, the same could hardly be said of the Powells; the Elms household fitting comfortably (or rather, uncomfortably) into Tolstoy's category of being unhappy in a special way. By this I do not mean that my grandparents' marriage was a disaster. That would be going too far; at least I think so. Marital feelings, rarely deducible from the outside, are not to be pronounced on with certainty after passing into history. Mutual lack of accord was not at all explicit; merely that both parties seem likely to have been better suited to a mate of rather different temperament.

On my grandfather's side, lack of harmony was latterly reflected by a day fairly regularly punctuated, from mid-morning onwards, with stiffish whiskies-and-soda as medium for keeping dejection at bay; although (bachelor jollifications of his youth apart) he was one of those men spoken of as never seen to be 'the worse'. My father once observed of his own father that 'he used to kiss everyone, but never had a mistress'; a statement that seems overpositive in a field where omniscience can be claimed only rarely. He may have been right, but, when some odds and ends of trinkets belonging to my grandfather were being sorted out years later, a screw of paper came to light inscribed in his handwriting 'Miss Lloyd's rings'. One was a wedding ring; the other bearing what appeared to be a cipher of combined initials. The owner must have possessed the tiniest of fingers. Of course the rings may have been left to my grandfather by a grateful lady patient.

My grandmother, a remarkable woman in her way, had (with perhaps a lesbian streak) a strongly developed taste for exercising power over other people. Without being a beauty, she must have offered a handsome armful in her prime, a personality full of attack. The latter quality was never entirely lost to sight, even when her daily life had turned to an utter indolence and feigned ill health. This trait—of an entirely different order from Laura Wells-Dymoke's hypochondria—took the form of diurnal repose on a sofa, or *chaise-longue*, where, robed in a négligé, she would spend the day reading books of the sort generically designated in those days 'French novels'.

The wife of a surgeon, and daughter of a decidedly selfmade local brewer (the trade itself, as the Peerage demonstrated, perfectly acceptable on a larger scale), was not likely, however amusing and presentable, to receive all the invitations open to her husband in his days as a popular bachelor. In addition to that—a very essential point—any circle to which my grandmother belonged was required to accept a fantasist of a high class even for that epoch of fantasism. If she had been based in London, with its wider opportunities, there is no knowing where she might not have found herself. Perhaps the situation would have been no different, the dose of personality too strong to be generally acceptable in any society not prepared for domination. My grandmother herself acknowledged a preference for (her own phrase) ruling in hell, rather than serving in such local heavens as might be available in a smartish county like Leicestershire; the nether regions of Melton falling easily under her sway.

In at least one instance, ruling in hell was diversified by what was undoubtedly serving there; though in one of the higher infernal echelons. This was under the roof of Lady Cardigan (widow of the Light Brigade's commander), who owned a house at Melton, but held court at Deene Park in the neighbouring county of Northamptonshire. An awful if undeniably prodigious figure—fantasist to put even my grandmother in the shade at that level alone—Lady Cardigan, having as an unmarried woman cohabited with her late husband while his first wife was still alive, was not received in Society. In 1909, Lady Cardigan took her revenge for this by publishing *My Recollections* ('ghosted' by a lively lady named Maude ffoulkes about whom my wife wrote a book), Memoirs that remain amusing to this day, if far from reliable.

Among other tokens of Lady Cardigan's friendship with my grandmother survives an autographed reproduction of her full-length portrait (the Earl leading the Balaclava charge in the background), its gilt-and-blue-velvet frame surmounted by the dual coronets of Cardigan and Lancastre; Lady Cardigan, after a second marriage to a Portuguese nobleman, Count de Lancastre, adopting the dubious style 'Countess of Cardigan and Lancastre'. This fancy did not at all please Queen Victoria, accustomed when travelling on the Continent incognito to use the subsidiary royal title 'Countess of Lancaster'; unhappy confusion of identities inevitably arising at foreign watering-places and spas. Of this picture, Flo Lambert (Constant Lambert's first wife), a beauty in a different mould, used to say that, whenever she felt untidy, she liked to gaze at Lady Cardigan's exquisite neatness, and make up her mind never again to fall short of it. The picture is not by Buckner, though Lady Cardigan too sat for him.

The recorded eccentricities of Lady Cardigan at Deene included wearing the cherry-coloured pantaloons of her late husband's fulldress 11th Hussar uniform, and having her coffin brought into the drawing-room to try it out for size. I don't know whether she did both simultaneously. Although the intellectual world was probably not much in evidence during my grandmother's visits to Deene, it is worth remarking that Lady Cardigan's brother, General de Horsey (a surname adopted from a remote mediaeval ancestor) settled in Venice on retirement, where men of letters like Henry James and John Addington Symonds stayed at his palazzo; the latter bearing away with him the General's strikingly handsome gondolier.

Mrs ffoulkes, in her own Memoirs, records Aunt Vi (my mother's youngest sister) as defending her from affront by some of the male guests, when they were both staying at Deene. Aunt Vi was a great friend of my grandmother, sharing her keen interest in the Occult and her more than average ability in telling fortunes. My grandmother also claimed the power of 'willing' a person to choose a given playing-card (its identity recorded before) from half-a-dozen others held in her hand. It was a curious sensation—possibly a trick though I think not—to feel the pasteboard fly up, almost physically attaching itself to a finger very lightly passed over the cards spread out like a fan. In the cabbalistic sphere my grandmother carried her principle of ruling in hell to what might be regarded as logical conclusions in not showing herself above such witchlike practises as burning salt, or invoking similar malevolent spells, to achieve the downfall of her enemies.

While my grandfather was alive, The Elms earned the name of a house where guests came for a week, and stayed two or three months, perhaps longer. Not a few of the visitors were odd fish. His partner, John 'Baba' McCraith, had married a Greek lady from Smyrna (now Izmir in Turkey), a circumstance that helped to maintain an international note among the company entertained in the house for longer or shorter periods. Babà (she always accented the last syllable of the nickname) was a great favourite with my grandmother, who treated his daughter as one of her own children; indeed appreciably better, as she was far from a devoted mother.

Among the exotic and lingering guests of The Elms was a character called Tommy Bury, said to have travelled much in foreign parts, who seems to have settled down for an exceptionally long season in one of the upper-floor bedrooms. On his travels he had become addicted to an 'oriental drug' (one assumes hashish), which at times somewhat deranged his mind. On account of this deleterious habit, he was detected one afternoon—presumably on account of the noise being made—furiously beating with a heavy club (no doubt also acquired in the course of wanderings in the East) the bed of one of the maids; fortunately unoccupied at the time. Nothing much seems to have been thought of the incident. At least it was never recalled—even by my mother—as anything but an excellent joke. Polly Hubbard, the cook (it was not her bed but a colleague's), would shake with laughter while recounting the story in her almost 18th century phraseology; speech which well accorded with an appearance and demeanour that continued to be charming and elegant into her eighties.

My Powell grandparents were adept at maintaining good relations with their domestic staff; tending to outdo the Wells-Dymokes (possessing the same endowment) in terms of sheer longevity, owing to living always in the one place. In addition to Polly Hubbard, was Lizzie Lane (early attendant on my father as a child, later parlourmaid), who also remained for close on fifty years, dying in her nineties, having survived the risks of Tommy Bury's club (it was her bed); a similar span of years being represented by the groom, Stephen Auger, who had begun life as a boy in a racing-stable, and at The Elms may have occasionally lent a hand at table. One cannot fail to notice the beauty of the names of these three.

I was first taken to The Elms when too young to remember the visit, and—my grandmother not caring at an earlier stage to have her children's children there to make her seem old—did not enter the house again until, long after my grandfather's death, I was twelve or thirteen. By then in her sixties, my grandmother had abandoned the unequal game of hide-and-seek with Time, except for remaining adamant on the point that, while admitting her year of birth (1858), she refused to agree that date made her the age she was. We always got on together pretty well, and she would from time to time tell my fortune.

In its palmy days, The Elms must have had something in common with the late Victorian households described in the novels of Ivy Compton-Burnett, my father always retaining that sort of idiom and manner of looking at the world; an atmosphere nerve-wracked, despondent, more than a little sinister, but—something to be emphasized in the light of much absurd legend grown up about the period—not in the least prim. The Victorians, my grandmother among them, had their own manner of discussing what were looked on as improprieties; within these merely semantic limits anything could be discussed. No doubt 19th century households existed in which a dreadful stuffiness prevailed. The Elms was not one of them; and, although each family faced life in a very different manner, moral stuffiness was not in the least characteristic of the Wells-Dymokes either. After my grandmother's death in 1929, The Elms, uninhabited for several years, was finally pulled down. A telephone-exchange now occupies the site of a house where life had not been lived without all style.

3

My father reversed the traditional psychoanalytical situation by being well disposed to his father; highly critical, not to say hostile, towards his mother. In principle, he regarded himself as having had an unhappy boyhood, neglected by his parents, brought up almost entirely by servants, educated any old way. He would have been the first to admit that the servants had also all greatly indulged him, especially his nurse, Lizzie Lane ('nanny' suggests too professional a figure), whose long anchorage at The Elms had thus begun. It was said that he was always angry if there were no tears in the servants' hall when he went back to school; a tradition he never denied, indeed took some pride in; one that certainly exemplifies his later attitude towards himself.

My grandfather seems to have felt that having his son 'blooded' out with the Belvoir at the age of nine absolved him from further parental obligations; everything now accomplished that could be required for a serious start in life. The glories of this initiation into foxhunting had, in fact, been somewhat impaired by the local paper publishing an illustration of the scene, in which my father was depicted as wearing a cap, instead of the orthodox bowler. My grandfather controlled his rage sufficiently to enable himself to ink in on the picture the crown and brim of more correct headgear.

Destined for the Royal Navy (both as grandson of a sailor, and because that career took a male child off its parents' hands in a respectable manner, at the earliest possible age, with a minimum of trouble and expense), my father failed the examination, then taken at twelve years old. This can only have been due to badly organized education, since he was relatively proficient at mathematics, the fence to bring down most naval candidates. At the same time, it would be true to say that he always showed signs of having sustained in childhood some sort of 'psychological bruise' which in an odd way affected his approach to things. He himself used to say that, when young, he could never make out what grown-up people 'were driving at'. This inability to master certain forms of comprehension always remained with him, seeming at odds with an ability that made him capable, in his middle forties, of taking a Second in Law, on leaving the army. After the naval débâcle his schooling continued in much the same hand-to-mouth fashion, followed by a longish stay with a French family at Saint-Servan in Brittany; terminating with a crammer's in London to get him into Sandhurst.

My father rarely spoke of his boyhood, but he seems to have found Saint-Servan tolerable enough. Though never at ease with the language, he developed a great love of France, especially Paris, and was always prepared to air a few French phrases, or pontificate on the ways of 'the Old Frenchman'. The crammer who prepared him for the Royal Military College (as it then was) used to drink heavily. His pupils, accustomed to their preceptor's occasional bouts of DT, would sometimes place a live toad at the corner of the table round which they sat for instruction. The crammer might from time to time throw that end of the room an uneasy glance, but, supposing a spell of delirium on him, was unwilling to make direct reference to the toad's jerky passage through the textbooks.

In spite of such moments of light relief, my father passed into the RMC, where he became a relatively successful cadet. Sandhurst—and his early years as a subaltern—established an identity he seems never to have achieved until that period of his life. Although hard to imagine in another profession, he was in many respects by no means a 'typical' soldier. At the same time, even if aware, intellectually speaking, that there were possibly subtler methods of approach, the manner in which a young officer looked at the world at the turn of the century remained for him—at least in the last resort—a standard to which he was apt to refer all problems of conduct. In the light of the knowledge and experience he had collected over the years in other fields this suggests a lack of moral self-confidence. It is perhaps worth mentioning, in this same connexion, that he did not at all like the writings of Kipling.

In March, 1901, my father was commissioned second-lieutenant in The Welch Regiment; its two battalions made up of the old 41st and 69th Foot. The Regiment had not been chosen on account of the family's Welsh origins (pretty well forgotten in a Leicestershire home, and never sympathetic to my father personally), but because regarded as both 'good' and inexpensive by a distant cousin, Major-General (later Sir Alfred) Turner. Possibly Alfred Turner, rather an eccentric figure, himself remembered the Welsh link as an additional consideration. (By an odd coincidence the General also sponsored for Westminster School a later friend of mine, Gerald Reitlinger, painter and writer on the economics of art.) My father was posted to the 2nd Battalion of The Welch, then serving in South Africa, where the Boer War was being fought. He was in action in the Transvaal a month or two after his nineteenth birthday.

The Galliers connexion making them as it were honorary cousins, my mother and her sisters often used to stay at The Elms. They liked the Powells, but so much hated the atmosphere of the house that, only a day or two after arrival there, were accustomed to write home asking to be told to return forthwith under one pretext or another. Nevertheless, these Melton visits resulted in my parents' marriage. Just when things took shape I do not know, but by the time my father sailed for The Cape feelings already ran strong.

Those who have succeeded in following the somewhat complicated chronology of the families of Powell and Wells-Dymoke will have noted that my mother, brought nearer to my father's generation by being daughter of a second marriage, was nevertheless child of an earlier generation. She was, in fact, well into her thirties when she and my father became engaged, a disparity of age that caused some consternation at the time; quite how much I have never known. The comparative indifference of my grandparents to their children's lives (even so, their daughter, Aunt Katherine, had to elope), combined with the fact that both were much attached to my mother, resulted in objection being finally waived. The marriage took place very quietly in December, 1904; relations with The Elms household afterwards settling down to what they had been before.

My parents' marriage was a wholehearted success. My mother, throughout her life, had no other aim than to make my father happy—no easy assignment in the light of his untranquil temperament—and, however difficult he might at times show himself, whatever rows he made, or wounding things he was prepared to say (one of his worst failings), he was completely broken up when she died; altogether incapable of reconstructing any sort of life without her.

As in all forms of stepping out of line, when human behaviour is concerned, life exacted a price. This was not, I think it true to say, that my father seemed ill-assortedly younger than his wife, although difference of age may have been more apparent when they were first married. In latter years there were times when he might well have been the elder of the two. In the main, the quittance was that my mother—who above all things detested having attention drawn to herself, even in a complimentary manner, or (though a very exceptional person) to seem in any way exceptional—was always acutely conscious of having taken a step at which the world might look critically. Of course I never knew this explicitly as a child, though always aware, in the manner that children are, of my parents' marriage being in some way 'different' from others.

In consequence of this circumstance, although my mother developed a workable technique for concealing her shyness, shyness was something that always tortured her when out of the company of those she knew well. She hated having to take the lead in any social duty, especially such as would inevitably have fallen to her lot had my father ever commanded the Regiment; and continued to be promoted. This extreme diffidence had no particular family connotation. Her eldest sister, Cicely, died when I was a baby, so I never knew her, but Aunt Vi—with whom I was on the best of terms—was completely at ease in ballroom or bar, palazzo or pension. Indeed, Aunt Vi's uninhibited delight in social life had obliged my mother to see her youngest sister through some fairly serious scrapes ('Aunt Vi has always been much too fond of people who amuse her', my mother would say), but the two sisters were very close to each other, letters exchanged as a matter of routine every two or three days.

My mother possessed none of her sister's (and mother-in-law's) fortune-telling flair, although in her younger days she too had not been at all averse from the Occult and its byways; she herself finally taking the view that such practices as planchette and séances were thoroughly bad for the nerves. To the end of her life she would always—from the Great Pyramid to *Old Moore's Almanac*—be enthralled by prophecy, in which inclination she was very much a child of the age. She also retained a lifelong interest in Christian Science; though never taking those beliefs on as a religion—religion profoundly occupying her inner life—remaining always a devoted member (Broad to Low) of the Church of England. My father accepted religion in a totally unquestioning manner, and would perhaps have liked to be High—anyway Higher—had not my mother been out of sympathy with much (though not all) of that particular religious commitment. Several writers come to mind (Jocelyn Brooke, V. S. Pritchett, Denton Welch) whose parents were to a greater or lesser degree involved with Christian Science. I have sometimes wondered whether emphasis on the unreality of 'matter'—as opposed to the omnipotence of 'Infinite Mind'—has the effect on a child of stimulating imaginative instincts, and, as in my own case, directing them into channels ultimately intellectual or aesthetic rather than religious.

During the first two years of my parents' marriage, my mother moved house nine times. The incessant dislocations of army routine, with attendant inconvenience, separations, expense, for the married of all ranks, are a commonplace of Service life, of which those whose professions keep them most of the time in one place are apt to be altogether unaware. Such displacements played a considerable part in the way in which I was brought up.

Index

Abercorn Place, St. John's Wood,
    Christopher Millard at, 52–53
Acton, Sir Harold
    at Eton, 75, 76–77
    and Eton Society of Arts, 66, 73
    at Oxford, 111, 118
    physical appearance of, 69
    writings of, 70, 79, 80
Acton, William
    as artist, 70–71, 79
    at Eton, 69–70, 75
Adcock, William, 194–195
Ainsworth, Harrison, novels of, 6
Alanbrooke. *See* Brooke
Albert, Prince Consort, on Eton
    Chapel frescoes, 78, 79
Albert Hall, site of, 3
Albert Memorial, The, 4
Alexander the Great, Veronese's pic-
    ture of, 61–62
Alington, Cyril, 26, 36
Allen, Geoffrey, 137
Allen, W. E. D., 137
Anderson, Sir Colin, 76
Antic Hay (Huxley), 107
Archer-Shee, Sir Martin, 23, 27
Arlen, Michael, 107
Auden, W. H., as influence on Con-
    nolly, 89
Auger, Stephen, 200

Baird, Sandy, 20

Bakst, Leon, ballet designs of, 9
Baldwin, Archbishop of Canterbury,
    168
Balfour, Patrick (3rd Lord Kinross),
    124
Ballad of Reading Gaol, The (Wilde),
    manuscript of, 55
Balliol College (Oxford), 111, 119
    character of, 109
    dons of, 112–115
    reputation of, 108
    students at, 120–127
Balston, Thomas, 21, 80, 123
    early life of, 22
    on New College, Oxford, 108
    personality of, 56–57
Banks, Thomas Christopher, 185
Barker's, Kensington High St., 5
Baronies by writ, 184–186
Beardsley, Aubrey, 8, 9, 50
Beaton, Sir Cecil, 83, 94
Beauchamp, Earl. *See* Lygon
Beerbohm, Max, 55, 144
Beggar's Opera, The (Gay)
    and Gay libretto, 51–52
    Lovat Fraser sets for, 50–51
Belgrade, visit to, 133–134
Bell, Clive, 58
Bell, E. A., 45–46
Bell, Kenneth, 107, 112, 113,
    144, 151, 159
    teaching methods of, 114–115

Betjeman, John, 27, 50, 125, 128
Bilibin, 11
Binks (cat), 16
Blair, Eric. *See* Orwell, George
Blakiston, Noel, 84, 85, 87, 124
Bordon Camp, Welch Regiment at, 12
Bowle, John, 125
Bowra, Maurice, 122
  on Hellenic cruise, 154–157
  on Kolkhorst, 128
  Oxford circle of, 141–148
  and rift with Powell, 151–153
Boyton Cottage (Wiltshire), Powells at, 23
Brideshead Revisited (Waugh), 129
Brilley (Herefordshire), Powell ancestors in, 172
Brooke, A. F., Jocelyn, 27
Brownell, Sonia. *See* Orwell, Sonia
Buckley, Denys (Lord Justice), 60, 61, 111
Buckner, Richard, 189, 199
Budapest, visit to, 134
Bungalow, The (Abercorn Place, St. John's Wood), 52, 53, 55, 56
Bury, Tommy, 200
Byron, 6th Lord, 183
Byron, Robert, 76, 77, 111, 118, 119, 130–131
  personality of, 71–72, 74
  as writer, 72–73

Cambridge, Powells at, 31
Cardigan, Adeline (Countess of), 198–199
Carter, John, 117
Cecil, David, 149
  at Eton, 39, 42
Cecil, R. W. E. (2nd Lord Rockley), 39, 42
Channon, Henry ('Chips'), 158
Cheke, Sir Marcus, 121–122, 138–139
Cheltenham College, 143
Cherwell, The (Waugh), 129
Chudleigh (Devonshire), 2
Clare College, Cambridge, Staff College at, 31
Clement ap Howel, 171
Clonmore, Billy (Earl of Wicklow), 36
Clutton-Brock, Alan, 74

Clyro (Radnorshire), Powell ancestors in, 172–173
Coel Hên Gautepec (Romano-British chieftain, 5th c., 'Old King Cole'), 168
Collins, Mrs. (Oxford landlady), 150
Conder, Charles, 9
Connolly, Cyril, 2, 27, 42, 94
  autobiographical writings of, 83–91
  on Brian Howard, 66
  at Eton, 81–82
  and Eton Society of Arts, 76
  on Orwell, 92
  at Oxford, 124–125
Connolly, Jean (*née* Bakewell), 92, 124
Connolly, William (Major General), 175
Corsica, visit to, 163
Cross, Bobbie, 121–122
Crowley, Aleister, 11
Crûgeryr Castle, the Eagle's Mound (Radnorshire), 168, 169–170
Curzon of Kedleston, Marquess, 61, 62, 63, 126, 127, 132
Curzon, Grace (Marchioness), 61, 63
Curzon: the Last Phase (Nicolson), 62
Cymbeline (Shakespeare), 26

Daintry, Adrian, 92
Dance, Eric, 42
Dance to the Music of Time, A (Powell), 13, 15, 60–61, 74, 159
D'Annunzio, Gabriele, and writer as man of action, 73
Decline and Fall (Waugh), 129
Dee, John (Dr.), 170
Deene Park (Northhamptonshire), 198–199
Deheubarth (the Southland), rulers of, 168
DeHorsey, General, 199
Derry & Tom's, Kensington High St., 5
Devils, The (Dostoevsky), 14
Digby, James, 194
Disraeli, Benjamin
  novels of, 184–185
  as writer and man of action, 73
Dostoevsky, Feodor, and *The Devils*, 14

Down and Out in Paris and London
(Orwell), 92
DRJ. *See* Jefferson, D'Oyly Ramsay
Dryden, John, 26
Duckworth's (publishers), 22–23, 56,
73, 89, 123, 160
Duggan, Alfred, 61
at Eton, 62–63
at Hypocrites Club, 115, 117, 118,
119
novels of, 127
at Oxford, 126
Duggan, Hubert, 82, 111, 118, 158
at Eton, 37, 46, 64
as model for Stringham, 60, 61, 159
at Oxford, 126, 130–132
personality of, 62
rebellious attitude of, 63
Dulac, Edmund, 9
DuMaurier, George, novels of, 189
Dunstall Priory (Kent), 96
Dymoke family, 179
Dymoke, Sir Edward, 181
Dymoke, Joan (*née* Marmion), 180
Dymoke, Sir John, 180
Dymoke, Margaret (*née* Welles), 179
Dymoke, Robert, 178, 179, 181–182
Dymoke, Sir Thomas, 178–179

Edward VII, funeral of, 7
Eliot, T. S., and *The Wasteland*, 122
Ellis Havelock, 48, 117
Elmley, Viscount. *See* Lygon
Elms, The (Melton Mowbray), Powells
at, 196, 199–201, 203
Enemies of Promise (Connolly), 76, 88
Eton
art studies at, 43–44
games at, 37
Goodhart's house at, 37–40, 42–43
homosexuality at, 40–42
myths about, 34–36
Eton Candle, The (Acton), 57, 64, 66,
67, 75, 79–80
Eton Drawing Schools, The, 43–44
Eton Society of Arts, founding mem-
bers of, 64–77
Evans-Pritchard, E. E., 117
Evans, Sidney, 10, 43–44, 70, 77

Felbrigg (former Wyndham family
seat), 125
Ferneley, J. E., 194
ffoulkes, Maude, 198, 199
Finland
Russian influence in, 135
visit to, 134, 136
First Edition Club, 56
Fleming, Ian, 9
Fleming, Peter, 9
Fleming, Robert, 9
Flower, Peter, 195
France, Anatole, 14
Fraser, Lovat, 50–52, 54–55
Fry, Roger, 77
Fulford, Roger, 121
Fuller, J. F. C. (Major-General,
'Boney'), 11

Galliers family, 177
Galsworthy, John, 106
Garsington, 149–150
Gathorne-Hardy, Robert, 42
Gay, John, and *The Beggar's Opera*, 50–
52
George III, coronation of, 182
George IV, coronation of, 190
George V, coronation of, 7–8
Gibbs, Mr., day school of, 20
Giraldus Cambrensis (Gerald the
Welshman), at Crûgeryr, 168
Gladstone, W. E., impersonation of, 38
Glendower, Owen. *See* Owain Glyndŵr
Gomme, James, 12, 192
Goodhart, A. M., 26
musical interests of, 39–40
physical appearance of, 37–38
on Powell, 44–46
speech of, 38
Gore House, 3
Gosse, Edmund, and *The Eton Candle*,
79–80
Gow, A. S. F. ('Granny'), 94
Grange, The (West Molesey, Surrey),
189
Gravesend (Kent), Powells at, 3
Grebby Hall (Lincolnshire), Dymoke
ancestors at, 178, 182, 186
Green, Henry. *See* Yorke, Henry
Grey of Fallodon, Viscount, 159

Gwriad (Celto-British chieftain, 9th c.), 167–168
Gwynedd (the Blessedland), rulers of, 167

Hambrough, Basil, 48
Hamburg, (Germany), visit to, 136
Hameen-Antilla, Captain, 136
Hare, J. H. M. ('Bunny'), 36
Hartley, L. P., 149–150
Haverfordwest (Pembrokeshire), Powell connections with, 174
Helsinki (Finland), in *Venusberg*, 134
Hemingway, Ernest, 187
Hephaestion, Veronese's picture of, 61–62
Hermon-Hodge, R. H. (2nd Lord Wyfold), 8–9
Heygate, Sir John, 36, 116
Hilliard, Arden, 120–121, 163
Holden, Inez, 93
Hope-Johnstone, C. J. ('Hopey', 'Hope-J'), 57–58
Horncastle (Lincolnshire), Welles ancestors in, 178
Howard, Brian, 76, 79, 80
    characterized, 66–67
    and Eton Society of Arts, 66, 74, 77–78
Howel ap John, 171
Howells, Thomas, 173
Howells, William Dean, Powell family connection of, 173
Hubbard, Polly, 195–196, 200
Hunt, Mr. & Mrs. (retainers at Hypocrites Club), 116
Hurt family, of Derbyshire, 183
Huxley, Aldous
    as Eton master, 79
    novels of, 107
Hypocrites Club, The, 71, 75, 115–119, 120

'If' (Kipling), Bowra's game of, 156–157
Isherwood, Christopher, 2

James, Henry, 199
James, Montague Rhodes, 36
Jefferson family, 190–191

Jefferson, DRJ (D'Oyly Ramsay), 191
Jefferson, Thomas Robert, 190
John ap Ieuan ap Llywelyn ('The Lear of Crûgeryr'), ode to, 171
Joyce, James, and *Ulysses*, 106
Judkins, Miss (governess), 17

Kensington Gardens, childhood in, 4–5
Kensingtons, The (13th London Regiment), 2–3, 5
Ketton-Cremer, Wyndham, 125–126
Kindly Ones, The (Powell), 13, 15
King's Champion, office of, 179–181, 182, 186
Kipling, Rudyard, 31, 96, 127, 177
Koestler, Arthur, and writer as man of action, 73
Kolkhorst, George ('Gu'g'), 127–128
Kyme, barony of, 181, 186

Lamb, Henry, 142
Lamb, Pansy (*née* Pakenham), 142
Lambert, Constant, 5, 11, 58, 59, 107, 132
Lambert, Flo, 198–199
Lambton, Ralph, 196
Lambton, William, 196
Lancaster, Marie-Jacqueline, on Brian Howard, 66, 74
Landshipping (Pembrokeshire), Powell ancestors at, 176
Lane, Lizzie, 200, 201
Lang, Andrew, 6
Lawrence, D. H., on Robert Byron, 73
Laycock, Sir Robert (Major-General), 60
Lempriere, John, 61
Lewis Glyn Cothi (bard), 171
Lewis, Wyndham, 66
Leyburn (Yorkshire), 21
Lincoln Minister, Dymoke tomb in, 182
Lindermann, Prof. (1st Lord Cherwell), 153
Lindsay, A. D. (1st Lord Lindsay of Birker), 111–112, 115, 122
Little Black Sambo, 6
Llowes (Radnorshire), 172
Lloyd, John ('The Widow'), 116, 117, 128

Llywelyn ap Philip (Llywelyn Crûgeryr, 14th c. Welsh chieftain), 169–170
Llywelyn Ddireid (Llywelyn the Mischievous), 169
Locke, W. J., 106
Locker-Lampson, Frederick, 36
'Londonderry Air, The' (Goodhart), 26
Longford, Earls of. *See* Pakenham
Loom of Youth, The (Waugh), 39
Lulu, of Zelli's, 139–140
Lyall, Archie, 132–133, 134
Lygon, Hugh
  at Eton, 60
  at Maugham's villa, 163
  personality of, 74–75
Lygon, William (7th Earl Beauchamp), 75
Lygon, William (Viscount Elmley, 8th Earl Beauchamp), 40, 60, 118

McCraith, John ('Baba'), 199
Machen, Arthur, 50
Mackenzie, Compton, and *Sinister Street*, 106
Maelienydd (Radnorshire), cantref of, 168
Mailer, Norman, as writer and man of action, 73
Malraux, André, as writer and man of action, 73
Mannerheim, Gustav (General Baron), 135
'Marmion' (Scott), 88, 185
Marmion family, 179–181, 185–186
Marmion, Philip, 179, 180
Marmion, Robert, 179
Marten, Henry, 45
Martin, John, 22
Martin Jonathan, 22
Massingberd, Elizabeth, 183
Massingberd, Thomas, 183
Maugham, Somerset, Powell on, 163
Mayfield, John S., 80
Melina Place, St. John's Wood (London), Powells at, 47, 49–50
Melton Mowbray (Leicestershire), Powells at, 192, 194–195
Messel, Oliver, 36, 71
Messel, Rudolph, 71
Meyrick, Sir Gelly, 172

Millar, H. A., 82
Millard, Christopher Sclater (Stuart Mason), 53–59, 80
Minns, Christopher ('Kit'), 76–77
Minns, Francis, 77
Mishima, Yukio, and writer as man of action, 73
Mitford, John (1st Lord Redesdale), 186
Mitford, Nancy, 70
Montgomery, B. L. (Field-Marshal, Viscount), 47
Moore (Wells-Dymoke butler), 192
Moore, George, 67–68
Morrell, Lady Ottoline, at Garsington, 149
Murray, Gilbert, 141–142
Muslick (Pembrokeshire), 174, 175

Napoleon I, at Brienne, 41
National Portrait Gallery, 55
Nelson, Horatio, 175, 183
New College (Oxford), 108
Nicolson, Sir Harold, and Curzon biography, 62
North Lodge, Melton Mowbray, Adcocks at, 194–197

Oates, Alberto, 11–12
Oates, Charlotte Florentia (*née* Galliers), 177
Oates, William Sidney (Major), 177
Olaf, Crown Prince (King of Norway), and Balliol, 123
'Old King Cole', 168
Orwell, Eileen (*née* O'Shaughnessy, 1st wife), 92, 96, 98, 101
Orwell, George (Eric Blair), 6, 27, 28, 76
  at Eton, 35, 36, 91–92
  novels of, 100–101
  personality of, 96–98, 102–104
  physical appearance of, 94–95
  and politics, 104
  at prep school, 83
  in Spanish Civil War, 99–100
  speech of, 93–94
Orwell, Sonia (*née* Brownell, 2nd wife), 103–104
Owain Glyndŵr (Owen Glendower), 170–171
Oxenham, John, 20

Oxford University
  attitude to women at, 121
  Powell's generation at, 109–110, 117–
    118, 129, 153, 157
  See also individual colleges

Pack My Bag (Green), 28, 29, 68–69,
    86, 148, 160
Pakenham, Frank (7th Earl of Long-
    ford), at Eton, 35–36
Pakenham, Thomas (5th Earl of Long-
    ford), 7
Pakenham, Thomas (Captain), 175
Pakenham, Violet. *See* Powell
Paris
  visit to, 138–140
Peel, Arthur (2nd Earl Peel), 39, 42
Pekoe (pekinese), 12, 16
Pennington, Georgiana (*née* Welles),
    188
Pennington, Roland, 188
Pennington, R. L. A. (Brigadier-
    General), as model for General
    Conyers, 15
Picasso, Pablo, 9, 70
Plutarch, 61
Pollard, Graham, 117
Ponsonby, Elizabeth, 120
Ponsonby, Matthew (2nd Lord), 120,
    121
Powell, Alice (*née* Moore), 174, 175
Powell, Anthony
  on American Civil War, 23
  artistic development of, 5, 10
  birth of, 1
  childhood reading of, 6
  early memories of, 2, 4–6
  at Eton, 34–37, 44–46, 60, 107
  in Finland, 134–136
  and foreign travel, 136–140, 163
  on genealogy, 2
  on Grand Tour, 132–134
  literary influences on, 106–107
  at Oxford (Balliol), 107, 108–119,
    120–127, 131–132, 152, 160
  in Paris, 138–140
  at prep school, 23–32
  in raid on Sandhurst, 130–131
  'real people' in novels of, 13–15
  and World War I, 19–21

Powell, Eliza Sophia (*née* Galliers),
    177
Powell, Elizabeth (*née* Turner), 175
Powell, Henrietta (*née* Howells), 173
Powell, Jessie Kate (*née* Adcock,
    grandmother of AP), 194, 197–
    198, 199, 200
Powell, John (son of AP), 155
Powell, John (Revd.), and founding of
    American Powells, 173
Powell, Katherine, 203
Powell, Lionel Lewis (grandfather of
    AP), 192–193, 196–197, 201
Powell, Maud Mary (*née* Wells-
    Dymoke, mother of AP), 1, 7–8, 9–
    10, 11, 57, 192–193
  and Christian Science, 205
  girlhood of, 191–192
  married life of, 12, 49, 203–204
  and occult, 16–17
  personality of, 33–34, 52
Powell, Philip, of Tyncoed, 173–175
Powell, Philip Lewis, of Jersey, 177
Powell, Philip Lewis, of Landshipping,
    175–176
Powell, Philip Lionel William (father
    of AP), 7, 24, 56, 57, 105, 108
  army career of, 202–203
  artistic tastes of, 8–10
  bohemian friends of, 10–12
  boyhood of, 201–202
  education of, 202
  on Eton, 34
  on family history, 1–2
  temperament of, 47–48
  in World War I, 19–20, 21, 31
Powell, Roger (Roger ap Howel), and
    first use of surname, 172
Powell, Thomas, of the Travely, 172
Powell, Thomas Joseph, and founding
    of American Powells, 173
Powell, Tristram (son of AP), 96
Powell, Lady Violet (*née* Pakenham,
    wife of AP), 96, 124, 155, 198
Powell, William, of The Broadheath,
    173
Powell, William, of Clyro, 173
Prometheus Unbound (Shelley), 59
Pryce-Jones, Alan, at Eton, 80
Purser, Clara, 2, 4, 5, 6, 7, 20
  family of, 3

Quennell, Peter, 58
  at Oxford, 122–123
Quest for Corvo, The (Symons), 53
Question of Upbringing, A (Powell),
  113, 159

Rackham, Arthur, 9
Radnor, Radnorshire, New Radnor,
  168, 169, 170, 172, 173–174
Ramsay family, of Bamff, 190
Ramsay, Alexander, 190
Ramsay, Sir Douglas, 190
Rattigan, Terence, and *The Winslow
  Boy*, 23
Reading Gaol, Wilde's cell in, 159
Redesdale, *See* Mitford
Rees, William, 169
Reitlinger, Gerald, 73, 203
Rhys ap Gruffydd ('The Lord Rhys'),
  167–170
Rhys Gryg (Rhys the Hoarse), 167,
  168, 169
Rice, David Talbot, 36, 73, 116, 118
Richard II, coronation of, 180
Road to Oxiana, The (Byron), 72
Ross, Robert, 53
Rothenstein, William, 77
Royal Military College (Sandhurst)
  Oxford raid on, 130–131
  P. L. W. Powell at, 202

Sacher, Frau, and Viennese Hotel, 137
Sadler, Walter Dendy, 194
St. David's Cathedral, 167
St. John's Wood (London)
  Millard at, 52–53
  Powells at, 31, 47, 49–50
Salaman, Michael, 58–59
Salisbury, Powells at, 23, 105–106
Sandhurst. *See* Royal Military College
'School at War, The' (Alington), 26
Scott, Sir Walter, 88, 185
Scrivelsby Court (Lincolnshire), Dy-
  mokes at, 178, 179–180
Service, Robert W., 102
Shakespeare, William, 26, 72, 91, 172
Shelley, Percy B., 59
Sickert, Walter Richard, 111
Sitwell family, original name of, 183
Sitwell, Edith, 56
Sitwell, Osbert, 79

Slater, E. V., 147
Smith, A. L., 111
Smith, Logan Pearsall, 42, 84, 91
Solomon, Simeon, 55
Spence, Roger, 66, 76–77
Spencer, John, 51, 71
  as model for Templer, 60
Spenser, Edmund, and *Faerie Queen*,
  26
Stapleton Castle (Herefordshire), 173,
  177
Station, The (Byron), 72, 73, 74
Stendhal, 25, 38
Stevenson, R. L., and *The Wrong Box*,
  147
Stone, C. G. ('Topes'), 112
Stonehurst bungalow
  fictionalization of, 15
  ghosts in, 15–17
Summers, Romney, 118, 136–137, 138
Sun Also Rises, The (Hemingway), 187
Sutro, John, 129
Sutton Coldfield (Warwickshire), 21
Svevo, Italo, and *Confessions of Zeno*,
  133
Swinburne, A. C., 79–80
Sybil (Disraeli), 184–185
Sykes, Christopher, on Waugh, 129
Symonds, John Addington, 199
Symons, A. J. A., 53, 56
Synnott, Pierse ('Piers'), 122, 123, 151–
  152

Talbot family (earls of Shrewsbury),
  167
Talboys, 1st Lord, 181
Thomson, Hugh, 9
Thorne (soldier-servant), 15
Three Men in a Boat, 6
Tolstoy, Leo, on families, 191, 197
Travely, The (Radnorshire), Powell an-
  cestors at, 172
Trieste, visit to, 133
Trilby (DuMaurier), 189
Trinity College (Oxford), 122
Turgenev, Ivan, 14
  and *Sportsman's Sketches*, 123
Turner, Sir Alfred (Major-General), 3,
  14–15, 203
Turner, Dawson, 175
Turville-Petre, Francis, 117

Tyncoed (Radnorshire), Powell ancestors at, 173–174

Uncle Remus (Harris), 6
Urquhart, F. F. ('Sligger'), 112–114, 119, 123, 124

Varda, Dorothy ('Varda'), bookshop of, 58–59
Varda, Jean (Janko), 58
Venusberg (Powell), 133–134
Veronese, Alexander the Great picture of, 61–62
Vienna, visit to, 136, 137
Vivian, Herbert, 11
Vivian, Olive, 11

Wadham College (Oxford), Bowra at, 141–142, 153–154, 155
Wagner, Sir Anthony, 102
Washington, George, Dymoke descent of, 181
Waterhouse, Anne (*née* Hurt), 183
Waterhouse, Elizabeth (*née* Massingberd), 183, 188
Waterhouse, Thomas, of Beckingham Hall, 183
Watts-Dunton, W. T., 37–38
Waugh, Alec, 27
    and *The Loom of Youth*, 39
Waugh, Evelyn, 60, 107, 121
    humour in, 129–130
    at Hypocrites Club, 116–117
    at Oxford, 110, 118, 128–129
Welch Regiment, The, 12, 20, 203
Welles, Wells, Wells-Dymoke family, 33, 178–187
Welles, Anne (*née* Waterhouse), 183, 188
Welles, Cicely (Wells-Dymoke), 192
Welles, Dymoke, 183–184, 185–186, 188

Welles, Edmund Lionel (Wells-Dymoke, grandfather of AP), 1, 33, 187, 188–190
Welles, Laura (*née* Jefferson), 190, 191
Welles, Mary Anne (*née* Galliers), 177, 189
Welles, Maud Mary (Wells-Dymoke).
    See Powell
Welles, Richard (7th Lord), 179
Welles, Violet (Wells-Dymoke), 192, 199, 204
Wellington, 1st Duke of, 62
Wells, Elizabeth (*née* Dymoke), 178, 179, 182
Wells, Thomas, of Horncastle, 178
Wells, Thomas (Revd.), 178
Wesley, John, 183
Whitman (retainer at Hypocrites Club), 116–117
Wickens, Miss (librarian at Boots), 106
Wilde, Oscar, 53
    portrait of, 55
    in Reading Gaol, 159
Willingham-by-Stow (Lincolnshire), Wells ancestors at, 178
Winslow Boy, The (Rattigan), 23
Wise, Thomas, forgeries of, 80, 117
Wyndham family, original seat of, 125
Wyndham, Violet, 158

Yorke, Henry (Green), 76, 111
    death of, 162–163
    at Eton, 64
    family of, 28, 35
    in family business, 160–161
    literary tastes of, 67–68
    novels of, 68–69, 86, 157, 161
    at Oxford, 124, 148–149, 150–151
    at prep school, 24–25, 29–31